DAY OF DAYS

DAY OF DAYS

SEPTEMBER 11, 2001

A NOVEL OF THE FIRE SERVICE

FRANK NAPOLITANO

Published by Toren James Publishing

Paperback ISBN: 978-1-7375201-0-8
eISBN: 978-1-7375201-1-5

Cover and Interior Book Design: Stewart A. Williams | stewartwilliamsdesign.com

 All proceeds from this publication will go to the 9 11 Tribute Museum and The Stephen Siller Tunnel To Towers Foundation.

This is a work of fiction involving elements of the Fire Department of the City of New York (FDNY) before and on September 11, 2001. The FDNY fire company designations used within it do not represent the actual FDNY companies identified by those numbers. All multi-unit fire departments have numbered company units and any resemblance to actual FDNY companies is completely coincidental.

Up to September 11, 2001, names, characters, places, and incidents are the product of the author's imagination or are used fictitiously. Any resemblance to actual persons, living or dead, events, or locales is entirely coincidental. The street names, locations of buildings, and chronology of events on September 11, 2001 are accurate. Novels need conflict and some of the conflict in this novel is invented, as are all of the villains.

I am proud to be a volunteer member of the fire service who, as fate would have it, found himself in lower Manhattan on September 11, 2001 and afterwards. The immeasurable bravery, sacrifice, honor, and call to duty I witnessed by my brother firefighters prompted this writing. September 11, 2001 may have been the fire service's darkest day, but it was also its finest. This book was written to commemorate those who made it such a day.

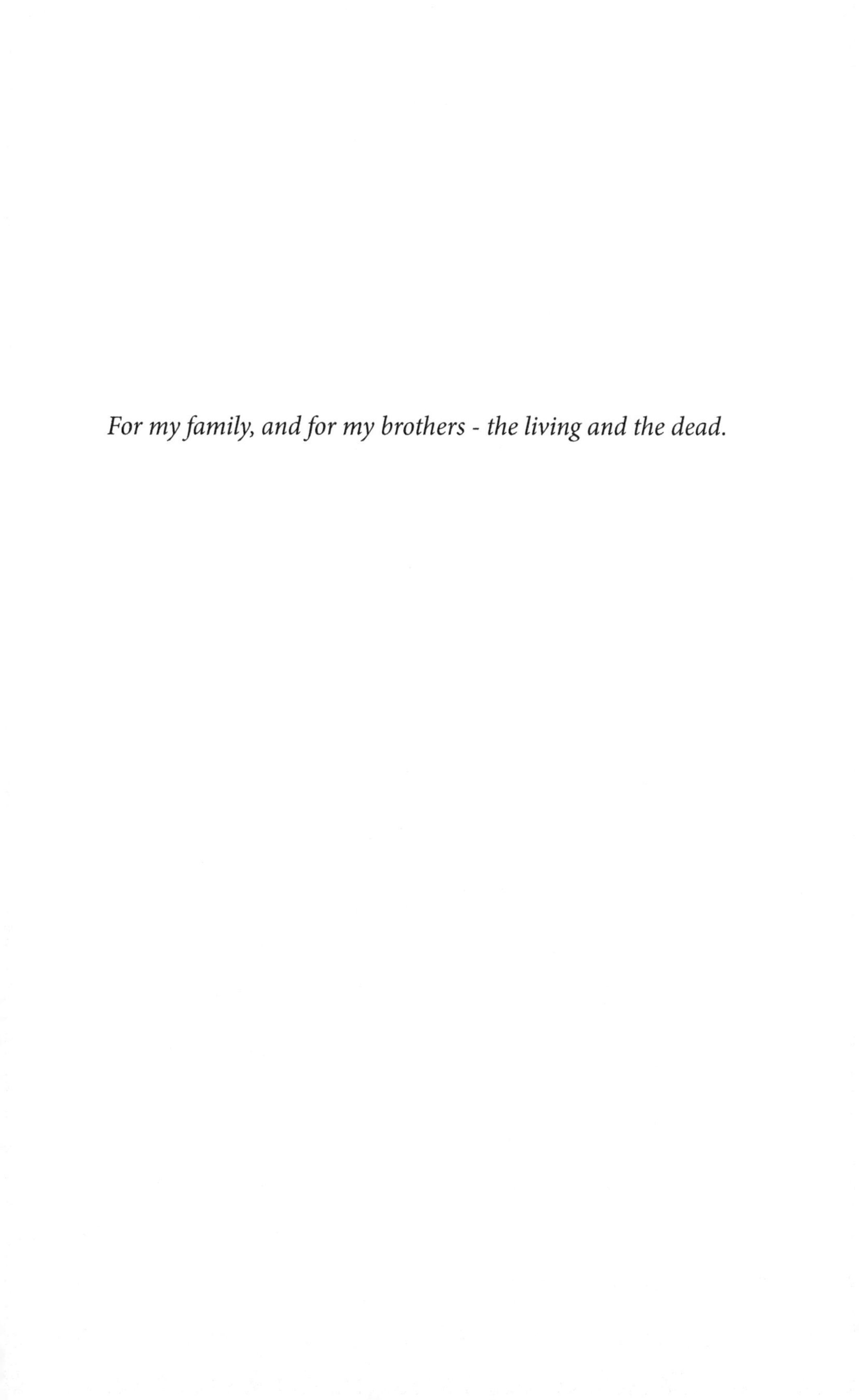

For my family, and for my brothers - the living and the dead.

A glossary explaining slang, fire department jargon, and technical terms has been provided at the back of the book.

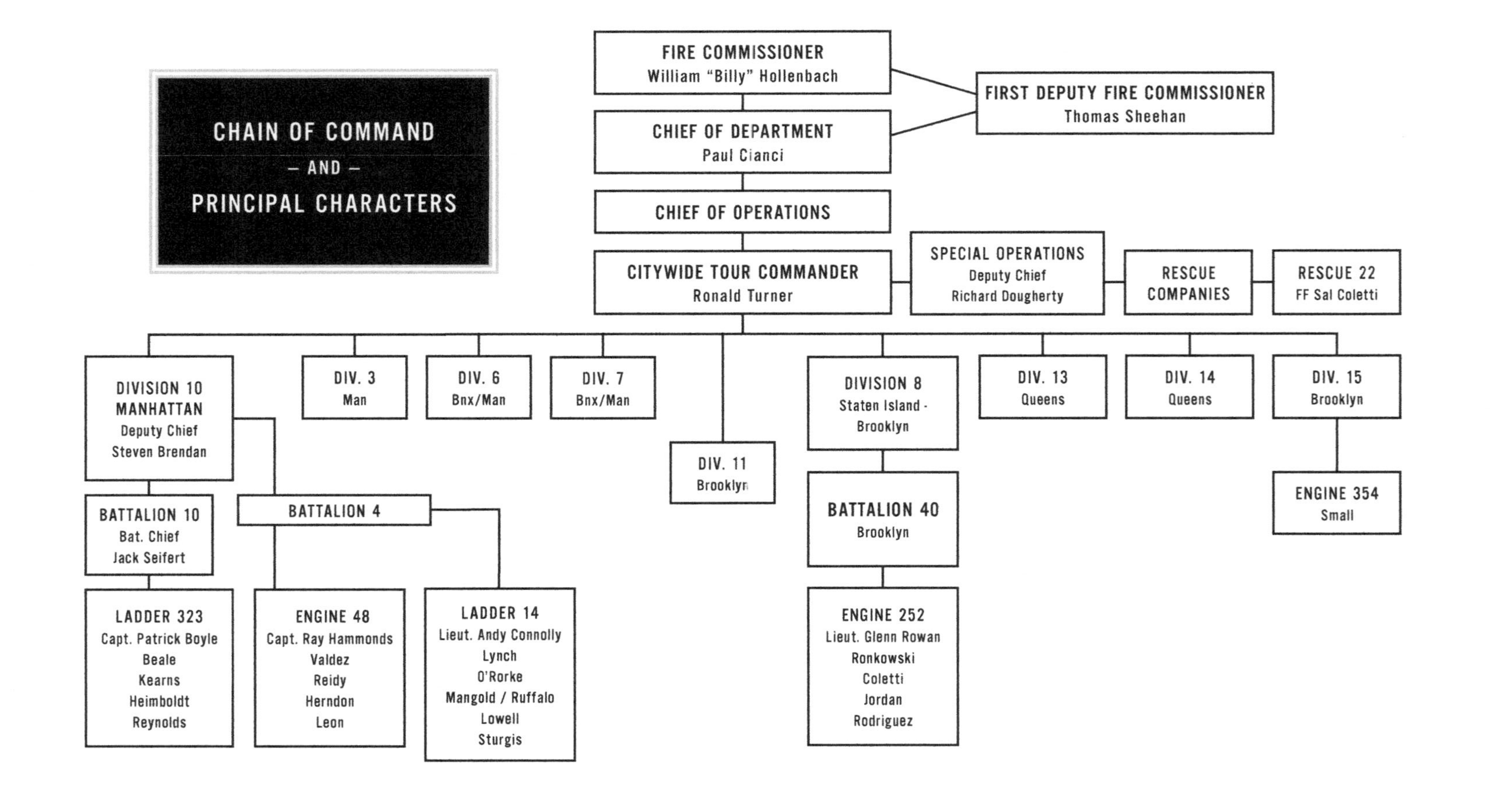

CHAIN OF COMMAND
— AND —
PRINCIPAL CHARACTERS
FIRE COMMISSIONER
William "Billy" Hollenbach
FIRST DEPUTY FIRE COMMISSIONER
Thomas Sheehan
CHIEF OF DEPARTMENT
Paul Cianci
CHIEF OF OPERATIONS
CITYWIDE TOUR COMMANDER
Ronald Turner
SPECIAL OPERATIONS
Deputy Chief
Richard Dougherty
RESCUE COMPANIES
RESCUE 22
FF Sal Coletti
DIVISION 10
MANHATTAN
Deputy Chief
Steven Brendan
DIV. 3
Man
DIV. 6
Bnx/Man
DIV. 7
Bnx/Man
DIV. 11
Brooklyn
DIVISION 8
Staten Island -
Brooklyn
DIV. 13
Queens
DIV. 14
Queens
DIV. 15
Brooklyn
BATTALION 10
Bat. Chief
Jack Seifert
BATTALION 4
BATTALION 40
Brooklyn
ENGINE 354
Small
LADDER 323
Capt. Patrick Boyle
Beale
Kearns
Heimboldt
Reynolds
ENGINE 48
Capt. Ray Hammonds
Valdez
Reidy
Herndon
Leon
LADDER 14
Lieut. Andy Connolly
Lynch
O'Rorke
Mangold / Ruffalo
Lowell
Sturgis
ENGINE 252
Lieut. Glenn Rowan
Ronkowski
Coletti
Jordan
Rodriguez

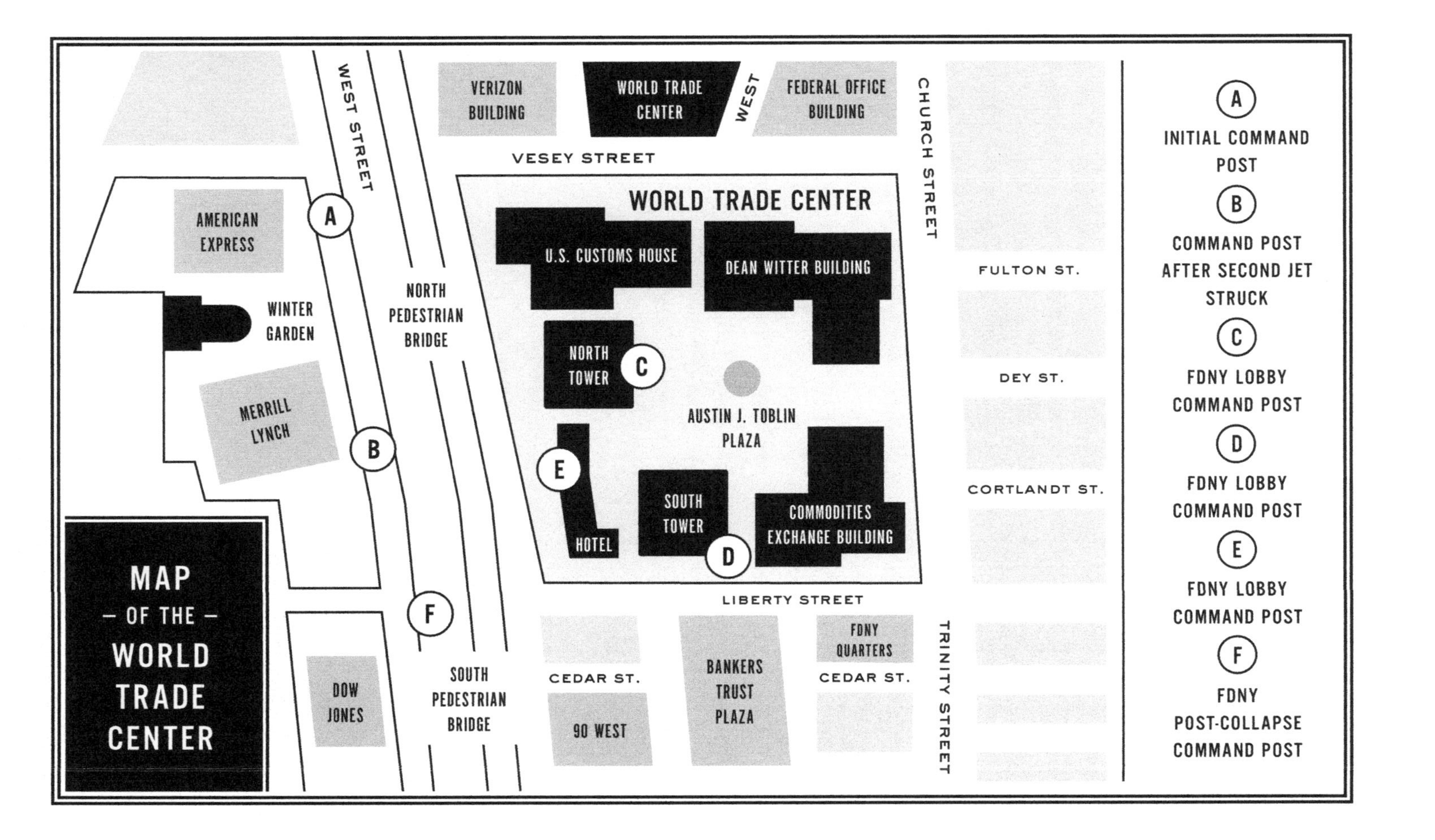
MAP
– OF THE –
WORLD
TRADE
CENTER
VERIZON BUILDING
WORLD TRADE CENTER
WEST
FEDERAL OFFICE BUILDING
CHURCH STREET
VESEY STREET
WEST STREET
WORLD TRADE CENTER
U.S. CUSTOMS HOUSE
DEAN WITTER BUILDING
NORTH TOWER
AUSTIN J. TOBLIN PLAZA
SOUTH TOWER
HOTEL
COMMODITIES EXCHANGE BUILDING
AMERICAN EXPRESS
WINTER GARDEN
MERRILL LYNCH
NORTH PEDESTRIAN BRIDGE
SOUTH PEDESTRIAN BRIDGE
DOW JONES
LIBERTY STREET
CEDAR ST.
90 WEST
BANKERS TRUST PLAZA
FDNY QUARTERS
CEDAR ST.
TRINITY STREET
FULTON ST.
DEY ST.
CORTLANDT ST.
A INITIAL COMMAND POST
B COMMAND POST AFTER SECOND JET STRUCK
C FDNY LOBBY COMMAND POST
D FDNY LOBBY COMMAND POST
E FDNY LOBBY COMMAND POST
F FDNY POST-COLLAPSE COMMAND POST

COLLECT

The sky bled. It rained in rivers of flesh and blood. The Brothers saw what they were up against, and slow-walked themselves silently into the towers. The thousands of fires they had fought over the years, from barge fires to jet plane fires, gave them all the experience they needed to get into those buildings, but nothing to deal with what they found. As the morning stretched on and the minutes tolled, the veterans sensed something was not right. Things did not fit into the normal course of events. The remoteness of the conflagration, so high up, made any thought of marshalling their extensive resources against the blaze a fleeting possibility. And with every passing second, they knew from years of fighting the Beast that, without their interdiction, it would grow stronger and more defiant, possibly unbeatable.

At the base of the towers, old friends, men who had fought thirty fires a night in the infected bowels of the South Bronx in the 1970s, and college-age probies, kids who'd never experienced as much as a campfire, found themselves conjoined, waiting for assignments from an increasingly overwhelmed command post. Some shot concerned, nervous glances to Brothers they hadn't seen in years, who themselves nodded back: *Yes, in all the trying days and countless, inconceivable emergencies Gotham could dish out, in all the catastrophic scenarios the geniuses on the Rock could ever devise, there was none like this one*, their looks said. This was the Big One.

Amongst the Brothers, many things were said at the base of the towers that morning.

And many things were left unsaid.

– An "old buffalo" at the World Trade Center.
September 11, 2001

ENGINEMAN

When they need help, they call us. But when we need help, all we have is each other. It's a brotherhood.

– Captain Patrick J. Brown, FDNY Ladder 3

CHAPTER 1

Coletti glanced out of the window of the 1992 Seagrave engine as it barreled northward toward Manhattan. The chassis bounced off the uneven pavement on the Brooklyn-Queens Expressway, knocking around the portable radios and air-pack harnesses fastened to the jump seats. Because he sat in his assigned seat, rear facing, officer side, Coletti couldn't get a good view of where the rig was headed. To do so, he would have to turn and crane his neck left out the door window or peer to his right through the windshield, past the lieutenant who sat in the front passenger seat.

Today, it didn't matter if he could see where the rig was headed or not. When he stared left out the cab window over Brooklyn, he saw a long horizontal tracer of black, angry smoke running high in the sky. It told him everything he needed to know. There was a large fire burning at the World Trade Center, and he was going to spend the rest of the day there. Maybe longer.

Smoke. It always started that way, he mused. Yeah, the call comes in, the alarm goes off, the gear goes on, and the rigs roll and pull up at the scene. But nothing really starts until the arrival of that collection of solid, liquid, and gas particles that appear when a material undergoes combustion. Smoke. It could be seen, smelled, or felt—on the skin, in the eyes, and in the nose. Once it materializes, it's clear the run is real and not a jerk job.

Coletti shook his head and glanced toward the driver's seat. Ronkowski, the burly engine chauffeur, gripped the steering wheel with his left hand. His other hand grasped a portable radio handset, pressed to his right ear so he could monitor tactical radio transmissions from the fire scene and relay them to his company officer seated to his right. Lieutenant Glen Rowan, the company officer, had his own radio glued to his ear, tuned into the citywide dispatch. Between the two of them, they would have enough information about any incident, ready to anticipate what would be needed when their rig arrived on scene.

However, on this box, no one in the rig could anticipate what would be asked of them or what they were going to do. And the radio traffic on the tactical channel made that painfully clear.

Ronkowski shouted over the engine's wailing siren. "Lieu, they're reporting jumpers from the tower. Fifth alarm assignment. Fire through the skin of the building on the ninetieth floor." Ronkowski raised his eyebrows slightly and cocked his head when he spoke. He put the handset down, grabbed the wheel with both hands, and expertly careened the rig around a minivan. *Good old Ronkowski,* Coletti observed. *That meaty Pole operates this rig better than the accordion he plays at the Sobieski Hall in Greenpoint on Saturday nights.*

Kelvin Jordan, a six-year nozzle man built like an outside linebacker, sat facing Coletti. He stared at Coletti with shock and fear in his eyes. "Damn. That shit's not right."

Coletti gestured to him with his right palm facing the floor of the cab. "Easy. It's gonna be a long day."

Ronkowski gunned the engine forward in the empty HOV lane

toward the Brooklyn-Battery Tunnel. The rig hurtled past packed express buses from Staten Island stranded on the side of the expressway because the cops had shut the tunnel down. Captive passengers and drivers sat there, transfixed, all eyes aimed at the inferno burning one thousand feet in the sky across the East River.

Coletti adjusted his turnout coat on his shoulders and eased his right arm through the strap of his air-pack harness. He did the same with his left arm, and then made sure the inhalation tube and regulator were attached to his face piece and dangled in front of him. The backup man, Rodriguez, sat diagonally across from him. He stared out the window at the World Trade Center. He lips weren't moving, but Coletti was sure he was praying.

This is going to be a hard, difficult day. Coletti's thoughts turned to more peaceful, happy times. Being with Ellie in an abandoned lighthouse on that little Italian island, Strombolicchio, came to mind. He bowed his head.

Shit. At least I had that.

CHAPTER 2

MARCH, 2001

The first time Coletti saw Ellie Deutsch, she was leaning against the railing on the traffic barrier of the Verrazzano Narrows Bridge, staring into the churning water below, one slender leg lifted, with her foot against the concrete barrier. What, he wondered, could cause her to want to end her life?

He and the crew on Engine 252 spotted Ellie as the rig rolled eastward on the bridge, out of Staten Island to Brooklyn. The crew was loose after a night of facing a four-alarm fire at a warehouse in Rosebank. The incident commander at the fire went to "defensive" early, pulled the crews from the building once he'd confirmed no one was inside. They'd spent the night protecting exposures, so the fire didn't spread to other nearby buildings. The chiefs let the Red Devil eat through all of the combustibles in the building and then the building itself.

Inside the cab, Jordan, who had transferred to the crew six months before from a company in Queens, eyed Coletti.

"Hey, man. I hear you play trumpet."

"Yeah, and?" Coletti replied, popping a stick of gum in his mouth.

"What does a trumpet player use for birth control?"

"His personality." Coletti grinned in response to the chuckles elicited from Lieutenant Rowan and the rest of the crew.

Jordan stared at Coletti for a moment, eyebrows raised. "That's right."

Traffic on the bridge slowed to around fifteen miles per hour as Ronkowski pushed the rig eastbound in the right lane. "Hey, Lieu, I think that girl's gonna jump."

Rowan peered right toward the bridge railing. He shouted, "Pull over."

Ronkowski did so and brought the rig to an abrupt stop.

"Coletti, Jordan, get out. We got a jumper," the lieutenant barked.

Coletti opened the cab door and jumped down from the rig. Jordan was right behind him. Rodriguez, fifth man on the rig, set up a trail line of flares behind the engine to divert traffic around them.

Rowan, handset to his mouth, stepped down from the rig. "Brooklyn Dispatch, this is 252 Engine. We're stopped on the Verrazzano Bridge, eastbound lane, lower level. Potential suicide attempt on the bridge. Twenty-year-old white female. Have NYPD shut down eastbound traffic and direct an EMS unit to this location." He motioned to Coletti to approach the young woman and held back Jordan.

Coletti was twenty feet from her. He eased over the abutment, onto the catwalk. She hadn't seen him or the rig. Last thing he wanted to do was startle her. He removed his bunker coat as he edged closer. "Excuse me. Are you alright?" he shouted to her above the traffic noise.

She continued to stare out over New York Bay. Wind gusts blew open the black cotton jacket worn over a white T-shirt. Lean legs covered in blue jeans ended in topsiders. Long, dark-brown hair swirled and shrouded her face. Her right hand held onto the railing;

her left hand stayed buried in her coat pocket.

Coletti glanced back at Rowan, who moved his hands in a circular motion. The message was clear—keep her talking. He edged closer. Too fast, and he might frighten her like a skittish bird with a broken wing. "My name is Phil. What's yours?"

Gaze fixed on the shimmering bay below, she said, "What's it matter?"

"Please. I really want to know."

After a pause, she exhaled and said, "Ellie."

Coletti forced a reassuring smile. "Pretty name."

Cars raced by in the single open lane. Several drivers honked and their passengers jeered. An NYPD cruiser pulled up behind the rig. The two cops inside remained there when they saw Rowan wave them off. Jordan inched his way behind Ellie from the roadway, out of her line of sight. The nozzle man used his position behind Ellie and the suspension cables that separated them to stay out of her view. Coletti needed to keep Ellie occupied.

He moved nearer. Slowly. "Okay if I ask you a question?"

Ellie held up a hand. "Don't come any closer." Despair evident in her expression. "I don't want anyone's help."

He put his right index finger to his ear and said, "It's really loud out here. I can't hear you. Okay if I take, say, five steps? Just five. Okay?"

Ellie turned away and nodded.

Coletti stopped three feet from her. Close enough to grab her if he needed to. Far enough not to crowd her into action. "I sure hope you're not thinking about jumping."

"What's it to you?"

"It's so final. You don't get any second chances, no do-overs."

Annoyance flashed on her face. "A do-over? Sometimes there's no such thing."

"Sure there is. Remember when you were a kid and you screwed up playing tee-ball or hopscotch, your mom would let you have a do-over. Everyone deserves a second chance."

Ellie pulled her long hair away from her face. Coletti got a good look at her and took a sharp breath. Her features were strikingly beautiful. High cheekbones and a perfect nose rose to meet radiant green eyes. Her well-formed lips and strong chin made her seem eminently kissable. Although her clothes were modest, she was slender and above-average height for a woman.

Doggie, you can't let her jump. "It's worth it. To you, and the people who care about you, who'd be crushed if you went through with it."

"Which is no one."

"A stunning woman like you? I don't believe it. Something else is going on."

"My boyfriend dumped me. Not that I blame him. I'm a freak." She pulled her left hand from her pocket. It was missing the ring and middle fingers.

In Coletti's peripheral vision, he saw Jordan behind the barrier, a few feet from her.

"So what? We've all got something that makes us not exactly perfect. Listen to me, Ellie. I'm Italian. Italian men know beauty when they see it." He gave her a sheepish smile. "Guess it's all those Renaissance painters' genes running through our veins. You're more beautiful than most of the women I've seen in the city. Hell, even in the tristate. And I'd bet a year's salary you're just as beautiful inside as you are out. You jump, that would hurt me." She continued to peer out toward the bay. Last thing he wanted to do was lose her. "It'd also be a waste of the gifts God gave you."

"Some gift."

"You'd never see another sunrise or sunset. Never hear another baby laugh. Or hold your own. What's better than that? Don't you want to stick around and find out what's going to happen tomorrow?"

Tears trickled down her cheeks. She took her foot off the barrier.

"My mom died last year. Then the boyfriend thing. I don't have anyone."

"Sure, you do. You have me. And him." He gestured toward Rowan. "That's Lieutenant Rowan. He saw you, and what you were thinking, and stopped the rig. Want to know why? It's not what you think."

Ellie glanced at Rowan. The anguished look on the middle-aged lieutenant's ruddy face stared back at her.

"Two years ago, his daughter killed herself. Ripped his heart right out of his chest. He swore if he ever had the chance to stop someone else doing the same thing, he would."

"Then why'd he send you to talk to me?"

"I *wanted* to talk to you. Besides, look at the guy. He's still torn up."

A siren whined in the distance, growing louder as it neared the scene.

Ellie shot a glance at Rowan then cast her eyes downward. "I wasn't completely honest."

"About?"

"My aunt Jesse would probably miss me."

"See? Funny who and what we forget when we're hurting."

Coletti flicked a glance at Jordan that said *stop there*, just as the nozzle man was a yard from Ellie. An FDNY ambulance pulled up and stopped behind the engine.

Coletti grew hopeful. "Listen, Ellie, I'll make a deal with you. You come away from the railing, and we'll cook a dinner for you at the firehouse. It'll be one of the best meals you've ever had. After that, you can stop by anytime, for a meal or just so we can enjoy your company. How's that sound?"

Still facing down, she nodded. "Okay."

Coletti silently, slowly released his breath. It had worked. He waved Jordan off. Coletti stretched his hand toward Ellie. "C'mon. I'll walk with you to the paramedics. They'll probably want to take you to the hospital. Give you a checkup. Let you get some rest." When she started to pull her hand back, he added, "It'll make me feel better. Okay?"

Ellie placed her hand in his and stepped back from the railing. He draped an arm gently around her shoulders and moved toward the ambulance. "Thank you, Ellie."

Back in the rig on the way to the house, Rowan wore a small, tight smile. He pivoted in his officer's seat. "Coletti, you did good today, kid. You did good."

Coletti nodded once as his eyes met Rowan's.

Jordan grinned and asked, "Where the hell did you get that smack about Italians and painters and genes?"

Coletti grinned back. "Gimme a break, rubber. You were itching to get those ham hocks you call hands around her. I had to say something to keep her attention off you sneaking up on her."

Rodriguez laughed.

"You got that right. That girl was F-I-N-E," Jordan responded.

They rode in silence over the bridge through the Brooklyn neighborhood of Bay Ridge, and to their own house in Sunset Park, one neighborhood north. Ronkowski backed the rig into their quarters at Seventy-Fourth Street, off Fort Hamilton Parkway. By the time Coletti stepped off the rig, his decision was made. He wasn't going to wait for Ellie to act first.

CHAPTER 3

Coletti could easily have been another jaded fireman, considering how much shit he'd seen on the Job. But he couldn't shake the desperation in Ellie's voice and utter despair in her eyes from his mind. Someone so strikingly beautiful should never be bereft of hope. No one should. As soon as Coletti's shift ended the next morning, he called dispatch to find out where the paramedics had taken her. He changed into his FDNY work shirt, navy-blue pants, and work boots, then made a few phone calls before taking a quick subway ride to get to Saint Raymond's Hospital in Borough Park, where she'd been held overnight for observation.

He started toward her room. Yards from her door, his steps slowed. Would she be as eager to see him as he was to see her? He cursed under his breath—his thoughts and motivation had been one track. But he had to see her. Had to make sure she'd be all right. Doing that was in his DNA, part of why he became a fireman.

He paused in front of her door, which was not closed all the way, took a deep breath, and knocked. At her soft "Come in," he inched the door open. Segments of the floor were drying in the sunlight streaming through the window. His nose wrinkled at the evergreen scent mixed with something else in the water used to clean the beige linoleum. He entered and found Ellie sitting up, her gaze fixed beyond the large glass pane. His eyes darted around, taking in the drab, sterile room; he cursed silently again for not thinking to bring flowers.

"Ellie? Okay if I visit for a minute?"

Ellie shifted her gaze from the window to Coletti. Her cheeks flushed when she recognized him. She folded her hands in her lap and focused her attention on them. The nod she gave was slight, but a relief to him.

He leaned against the wall opposite the foot of her bed. "How's it going?"

She shrugged. "Okay. Sorry about yesterday." The color in her cheeks deepened.

Coletti smiled. "I'm just happy you changed your mind. And relieved."

She studied his face for a moment. "Me, too."

A nurse bustled into the room and stopped short. She smoothed her hair and smiled at Coletti before moving to stand by the bed. "Ms. Deutsch." She held up a bottle of pills. "The instructions are on the bottle, and your attending doctor signed your release. Be sure to keep your appointment with Dr. Nehas. Thursday at eleven. Her office." The nurse turned her attention to Coletti. "It isn't every day a patient is taken home by a fireman. Lucky you."

Ellie's eyes grew wide, and her complexion paled.

Coletti stepped away from the wall. "That's good news. Won't take longer than a few minutes to be ready to leave. Right, Ellie?"

Ellie's eyes met his. "Right."

"I'll wait outside your door." As he pulled the door closed behind him, Coletti decided the thing to do was make sure she got home okay—no detours to any more bridges. He pulled a card to a car service from his wallet and ordered a car. Told them he needed one there as soon as possible.

Ellie joined him several minutes later. They walked in silence to the elevator and didn't speak until they reached the lobby.

Coletti held the door open for her. "Where do you live?"

"Bath Beach." She added the specific address.

The black Lincoln, engine running, waited at the curb. He opened the rear door and smiled at her. "I'll ride along, if that's okay with you."

Ellie focused on his face for a moment, nodded, and got in.

Coletti watched as she slid all the way to the opposite door. The paleness of her face stood out in the shadowed interior. She was a long way from being whole.

He paused outside the car. He knew what he was doing, starting to get to know this girl, and he knew he couldn't help himself. *You are such a softie, bro. Why can't you be harder, like the other guys? You really have a fucking savior complex.*

From the back seat, Ellie studied him, her expression quizzical. His hesitation had been noticed; trepidation mixed with pain in her eyes. He sighed, got in, closed the door, and repeated the address to the driver. He gazed out the window so Ellie couldn't see the wistful smile on his face.

CHAPTER 4

As the radio car brought her home, events of the last twenty-four hours raced through Ellie's mind. She thought of how she'd felt just before she did it, that she couldn't take it anymore. There were so many letdowns, so many disappointments; she couldn't get up in the morning. The emotional and physical pain were almost unbearable. She felt like she was tied to a stone at the bottom of the ocean. Even daylight had reflected differently in her eyes. The off-white clarity of the morning had given way to a gray smear, no colors, just different degrees of darkness.

She'd been in New York City five years. Had left LeMoyne, Ohio, like so many others eager for fame and fortune in the big city. And like so many others, it hadn't happened as anticipated—all her fault. Her dream of a career in fashion as an accomplished designer diminished then ended when she fell in with the wrong crowd at the Fashion Institute of Technology. It wasn't long before the booze and drugs caught up with her and she dropped out of school in her third year, taking a retail salesclerk job.

She blamed it on low self-esteem. But even *low* was too high for what the truth was. She'd let her dream falter when that particular group of FIT students had welcomed her in, as though her birth defect was nonexistent. Not like the kids in high school. They would see her face and do a double take, stricken by her unbelievable beauty and figure. That was, until they noticed her hand, and then they didn't really know how to act. She was a novelty. The strikingly beautiful girl with the deformed hand. Perfect, but imperfect.

Guys in New York had been willing to overlook her hand as long as they got what they wanted from her. Until David Walsh. A graphic designer who'd treated her differently, enough so that she stayed with him a year and a half. Enough so that she moved into his apartment. She'd come close to letting her guard down with him. They both drank, and it wasn't long before she discovered he didn't handle alcohol well. Soon after they met, his darker side emerged, and with it came physical abuse. Beatings were accompanied by verbal epithets about her disfigurement, hurting more than the blows. Then, one night after a fight, he threw her out. She found the apartment in Bath Beach in the classifieds and holed up there to lick her wounds, hiding more from herself than the world. After three months, she convinced herself it was the end of the line, with nowhere else to go but out. The bridge had seemed the easiest, surest way to get it over quick.

She glanced at Coletti.

I'm glad I didn't go through with it.

Her feelings were mixed about this fireman. He was attractive. Above-average height with a muscular, toned body. He had an easy smile and dark, almond-shaped eyes that didn't turn away much. His chestnut hair and olive skin gave away his Italian ethnicity instantly; his soft, nurturing voice convinced her it was incapable of uttering insults or criticisms. But she didn't know him or what he wanted from or with her. Uneasiness crept up her spine. She told herself to stop it. That if it hadn't been for this guy, she'd be in the morgue.

Truth was, she did feel somewhat better today than yesterday.

The ride was made in silence, until the car pulled to a stop in front of her apartment. Coletti paid and then exited. Ellie slid from the back seat and started toward the entrance. She stopped, shoulders drooping.

"What's the matter?" Coletti asked.

"I hadn't planned on returning. The key's inside."

"Which apartment is yours?"

Ellie pointed to the window left of the brick steps leading to the first floor.

Coletti glanced at the window and the garbage cans stacked beneath. "Any chance you left a window unlocked?"

"Olga has a key." At his expression, she added, "Landlady."

Coletti followed her up the steps to the first door on the right.

Ellie knocked. Olga opened the door, cell phone pressed to her ear.

"I locked myself out."

Olga's eyes took in Coletti. Scowling, she opened a closet door, retrieved a key, handed it to her, and said, "Bring it back," then closed the door hard.

Ellie slipped the key into the lock.

Once inside, she hurried to the vanity in her bedroom, where she'd left the suicide note. She quickly ripped it up and dropped it into the trash can in the kitchen, then opened the door and gestured for Coletti to enter.

"Sit if you want. Can I get you a cup of coffee?"

"Yeah, thanks. Milk and one sugar, if you have it." He chose the loveseat positioned in front of the window in the sparsely decorated living room.

A few minutes went by, silent except for sounds from the kitchen. Ellie crossed the room and handed him a mug, then sat, mug in hand, in the chair arranged at a ninety-degree angle next to the loveseat.

Coletti took a sip. "Where are you from?"

"A small town in Ohio you've never heard of. How about you?"

"Here, Brooklyn. Grew up in Bensonhurst." He sipped his coffee.

"Big Italian family?

"No, just my brother and me. My mom and dad still live in the neighborhood. I've got my own place in Carroll Gardens. You familiar with that neighborhood?"

"Not really. Brooklyn is a big place."

"You got that right."

Ellie studied Coletti. She noted his ease as the sunlight spilled through the window. As though he was unwinding from a long day. As though any discomfort or thought of needing to rush had been left outside.

"Thanks for taking me home. I don't know how…"

Coletti put up his hand. "Don't mention it. Yesterday is ancient history. How about we put it all in the past and start with a clean slate?"

Her smile was small but genuine. She placed her mug on the small table, then held out her hand. "Okay. Hi, I'm Ellie Deutsch."

He grinned and shook her hand. "Phil Coletti."

"So, Phil Coletti, how long have you been a fireman?"

"Twelve years."

"When did you start working, when you were eleven?"

He chuckled. "I was a volunteer when I was sixteen. Went on the Job—I mean, became a New York City firefighter—at twenty-one."

"Sixteen. That's kind of young, isn't it?"

"I know. My dad's a fireman so I guess it's in the genes. I never really wanted to be anything else." He drank the remainder of his coffee and held up his cup. "Should I put this in the kitchen?"

"I'll get it."

He placed the cup on the table next to him, slapped his thighs, and stood. "I should be going. Thanks for the coffee and the company."

Ellie froze, fear flashed across her face. She saw that Coletti immediately picked up on it.

"Listen, Ellie, you need to take baby steps, day by day. How about I come back tomorrow morning, after work, to check in? See how you're doing. I said I'd help you and I will. Okay? Only thing you need to do right now is take the prescription the doc gave you and keep appointments with her." He glanced out the window, then smiled to her. "It's beautiful out. If you feel like it, maybe take a walk or sit in the sun on the steps. I'll come straight here after I get off shift at nine tomorrow morning. You'll be here?"

"I'll be here."

"Should I bring coffee? Or maybe you'll fix me a cup?"

"I'll fix you a cup."

He walked to the door. Hand on the knob, he turned. "Try not to think about things. You know?"

"I don't know what to think about."

"Maybe I can help with that. See you tomorrow."

She watched the door close. *Just need to get through till tomorrow.*

CHAPTER 5

Ellie's alarm jangled at eight thirty. She moaned, stretched, noted the ache throughout her body from the extreme stress of the prior two days, tossed the bedcovers to the side, and padded barefoot to the front window. She knelt where *he'd* sat the day before. Phil Coletti. Nice name. Nice guy. She opened the blinds and peered out at the overcast sky. *Maybe he won't show up. Maybe he decided I was too much trouble.*

She put a pot of coffee on the stove then flicked on the radio. The last thing she wanted to do was get dressed. But if he did show up, she wouldn't want to be caught dead in her pajamas. This made her chuckle for two seconds before tears welled in her eyes. Fresh jeans and T-shirt on, she ran a brush through her hair, stopping mid-stroke when the doorbell rang.

The clock showed the time as nine thirteen. It couldn't be him. But what if it was? She checked her reflection in the mirror, ran the brush over her hair with a few quick strokes. A hard knock on the door caused her to drop the brush and hurry to the living room.

She inhaled and blew out the breath, then opened the door. He was dressed in his navy work clothes.

He gave her a weary smile. "Hi there. Hope the coffee's on."

"Yes, it is. Come in."

He stepped in far enough for her to close the door and held the box out. The odor of smoke followed him. "I hope you like Italian pastries. These are fresh from my cousin's bakery." He sniffed. "Coffee smells good."

She carried the box to the kitchen table, took out a plate, and placed it next to the box.

Coletti placed the pastries on the plate while Ellie poured their coffees. He waited for her to sit and then took the chair across from her. He selected the round, lobster tail-shaped pastry, dunked it into the coffee and took a bite. "Mmm."

Ellie chose one of the same and bit into it. "Oh, that's good. What's it called?"

"*Sfogliatelle*."

"Solatelly?"

Coletti laughed. "Be glad I don't ask you to try to spell it." He took another sip of coffee. "Coffee's good," he said. "You'd hold your own at the firehouse."

Her lips widened into a full smile. "One thing my mom taught me was how to make a cup of joe."

"That she did." His expression shifted in a flash. "How're you feeling now?"

She swallowed hard. "Better."

He made and kept eye contact. "You mean that?"

She nodded.

"I promised to help you. You're not going to get to a better place psychologically unless you get into a routine and stick with it every day. That way you won't think about the down stuff. Know what I mean?"

Ellie cast her eyes down. "I think so."

"I want to help you know so."

He removed a pen and small notebook from his shirt pocket and started writing. She sat silently as the pen scratched quickly across and down the small page.

Coletti tore the page off and handed it to her. "This is the routine I'm asking you to follow. It's not a lot, and it'll give some structure to your days. Okay?" When she nodded and turned the page to read it, he said, "Best if you start today."

Ellie took the note and read it aloud.

WEEK 1
GET UP AT 7. EXERCISE (STRETCH OR YOGA)
EAT BREAKFAST.
GO TO LIBRARY. READ.
WALK HOME. EAT LUNCH.
1:00 P.M. VOLUNTEER AT ST. RAPHAEL SOUP KITCHEN 87TH AVENUE AND 8TH STREET. (SEE FATHER GIUNTA)
RETURN HOME AT 6:00. MAKE DINNER.
CALL PHIL AT 8 P.M. AT HOME OR THE FIREHOUSE.
IN BED BY 9:30.
NO ALCOHOL, EXTRA SUGAR, OR SMOKING.

"I think I can do this. But ..."

"What?"

"Rent's due tomorrow." Tears filled her eyes. "I don't have it."

"I don't want you to worry about that. I'll talk to your landlady." He tapped the list. "You can do this. At the end of the week, I'll give you a new list." He drained the coffee from his cup, wrapped a cannoli in a paper towel, and got up. "Sorry to run. I've got my own routine to get going on."

She followed him to the door. "Thanks for the pastries."

"After you finish the one left in the box, that's your sugar limit for the day." He reached for the knob and stopped. "Okay, gimme a hug."

Ellie nodded and leaned into him. He wrapped his arms around her, gave a quick squeeze, and released her. "Remember to call me tonight."

"I'll remember."

She closed and locked the door, and leaned against it, waiting for the knock on Olga's door and the hum of his voice, the door too thick to hear his words. She stayed there until she heard Olga's door close and then the front door. She smiled and rubbed her arms. For the first time in a long time, she started to feel calm around a guy.

✦

After a shower and getting dressed in nicer clothes, she walked the six blocks to Greenwood Library and spent the rest of the morning reading a book about the history of fashion. It was eleven thirty-seven when she headed back to her apartment to have lunch. Afterward, she made her way to Saint Raphael's Church.

She followed the signs labeled Soup Kitchen to the basement. Inside, she took in the room lined with serving tables laden with chafing dishes and stainless-steel pots. Six volunteers stood behind the tables and doled out food to dozens of homeless people in line. Another two-dozen people sat at folding tables eating.

A middle-aged African American woman dressed in an apron, holding a serving spoon in her hand, stepped away from the nearest table and approached her. "You're Ellie."

Eyes wide, she asked, "How did you know?"

"That good-looking Phil Coletti said to watch for a real head-turner coming today to help out." She switched the spoon to her left hand, wiped her right hand on her apron, and held it out. "I'm Evelyn. Put your stuff in the kitchen and slip on an apron. George is back there. Tell him to get you started on cutting bread and ham." She glanced around the room. "These folks got a good appetite on them today."

Ellie prepared food for a seemingly never-ending line of hungry people. Remarkably, she was comfortable in the role and in the place. The volunteers were friendly, kind, and nonjudgmental, which was an unfamiliar sensation for her. They showed her the ropes, never displaying impatience when she asked questions, and treated her as though she'd been one of them for a long time.

After two hours in the kitchen, Evelyn stood in the doorway. "Hey, El."

Ellie glanced around to see who would answer. No one did. She cast puzzled eyes toward Evelyn.

"Yes, ma'am, I'm talking to you. How 'bout you switch to serving for a while?"

Things slowed around five twenty when Evelyn announced it was time to eat. Ellie followed her to a table and loaded turkey, mashed potatoes, and asparagus onto a plate. George joined them in companionable conversation at one of the empty tables. At the end of dinner. they refused to let her help with clean-up, high-fived her, and told her they expected to see her the next day.

They hadn't needed to express their expectation—she was eager to return. Often. For the first time in ages, she had a sense of purpose.

That night, when she got home, she called the firehouse. She didn't feel nervous making the call.

"Phil Coletti, please."

"He's out on a run."

"Please tell him Ellie called."

"Will do."

She'd hoped to hear his voice, to hear how pleased he was that she'd called, to have him listen attentively as she told him about her day. Perhaps he'd call later, though she had no idea how long a run might last. Tension crept up her spine—she hoped he'd be safe. More tension was added when she remembered the rent was still due. Whatever he'd told Olga, she prayed it had worked.

✦

The phone rang, causing Ellie to lurch up in bed. The clock showed it was 6:20 a.m. Sunlight seeped around the window shades. Half asleep, she reached for the phone and croaked out, "Hello?"

"Mornin' Ellie. It's Phil Coletti. Sorry I missed your call. Had a three-alarm that took all night. Just got back to the firehouse."

Relief at hearing his voice woke her up even more. "Hi, Phil." She smoothed hair from her face.

"How'd it go yesterday?"

"Really good. I liked everything. You were right. Nothing was too much. It was just right."

"Glad to hear it. You'll repeat it today, right?"

"Yes. The only flaw is—"

"I know what you're going to say, and I told you it was okay. Olga's not going to bother you about it for thirty days. Consider this kind of a vacation from worrying about it."

"I'll have to worry about it at some point."

"Not yet. Listen, some of us are having an early spring cookout at the house this Saturday. How about you join us?"

A seed of tension rose in her chest and began to spread.

"Ellie?"

"What?"

"It'll be casual. Fun. Say you'll come."

"What time?"

"Show up around three. You don't need to bring anything. We've got it covered. The house is at Fort Hamilton Parkway and Seventy-Fourth Street. You got that?"

"Yes."

"You'll come?"

"Okay." A commotion grew louder in the background.

"Gotta run. See you Saturday."

He ended the call before she could bid him good-bye.

She returned the receiver to the cradle and lay back in the bed, her gaze fixed on the ceiling. Her hands became clammy. She considered whether she should go. She could play it safe and stay home. But she felt she should show him some thanks for what he had done for her. It was just a picnic. It was too soon to know if she desired more than friendship with him. She liked him but still didn't know what it was he wanted from her. Maybe this was a sport or some kind of hobby for him. Take pity on the girl who tried to kill herself, just long enough to make sure she won't do it again. Maybe it was nothing more than extending his accomplishment a bit longer.

He told you not to think about anything that drags you down.

She yawned, kicked off the covers, made a quick trip to the bathroom and, still in her pajamas, did her stretches.

CHAPTER 6

Coletti's home away from home was the century-old, three-and-a-half-story brick-and-granite building, known by the firemen who occupied it as the Big House. The turn-of-the-century building housed two engines, a ladder truck, and a battalion chief's car. The firehouse was shared by Engine 252, Engine 294, Ladder 218, and the Eighth Battalion. On any given shift, twenty-one firemen and officers cooked, cleaned, milled, fraternized, trained, and readied for incoming calls that would send Engine 252 to South Brooklyn, Queens, or Staten Island. The guys referred to themselves as "The Wanderers," because of the road time they put in on the rig while chasing calls in the three boroughs. Camaraderie was absolute. Hijinks or pranks instigated by one company on another, usually with tacit approval from officers, kept the guys loose and eased the stress that came with the Job.

The weather was unseasonably mild that Saturday in early April, and the baseball season was underway; two factors that elevated moods in the house. That's all it took to throw the first cookout of the year. The guys appropriated McKinley Park, directly across from the Big House, which made it easy to prep food in the firehouse kitchen and then barbecue in the park. It also let the guys on duty get to the house quickly if a call came in.

Coletti arrived early, ready to help with food preparation. Bruno Tazik, a truckie on 218, who was also a sous chef at a Lower Manhattan restaurant, was in charge of the kitchen and the day's menu. Tazik wasted no time putting Coletti to work chopping vegetables to go with the burgers and sausages.

His junior man, Rodriguez, approached him. "Rowan wants to see you in his office."

Coletti wiped his hands on a dishcloth and said, "Take over here for me." He headed to the lieutenant's cramped office located next to the house watch at the front of the building.

The lieutenant, hazel-eyed and with a receding hairline, was sitting at his desk completing run sheets from the night before. The cuffs on his white shirtsleeves were darkened by the ink he laid down on those sheets at the end of every shift.

Rowan finished writing and looked up. "Phil, sit down."

Coletti lowered himself into the metal folding chair two feet from the desk.

"Have you given any more thought to my suggestion about taking the lieutenant's test?"

"Yes, sir."

"And?"

"I don't think I'm ready for it, sir."

Rowan frowned. When he did so his brow creased, and his roundish face contorted like a bulldog's. "Why not?"

"I'm not sure I have what it takes to be an officer."

"Bullshit. I know what it takes, and you have it."

Rowan leaned back in his metal swivel chair, placed his hands behind his head, and studied his control man.

"Let me take a wild guess. It's Sal, isn't it?"

"Excuse me, sir?"

"Your father."

"Well, yes, sir."

"He doesn't want you to take the test, right?"

"He's not keen on officers and I don't think he'd take too well to his son becoming one."

Rowan nodded. "Phil, listen to me. The other day, you showed real poise on the bridge. That girl was gonna jump, for sure. I know. I don't know how you got to her, but you did."

"Thanks, Lieu."

"You've got the skills to lead these guys. You know how to talk to them, get the job done, and get others to do their jobs. They respect you. All the guys do. That's leadership."

"Lieu, I'd like to take the test, but my dad's been a real pain in the ass about it. Otherwise …" Coletti shrugged.

Rowan swiveled in his chair and fixed his gaze on a grainy black-and-white photo of 252's crew. The year "1980" was printed underneath the photo. Coletti noticed the picture. It captured a younger, slimmer version of Rowan operating a two-and-a-half-inch handline at an apartment fire in Bensonhurst. He faced Coletti. "I've got a proposition. Study and take the test. When you get the results, let's talk. If you pass and still don't want to apply, I won't press it. Deal?"

Coletti pursed his lips. "Okay. Sure. Just don't expect me to change my mind."

Rowan leaned forward and smiled. "Just do that much, and I'll be happy."

✦

It was a little after three thirty when Ellie arrived at the house, holding a plate of Russian pastries. She was wearing a lime-green blouse, blue pastel skirt, and flats. Her hair was pulled back with a hair tie, letting the midday sun highlight her wide, open face. She drew in a deep breath and told her feet to move, which brought her inside to the apparatus bay.

The guy in the house watch whistled low, but eased up when he saw her blush. He stepped out. "Can I help you?"

"Hi. I'm Ellie. Is Phil Coletti here?"

"I'll get him." He returned to the house watch, used the intercom to page Coletti.

Ellie studied the engines and trucks parked in their bays.

The watch room fireman bounded back to her. "He should be right up. I'm Fred DeBellis. Can I—?"

Coletti's voice sounded behind him. "Thanks, Probie. Rodriguez needs help with the garbage."

"Yeah. Okay. I get it." DeBellis skulked away.

Coletti watched him depart.

"I thought his name was Fred," she said.

"What?"

"You called him Probie."

He grinned wide. "Nah. Probie is short for probationary firefighter - rookies. It's what we call them."

Ellie studied Coletti. Loose jeans, button-down collared shirt, black boots—all fitted him in a way that confirmed her impression of him as well-proportioned, muscular. If he had any body fat, she couldn't see it.

She balanced the plate on her left palm and held out her hand. "Hi."

Coletti took her hand and gave her a quick kiss on the cheek. "I'm glad you could make it."

Ellie held the plate out. "Pastries. For the guys."

He took the plate from her. "Thanks. But I told you you didn't have to."

"I wanted to."

His grin widened. "C'mon. The cookout's across the street, in the park. I'll introduce you to the guys."

He led her through the building, past the gear lockers and

equipment stands, through the kitchen, out the side door, and across to the park. Fifty or so people clustered near roasting meats and vegetables. Those aromas, mixed with spices and condiments, wafted toward them.

Ellie slowed her steps. "There are a lot more people here than I thought. I thought—"

"I should have said." He gestured. "Firemen, wives, girlfriends, kids. The usual." At her hesitation he added, "It'll be fine. Good food, good company. Only a few of us know what happened, and our lips are sealed. Okay?"

Ellie nodded and followed him. The tall African-American fireman who was on the bridge with Phil stood next to the grill, hands holding a plate of burgers, hot dogs, and a healthy helping of potato salad. He smiled when Ellie and Coletti approached. "Hey, girl. You're lookin' better. Hope you brought your appetite."

Coletti said, "Ellie, this is Jordan."

Ellie's cheeks pinked. She gave him a small smile. "I could eat, especially now that I smell the food."

Coletti elbowed Jordan. "That was *almost* smooth enough." He pointed his chin at the plate. "Feeding the bears at the zoo?"

"Ha-hardy-ha." He leaned in toward Ellie. "Listen, if this guy gets out of line, you let me know, and I'll feed *him* to the bears."

Ellie laughed then bit on her lower lip.

"Go, Jordan." He waved him away. "Go feed the bears."

"You guys have a funny way of talking to each other."

"Really? I didn't notice," Coletti responded with a chuckle.

It didn't take long before other guys came up to Coletti and asked him who his friend was. All of them were polite, but curious.

"Find us a table, and I'll bring the plates," Coletti said.

One table had room enough for both of them. She nodded and smiled at the people seated around it. Introductions were made. Shyness colored her face, so the others spoke but didn't throw questions her way.

Moments later, Coletti slid in next to her on the bench. Almost as though they'd been waiting for him, the stories about the Job, and some of the dumber things they'd seen, mostly done by civilians, became the conversation topic.

Sean Hurley, whom Coletti had introduced as the can man on 218, said, "I mean, do you have to be a rocket scientist to know you shouldn't place a miniature Christmas tree over your oven's vent hood?" he asked rhetorically. "Like how long do you think it's gonna last when you're cooking ribs on the stove? Shit, some people make my four-year-old look like Albert-fucking-Einstein."

His contempt was palpable. The crew around him, Coletti and Ellie included, roared at his diatribe.

"So, when I ask this guy why he put it up there, you know what he says? He tells me he didn't want to put it by the heater in the living room because he thought it might catch fire. You can't make this shit up."

The tales stretched across the next hour or so. Ellie whispered to Coletti, "These stories are something else. I never know what I'm going to hear next."

"We never know what we're going to find next." He studied her face. "You look relaxed."

She beamed a smile at him. "I am. I was afraid I wouldn't fit in. That I'd be uncomfortable, but it's the opposite."

He nudged her with his shoulder. "I'm glad."

The shrill sound of the firehouse alarm pierced through the afternoon air like a dentist's drill. The guys wearing their blue work uniforms immediately got up from their tables and headed into the firehouse. A male voice came over the intercom.

"Engine 252. Ladder 128. Smell of smoke. Five-four zero seven. Bay Parkway."

"Sounds like a bullshit call to me," Hurley quipped.

Coletti winked at Ellie. "You never know. Could be the Big One."

Hurley continued his analysis. "Smell of smoke. Probably food on the stove. Shit, I smell smoke right here." He gazed toward the grill. "And now I know why." He shouted, "Tazik at the grill. Sound a full assignment. Five alarms."

Guys at their table shook their heads and chuckled. One of them shouted, "Hey, Tazik. Hurley's cutting you up."

Tazik glowered at the group. "He wishes he could be as funny as good as I cook," the truckie responded through a thick Polish accent.

Coletti stared at Hurley. "Ellie, I apologize for some of the behaviors exhibited by this bunch of New York's bravest."

"No apology needed. He's entertaining. Reminds me of when I watch *Sesame Street*."

Those at the table, including Hurley, erupted in laughter.

Coletti smirked. "Nice comeback." He wiped his hands on a napkin. Sirens from the outgoing engine and truck put a momentary halt to the conversation. "How about the five-cent tour of the house?" he asked Ellie.

"I'd like that."

After eating they returned to the firehouse. Once inside, he asked, "Where do you want to start?"

"Coats and pants."

"Turnout gear. Let's go."

She followed him across the now-vacant apparatus floor, to the row of metal gear lockers against the far wall where they stopped at a dented gray locker with his name written in black marker on a faded strip of masking tape. He opened the door and pointed to each item. "Bunker gear, boots, turnout coat, helmet." His "New Yorker"-style helmet faced forward. The once-shiny, eagle-shaped brass shield holder was now singed the same color as the patina of one of Tazik's charred hot dogs. The shriveled leather shield with curled edges—the result of heat exposure at countless fires—revealed a barely discernible "Engine 252" embossed on it. He removed the helmet. "Try this on."

She took the helmet. "It's heavy." Slid it over her hair. "You put this on every time you're called to a fire?"

"Yeah. But a Nomex hood and facemask has to go under it."

"Can I try on your pants and coat?"

"You really want to?"

She nodded.

He helped her get into the bunker pants with red suspenders and then his boots. Then he placed the turnout coat over her shoulders, added the equipment, and took a step back. "Not bad. You could pass for a probie."

She patted the pockets and sniffed. "What's that smell?"

"The smoke from way too many fires. Doesn't matter how many times you wash the gear; it never goes away."

Ellie returned Coletti's smile, saluted, and said, "Probie Deutsch reporting for duty, sir."

Coletti nodded and chuckled. "At ease, Deutsch. Let's get you out of that gear. I'm sure it's getting heavier by the second."

As they removed and stored the gear, radio transmissions from the engine and truck that had responded to the call echoed from the house watch. Sunlight beyond the open bay doors began to wane. Coletti touched her arm. "C'mon. I want to show you something."

He led her to the doorway and up the worn, bowed metal stairs behind the house watch.

"Gosh, these stairs are old. They're so beveled."

Coletti nodded. "Yeah, a lot of years of guys pounding down on them, scrambling to get on the rigs."

Coletti and Ellie ascended four flights until they reached the roof where Coletti opened the roof door and motioned to the parapet wall. "Take a look," he said.

Ellie took in the sweeping view of New York Harbor and the Atlantic Ocean. Manhattan's skyline rose in the distance. Late afternoon sun reflected off the buildings, like golden illuminated fingers rising out of the harbor. "What a view."

He leaned against the parapet wall, facing her rather than the view. "Yeah, I thought you'd like it." He placed his hand on her elbow and gently drew her toward him. Ellie hesitated at first then moved closer, her face no longer as relaxed as it had been. "I'm really glad you've kept the daily routine. It's been helpful, hasn't it?"

"Yeah. I don't know what, but it's okay."

"I'm sorry I couldn't take your calls sometimes. We've been getting a lot of runs lately. I'll always check in the next morning, though."

"I know. I understand."

"Tomorrow is Sunday. Just keep doing the same routine. If it's working, you don't need to fix it." He smiled a little. "Know why I wanted you to see this?"

She shook her head, which she lowered, and bit down on her bottom lip.

He used his other hand to raise her chin. "Because it's beautiful—like you." He ran his index finger down the side of her neck, across her collarbone, to her shoulder.

She moved a half inch closer then stopped. Swallowed hard, then broke away from his face and eyes that held her gaze. "Thanks for the tour. And the cookout and all. I enjoyed spending the afternoon with you, but I think I should go now. I hope you understand."

He kept eye contact with her for several moments, then smiled. "C'mon. I'll get you a car to take you home."

CHAPTER 7

"What a dumb idea. What a clusterfuck of a dumbass idea." Sal Coletti spat tobacco-laced saliva. He rested his back against the gunwale of his boat and fished a matchbook out of his front pants pocket. He yanked off one of the matches, struck it hard against the abrasive brown band, and held it to the tip of his half-smoked Hoyo de Monterrey cigar. The twenty-five-foot center console with twin outboard engines bobbed gently off its anchor in the Atlantic Ocean. A red-orange sun began its ascent over the horizon.

"Well, that's not what the lieutenant thinks," Phil Coletti shot back.

"Rowan? Son, he couldn't find his ass with both hands." Sal inhaled on the cigar and threw the match in the water.

Coletti watched his dad, sixty-one, leaner and more fit than most twenty-five-year-olds on the Job. He picked up the bait knife and sliced into the moss bunker on the bait table. "He's a good fireman. And a good officer."

"C'mon, 252 is nothing to write home about. It's second due on everything," Sal scoffed, referring to Engine 252's habit of arriving second to alarms, thereby relegating it to water-supply duty rather than immediate fire suppression.

"Yeah, if you're not on a rescue rig, you're not a fireman, right, Pop?"

Sal picked up the black eight-foot casting rod in one hand and kept his gaze fixed on the ocean. He spit again. "I have thirty-eight years on the Job. What the hell kind of answer do you expect me to give to that lame-ass question?"

Coletti stood up in front of the bunker steaks laid out on the fish tray ready for baiting. He took one and baited a bluefish hook on his casting rod.

"You know what I think, Pop?" Coletti held the rod behind his head, bunker chunk dangling on the end of the line, ready to cast it.

"Yeah, go ahead, Miles Davis, hit me with another bright idea."

Coletti held the rod in two hands above and behind his head, the monofilament line pressed between the rod and his right index finger, the bait and tackle dangling at the end. In one motion, he swung the rod forward and released his index finger. The line sailed fifty yards in the air and splashed in the ocean. "I think you can't handle it if your boy, the one you did *not* want to go on the Job, became an officer. That would be too much for you."

"What a stupid boot," Sal scowled. "You think I'm threatened by you making lieuie? C'mon. You're not such a smart guy if that's what you think. You haven't even yet learned what I've forgotten about the Job. If you stopped to—"

Wheeeeeeeeeeeeeeee. The star drag on Coletti's rod whined as the line ran. A bluefish had taken the bait near the surface and was diving fast.

Sal reeled in his own line. "Don't pull up. Let that cocksucker set the hook in his throat."

"I know," Phil said. He held the rod near the surface of the ocean.

The spool was getting smaller by the second as he let the fish go deep. Within ten seconds, he'd be out of line. He waited another five seconds and then raised the rod fast, tightening the star drag to slow the unspooling. He felt the tension of the fish, its weight and speed, against the line. He raised the line higher. The whining stopped.

"He's turning." Phil held the rod up. Its pliant end bent like a shepherd's staff.

Suddenly, the line went limp. The rod snapped back to upright. No more tension.

"I lost him," Phil said, lowering the rod.

"Nah, I don't think so." Sal peered out over the water, the two-inch butt of the cigar firmly planted in the right side of his mouth, a fish gaff in his left hand. "He's coming at you. You better hold on to that rod."

"I lost him."

"If I were you, I'd reel in."

Coletti reeled the line in slowly.

"He might have taken the hook and leader—" Suddenly, the line became taut again. The rod heaved toward the water. Coletti tightened his grip on the rod a second before it was nearly ripped from his hands.

"Told you," snickered Sal, watching his firstborn fighting the wily blue, which was so far getting the best of him.

Coletti lifted the rod over his head, its business end whipping down as the bluefish dove under the boat. Sal moved to the stern as Coletti walked forward to the bow to work the fish around the boat, rod in hand, reeling slowly.

"I hope he doesn't foul up the anchor line," Sal quipped.

Coletti held the rod straight up, now confident that the hook and bait were firmly planted in the fish's throat. The tension of the line on the fish had reduced the blue's resistance. It was moving more slowly through the water. He dropped the rod to slacken the line so he could reel up, and then raised it back over his head. The fish was now close to the boat.

"C'mon, Philly boy. Let's see if you learned what the old man taught you."

Phil kept the tip of the rod up and reeled in slowly. The fish broke the surface about twenty feet off starboard. Sal leaned over the starboard gunwale with the gaff ready to spear the fish and pull him in. Phil kept reeling.

"Keep it up. They always spook closest to the boat," Sal said, keeping his eyes on the fish.

"I know. Do you think this is the first fish I ever caught?"

The fish was now close to the boat, on the surface. "That's a good-size fish, like twenty-five pounds," Coletti said.

"C'mon." Sal waited, with the gaff cocked. The fish was now next to the boat. Sal gaffed the fish and yanked it up and over into the boat in one movement. The fish writhed, bouncing angrily on the deck, and gnashed its teeth in an attempt to bite anything it could latch onto.

Sal grabbed a billy club and brought it down on the blue's head, intent on beating the fish into submission. Blood splattered everything nearby—his clothes, cheeks, arms, and cigar still tucked firmly in the corner of his mouth, until the fish lay motionless. Sal sucked in a breath of sea air and eyed his son. "What I was gonna say before is that if you stop and think about it for even one damn minute, you'd know the Job isn't for you." He pointed the club at Coletti. "Do something else." He aimed the club toward the shore. "Let's go in."

OFFICER

We cannot understand firemen; they have risen to some place among the inexplicable beauties of life.

– Murray Kempton, *New York Post*, August 3, 1978

CHAPTER 8

MARCH, 2001

Lauren Moore toyed with a strand of her shoulder-length amber hair as she sipped coffee from a china cup in the living room of her coveted multi-million apartment on Fifth Avenue. With her back against the plush Chippendale sofa, feet propped against the antique coffee table purchased in France, her hazel eyes watched the morning sunlight spill through the nearly floor-to-ceiling window that looked out over Central Park. Her cell phone hummed against the coffee table's surface under the latest issue of *Harper's*. She checked caller ID—Amy Heller. She smiled and answered. "Hey, Amy. What's doin'?"

"I can tell by your tone … you haven't heard about Pat."

Lauren sat with her spine straight. "Heard what?"

"There was a fire last night. Lower East Side."

Stay calm. "Pat's been in lots of fires. He knows how to handle himself."

"He's in the hospital. It's on the news."

Lauren's skin grew clammy. "I haven't turned anything on yet."

"Is Ross there?"

Lauren heard footsteps behind her and swiveled. Her fiancé, Ross Challinor, entered the living room. She made eye contact with him and said, "Yes."

The blue-eyed, 6-foot-tall business mogul leaned over the back of the sofa and kissed her forehead. "Who is it, honey?"

Lauren fixed her eyes on the Persian rug that filled most of the marble floor.

He walked around the sofa, stopping a few feet from her. "Who's on the phone?"

She held up her hand to silence him. Into the phone she said, "Yes. Thank you. I'll call you later."

Ross went to the foyer and stood in front of the full-length mirror mounted in a gilded frame. He adjusted his platinum cufflinks. Turning side to side, he checked the lines of his custom-tailored, blue pinstriped suit and smoothed the solid maroon Hermès tie resting against the crisp white Brooks Brothers shirt. "Who called?"

"Len. Apparently there's a problem with some of the pieces that arrived for the museum's upcoming Phoenician art exhibit."

"Oh." He walked to the adjoining kitchen; the subject apparently already forgotten. Hardboiled eggs, a fruit medley, coffee, and juice were prepared and waiting for him at the breakfast table.

Lauren trailed him in, cell phone tucked into a pocket. "Looks like I'll have to work late tonight."

"That works out for both of us. I have a dinner with the Brooklyn Democratic Party chairman. Word is, he's not committed on the election. With the right persuasion, I'm sure I can get him to support me."

Persuasion, she thought. *I have a good idea what that entails.* "I'm sure you'll bring him around." She poured more coffee into her cup, sat at the table, and added a teaspoon of sugar to her cup. "Ross, I've been meaning to ask you something."

"Shoot."

"You have more money than just about anyone in this city. Why would you want to go into public service? What do you need it for?"

Ross looked up from his eggs, fork in his hand. "Well, I've assessed the quality of civil servants in the government and I've always wondered if we could take our business skills that make millions, billions of dollars, and apply them to government, couldn't we do better than the hapless bunch of incompetents currently on the job?"

Lauren listened, studying him with probing eyes. Ross put down his fork.

"I mean, wouldn't it logically flow that we could deliver better service to more people for what it should cost and no more?"

Lauren nodded slightly. Ross always spoke so convincingly on the things he was sure of, she thought. It was why she said yes to his marriage proposal. He convinced her they were a great fit together.

Ross checked his watch. "I better get going." He hurriedly downed the rest of his breakfast and, leaving his dishes on the table, strode to the intercom positioned on the wall next to the kitchen entrance. He pressed one of the buttons.

A deep voice said in response, "Good morning, sir."

"Louis, can you pull the car around? I'll be down in a moment."

"Yes, sir."

He returned to where Lauren sat, kissed her on the cheek. "Don't let Len get you down, honey. There's no problem too big to be solved."

She gave him a slight smile, which he didn't see, and remained fixed in placed until she heard the foyer door close behind him. Quickly, she hurried to the mahogany-paneled study, opened the TV console door, grabbed the remote control tucked inside and turned on the TV. She sank into the high-backed leather chair Ross had purchased in England; eyes aimed at the screen. A reporter stood in front of a burned-out storefront amid fire trucks and police cars. The banner at the bottom read: *Two firefighters seriously injured in Lower East Side fire.*

Microphone raised, the reporter said, "Fire officials as yet have no knowledge of how the fire started. When emergency personnel arrived on the scene, they encountered a fully involved storefront with victims trapped inside the apartments above it. Two firefighters were injured while rescuing victims from the floor above the store. The ceiling of the store, which was the floor they were on, collapsed, plunging them into a storage room adjacent to the store."

Tears welled in Lauren's eyes. Her hands went instinctively over her heart.

"We're told the two firefighters suffered life-threatening injuries. They were rushed to Metropolitan Hospital, where they remain in critical condition." He raised a folded piece of paper and read from it. "I'm told their names are Captain Patrick Boyle and Firefighter Dennis Andrews."

Lauren brushed tears from her cheeks, rose to her feet and paced. *God, if you can hear me, please don't let Pat die.* She had to see him, but it wouldn't be easy. Her life was already complicated enough.

Life had not prepared Lauren for such situations. She particularly had no idea how to deal with this one. Her wealthy shipping-executive father had given her an upbringing of privilege in Philadelphia. The daily struggles of others never crossed into her world. Except the one time, when she was in grade school. Her father's chauffeur had driven her past a horrific car accident. She was told not to look, but she did—at the ambulances with their flashing lights; at the injured on gurneys and the deceased on the ground; at the drawn, sullen faces of those trying to grasp what had just befallen them. It was a tragedy on the other side of her tinted window, close in proximity but remote in experience. Almost like watching a movie too close to the screen.

Now, someone close to her was hurt, and seriously. And to complicate the situation, it was not her fiancé, but her former lover. Here she was living on Fifth Avenue with her fiancé, the billionaire Ross Challinor, who was on the verge of being elected governor of New York, while the man she truly loved—The Man Who Got Her—was lying gravely ill in a municipal hospital bed less than thirty blocks away. And she could not go see him. The intensity of the conflicting emotions made her extremely anxious. *Settle down. Get in control.*

She pulled her phone from her pocket and hit speed-dial for Amy. At the same moment her friend answered, a knock at the open door startled her. She whipped around, afraid it was Ross, and released a breath. Into the phone she said, "Hold on a moment." She turned off the TV. To the woman standing in the doorway, she said, "What is it, Rosa?"

Short and stocky, the Dominican cook smoothed a loose strand of black hair behind her left ear. "Need anything, Miss Lauren?"

"No. Thank you."

"There's some coffee left, if you'd like me to pour you a cup."

"I'm fine. Please close the door behind you."

The cook nodded and pulled the pocket doors together.

"Sorry about that, Amy. I just caught a brief snippet of news, enough to know he's at Metropolitan. Have you heard any more?"

"One of the cops I work with said Pat and Denny have third-degree burns. They're both in surgery. The mayor's at the hospital, getting ready to have a press conference soon. That's all I've got at the moment."

Lauren's stomach knotted. "God. I hope it's not his face. Please don't let it be his beautiful face." She sank onto the sofa. "My poor Pat."

"Lau—I'm sorry. I don't know anything more specific. Soon as I get more information, I'll call. In the meantime, keep your TV on."

Call ended, Lauren dropped her face into her hands and sobbed.

Collecting herself, she turned the TV on. A morning talk show was on. She stared unseeing at the screen, allowing a replay of when she and Pat Boyle had met occupy her mind. A meeting that led to blissful nights shared in intimacy. Eyes closed, she pictured his steely blue eyes and the way they sparkled when she told one of her not-so-funny jokes. She wondered if he—or they—would ever be the same.

SPECIAL REPORT flashed on the screen. Ashen-faced, Ronnie Pisani, NYC's mayor, approached a podium cluttered with news microphones. Behind him stood Bill Hollenbach, city fire commissioner, equally somber.

Pisani cleared his throat. "Early this morning, firefighters from seven stations out of Manhattan and Brooklyn responded to a three-alarm fire at 153 Avenue C on the Lower East Side. They found the storefront in flames and occupants trapped on the upper floors above the store. While engaging in rescue operations, two of our veteran firefighters, Captain Patrick Boyle and Firefighter Dennis Andrews, suffered grave injuries. They were on the second floor, which collapsed beneath them." The mayor paused to study the paper in his hand.

Lauren gripped the sofa arm, digging her nails into the leather.

"Boyle and Andrews were brought to the Metropolitan Hospital Burn Unit, where doctors rushed to stabilize their injuries. Unfortunately, injuries suffered by Dennis Andrews were too severe. He succumbed at four twenty-eight this morning. His family has been notified."

Oh, God, here it comes.

"Captain Boyle is in critical condition. He suffered bruised ribs and third-degree burns on his legs. Doctors indicate his prognosis for a full recovery should be good but will take a while." He put the paper down. "I'll take a few questions."

Lauren rested her head against the back of the sofa, stared unseeing at the ceiling as tears streamed down her cheeks. She released the breath she'd been holding then returned her gaze to the screen.

Pisani glanced to his right, leaned forward slightly, as he listened to a reporter's question. "It's my understanding that they'd cleared the floor above the fire of four occupants—three children and their mother. When they returned to continue their search for another trapped victim, the floor opened up on them, and they fell into a storage room in the back of the store. They were rescued by other firefighters who were able to gain access to the storage room from an alleyway behind the store."

The mayor paused again, listening, then nodded earnestly.

"Yes, that is the same Captain Boyle. The doctors say his condition is critical and he will take time to recover. If any of you know Captain Boyle, you know he's one of the most experienced, decorated firefighters in the city. I don't doubt that he'll be back to work as soon as he can, but it's going to take a while."

The mayor put up his hand and leaned toward the microphones.

"We should all take a moment to think about our firefighters, police, and EMT crews who put themselves in harm's way for all of us in our city, every hour of every day. Please remember to keep the family of Firefighter Andrews in your prayers and thoughts. They're going to need them in this difficult time. I'll let Commissioner Hollenbach answer any other questions."

The scene shifted to a reporter for the local station, who stood in the foreground, microphone at the ready. Lauren's cell phone vibrated in her hand—Amy. "I watched it. Do you know anything they didn't say?"

"He's conscious, in a lot of pain, so they've given him some serious drugs."

"You sound so much calmer than I feel."

"When you're press liaison for the New York City Police Department, you get a lot of practice. One time too many, far as I'm concerned."

"I want to see him."

"No visitors other than immediate family, at least for now, and even then, it's for like a minute." She paused. "Lau, you sure you want to do this?"

"I must. What if I go there late tonight?"

"FDNY medical support are on duty outside his room, but I'll notify them. They'll have your name but be sure to mention mine to them."

"Thanks, Amy. For everything."

"He's in the burn unit. Third floor. Turn right when you get off the elevator and go all the way down the hall. Last room on the right. Be careful."

"I will."

Lauren ended the call. Her shoulders relaxed. Pat would be all right. If anyone could bounce back from injuries, it was him. As much as she wanted to see him, uneasiness kept a grip on her. It wasn't right to have these intense feelings for him when she intended to marry someone else. How many times had she asked herself why she didn't feel the same about Ross?

Too many.

✦

Third Avenue traffic was light in the late-night hours. It was eleven thirty when Lauren's taxi pulled up in front of the nearly deserted lobby of Metropolitan Hospital. Lauren paid the cab fare then walked into the lobby. She went directly to the elevators. When she emerged from the elevator, she followed Amy's directions, walking past the nurses' desk.

The duty nurse saw her walk by. "Sorry, ma'am, visiting hours ended at ten."

"I know. I'm sorry. My visit will be brief. It was prearranged," Lauren answered. She adjusted the mink collar of her tailored suit jacket. "I'm expected. And as I said, it'll be brief. It's the only time I could get here." She let her eyes do the rest of the pleading.

"All right. But be quick."

She continued to the end of the dimly lit hallway, espying two firemen wearing navy-blue shirts and work pants outside the last room on the right. They'd been leaning against the wall but stood up straight when they saw her approaching them. She did her best to ignore the rhythmic tolling of heart monitors and respirators coming from open or mostly open doors as she passed them, finally coming to a halt outside Pat's room.

She glanced at the door that was ajar, made eye contact with the first man, a tall, square-shouldered, thirtyish guy with deeply set eyes. She held out her hand. "I'm Lauren. Amy Heller said she'd arrange for me to stop by."

"Ken Kearns," the fireman replied, taking her hand. The other fireman, forty-something with male-pattern baldness, extended his hand.

"Noah Beale."

How's Pat doing?" she said to the second man, shaking his hand.

"Sleeping. Finally. You still want to go in there?"

"Yes."

"Gotta wear these." Beale handed her a surgical mask, gown, booties, and thin rubber gloves.

She placed her purse down on a chair in the hallway. She slipped the booties on, then the gown, followed by the mask and gloves, then picked up her purse.

"Go in, but stand near the door. No closer."

She nodded, inhaled a nervous breath as he opened the door, and entered. The odor was like an assault—antiseptic over the stench of burnt flesh. The bed was to her right, centered against the wall, just beyond the bathroom. Pat lay on his back with an IV in his left arm dripping saline from a bag suspended on a metal pole. Next to the pole, the monitor console tracking and showing his vital signs flashed numbers and graphs, making occasional beeps. Sterile gauze bandages encased his left leg from thigh to foot. Bandages covered his right calf only. A hospital smock covered his torso. His left hand was bandaged as well. She sighed in relief to see that his face, though it had bruises around his closed eyes, was unmarred in other respects.

Seeing him in the bed in this condition reminded her of the first time they were together. How, when he took off his shirt, she was shocked by the number of scars on his body. His back had a burn scar running across the width of it. He had a scar from a gunshot wound in his shoulder, a scar from a puncture wound in his thigh, and various blemishes from other bruises and injuries. She remembered that Pat noticed her expression of shock and told her not to pay attention to them. He had told her they were old injuries, that she could touch them. She thought about how, when their bodies were against each other, she could feel the roughness of the scar tissue. Now, seeing his bandaged legs, she didn't have to imagine how they would feel against her.

There was a chair propped against the wall just to her right. She sank into it and placed her purse on the floor. This was the only place she wanted to be, right now, right here. With him. Although she was nonreligious, she'd prayed to the God she believed was good and fair, and who listened whenever she asked Him for something, like this morning. Like in the taxi coming here. Like now.

Faintly, she heard voices from the hallway. It was the two firemen, talking in hushed tones, as if they were in a confessional. She cocked her ear.

"He better make it." Kearns said. "If there's a god, he better make it."

"Ken, he always does, but those are some serious burns."

"Do you remember that job in Alphabet City? The chief shut it down because it was too hot and he went back inside and pulled two kids out, stuffed in his coat?"

"Yeah. He got a James Gordon Bennett Medal for that one."

"Shit. He has five Bennetts. *Five*."

"Beyond unbelievable."

"You know, if he lives, they're gonna rip his ass downtown for this one. Say he takes too many chances—total bullshit."

Lauren could hear a chair move, followed by steps.

"Noah, you've known him longer than anyone. How does he do it? The guys will follow him anywhere."

"He's just hard-wired, I guess. Did you know when he turned eighteen, he joined the army and *asked* to go to Vietnam? Did you know that?"

"Geez."

"And he got the Silver Star."

The fuckin guy is on a different plane. You ever see him in a fire? It's almost like the fire's afraid of him."

"No one would believe it."

"No one."

Inside the room, Lauren closed her eyes and returned to her prayer. She talked to God for several minutes, until she heard movement. She wanted to jump to her feet but resisted the impulse and opened her eyes.

Pat moved his head from side to side and then opened his eyes, his gaze fixed on the ceiling.

Softly she said, "Pat?"

"Hey. When'd you get here?" His pronounced Brooklyn accent was muted by pain and medications.

"Not too long ago. How are you feeling?" She bit down on her lower lip and said, "What a stupid question."

"It's fine. I'll be okay." He coughed up dark phlegm, grabbed a tissue from the box next to him on the bed, and spit into it. "Sorry." Pain echoed across his face from the movement. Tentatively, he rubbed his ribs. "They told me about Denny."

"I know. I'm so very sorry."

"He was like a kid brother. I can't believe it."

He peered out the window at the city lights across the East River in Queens. Lauren looked down at her hands in her lap and remained silent.

"We heard another guy in there. So we went back in. Even though the conditions were bad." He paused. "Real bad. Damn it.

I should have let it go." He draped his right forearm over his eyes.

Lauren glanced left. Neither fireman standing post was watching. She crossed to the bed, pulled his arm away, lowered her mask, and pressed her lips to his forehead. Her eyes glistened with tears. Voice lowered, she said, "I could get kicked out for doing that, but I had to." She kept her face inches from his. "Pat, I know you won't listen to me, but I'm going to say it anyway. Don't do it. Don't take this one on. It wasn't your fault," she said softy.

Pat looked up. Her hair gently brushed his cheek. He raised a hand and let his fingers clear the strands falling in front of her face. "Still using Jean Patou. Much better than the soot smell I'm giving off right now." She nodded. He continued. "Reminds me of that night we went to the Boathouse in Central Park. And afterwards, at your apartment." He smiled, then winced in pain.

She pulled up the chair next to the bed, sat down, and took his right hand in hers.

"Pat, don't try to speak. Please listen to me. I know I will never know, never really know, what you are going through." As she'd so often done when they were together, she stroked the veins on the top of his hand with a gloved finger. "And I could remind you how tough you are, because you are, but that won't help. So, what I want you to know, what I *need* you to know, is that some of us cannot live without knowing you're there, out there, somewhere, doing what you love to do. And I can't bear to see you hurt yourself, because this world has done enough of that already."

Lauren tilted her head toward him. She hoped half the words would sink in. Pat bit his lip. He stared at her perfectly shaped gloved hands holding his.

"I'm glad you came," he said.

Lauren breathed in a little deeper than normal. "I had to, though I didn't know how you'd take it." She put his hand on his chest.

"When's the wedding?" Pat asked, his eyes cast to the window.

"It's in December."

"Did you tell him about us?"

She hesitated a moment and lowered her head. "No." She paused. "No, I didn't."

"I guess it doesn't matter. It's ancient history."

"Is that what you think it is?"

"Not like I had a choice, was it?" he said with forthrightness, one of his strongest traits. Uncomplicated and true, Pat called it like it was, she thought. "Ross came waltzing back into your life last year, and that was that."

Lauren lowered her head. She knew she was matched. He was right. She hadn't given him any choice. She abruptly stopped seeing him when Ross came back into her life last year. Since that time, and the hectic pace of her reunion with him, the marriage proposal, the publicity surrounding his run for governor, she didn't have time to think about Pat and how she had truly felt about him—until this morning. When she got that call and turned on the TV, the feelings she had for him rushed at her like a tidal wave.

"No, it wasn't."

"It's okay. Some things are never easy. Besides, if we were still together, in the state I'm in, I'd be no kind of date to the swanky society parties you like to go to."

She studied his face. She always thought she had a stolid demeanor, but it was nothing next to his. Here he was in a city hospital bed, fighting painful third-degree burns, grieving the loss of a brother firefighter, and talking to her like they were having tea at Lespinasse—and letting her off easy. The captains of industry and Wall Street whales she knew, were they in Pat's condition, would have told her to take a hike when she dared to show up. Not Pat Boyle. A gentleman through and through.

She remembered when they first met how fascinated she was by him. Not really him, but his life, the life he lived and how he lived it. She had never met anyone who was so comfortable in his station in life: no reaching, no airs. She remembered the pace and meter of how he carried himself; his body language exuded such a sense of place and bearing, but without conceit or ulterior motive. It was foreign to her. So many men she met were always striving, achieving, competing, seeing her as a trophy to be won.

Damn, how can you not love this man? He's a man; the rest, including Ross, are boys.

Both of them glanced toward the small entrance hall as rubber soles slapped against linoleum. A nurse entered and stopped. Her smile slipped to a stern expression. Noah Beale stood behind her. She said, "Captain Boyle needs his rest." She frowned at the fireman and turned back to Lauren. "You shouldn't even be in here, especially at this time of night. Time to go."

Lauren got to her feet and rested a hand gently on Pat's forearm. "I know you'll recover quickly, but please take care of yourself. Think about what I said."

He nodded. She could tell his eyes drank her in.

Lauren picked up her purse and exited. She placed her purse on the floor and removed the protective garments, handing them into the outstretched hands and arms of Ken Kearns, who'd remained outside the door.

Walking toward the elevator, she got that feeling she was afraid she would get. It made her feel warm and safe. It was the feeling of balance—order in the universe. She hated seeing him there, like that, but she knew this was the reality of life, his life. She knew that with every grab, every attempt at a rescue, Pat and his brothers ransomed total strangers back to life. They were like a dark, inexorable force brought forth when needed and returned to obscurity when not. These men couldn't do anything else. It was their destiny, and her comprehension of that fact gave her extraordinary comfort and understanding. *God, how inadequate I am compared to that man*, she found herself thinking.

Lauren opened the door to her apartment a few minutes after 12:30 a.m. She removed her heels and made her way to the master bedroom, decorated in French Provincial. A small lamp cast a dim, yellow glow in one corner of the room. She walked to the sixteenth-century armoire Ross had purchased for her at Sotheby's and undressed. Bedcovers rustled behind her. She glanced over her shoulder.

Ross yawned, opened his eyes halfway, and said, "Where have you been?"

"Dealing with the exhibit fiasco, then coffee with Amy. She'd had a rough day and wanted to talk."

He yawned again and rolled onto his side, facing away from her. "Come to bed. There's a mayor's benefit tomorrow night. Need to bring our A-game if we want to live in the Governor's Mansion."

She slipped a silk gown over her head and went into the bathroom to brush her teeth and pamper her skin. She turned out the light there and on the small lamp, got into bed, and stared at the back of Ross's head. He wanted to be governor, yet she wondered if he knew how real people in the five boroughs and upstate actually lived. She fixed her eyes on the ceiling. With Ross she had every luxury and amenity she could want, and with the promise of even more to come. She thought of Pat and the time they had together. How elemental it was, the feelings she had for him. Seeing him tonight brought it all back, the truth of it. It resolved nothing in her, and that troubled her deeply.

✦

Boyle grinned when Gordy Ryan entered his hospital room. The six-foot-three, former all-state basketball player and track star-turned-fireman was a welcome sight. "Here he is. FDNY's calendar guy favorite three years running. You wear that gown like a minidress. And how'd they find booties to fit those boats you call feet?"

Ryan chuckled past his dark-brown bushy mustache, hidden by a mask, and moved closer to the bed. He lifted his leather jacket that was draped across his left arm to reveal two cans of Harp Lager he'd smuggled in. “Thirsty?”

“Wish I could. Drink them for me, brother. How’s it going for the lieutenant of the busiest house in the city?”

“You know how.” Ryan opened a can and sipped. His smile faded. “Coroner’s starting Denny’s autopsy tomorrow.”

“I heard.”

“Knox is calling for an investigation. Says you shouldn’t have gone back in.”

“No surprise there. He’ll do anything to get in good with the brass downtown. Anything to boost his career.”

“Except put out a fire.”

Boyle laughed and said, “You got that right.” He rubbed his eyes with his right hand, winced. “I wouldn’t do it any different. Couldn’t. There was someone in there. Denny didn’t hesitate when I told him we had to go back in.”

“I hear you.” Ryan placed the beer can on the floor. “You know the drill. Commissioner and the brass downtown will investigate. Try to show you took too big a risk. You’ll get slapped on the wrist and sent back to work.”

He faced Ryan. “Yeah, I know. And the loudest are the ones I never see at a job.”

“Knox will use it to make division chief.”

“That he will, brother. That he will.”

Ryan picked up his beer, held it up in a salute of mutual understanding, and sipped the rest of it in silence, each man’s thoughts kept to himself.

CHAPTER 9

Patrick "Paddy" Boyle belonged to that small, elite club of firemen who had achieved the rare distinction of earning their reputations through acts of bravery and sacrifice without letting those achievements go to their heads. Loved by his men for his dedication and courage, he was as knowledgeable as any instructor at the "Rock"—the FDNY training facility—in tactics and strategy and had more fireground experiences than all the teachers combined.

A man of average height, athletic build, and rugged good looks, Paddy could have been mistaken for a soccer or baseball player. At forty-six, his temples had started to gray below a full head of dark-brown hair. With bushy eyebrows, dark-blue eyes, and strong chin, it didn't take long for young ladies to notice him when he stood outside his firehouse on Twelfth Street in his fire officer's uniform, having a cup of coffee.

There had never been a shortage of women in Boyle's life who wanted to be more than friends, but those relationships never lasted. They'd reach a point of intensity and then fade—for him, not for them. No matter how long any of them stayed in his life, one thing was clear: the fire service was and always would be his first love.

That was until he met Lauren that one particular summer covering at a house in Kips Bay on the East Side. He'd heard yoga improved the mind and spirit as much as the body and decided to take a class. He'd gone in there with a somewhat cocky attitude, believing he was physically fit and filled with stamina from the Job. Yoga. A piece of cake.

The class had darn near killed him, with all the contortions he was asked to put his body through. But he stuck with it.

It was during his second class when they met. Boyle was on his mat at the back of the room, in a downward dog position. Lauren came in late and took the last available spot, next to him. Without either of them glancing at each other, they continued with the warm-up routine. Until he lost his balance and fell into her.

"Sorry," he muttered with a disarming smile.

Lauren, glaring, righted herself, and then beamed a smile at him.

The instructor reprimanded them. They returned their focus to the class without another word between them.

Probably for the best, he told himself. *She's from uptown.*

A few classes later, Boyle spotted her sitting, book in hand, on a bench outside the changing rooms. He moved closer, tilted his head to read the title—*The Unbearable Lightness of Being.*

Her beauty made him forget about the bandage wrapped around his right forearm and the dressing taped to the side of his neck. He cleared his throat. "He reads easy."

She looked up, realized who it was, made a quick glance at his bandages, and asked, "You like Kundera?"

"Never read him. It's just what I've heard."

Her eyes brightened. In her best fake Brooklynese, she said, "Ya heard right."

He extended a hand. "Patrick Boyle. People call me Paddy. That's with two Ds."

She took his hand, and in her usual accent tinged with sophistication replied, "Lauren Moore. That's with two Os."

He gestured to the bench, a silent request to join her. When she shrugged, he sat and removed his shoes. "I'm in over my head next to you super-yogis here."

Lauren glanced again at the bandages. "I have a feeling you can hold your own."

"With that vote of confidence, maybe I can do anything."

She motioned toward his forearm and neck. "What happened?"

Boyle shrugged. "Occupational injury."

"What do you do?"

"I'm a fireman," Boyle said, under his breath, as if he was divulging a personal shortcoming to a confidante.

Lauren raised her eyebrows, nodded.

"I can't imagine what you have to deal with," she said.

He gave her a small smile. "I hope you take this the way I mean it—I'm glad you can't."

She tilted her head and studied his face. "Why do you say that?"

"Because I'd like to know that someone as beautiful as you has never experienced the things I've had to on the Job." He stood up in his sneakers. "I'm going in to do some warm-ups before the warm-ups. Catch you later." From the corner of his eye, he saw her shake her head. He was sure she was following him with her eyes—and that he'd landed a good one.

When class ended, he asked her out for a cup of coffee. It lasted two hours. He walked her to her apartment door in Gramercy Park. She let him kiss her on the cheek and gave him her telephone number. He walked north to the firehouse struck by the poise and balance of this elegant, intelligent woman. He could sense strength in her and it intrigued him in a way he never felt before.

CHAPTER 10

Early sunlight crested above buildings in the borough of Queens, bouncing light rays on the East River and westward, down the length of Fourteenth Street in Manhattan. The light from the east cast shadows on the façade of a Romanesque Catholic church just west of Avenue A, which had occupied that spot in the city for 140 years. Sixty-five-year-old Father Joseph Kelly, wearing a white chasuble, faced the congregation of a couple of dozen parishioners from behind the altar. Light filtered through stained glass in easterly windows, painting the sanctuary floor with a prism of colors. One ray illuminated his blond hair mixed with silver that looked more like natural highlights than evidence of years and life events. He held a round, unleavened communion host in front of him as he recited consecration prayers during the early morning mass.

In a clear voice, he said, "On the night He was betrayed, He took the bread and gave You thanks and praise. He broke the bread, gave it to His disciples and said, 'Take this all of you and eat it. This is my body which will be given up for you.'" With both hands, Kelly raised the host high above his head, believing, according to his faith, that the wafer transformed into the Eucharist, the body of Jesus Christ, the Redeemer, so that His faithful might absorb His essence, become more Christlike, and have everlasting life.

Today, his mind and heart bore the weight of news he'd received as he'd readied himself for mass. As an FDNY chaplain, it was his task and his burden to be notified that Dennis "Denny" Andrews had perished from injuries received in a fire, and that his good friend, Captain Paddy Boyle, had been injured as well. With the host raised, he offered a prayer for Denny's soul, and for his wife and their children.

Kelly knew this duty well. In the forty years since he was ordained, he'd buried more than half a dozen firemen. He knew how to talk to these men, but more importantly, he knew how to listen. At this time, when the wounds were still open and the emotions still raw, he knew that the ministry of presence is the best ministry a priest can offer the bereaved.

A tall, imposing frame of a man, when Kelly walked into a room wearing the black clerical suit and Roman collar, there was never a question that God's emissary has arrived, and he used it to his advantage when he had to, like today. He knew that by just showing up, the brothers would be consoled and begin to feel better. His calm, baritone voice tinged with a faint brogue acquired from his childhood growing up in County Wicklow, could salve the grief and psychological injuries that the Job inflicted on the brothers and their families alike.

He completed the mass, dressed for his next task, left word where he'd be, and departed.

✦

Kelly approached the Twelfth Street firehouse and stopped a few yards away. Hung over the garage doors of the 1929 two-story brick-and-stone building housing Ladder 323 and the battalion chief for the Tenth Battalion was the anticipated black-and-purple bunting. The flag was lowered to half-staff. Yesterday morning, the firehouse had been its typical welcoming place for people in the neighborhood. Today it was somber, silent.

He continued forward, crossing the bay floor, to the kitchen. Firemen hunkered around the table. Worn out and feeling beaten, some remained in their bunker gear, leaving the grime and char of the previous night's engagement on them, as if to clean up and change would wash away the memory of their fallen brother.

Kelly entered the kitchen. All at the table rose to their feet. Firehouse policy was to give a cup of coffee to any visitor, a tradition going back generations. A probie moved toward the coffee urn and filled a cup as Kelly worked his way around the table to shake hands and hug each man. He'd officiated at the weddings of many of them, had baptized their children, heard their confessions, counseled them through affairs and marital troubles, and enjoyed many summer barbecues at their homes. This was his family.

Walsh, a retired fireman, offered Kelly his chair at the table. Kelly studied the face of the older man dressed in civilian clothes. The last time he'd seen him at the firehouse was seventeen years ago, when there was a line-of-duty death. Heavy wrinkles around the man's eyes, plus a barroom tan, indicated Walsh was dealing with this recent loss with the aid of more than mild restoratives. He thanked the probie, who handed him the cup of coffee.

"Who's with Michelle?" he asked. His right hand fingered the lip of the ceramic coffee cup.

A young, slender, square-jawed lieutenant answered, "Chief Brendan and Chaplain Marcchione went out to break the news."

Kelly nodded and said a prayer, remembering the last time he had to make The Knock every fireman's wife dreaded. "I'll go there later this morning. How's Paddy?"

The lieutenant rubbed the side of his nose. "Third-degree burns and bruised ribs. Lots of pain, but the docs say he'll make it."

Kelly glanced around the room, sipped his coffee, and waited. "What happened?" he said to anyone, no one.

Heimboldt, a short, stocky truckie with a crew cut and narrow-set eyes, leaned against the radiator. He sighed and said, "I cut open the shop's back door with my partner saw. We pulled back the grate and …" He squeezed his eyes shut and lowered his head. "Paddy and Denny were lying there, flames all over them." Tears streamed past his eyelids, down his cheeks. "I pulled him out but …"

The fireman standing next to Heimboldt wrapped an arm around the man's shoulders.

Kelly said, "Get it all out, lad." He turned his gaze to the ashen-faced truck chauffeur, Noah Beale, who sat across from him. "Noah?"

Beale grimaced and adjusted the radio in its shoulder strap still slung across his chest. "When we pulled up, the first floor was rippin' pretty good. On the way there, command reported occupants trapped on the upper floors." He moved his head slowly from side to side. "Paddy told me to make the roof. He and Denny had their masks on, got off the truck, and headed for the second floor." He halted, gaze fixed on the table, and swallowed hard several times in the silence that surrounded him. "They made some good grabs right away—a mother and three kids. Paddy told Denny and Chief Brendan there was still someone in there—you know how he is." Heads nodded in confirmation. "The two of them went back in. That's when things got bad.

"The fire just took off, you know? Flames blew out the second-floor windows. Chief Brendan tried to raise Paddy on the radio but couldn't. Some of the guys wanted to go in, but the chief said no. He ordered a hose team to the second floor and told Heimee and Russo to get down the fire escape and open up the back of the store. Fifty-two found the guy on the back fire escape."

Kelly, clasped hands resting on the table, waited. They had to talk it out. To recount blow by blow what they'd experienced. It was the only way to come to grips with the tragedy. The only way to get right in their minds and hearts so they could get back on the rig and meet the Red Devil face to face again. "Lads, I don't need to tell you what you already know, but you know me well enough to know I will. It'll be tough for a while. Denny was a good man, good husband, good father. A lousy cook, but—" He waited for their chuckles to cease. "But a good family man and fireman. We're going to miss him dearly, but not his cooking."

Kelly breathed in and glanced around. Keeping his voice even, he said, "Go ahead. Think all that you want. They call it survivor's guilt. It's normal. You understand?"

The brothers nodded. One sobbed silently. Kelly continued. "If you need to go off in some corner and lick your wounds until you begin to feel even a little better, do it. You won't be the only one. Then remind yourself that we all rely on each other; that we have to. Then close ranks. Michelle will need all the help she can get, especially now, and from all of you. I'll help her as much as I can as well. But we each need to take it one day at a time. Show up and do your job. The Lord will sort out the rest, I promise you. He'll heal your broken hearts and bind your wounds."

Kelly sensed he was getting through. Shoulders relaxed a half inch. Some who hadn't moved since he'd entered the room shifted their positions. Brothers exchanged looks with brothers. The mood in the room was lightening.

Kelly leaned forward. "But what I don't want anybody doing is letting what happened get inside your head and stay there. We're gonna honor our fallen friend at his wake and funeral. We'll take care of his widow and his kids. We'll give Paddy the support he needs until he gets back on duty, and I can't fathom what that is, because as long as that tough old bastard is alive, the only support he needs is from his jockstrap, and we're gonna keep serving the people in this community, because that's the only thing we know how to do. Does that make sense?"

He waited for the limited affirmations he anticipated, then pointed to Walsh, who'd moved to stand with the guys near the refrigerator. "Retired Chief Walsh is here for you, just as he's been after every line-of-duty death over the last twenty-five years. With him here, you don't need me, so I'll be on my way." Kelly got to his feet. "Any of you want to go for a cup of coffee, call the rectory. They'll know where to find me. Please stand for a prayer."

Men shuffled to their feet or adjusted their posture. Hands clasped, heads lowered, they listened as Kelly led them in the Lord's Prayer.

They fixed their gazes on him when he said *amen*. He raised his right hand and made the sign of the cross in the air. More handshakes, pats on the back, brief hugs, and thanks were exchanged as he started for the bay.

He made his way onto the sidewalk, into the sunshine. It was going to be a long week for all of them.

CHAPTER 11

A cold, early spring drizzle laced the pavement and concrete on Fifth Avenue peppering the face of Deputy Chief Steven Brendan. The sandy-haired, slightly built, fifty-five-year-old chief stood amongst the throng of firemen, public officials, clergy, and family members gathered in front of Saint Patrick's Cathedral ready to receive the casket that carried the body of Firefighter Dennis Andrews. Two thousand blue uniforms, topped with navy-blue bell caps, lined the avenue for blocks, quietly waiting for the solemn centuries-old ritual to commence. Traffic had been diverted to cross streets casting a rare silence down the cavernous boulevard.

Brendan slipped on his white dress gloves, fastened the wrist snap on each one and straightened his uniform jacket. He was reminded how uncomfortable his uniform felt when he put it on for a line-of-duty funeral, and how comfortable it felt when he marched over this very same ground with the department on Saint Patrick's Day.

Across Fifth Avenue facing the cathedral stood the FDNY color guard detail in front of dozens of white-capped uniformed fire officers, twelve rows deep. Behind them, two ladder trucks sat, their aerial ladders raised toward each other at forty-five-degree angles. An American flag hung from the apex between them.

Brendan wanted to stare at the flag and forget why he was there, but he knew his duty. He was there to bury one of his own, a longtime friend, who he sent into a burning building to attempt to rescue a trapped civilian. He couldn't start to process that loss for himself, not today.

He glanced to his left. A vacant-faced Michelle Andrews, Dennis' widow, stood near the cathedral's entrance, clutching the hand of her daughter, her sons next to her, surrounded by extended family members. Brendan recognized that look on her face because he put it there, two mornings ago, after he showed up on her doorstep with Monsignor Marcchione to deliver the news that her husband was dead. After hearing her heart break and picking her up off the floor, after the tears and sobs and screams, her face turned ashen-white and hadn't changed since.

She'll get some color back after a month.

A firm hand squeezed the blue-eyed chief's left shoulder. Brendan looked back to see the face of Firefighter Bryan O'Rorke towering over him.

"How you holdin' up, Chief?" the thirty-year-old fireman asked.

Brendan offered a grim smile. "I don't have to tell you."

"No, you don't," O'Rorke answered, scanning the cathedral over their heads. "It's like it was yesterday, standing here."

"I know. For me, too."

O'Rorke fixed his gaze on the widow and children, their tear-stained faces.

"Man, it never ends," he said tightly.

"How's Mom?" Brendan asked, trying to bring O'Rorke back.

O'Rorke broke his stare. "She's good. You know how tough she is."

Brendan nodded, smiled. "Tell her I was asking for her."

"Will do, Chief." He started to move away, then stopped. "Chief, you need anything, call me. I mean it. You know?"

"Bryan, I will. I wouldn't hesitate."

O'Rorke nodded, moving away. Brendan watched the big truck man head off, following his large frame until it disappeared into the sea of blue uniforms on the sidewalk. How different O'Rorke looked, he thought, from the last time they both were here, twenty-three years earlier, in front of the same cathedral, on the same piece of pavement, for the same reason, to bury a fireman—O'Rorke's father.

A limousine pulled up in front of the cathedral. Mayor Pisani and Fire Commissioner Hollenbach stepped out and greeted the Andrews family. In keeping with century-old protocol, no one entered the church until the deceased firefighter's coffin was carried in by the pallbearers, each a member of the fallen's fire company.

From a distance north on Fifth Avenue, the cadence of the FDNY Pipes & Drums' snare drums echoed through the canyon of structures reaching into the sky.

At the top of the stairs in the opened doorway of the 122-year-old gothic cathedral waited Cardinal Reagan, the towering archbishop of New York with the deep, baritone voice, dressed in a white chasuble, his scarlet zucchetto cap covering his crown of golden hair. Next to him stood his sacristans and acolytes in black cassocks and white surplices.

Engine 61, draped in black-and-purple bunting, moved south on Fifth Avenue, rolling ever closer to the cathedral. Acting as a caisson, the engine carried the flag-draped casket on its hose bed. Two of Dennis Andrews's brother firefighters stood at attention on the back step, flanking the casket. Surviving members of the honor company, Ladder 323, marched behind. With Paddy Boyle still in the hospital, the duty to lead the company fell to Brendan.

The caisson drew up to the cathedral and stopped. The firefighters on the back step removed the casket with care and some difficulty and handed it to other members of Ladder 323. Six pallbearers took the casket firmly in hand and then turned in unison toward the church entrance. With measured steps, they proceeded to the foot of the cathedral and came to a halt, where they faced the Archbishop of New York. Brendan emerged from the crowd and stood at attention behind the casket, facing the archbishop. Brothers-at-arms against the Red Devil had come in peace to present their fellow fireman to God, for the commendation of his soul and its return to his Creator. The good and faithful servant was going home.

Cardinal Reagan descended the steps. His sacristan followed, carrying the brass aspersorium containing holy water and aspergillum. He reached the foot of the steps, took the aspergillum, and circled the casket slowly as he sprinkled holy water over it. With the blessing completed, he ascended the steps. Pallbearers, with sure grips on the casket, ascended behind him. Brendan and the Andrews family followed, trailed by friends and the thousands of brothers. The century-old hymn, "The King of Love My Shepherd Is," played to the Irish melody of Saint Columba, burst forth from the 7,855-pipe organ.

Brendan moved slowly behind the casket. Thoughts raced through his mind, watching the men he lived and fought the Beast with on a daily basis honor their fallen brother. He thought of Andrews. How he was a good fireman, a good father, and a mild prankster who kept everyone on their toes at the house. As the music swirled in the upper reaches of the cathedral, he gazed toward the altar and the statue of the crucified Christ, with head bowed, a haunting reminder of the sacrifice on Calvary thousands of years ago. *Denny gave the same. He gave the same.*

During the mass, Brendan sat pensively in the second row, attempting to collect his thoughts prior to giving the eulogy, as Michelle had requested. That morning, when he told her, she had taken his hands during that request, tear-filled eyes aimed at him as she told him how much her Denny admired his cool composure in any emergency, how he'd said if he ever made it to chief, he wanted to be just like his own chief.

Brendan cleared his throat and fought back tears. Denny would never get that chance. Never live to prove he could match the man he admired—or surpass him.

What could he say to any of them? A line of Shakespeare from *King Lear*, read and remembered in eighth-grade literature class at Our Lady of Grace School in Breezy Point, flashed through his mind:

The weight of this sad day we must obey. Speak what we feel, not what we ought to say.

After communion had been distributed and mass concluded, Brendan rose from the pew and walked up the steps to the centered altar. He faced the congregation, each pew filled and people standing at the back and sides. He glanced to his left, at the archbishop, who gave one slight nod. Brendan cleared his throat.

In turn, he eyed each person as he said their names. "Michelle, Aidan, Kelly, and Sean, Cardinal Reagan, Mayor Pisani, brother and sister firefighters, family and friends, we come here today, to this cathedral, to honor the life of our fallen brother, firefighter Dennis Andrews. Denny, as we knew him at the house, was an excellent fireman. He was the type of firefighter you wanted with you on the toughest job—calm, cool, and collected. When things got hot, that's when you wanted Denny around. He knew what to do before you asked. And you knew, whatever you asked, he would do it. He had that youthful heart that made him a real pleasure to be around."

He directed his gaze to the family. "Michelle, we both know there's nothing I or anyone can say to take away your pain and grief. Denny cannot be returned to us. Like you, we cherished the time he had with us, whether that was at the firehouse, your house, on a bad job, or just shooting the breeze. He was always talking about his kids and how proud he was of them. He called them his 'three marks.' His marks in life.

"We'll have to learn to move forward without him, which we'll be doing together. Each day will bring its own challenges. Aiden, Kelly, Sean—I know, as sure as we're here today, that your father would want you to go forward and make your own marks in life. It won't be easy at first, but we—all of us who knew your father—will be with you every step of the way. That's a promise.

"As we look back on Denny's life and commend his spirit to God, let's always remember the good he showed us. I know I'll remember." He lowered his head then looked up, as if something triggered in his mind.

"But there is something more about this day and why we are here that needs to be said. We can speak of how special Denny was to us, because he was. We can speak of how we will miss him dearly, because we will, and we can speak of how we will see him again, because we will. I can assure you we will."

Brendan paused. The cleft-chinned deputy chief narrowed his eyes. "Brothers, I want to talk about a place. The place in which we live, where few others do. You must remember, when the alarm goes off and we get on the rigs, we enter a realm, a void, where others do not go. That is when time splits in half. On one side is life, with all its beauty, warmth, safety and comfort. On the other side is death, our cold, relentless, jealous foe, who cruelly relishes every hapless soul he can harvest from us, through the misfortunes the helpless find themselves in.

"Those innocents we have sworn to protect who have called us for help, they find themselves in this place, where their lives are up for grabs, their fate uncertain and, with every minute that passes, if we do not retrieve them for life, death will claim them."

Brendan lowered his head, exhaling.

"That is where we live—in that place—between life and death. It is a dark arena, where a game is played against a malicious enemy who never stops seeking victims. And sometimes, we have to make the trade. We have to trade ourselves for those we've sworn to serve."

The cathedral was deathly quiet. Brendan's words, spoken in his soft Queens accent, sounded more like a cautionary warning than a panegyric for his fallen friend.

"Denny died in this place, where he was hot, dirty, and exhausted, trying to rescue a stranger. What he did, he did for a special reason. Some could say he did it because it's his job, and that's how he put food on the table for his young family. That would be true.

"Others could say he did it because he gets a thrill from the work, the adrenaline rush that comes with the pressure and unpredictability of the job—and maybe that's true, at least for some of us.

"But Denny did it for a simple reason: to help other people. For those of us who call ourselves Christians, we know the commandment given by our Savior: 'There is no greater love than this. To lay down one's life for one's friends.' Denny went further. He laid down his life for a stranger.

"Now, brothers, I need you to listen. I need you to understand this. This war we are in never ends. Some battles we win, others we do not. And the only way we prevail, the only way we can beat the devil and redeem and honor our fallen brother is for us to get back on those rigs, go out those doors, and race to that place between life and death, where we fight the Red Devil. There is no retreat. And no surrender. We know our enemy, and he knows us.

"Last Sunday, the enemy took one of our own. But his victory is fleeting. Because he may have taken Denny's life here on earth, but he did not get Denny's soul. Michelle, Aidan, Kelly, and Sean, you know better than the rest of us, your father is with God and the angels in heaven, where he will wait, hopefully, for the rest of us."

Brendan surveyed the congregation and smiled.

"Death cannot celebrate the loss of Denny. His victory is hollow. Denny's spirit lives and carries on with each one of us. So, brothers, I ask you to join me right now, here in swearing an oath to Michelle and her children. Stand up and repeat after me with your hands on your hearts."

The firemen in the pews, almost two thousand of them, stood up and placed their hands on their hearts.

"We promise you, Michelle and your children, that we will never waver in our duties. That we will respond to every call and, if called to do so, will give our lives, like Denny did, so others might live. We do this because it is our sworn duty, and to honor and remember our fallen brother, your husband and father, Firefighter Dennis Andrews, so help us God."

The good chief returned to his pew. Amid sniffling and sobs, someone began to clap. Then another and another, until applause filled the sacred space.

The brothers somberly filed out of the cathedral and formed a line of honor on Fifth Avenue. As Denny's casket was hoisted by his grim-faced brothers onto the vacant hosebed of Engine 61, the thousands in the line of honor raised their arms in salute to Andrews. The engine slowly rolled down Fifth Avenue, the main thoroughfare through America's Gotham lined with firemen four-deep for over a dozen blocks.

Brendan, staring straight ahead, marched behind the caisson in front of 323 Truck's crew. Behind his company marched Denny's widow, children, and family members. He detested the fact that he knew, from experience, how this would go. He knew Michelle would, at first, after the initial shock wore off, "accept" that Denny was gone. Then, as she began to heal and learn to live with the reality of the loss, she would want to know exactly what happened. She would become angry, upset, and ask why this happened to her, how it was unfair, and she would blame Brendan for his death. Brendan knew this was coming. He'd seen this before, up close. It was part of human nature, part of the grieving and acceptance process, he told himself, but it still wasn't easy.

The cortege processed six blocks down Fifth Avenue. At the end of the line, as happenstance would have it, 57 Truck was just returning from a run. The crew had dismounted from the truck and was standing at the end of the line, in full bunker gear, saluting their fallen brother. Not much got to Brendan. He'd seen a lot in his thirty-five years on the job. But seeing the young brothers in bunker gear, at the end of the line, was such a fitting, serendipitous tribute to Denny Andrews, a good truckie, that he welled up, at least for a moment. *God sure loves firemen*, he thought.

The engine turned east on Forty-Second Street and proceeded toward FDR Drive, where Denny's remains would be taken to Saint Raymond's Cemetery in the Bronx, to be interred after a private graveside ceremony. Brendan and the company fell out and headed for the lounge at the Fitzsimmons Hotel on Fifty-Fourth Street, where they'd toast Denny and others, and hope whatever they drank would soothe them for a while, knowing it wouldn't.

PROBIE

Until the day of his death, no man can be sure of his courage.

THOMAS À BECKET, IN JEAN ANOUILH'S *BECKET* (1959)

CHAPTER 12

Harry Sturgis plopped into the easy chair in the living room of his mother's house on Lurting Avenue in the Morris Park section of the Bronx. Seventeen, a senior in high school, loner, and latchkey kid starting at age ten, he did what he did every weekday when he got home—watch reruns of *Knight Rider*, talk shows, or soaps. Around five o'clock, his mother, Anita, would return home from her nursing shift at Mount Sinai Hospital, don her waitress uniform, chat for a moment, kiss the top of his head, then leave for her night job at the Throg's Neck Diner.

His father abandoned the family when Harry was ten. Before that time, there were no father-son games of catch in the park or other such sharing of time together, with one exception: his father would take him for ice cream at the Carvel on East Tremont Avenue. Cone in hand, Harry stood nearby while his father used the payphone out front, talking in soft tones, purring to whomever he was talking to: "No, baby, I can't. I gotta be home that night. I'll see you next Tuesday."

It was only a few years later that Harry realized his dad was talking to another woman—his girlfriend. When he asked his mother why his dad left, she stared away, into the distance. After a moment, she said, "He must have had a girlfriend he wanted to be with more than us." When she told him this, her brown eyes became glassy and the wrinkles on her face darkened, as if the shadow of a dark image had just passed over her.

Sometimes at night, he could hear her crying softly in her bed. He wanted to go to her, but he knew it would upset her that he knew she was crying. She was tough, so much tougher than him or his dad, and Harry loved her for her toughness. But he knew she was proud and didn't want him to know that she was affected by his father's desertion and the divorce.

When the divorce was finalized, Anita got to keep the house. She worked two jobs and her parents helped out where they could. She really needed Harry to step up and get a job to help bring in some income, but the kid wasn't into it. All he wanted to do was watch TV and play video games. Harry had no close friends at school or in the neighborhood, no girlfriend or demonstrated interest, no inclination to get a part-time job to add to the family's income, no interest in sports or extracurricular activities. He'd closed everyone out, except his mother.

It showed in his physical appearance. Harry's dark-brown hair was always matted over his forehead and ears. Acne sprouted over his face and neck that led down to a gawky frame, usually clothed with ripped corduroys, button-down patterned shirts, and Puma sneakers—a lanky, brown-eyed nerd. Bullies named him the Nothing Man, which other unkind students repeated.

Harry found it easy to escape through the TV. He'd watch whatever was on, but he preferred science fiction and shows dealing with the paranormal. He could recite every episode of *The X-Files* if he were asked to, and would be quite happy doing so.

It was Wednesday afternoon, and Harry turned on the TV,

cracked open a Coke, and sat down to an episode of *The Jerry Springer Show.* The topic of the segment was "Men who beat their wives, and the women who love them." On the screen, a burly, bearded truck driver sat on the couch next to two women, his wife and girlfriend, both routine victims of his beatings. Harry shook his head. "I wonder what makes a woman stay with a guy like that," he said.

Although the talk show was quite entertaining, something made Harry glance outside the picture window. A group of people were standing outside the apartment house next door wearing only their house clothes in the mid-December cold. At almost the same time, he started to smell something, a burning odor. He got up from his chair to get a better look at the scene. The crowd of pedestrians was focused on the roof of his house.

The house can't be on fire.

Harry exited the front doorway, ran down the steps into the street, and turned toward the house. About two stories above the roof of his mother's house, flames crackled out of a window in the adjacent apartment house. *Would you look at that. So that's what a real fire looks like.* Now kids gathered in the street, marveling at the flames. In the distance, the wail of a fire truck's siren could be heard, interrupted by the intermittent bursts of its throaty horn, as it plied its way through traffic.

He turned his attention back to the fire. Flames licked the window eaves and darkened the exterior brick of the apartment building and smoke now rose from the front windows on the floor of the fire. Tenants continued to exit out of the building. Sirens grew louder, which prompted Harry to cross to the opposite sidewalk.

It was no more than three minutes since Harry left the house before Engine 193 pulled up and parked just beyond Harry's house. Before the engine came to a stop, the officer's door opened, and a white-shirted firefighter with a radio jumped to the ground, turning to face the fire in one motion. Harry murmured, "Wow," to himself, impressed by the fluid, nearly singular movement. Another fire truck, Ladder 94, rounded the corner and came up right in front of Harry's house.

The officer on the ladder truck emerged from the front passenger seat of the rig and put on his mask and hood. Two firemen carrying tools and long hooks stepped out of the truck's cab and quickly walked into the entrance to the apartment house. The driver opened a panel on the side of the truck and hit a button causing hydraulic jacks on the ladder truck to extend out from the sides of the truck. A firefighter holding a fire extinguisher and a long hook, stood near the lieutenant. Down the street, a second ladder truck, Ladder 89, pulled up behind Ladder 94, its own crew also emerging from the cab.

The crowd had swelled to more than fifty people. A firefighter built like a longshoreman from the 193 Engine approached Harry. He dragged a large hose from the engine. "Son, I need you to move," he said.

Harry glanced down and realized he was next to a fire hydrant. Transfixed, he watched the engineman use the largest wrench he'd ever seen to give a hard turn to the pumper nozzle cap until it spun freely off its threads. In no time, the engineman threaded the large hose's coupling onto the hydrant's nozzle and placed the wrench on the operating nut atop the hydrant's bonnet. Harry, eyes wide, followed the engineman's focus, which was on the pumper where the chauffeur had coupled the other end of the large hose line.

A young African-American woman rushed toward the engineman, screaming, "Jayden's in the house. Jayden's in the house."

The engineman leaned toward her. "Who's Jayden?"

Harry's head turned back and forth as he watched the engineman and woman.

"My baby." She pointed upward. "He's on the fourth floor."

The three of them fixed their view on the floor above the charred window, where flames shot out with a vengeance.

To her, the engineman said, "Come with me." To Harry he said,

"Will you help me?"

"Yeah," Harry muttered.

The fireman held the handle of the hydrant wrench that sat on the hydrant bonnet. "What's your name, kid?"

"Harry."

"I'm Murphy." He pointed to the chauffeur in front of the pump control panel. "Okay, Harry. I've got to go back to the engine. I need you to watch this hydrant wrench so nobody takes it. Can you do that?"

"I think so."

"I need you to know so."

Harry swallowed hard. "I got it."

The engineman lightly punched Harry's shoulder. "You look like you can handle this."

The engineman took firm hold of the frantic woman's arm and hastily walked her to the white-shirted engine officer.

Murphy exchanged words with the officer, who stiffened, then shouted into his handie-talkie radio mouthpiece, "Eighty-nine, get to the floor above the fire now. There's a kid trapped on the floor above. Exposure 4-side."

"Received, Chief," emanated from the engine radio. Two firemen headed from the sidewalk through the front door just before glass splintered, shattered, and fell from the second-floor windows. Harry stared open-mouthed as he watched firefighters inside the building break windows with their tools.

On the street, three enginemen stretched a hose line from the engine to the front entrance of the apartment house. The line rested limp on the street like a long, thick, bunched strand of spaghetti. The crew donned facepieces, masks, and helmets. The lead man, holding the nozzle, pressed into the building, the backup man behind him, carrying the flat coil of hose. Another engineman fed the line from the engine to the doorway, spreading out the dead hose so it wouldn't tangle on anything.

It wasn't long before the adrenaline of the situation caught up with Harry. He realized he was not just watching this drama unfold on his street, in his neighborhood, right in front of his home. He was *in* the drama. He realized that he had a very simple but important job to do, one that several lives would depend on. If the firemen could not get the hydrant open and water flowing into the hoses, they could not put out the fire. He never felt this way before. *This is cool*, he thought.

A barked, shouted, "Hey, Harry!" split the air. Harry shifted his gaze to see Murphy heading his way. "Okay, Harry, look alive, and give us the water."

His attention flew to the building. Flames broke through the second window on the third floor. "Shit!" He grabbed the hydrant wrench with both hands and started the turn, feeling the strain of seldom-used muscles. On the fifth turn, there was a hiss, followed by a rumble. Water raced from the main ten feet below, like an oil gusher. The large hose came to life. It popped off the pavement as a thousand gallons of water per minute zoomed to the engine. The chauffeur boosted the idle on the engine and pulled the intake valve and filled the pumper's water tank. The pumper rattled on the pavement just as its tank topped off with water.

The driver shouted into his handie-talkie, "Ready with the water."

A brief silence was broken by a voice on the radio saying, "Start water."

"Ten-four." The chauffeur pulled the pump discharge valve, then increased the water pressure. The taut hose line off the engine snaked on the ground as the pumper delivered the "City Gin" to the engine crew inside the house that was quickly starting to resemble a brick oven.

✦

On the fourth floor, Bryan O'Rorke and Jimmy Leary, Truck 89's Vent-Enter-Search team, looked for the trapped kid. They knocked in doors and scanned openings for any signs of a civilian inside the now-dark apartment house. O'Rorke used his halligan tool to pry the lock on an apartment door, then pushed into the first room on his hands and knees. "Go right," he told Leary, who was immediately behind him.

They stayed low against the wall and moved across the floor, swinging tools in an attempt to strike a leg, arm, anything they could recognize as a human being. O'Rorke, through his facemask, surveyed the room illuminated solely by his helmet lights, spied an interior hallway, and moved toward it.

"The engine better knock this down soon, or we're done," he said to Leary. Through a smoky haze, a window down the corridor allowed light off the street to frame the walls of the hallway beyond the room they were searching.

"If it goes to shit, we'll make the window," O'Rorke said.

He could feel Leary's hand on his ankle as he crawled across the room toward the hallway.

"Probably in the bathroom," O'Rorke guessed.

Now in the apartment hallway, they came to a locked door. O'Rorke shoved his halligan between the door and jamb, and with one sure twist, pried it open. He pushed the door into the room. At about eight inches, it stopped, as though a sandbag blocked it. He reached around the door and felt what he took to be an arm, shoved his way farther in and found a child, he guessed around ten, unconscious and slouched against the door.

To Leary he said, "Room's getting hot." He pulled the mouthpiece of his radio mike to his mouth. "Eighty-nine Outside Vent to command."

"Go ahead, eighty-nine."

"We've found a ten-forty-five, unconscious, about ten years old. We'll take him down the stairs."

"Eighty-nine, negative. Conditions are not tenable below you. Can you make a window?"

“Eighty-nine Outside Vent. Proceeding to window on side one, fourth floor.” He dragged the child from behind the door and handed him to Leary. “Make the window.”

Leary grabbed the kid and dragged him to the window. The tinny whine of Tower Ladder 94’s hydraulic motor was a welcome sound to O’Rorke. It let him know the truck chauffeur was extending the bucket toward the building.

O’Rorke stepped over Leary and the boy, reached the window, smashed the glass, and ripped the sashes to clear the opening. Through the window he saw the bucket at the end of the tower ladder reaching up to the fourth-floor window.

The chauffeur on the turntable forty feet below placed the bucket one foot shy of the window. O’Rorke stepped out of the window and stretched down until his foot reached the base of the bucket. He planted one boot and then the other firmly onto the bucket and turned around. From inside the window, a gloved hand and coat-shielded arm handed the limp child to O’Rorke.

A collective gasp followed by cheers and applause erupted from the crowd.

O’Rorke made room for Leary, who joined him in the bucket. The chauffeur backed the bucket away from the building, lowering it with a slow, steady motion.

✦

Inside the building, the 193 Engine crew had dragged their uncharged line up the stairs to the third-floor landing. Nozzle man Al “Kaz” Kazmierski, a broad-shouldered, former steamfitter, cradled the smoothbore nozzle—the *knob*—as though carrying a cat. Phil Coletti, detailed to the company as his backup man, wasted no time snaking hose right behind him.

Coletti had heard about Kaz before he took the detail for a buddy taking time off. Kaz had been on the Job twenty-nine years, all of it in the Bronx. He’d been inside more tenement fires than anyone in the FDNY and was known as a "Brunt Man" because he lived through the War Years in the seventies, when the whole borough was thought to be going up in flames. On a *good* weekend back in the day, the companies in the Bronx got over thirty fires *a night*. Kaz had seen it all, done it all, hated it all. To Coletti, this fire was not a problem. Simple shit. But he knew Kaz had been on the Job long enough to know every job was not the same. Think that and the chances of getting jammed up go way up, leading to another two line-of-duty deaths to be written about in the morning tabloids.

Kaz halted and peered down the hallway of the third-floor landing. Nothing showed in either direction, though smoke collected in the middle of the corridor.

"We've gotta move on this thing," he barked to Coletti. "I'm not waiting on that greenhorn lieutenant from Forest Hills."

Kaz drew in a quick breath through his nose. "Mask up," he told Coletti.

Coletti nodded, donned his facemask, and opened the valve on his air tank. He gathered the line behind him and waited for the order to advance.

The covering lieutenant emerged from the darkness behind them and kept one hand on the hose line. He nodded to Kaz.

Kaz crawled toward the dark smoke, then into it, slowly, blindly, with the attack line in his hand. His survivor light was useless, as it reflected and dispersed its beam off the thickening haze.

Behind him came the sounds of Coletti flaking out line as they advanced.

The nozzle man pressed forward. This smoke was only the prologue to the main event. The only way to knock this thing down was to reach the seat of the fire. But the Beast had yet to reveal itself. Kaz reached the end of the hallway, enveloped in black, sooty smoke. He turned to Coletti and said, "It already flashed," referring to the combustible situation in the room where the fire was, wherever that was. Through the smoke, he saw a flicker of light. A thin sleeve of light was shining from under the doorway of an apartment.

Kaz pointed to the floor. "Here," he said to Coletti, as if he was a treasure hunter who had found the right spot to dig for booty. Coletti nodded and retreated to survey the line, making sure it wouldn't bend or crease when it was charged.

The chauffeur's voice crackled through the lieutenant's radio. "Ready with the water." Kaz touched the apartment door with his left, gloved hand, then retracted it from the heat. He moved left of the doorway, put his back to the wall and his left shoulder against the door's molding. He clutched the knob with his right hand, and the nozzle handle with his left.

The lieutenant came up from the stairwell and made a circular motion with his hand. Into his handie-talkie he ordered, "Start water."

Coletti knelt behind Kaz, holding the flaked-out hose. The two firemen waited for the attack line to fill with the wet stuff. Suddenly, the line tugged and moved as it filled.

Kaz opened the nozzle a crack. The eerie, pressing *hiss* emanated as the hose released air ahead of the water. He shut the nozzle back tight. It was only a matter of seconds before water would arrive. He placed his left hand on the doorknob and clutched the line and nozzle with his right. The hose line grew taut, straining to pull away from his grasp as maximum pressure pushed through the line. He and Coletti tightened their grips.

Kaz twisted the doorknob with his left hand, then pulled back the door. The opening lit up, illuminating the hallway like the sun on the city streets at noon. Tongues of flame shot out and darted around the opening. The apartment contents crackled like kindling at a college bonfire.

In unison, Kaz and Coletti swung around on their knees and faced the doorway. Coletti pushed his shoulder into Kaz's back and held the line down firmly, to absorb the inevitable recoil when Kaz opened the nozzle.

The veteran nozzle man positioned himself nearly prone on the floor. He kept his head down. Seeing any damn thing through his facemask would be impossible until he knocked the fire down. He pointed the nozzle up toward the ceiling, where the fire was pushing through into the floor above. He pulled back full on the nozzle handle. Two hundred pounds per square inch of water shot toward the ceiling, attacking the thermal balance of heat, fuel, and air that kept the Beast alive.

This was Coletti's favorite part—kicking the Beast in the ass. To him, it was a living, breathing organism, ready to consume whatever it could, on its own terms. It sought its quarry anywhere and everywhere. Once fire ignited, it needed air, fuel, and heat to survive. Take any one of those away, and it was history. When water hit it, the Beast reacted violently, like a grizzly bear poked with a stick. Its nature was to race away from the water and push heat toward the guy on the knob. That's the best way to subdue it: introduce water to the combination of gases, heat, and fuel at the ceiling of a burning room and take away its food supply.

Kaz pressed the hose line under his right armpit. He moved the nozzle slowly in a circular motion, painting the ceiling with water, cooling the fire below its ignition temperature. A loud *whoosh* and *pop* erupted from the ceiling where water hit flaming wood and combustibles. White smoke and heat rolled toward Kaz and Coletti. They bowed their helmets to protect themselves, then crawled into the room, advancing the line with them.

Kaz moved the stream along the walls and over the burning furniture. He couldn't let up now. Otherwise, the Beast would shift its strength to another part of the building. He had to kill it. As he had done dozens of times before, Coletti stayed with his nozzle man. When Kaz aimed high, Coletti pushed the line low. When Kaz brought the smooth bore down, Coletti raised the line high and pivoted to reduce the pressure the attack line placed on his brother engaged in mortal combat.

After 120 seconds of water suppression, the conditions began to improve. The room grew darker, quieter—no more *snap*, *crackle*, and *pop*. The smoke lifted. Coletti saw the contours of a window and doorway. He removed his helmet, mask and hood to let the heat touch his ears. It was hot, but not unbearable. He surveyed the charred, almost unrecognizable contents. "What a shithole."

The lieutenant poked his head into the room, raked his eyes across it floor to ceiling. "I'll call a truck up here for salvage. What a mess," he told Coletti and the Brunt Man.

"You do that," Kaz responded. He didn't bother to keep disdain from his voice for the green company officer twenty years his junior.

The lieutenant spoke into his radio. "Need a truck to third floor to assist engine crew with salvage and overhaul of the fire room."

✦

Muscles tight, Harry watched the 94 Truck's aerial platform descend from the fourth-floor window holding two firemen and a child. *Oh, man*, he thought. *This is bad.* Harry's focus shifted for a moment, away from the trio to the boy's shrieking mother, who strained to break free of the arms of two neighbors trying to console her.

One of the firemen ripped off his gloves and turnout coat as the bucket reached the truck bay. The name "O'Rorke" was stitched on the back of his coat. The other fireman leaped from the platform.

O'Rorke lowered the boy into the arms of the other fireman who placed the limp body flat on the street and took a position to begin CPR. He had the name "Leary" stitched on the back of his coat. O'Rorke joined him and cupped his fingers around the child's mouth. Leary used his grimy, muscular hands to do compressions on the small chest. Sweat dropped from his face onto the boy's Knicks jersey as the seconds ticked by.

Four NYPD patrol officers stretched crime scene tape across the street and around the two fire apparatuses, keeping onlookers away from the emergency scene. One of the officers broke away, went to the grief-stricken mother, and spoke to her in low tones. Her expression shifted from one of ultimate grief to disbelief.

An ambulance used its siren to move onlookers out of the way. EMTs emerged from the vehicle, heading straight to the boy and the two firemen still working on him. Another officer ordered the people in the street to disperse. A few moved back but stayed. Others slowly walked away.

Harry barely breathed as the firemen tried to revive the child. A team of emergency medical technicians moved in to take over. He jumped when he heard someone call his name.

Murphy, at the hydrant, spun the hydrant wrench around the bonnet and shut down the flow. He nodded and said, "Nice job, Harry."

"Thanks," Harry responded before returning his gaze to the boy, hoping to see the kid come around.

Murphy stood up straight and surveyed the scene. "Not lookin' good, is it?"

Harry shook his head.

The large hose line between engine and hydrant collapsed as the 193 driver pulled the engine's discharge lever and dumped water onto the street. Murphy spun the line off the hydrant thread. "You never know what you're gonna get in this business."

Harry trailed Murphy with his eyes. The fireman methodically walked on the line forcing water out one end of the hose onto the street with each step he took.

The engine lieutenant came around the back of 94 Truck and crossed the street, stopping a few feet from Harry. He shouted, "Hey, Murphy."

Murphy paused and glanced back.

Scowling, the lieutenant asked, "You let this civilian handle the hydrant?"

Murphy glanced at Harry and then back at the red-faced lieutenant. "I took care of it." He turned and continued with his task.

"Son, did that fireman ask you to handle the hydrant?" the lieutenant asked Harry.

Harry swallowed hard, felt sweat pool in warm places on his body. "He took care of it," the seventeen-year-old responded. He lowered his head and shot a surreptitious glance at Murphy, who cast back the faintest smile.

The lieutenant, eyes aimed at Harry, shook his head, then headed to the engine.

Harry took a few steps toward his house and then stopped. One of the firemen who'd done CPR—O'Rorke—was standing at the back of the ladder truck, his face flushed purple, like he'd just run a sprint. His eyes were sunken, sallow, and darted around as if he wanted to scream but couldn't. His mouth was open, taking in gulps of air.

Another fireman approached him. "O'Rorke, you okay?"

O'Rorke waved the guy off and staggered farther behind the truck, still sucking in air. Harry turned away, feeling guilty for having observed him in that state.

TRUCKIE

To the men of the fire department
of the city of New York
who died at the call of duty,
soldiers in a war that never ends,
this memorial is dedicated
by the people of a grateful city.

– Inscription on the Firemen's Memorial,
Riverside Drive at 105TH Street, Manhattan Dedicated 1913

CHAPTER 13

MARCH, 2001

O'Rorke stood on the south side of West Thirty-Fifth Street between Sixth and Seventh Avenues, staring at the weather-beaten bay doors on the firehouse across the street. They could really use a paint job, he thought. The house, located in the Garment District, sat on a block occupied by factories, warehouses, and tenement buildings. It had been built in 1895, an old Romanesque Revival beauty, designed by Napoleon LeBrun, the firehouse architect. Rough-cut stone blocks buttressed two iron-framed, red wooden doors that housed Engine 48 and Ladder 14. Above the first floor, terra cotta sections enhanced a three-story, orange-brick façade separated by stone trim around arched windows, capped by an ornate, arcaded cornice.

It may have been a beauty from the outside, but inside, the house was a different story. The plumbing and electrical hadn't been updated since at least 1940, the stairs groaned on every step, and the dormitory beds were army surplus from the Korean War. And the guys stationed there swore the house was haunted by the ghosts of dead firemen—ill-fated inhabitants who were lost on the Job many decades ago. The guys called them "the Owners." They'd been known to knock over gear, undo hose beds, and close compartment doors when they felt restless.

O'Rorke chuckled to himself. *Everybody in this house is nuts—dead or alive.*

He checked his watch: 9:18 a.m. The cold March morning made him zipper his black, quilted jacket to his chest. Out of habit, he fingered the Saint Florian Medal on the silver chain around his neck. Saint Florian: Patron Saint of Firefighters. His mother had given him that medal when he graduated from Ridgewood High School in Queens just before he set out on a motorcycle trip to work a fishing boat out of Seattle. It was the medal his father wore the day he died on the Job when O'Rorke was seven years old.

The side door to the firehouse opened. Selso "Exxon" Valdez, the chauffeur on 48 Engine, stepped out of the doorway, lit up a cigarette, and leaned against the building. O'Rorke watched him take a long drag, curious to see how long before the engineman noticed him across the street, and how long before the guy asked him about the job last night.

Valdez' attention focused on a boosted Honda Civic blasting rap music coasting down Thirty-Fifth Street, right past O'Rorke. O'Rorke had noticed the street race also. When O'Rorke glanced back at the firehouse, the short, portly, forty-year-old engine chauffeur was traipsing toward him.

"Hey, O'Rorke. I heard some crazy shit in there about you last night. Is that true?" Valdez pointed his right thumb over his shoulder as he walked.

"Depends on what you heard, Valdez."

"You were at that job on Thirty-Seventh?"

"Yeah."

"I heard Viterbo and Herndon were stretching a line on the second floor when the ceiling collapsed cutting them off from the stairs, knocking out Lieutenant Raines."

O'Rorke nodded. He stood a good foot over the engineman.

The bald driver wiped his head as if to smooth imaginary hair. "And you straddled the hole so Viterbo could drag Herndon—who was fucked up—*across* your back. That's what I heard."

"You forgot one thing."

"What's that?"

"The crew on 323 reeled me back in or I'd have fallen into that basement and roasted."

Valdez abruptly turned away. 'You guys on 14 are certifiable."

O'Rorke chortled. "Got to keep our reputation up. You know whenever the scene is about to turn to shit, they call 14 Truck."

"Nah. It's you truckies in general. How guys built like you can shimmy up fire escapes, cut holes in slate roofs, make so many grabs …" Valdez shook his head. "Man, I don't know."

O'Rorke curled his lip. "You'll never know," he sneered.

"What?"

"I said, 'You'll never know.' Because there are two types of firemen in this world, truckies and—"

"—those who want to be truckies." Valdez nodded, dejectedly. "I know. I know."

O'Rorke stepped back, gazed down the street. "But hey, you guys on 48 hold your own. I mean, I don't know another engine company that could keep up with a wildcat truck like 14."

Valdez brightened at the compliment. "You think so?"

"Yeah, you guys are always trying to be first on the scene, anywhere."

"Then—"

O'Rorke leaned down. "—But you'll *never* be truckies." O'Rorke brushed past Valdez and headed for the firehouse.

"Aw, screw you, O'Rorke." Valdez followed O'Rorke across the street. "Midol wants to talk to you."

O'Rorke's hand was on the doorhandle. He shot a glance at

Valdez. "Why?"

Valdez shrugged his shoulders. "He didn't say."

✦

O'Rorke entered the firehouse and walked past the house watch, a small room occupied by a desk, a couple of chairs and the FDNY dispatch radio transmitter. Two junior guys from 48 Engine sat there, talking. When O'Rorke's large frame moved by them, they went silent. O'Rorke didn't pay them any attention. He headed to the kitchen where 14 Truck's chauffeur and his friend of eight years, Eddie Lynch, sat at the table reading the *Daily News*. The sandy-haired, bushy-eyebrowed veteran didn't look up when O'Rorke entered and poured himself a cup of coffee.

"What's the word on Herndon?" O'Rorke asked, holding a ceramic mug with the words "Bite Me" displayed on one side.

"Heard he broke his leg, two places."

O'Rorke raised his eyebrows slightly. "He'll be okay?"

"I guess." Lynch turned the pages of the paper. "Maybe he'll send you a thank you note," the veteran deadpanned.

O'Rorke snorted. "If he does, I'll shove it up his ass. Raines?"

"Concussion, that's it." Lynch raised his eyes over the paper. "Did you he—?"

"—yeah. I'm going up now." O'Rorke downed the rest of his coffee, exited the kitchen, and headed up the stairs to the captain's office.

As O'Rorke approached the office he could hear the sound of an AM radio playing from inside. He rapped on the door jamb and waited in the doorway. Inside, fifty-six-year-old Captain Ray Hammonds—called "Midol" behind his back by the guys—stood by a filing cabinet sprinkling fish food into a tropical fish tank. The tall, wrinkled-faced captain didn't look up when he heard the knock.

"Come in. Take a seat," the house captain sighed.

O'Rorke entered the room and took a seat in front of the desk.

The room resembled a storage closet more than an officer's den. File cabinets and bookshelves with call logs going back to the 1950s stood against the wall. Most of the overhead fluorescent lights were out and a film of grime covered just about everything except the fish tank.

Hammonds continued to tend to the fish tank. "Bryan, I heard about the job last night."

"Yes, Captain."

"That took balls. What you did."

"It seemed like it had to be done," O'Rorke admitted.

Hammonds put the fish food down, made his way to his desk chair and sat down, across from O'Rorke. "Did you think it might not have worked?"

"Sir?" O'Rorke sat up a little straighter in his chair.

"I mean, what if the floor gave way when Viterbo and Herndon were on your back?"

O'Rorke didn't say anything. *Monday morning quarterbacking, here we go.*

"Did you think about that?" Hammonds asked.

O'Rorke stared at the fish tank. Swordtails and neon tetras swam aimlessly amongst the coral. "Well, sir. When Herndon was rolling around clutching his leg the only thing I wanted to do was get him out of—"

"—the only thing? Bryan, you didn't think. That's the problem." Hammonds exhaled, leaned back in his chair, pursed his lips. "I should transfer you back to the marine division. You want to go back to working on a fireboat?"

O'Rorke continued to stare at the fish. *Big show. He's got to do his job. I'm not going to take the bait.* "No, sir. I've had enough of boats," he finally said. He knew Hammonds was studying him.

"Let me ask you a question," the house captain said. "Are you trying to prove something?"

O'Rorke cocked his head and eyed Hammonds. "Excuse me, sir?"

"Some of the stuff you pull makes me think you're in competition with someone or something."

"Cap, I don't know what you're talking about. I give 100 percent and expect 100 percent out of every guy on my rig."

Hammonds shook off O'Rorke's deflection. "Bryan, did you know I was on overhaul at the A&P fire?

O'Rorke stared straight at Hammonds. "No. I didn't."

"They had already brought your father and the five others out when we got there." Hammonds squinted toward the rusted, corroded blinds in front of his office window. "Think about that day more than I care to."

O'Rorke studied his boots. "So do I."

"Next time, I need you to think before you try something no one has ever done before. I don't need to have to see that look on your mother's face again. She does not deserve that. Okay?"

O'Rorke shot Hammonds a knowing smile. "Understood."

Hammonds motioned to the door. "You can go. Oh, and I'm still gonna put you in for a medal. You earned it."

O'Rorke stood up and exited the captain's office. He took his time walking down the stairs, past the photos, banners, and trophies the house had garnered over the years, recognitions for distinguished service from years gone by. He shoved his right hand into his jacket pocket and made a fist. He didn't know whether he wanted to tear everything down off the wall or swell with pride knowing there'd be another award up on that wall soon with his name on it.

Dad, thanks for being there last night.

CHAPTER 14

Outside the Irish flag-draped Clancy's Pub and Restaurant on Manhattan's Second Avenue, a boisterous green-clad crowd of youthful bar-hoppers waited to be allowed in. A bouncer guarded the door as he kept track of the pub's occupancy, intent on controlling the flow of patrons, young and old, but especially young, single people, ready to celebrate.

Twenty-five-year-old Melanie Haynes stood outside the doorway with her friend, Dara Vincent. It would be their turn to enter next.

Dara said in her Tennessee twang, "Remind me why we're doing this."

With a similar accent, Melanie said, "Saint Patrick's Day in New York is like Mardi Gras for northerners."

"Well, this waitin' in line thing gets old pretty fast. I'm gettin' tired of waitin'."

"If we're not let in in another five minutes, we'll go."

Dara blew out a breath, blowing a loose curl from her forehead. "I can live with that."

The bouncer's attention focused down the line, his gesture clear that he'd called someone to him.

Melanie watched two firemen dressed in their blue uniforms come forward. Loud enough for the two men to hear, she said, "Guess we can't expect firemen to have manners on Saint Pat's Day."

Bryan O'Rorke put his hand on Jimmy Leary's arm, nodded, and then turned to the two young women. "There you are. You beat us here." To the bouncer he said, "They're with us."

The experienced bouncer grinned and let them in.

Once inside, O'Rorke raised his volume over the din and said to Melanie, "What's that about firemen's manners?"

"Guess I spoke too soon."

She turned to Dara and mouthed, "He's so handsome."

Dara said into her ear, "They both are. Tall and big too."

Melanie felt a tap on her shoulder and turned.

O'Rorke held his hand out. "I'm Bryan."

She placed her small hand in his. "Melanie."

They completed the introductions. O'Rorke said, "How about my buddy and I buy you ladies a drink?"

"Sounds good."

O'Rorke said, "Follow me." He guided the other three to the bar, finding a place to squeeze in, and ordered four whiskey shots.

Melanie leaned in. "You Yankees sure know how to party."

O'Rorke grinned at her and then glanced at the other two. "They're talking like they've known each other a long time."

"That's Dara for you. She never met a stranger who stayed one for long."

He handed each of them a shot glass filled nearly to the top.

Melanie said, "There's every chance this is going to end badly."

O'Rorke laughed. "Nah, that's a small one." He made eye contact with each and said, "Down them on three. Ready? Three."

They handed their empty glasses to O'Rorke, who placed them on the bar.

Melanie tilted her head a few degrees and said, "Is this your M.O. or something?"

"What do you mean?"

"You pick up girls in a bar and get them drunk?"

O'Rorke's gaze went from her to whatever was beyond the front window. "Come with me." He nodded at Jimmy and said, "C'mon."

"What's up?"

"Just spotted Sean Maloney with his pipes."

They made it through the throng and onto the sidewalk, where a group of bagpipers clad in white shirts, green kilts, and matching berets stood in a circle. Amid them was Maloney, the stout, brick-red-faced chauffeur from 135 Truck.

Melanie said, "His sideburns—I forget what they're called."

O'Rorke grinned. "Mutton chops." To Maloney he said, "Tell your guys to follow me." Maloney did so. O'Rorke stepped into the street, with Leary and the two young women behind him. The pipers formed a single-file line behind them and followed O'Rorke, who crossed Second Avenue, causing southbound traffic to come to a halt. He continued down the sidewalk, stopping in front of Tate Malone's Bar.

The doorman leaned to the left, visually tracking the line of pipers.

O'Rorke said, "I'm bringing them in."

The doorman opened the door and stood out of the way.

The bagpipes groaned as the pipers pushed air through the bags and fingered the pipes. They marched into the bar to the tune of "The Minstrel Boy," raising rowdy cheers from patrons.

Melanie shouted to O'Rorke, "Won't see anything like this in Nashville. You crazy Irishmen are fun."

He laughed. "We're just getting started." To the three of them he said, "I'll get a round of beers," then disappeared into the crowd. He returned a few minutes later, handing each a pint of Guinness.

They tapped their mugs in salutation and sipped. O'Rorke

surveyed the scene. "Now this is how to celebrate the day—beer, pipers, and my brothers in the company of fine lasses such as yourselves."

Patrons erupted into applause as the song finished. The pipers played the "Marine Corps Hymn."

O'Rorke smiled at Melanie. "Did you come to the Big Apple to celebrate this holiday?"

She shook her head. "We moved here six months ago. You know, Bryan, you make quite a first impression."

"Some would say that. Some might say otherwise. Drink up, lass. We've got four other bars to go to."

The four, accompanied by the pipers, made their way north on Second Avenue, each bar and patrons welcoming them in, paying for their beers, until the moon replaced the sun in the sky.

O'Rorke asked Melanie for her phone number. She wrote her office number on a bar napkin. He and Leary walked with them to a street free of partygoers and hailed a cab. Brief cheek kisses were exchanged, and then the young women got into the cab. Melanie gave the driver the address of their Upper East Side apartment on First Avenue, both women waving at O'Rorke and Leary as the cab drove away.

Melanie sat back and said, "Wow. What the hell was that?"

Dara stared out the window. "Before I came up here, my daddy said, 'Be careful. Ya never know who ya gonna meet on the streets of New York.' And who do we meet? Strong, good-looking Irish firemen." She fanned her face with her hand and faced Melanie. "That was a different kind of heat, for sure."

Seconds later, they were laughing and exchanging high points of their interactions with O'Rorke and Leary.

✦

Melanie hurried down the hall, toward her small cubicle at Sterling and Black, the white-shoe investment bank where she worked as a junior financial analyst. She had a full night's work ahead of her. A prospective merger transaction was heating up, and there was a lot to get done for the deal to close as planned. She was a yard from her cubicle when her desk phone rang. She frowned at the interruption. This was no time to talk to anyone. But the darn thing kept ringing. Still standing, as though sitting to take the call would give permission to the caller to waste her time, she picked up the receiver, said hello, and waited.

"Can I speak with Melanie, please?"

She recognized the thick Queens accent and the unusual way he pronounced her name. "Hello, Bryan." To her right, three cubicles away, she heard a chair squeak and glanced at Dara, leaning far back in her chair, who grinned and gave her a thumbs-up.

"How's it going, southern lass?"

"Kind of hectic at the moment." She pulled her chair out and sat. "It's nice of you to call."

"Saint Patty's Day was so much fun. How about getting together this Friday night for dinner?"

"I'm sorry. I have plans."

"Guess you'll have to break them."

"Excuse me?"

"You didn't say you had to help your mother or a sick aunt or wash your hair. Plans—that's girl-code for a date. That's not gonna happen. What is it, a first date? Bet it is. I'm right, aren't I?"

"Are you always this direct?"

"Only when I need to be."

She stayed silent, torn.

"Meet me in the lobby of your office at six thirty Friday evening. We'll go for a drink. One drink, Melanie. You pick the place. If it doesn't work out, you can get Smedley or Tucker to take you out another night."

"His name's Allan, from mergers and acquisitions."

"Same difference."

"You're also persistent."

"So, it's a date?"

She nodded. "It's a date."

"Good lass. You won't be disappointed. See you then."

She listened to the dial tone a moment and then cradled the receiver. "Damn Yankees."

CHAPTER 15

"What made you decide to become a fireman?" Melanie asked Bryan, pulling the glass of bourbon on the rocks closer to her. Her question was almost swallowed up in the Friday night din of the crowded Wall Street bar, the Margin Call.

O'Rorke peered at her, perplexed. "Uh, to help people," he responded.

"But the pay isn't that good, is it?" Melanie asked, running her finger along the edge of the glass.

"No. I guess the pay is shit to a lot of people," Bryan said, averting his eyes as he popped a fried mozzarella stick in his mouth. The waitress placed an order of nachos on the table. Melanie took a sip of bourbon and chuckled.

"But it's real expensive to live here. How do you do it on a fireman's salary?"

Bryan ran his tongue along his molars as if he were trying to remove a piece of food from his teeth while he pondered the interrogation he was receiving.

"Well, most guys have second jobs to bring in more dough."

Melanie shot him a quizzical look. He couldn't tell if she was toying with him or genuinely interested. "I'm just curious. When did you know this was what you wanted to do?"

O'Rorke tapped the table with his fingers. *Is she auditioning to be a shrink?* He glanced past her to the bar. "I guess it was when I was nineteen and I was riding my Harley home from the West Coast," he said. "I—"

From his left a voice said, "Melanie?"

Both of them turned toward the voice. A twenty-something guy wearing an expensive navy suit—tailored—and a two-hundred-dollar haircut approached them. O'Rorke took in the man's hands, which had never seen hard work, the manicured nails, the Rolex watch. The half-empty tumbler of scotch in the man's left hand.

Melanie shot a surprised smile at the intruder. "Hey, Allan. I didn't know you came in here."

Allan nodded. "I don't. But Hunter on my desk just got engaged and the guys wanted to celebrate. Had to stop in for one." He glanced at her date.

Melanie gestured toward O'Rorke. "This is my friend Bryan." To O'Rorke, she said, "Bryan, this is Allan."

Allan raked his eyes over O'Rorke and extended his hand. "Nice to meet you, sport."

O'Rorke gripped the hand a little harder than necessary. "Likewise."

"What's your line of work?"

"Fireman."

"Whoa, bet you've seen things no one else in this bar has."

A departing patron opened the door, letting a breeze waft towards their booth. The fresh air carried the scent of cologne from Allan. *Probably expensive stuff,* O'Rorke thought. *Probably French.*

Allan bent down a bit, placing his face eighteen inches from O'Rorke's. "So, *Bryan*, how much college is needed to become a fireman?"

O'Rorke smelled the scotch on the man's breath. From the ruddiness of his cheeks, he'd likely had a few before this one. Maybe even one too many.

Melanie frowned. "Allan. Please."

O'Rorke smiled at Melanie and said, "How about sliding over a little?" She did. To Allan he said, "Have a seat, so we can talk."

"Sure, bro. I like the idea." He slid in next to Melanie.

O'Rorke took a sip of scotch. "Sixteen weeks at the Fire Academy."

"Hmm. That doesn't sound like a lot. Tell me, I read in the paper that you guys are asking for a raise, and the average fireman's salary is $47,000. Is that true?"

O'Rorke glanced at Melanie, who kept her head lowered and a death grip on her glass. "That's about right," he said.

"Me? I don't know how any of you can live on that. Right, Mel?" She didn't look at him.

O'Rorke took another sip. "Allan—that's your name, right?"

Allan held up his glass and said, "*C'est moi.*" He took a healthy swig of scotch.

"My turn to ask a few questions." O'Rorke sat forward.

Allan grinned and elbowed Melanie, prompting her to glance at him. He winked at her. "This should be good."

"First, let's sort out a few things. You're not my brother. My brothers have my back—and I don't mean like at a poker game or at a bar, though they've got my back there too. I mean like when I'm crawling in a basement that's pitch black, looking for some three-year-old whose crackhead mother decided to set the bedroom drapes on fire because she's mad at her landlord and doesn't want to pay the rent. I know my brothers will do whatever they can to come and get me if I'm stuck giving the kid mouth-to-mouth when my mask runs out and the fire is rolling over my head. And, for some reason, I just don't see *you* doing that."

Melanie turned wide eyes to him. O'Rorke made eye contact with her and then glowered at Allan. "That's why you're not my brother."

O'Rorke tipped the rim of his glass toward Allan. "Now for a few questions. You make a lot of money, am I right?"

Allan's expression made clear he was no longer enjoying himself. "I do all right."

"Probably better than all right. All right is living in Rye and sending your kids to public school. That Rolex on your wrist? The suit you're wearing, your haircut, et cetera? Probably pulling in seven figures."

Allan made a sound like someone trying to clear something stuck in his teeth. He shrugged. "So what? What's your point?"

"So, now stay with me here. Have you ever breathed in someone's last breath? Like, I mean for real. Like just before they died. Have you?"

Allan shook his head. Melanie was transfixed. Bryan was the same age as his audience, but he felt like he was talking to teenagers.

"I didn't think so. Well, you see, when a person dies, they lose all control of their bodily functions, and they get real heavy. That's why they call it dead weight. So, when you start to do CPR, it gets kind of messy, and it's difficult. And you've only got six minutes before they start turning blue, and then you've lost them—for good."

Bryan spread his hands across the table.

"Forever. So, you have to work fast to save them. You got it?"

Allan nodded.

"Now, let me ask you a question. When you're an old man, near the end of your days, looking back over your life, after you've made your millions, bought your penthouse suite on Park Avenue—" Bryan pointed to Melanie. "—married your attractive trophy wife, sent your kids to Fieldston and Princeton and you have all you'll ever need, no money worries, vacations, everything. Let me ask you this: at that time, when you're staring eternity in the face, what do you think is gonna matter to you more—that you made millions? Or that you saved six people's lives? That those six people are walking the earth, getting married, having kids, their kids are having kids, calling you up every Christmas to thank you for saving their lives, for saving their parents' lives. What do think is going to matter more?" Bryan reached across the table, took Allan's cocktail glass, and moved it to the left. "The millions?" He moved his own scotch glass to the right. "Or the six people?"

A bitter silence followed. Melanie stared at her drink. Allan sat back in his chair, locked his arms around his head and smirked at O'Rorke. "I'll take the millions."

Bryan shook his head. "Yeah, that's what I thought. You could never be a brother." He pulled a twenty-dollar bill out of his wallet and threw it on the table.

"Here, kids. This should cover my share. Screw the both of youse." He abruptly got up from the booth and made his way to the door.

Outside the bar, Bryan lit up a Winston and walked down the street. He thought about how clueless civilians were—and how the Job screwed with his head to make him short and cranky—like he was in the bar. The fact that he got like that with this girl he sort of liked made him angry.

He thought about how the Job takes its toll on everyone—the grim, predictable unpredictability of it. In one instant, you're helping someone who locked their keys out of their car, and at the next call you're dragging a lifeless five-year-old's body down a hall with the hope of giving the kid a shot to live the years you already have. Or the fatals, where you can't do anything but wait for the meat wagon to show up, knowing someone's son or daughter is dead and you know that before they do. It's unseemly, intrusive, a violation of the family's right to privacy. Like when you show up at a messy car accident at 2 a.m. on a Saturday night and cut some nineteen-year-old's body out of a car with a Hurst tool—only to see the kid's cell phone on the ground light up with the word "Mom" on the screen. You know her parents were home blissfully asleep and they're going to get a call. You'd like to send them on a trip around the world for a year before they got that call. But that's not how it goes. They're going to get that call—soon—and you know it. It's the fringe benefits of being in the "I'm-having-the-worst-day-of-my-life" business. O'Rorke bristled thinking about it.

After a while, you realize it's an endless war. And you have to deal with its influence on your body and soul, the way a heroin junkie manages his addiction. You can't get away from it, so you manage it. You work your life around it, around its grip on your life. You work out. You run. You smoke, drink, fight with your wife, chase skirts, or go see the chippies. You've responded to so many emergencies, you know what to expect at most of them—the fire, smoke, mayhem, death, and life, but it doesn't make it any easier. You never really get used to the grief and loss on the Job, and it works its way into your bones, becoming a dark picture frame around your workingman's life.

Bryan chuckled. *And then they wonder why the brothers drink, smoke, and chase pussy,* he thought. *That skirt was clueless.*

He reached the corner and stopped for the Don't Walk sign. Across the street at the curb sat a Harley-Davidson motorcycle, a softail like the one he used to have. He thought of what Melanie asked: *When did I know I wanted to do this?*

✦

A nineteen-year-old Bryan O'Rorke pushed his Harley Softail east on Interstate 40. The lonely open road stretched before him. Rock formations rose from the painted desert floor. Cacti and scrub brush littered the landscape on either side. Last year, he'd been the six-foot-two varsity tight end at Ridgewood High School in Queens, New York. Now, he didn't own much and wanted less. Except to get through the desert to a roadside motel in Gallup, New Mexico, before nightfall.

Saddlebags flanked the sides of the bike. A leather sleeve held a Springfield 30-aught-6 hunting rifle, the rifle and bike being his sole possessions of any real value. It was late afternoon, and the day's heat was beginning to taper off. Long brown hair waved under his cruising helmet, and sunglasses shielded his blue eyes from the glare, dust and sand. His tanned, freshly tattooed arms turned even more brown as he made the ride wearing a sleeveless leather vest. The ink of a Celtic Cross over the date July 2, 1863 displayed on his ripped left bicep. A Maltese Cross above the date August 2, 1978 covered his right one.

Up ahead, a late-model Toyota sat on the side of the road with its hood up. Behind it was a beat-up Chevy sedan, empty of passengers. Didn't like what he saw. *Not everyone is a Good Samaritan.* O'Rorke slowed his speed and eased off the road, pulling up behind the second car. He removed his helmet, put the kickstand down, and used his portable CB radio to call the highway patrol. He dismounted and slowly approached the Toyota, the only sound made by his black leather motorcycle boots that softly clanged on the blistering pavement.

A man and a woman sat in the front seat of the first car. O'Rorke leaned over and peered in. The man was behind the wheel. O'Rorke guessed his age at around twenty-five; had a ratty, disheveled appearance with unkempt hair and scruffy beard. The woman in the passenger seat was close to forty, wearing business clothes and a distressed expression. "Excuse me. Need any help?"

The man answered, "No thank you, sir. Triple A should be here any minute."

O'Rorke nodded. "Good. While you wait, how about I take a look at the engine?"

"No need. Alternator burned up. We're done."

"That's not good. Think I'll check it out anyway." He walked to the front of the car, touched the alternator—hot, but not unusually so. He sensed something was off; he put the hood down and returned to the driver's side, positioning himself to see both people inside the stifling hot car. "Probably best if I wait with you."

The man pressed his lips together. A bead of sweat broke free from his temple and slid down the side of his face. "Not necessary. We're okay here."

O'Rorke eyed the woman, panic evident in her eyes and face. "That okay with you, ma'am?"

The man turned his face to her. She swallowed hard. "I'm—we're okay. It's okay."

O'Rorke nodded. "All right then."

O'Rorke walked back to his bike. Just as he got there, he heard a car door open. He grabbed the 30-aught-6 from its case and turned around to see the driver exiting the car, a Walther .38 in one hand. He dragged the woman by her hair out the door with the other.

The man, eyes bulging, said, "Don't even think about it, asshole!" He shoved the woman to her knees and held the pistol to her head. "Drop the gun, or I'll kill this bitch."

In a fluid move, O'Rorke lined up the man's head in the rifle scope's crosshair. "Make a move, and I'll vaporize your fucking head."

"I mean it. I'll shoot her."

O'Rorke's finger, visible to the man, eased the safety off. "And someone'll be hunting for pieces of your head for weeks."

The man pressed the pistol hard against the woman's head. "Last chance."

Tears streamed down the woman's face as she sobbed.

White rage coiled up O'Rorke's spine. "Listen, cheese-dick, this is going to end badly for you, one way or another. I called nine-one-one before I got off the bike. Highway patrol will be here soon. You can do something stupid, and I can end this now, or you can let her go and maybe get off easier. Your choice."

"You're lying. You're full of shit."

"Oh yeah?" O'Rorke asked, before flashing the brigand a wry grin. "Let's wait it out."

In his peripheral vision, O'Rorke's gaze flickered toward his right rearview mirror, tilted up just enough for him to see a black-and-white Crown Victoria approaching. One *whoop* of the siren announced the patrol's arrival.

The troopers' car pulled up a couple yards behind O'Rorke's motorcycle. Over the loudspeaker boomed the words, "Put the guns down. Now!"

The man let go of the woman and sped to the Toyota.

O'Rorke kept his rifle aimed toward the car. Behind him, one of the troopers radioed for backup.

Both troopers' doors opened but didn't close. "Put the rifle down and get on the ground. Do it!"

O'Rorke lowered the rifle, eased onto his knees, placed the rifle on the asphalt with his left hand, and then placed his hands behind his head.

"Face to the ground."

As O'Rorke sank all the way to the ground, the officer grabbed the rifle. Footsteps ran past him—the other officer, pistol out, running toward the Toyota.

An hour later, O'Rorke lay on a cot in the state troopers' holding cell. Footsteps came closer. He sat up as the sergeant approached the deputy outside the cell. "Let him go. The woman confirmed his story."

The deputy unlocked the cell. O'Rorke wasted no time leaving it.

The sergeant gestured toward the hall to the right. "You can get your things out of property. Your bike's out back." They walked in silence for a few moments. "Had to check you out, of course."

"Of course."

"New York City. From a fireman's family. Sorry about your dad. Lost on the Job, I saw."

"Thanks."

They approached the window. The sergeant gave the order to the clerk, who retrieved a box with O'Rorke's personal items. The clerk announced each item, simultaneously making check marks on the property list in the box.

The sergeant picked up the Saint Florian Medal on a silver chain, checking both sides before handing it to O'Rorke.

O'Rorke slipped the medal over his head, tucking it under his vest.

"Where you headed?"

"Back home." O'Rorke slid his wallet into his back pocket.

The sergeant chuckled. "Going on the Job?"

O'Rorke nodded. "A family thing." He slipped his sunglasses on, grabbed his helmet and rifle, and faced the sergeant.

"Bike's this way."

He followed the sergeant out the station house door to a back parking lot. A quick walk around his bike and saddlebags showed that everything was in order. He slid the rifle into its holder, combed his fingers through his hair, and put the helmet on.

The sergeant rested his thumbs on his belt. "Nice piece of work out there."

"Thanks."

"Why'd you stop, get involved?"

"I don't know. Why do you?" O'Rorke tossed his leg over the bike, righted it, and started the engine. "Guess it's just in us."

The sergeant nodded, waved. Bryan Edward O'Rorke eased the Harley around the building and onto the road, heading east into the descending daylight.

✦

"Bryan." The loud female voice got his attention. He looked down. Melanie stood next to him. "Can you hear me?"

O'Rorke nodded. "Oh, excuse me. I was thinking about something you said."

"Bryan, I'm so sorry. I work with him."

"Yeah. Mergers and acquisitions."

"I'm new there. He's one of the VIPs. That's no excuse, I know, but I hope you can understand. It was awkward for me."

The light changed. O'Rorke started across William Street. Melanie followed him, sped her steps to keep up.

"Bryan, please wait. We didn't get a real chance to talk. I'm not like that, shallow, the way I was in there."

O'Rorke took a long drag on his Winston, blowing smoke out over the street. Melanie pursed her lip.

"Bryan, please listen to me. I grew up in a trailer park in a dirt-road town in Tennessee. My mother died when I was ten and my father worked three jobs to give us enough money to put food on the table for me, my younger sisters and brother, and I had to basically raise them. I got a partial scholarship from the Salvation Army to attend the University of Tennessee and put myself through college waitressing and bartending. I came up here to New York because this is the big time and I have one shot, one shot to make it here. Sometimes, with all the noise and commotion of the big city, I miss seeing the real things and real people around me—like you. I'm sorry."

O'Rorke halted in front of McPherson's Irish Pub and faced her. "One more chance. Any bullshit and it's sayonara." He opened the pub door and entered. Melanie trailed in after him.

They found a table and ordered. The silence between them was uncomfortable, until she made the effort, asked questions, listened to his answers, studied his eyes and expressions.

"I want to confess what you already know," she said. "From the first, I realized you were someone with substance, *of* substance." A small smile played on her lips. "I had to tune my ears to your Queens accent. Still getting used to all the accents here and how fast some people talk compared to back home."

He returned her smile. "I noticed."

"And I noticed you have insight, clarity. You get to the heart of things without taking any detours. You have a real purpose in life and don't walk around with any kind of affectation." She chewed on her bottom lip a moment and then added, "I just wanted to say that to you."

He studied her face and the sincerity in her eyes. "Let's just say we got off to a bad start. But that's behind us now." He gently placed his right hand on top of hers. "Let's order some food and try to—what did you say?—get to the heart of things?"

Hours later, they were still talking.

CHAPTER 16

It had been several weeks since her suicide attempt. Ellie kept up with the routines Phil Coletti had prepared for her—got up early, did yoga, read at the library, helped at the soup kitchen, took her meds, met weekly with the psychiatrist, who, at her last appointment, told her that from then on she was to from then on see her once a month for the next three months. Each day, she felt a little better physically and mentally. Mornings at the library were the most peaceful times of the day. Good books took her out of her thoughts, like a mental vacation. The depression that had gripped her for so long was beginning to loosen its grasp. At the church, she was such a reliable volunteer, the pastor hired her to answer phones and work the front desk three evenings a week.

Still, the high point of her day was the soup kitchen. Each day made it easier to start a conversation with the people who came there. Made it easier to note their appreciation as she ladled food for them. And now she'd formed friendships with Lena, an elderly Polish woman; Juan, a recovering Dominican drug addict; and Stu, a tall, articulate, middle-aged African American. Her lunch club. Their first real conversation happened one day after she'd finished serving and had helped clean the kitchen. She'd grabbed a cup of coffee and joined them at a table, listened to their stories of how they'd ended up at the soup kitchen. This coffee-and-chat time soon became an everyday event for them. Had anyone asked, she would have found it difficult to explain what she was feeling—like life was becoming more balanced, like something about her life was evening up. It was as though her suicide attempt was nothing more than a portal she'd walked through, carrying her to another world just on the other side, one she'd never noticed before.

As requested, she called Phil every night at the appointed time, sometimes reaching him at home, sometimes having to wait when he was at the firehouse, sometimes having to wait until the next morning. But she didn't return to the firehouse, nor had he asked her on a date. She hadn't seen him since the barbecue.

On the calls she'd tell him about her day, he'd fill her in on what was happening at the house, the stunts and stupidity they got up to. He'd told her about his side job, playing the trumpet; told her about his dad and mom. In one of their recent calls, he told her he'd taken the lieutenant's test and was waiting for the results, how his father had come around about him going for lieutenant and even gave him study books for the test. It pleased her that he never sounded bored or uninterested when it was her turn, which made opening up not only easy but anticipated.

Their paths crossed again during rush hour on the Thursday of that week. She was on her way home from the soup kitchen. Engine 252 passed her, going in the same direction. The rig stopped at the intersection, and the rear cab door opened. Coletti exited in full gear, minus his helmet. His face was smudged with char and grime. He stepped onto the sidewalk. "Hey, stranger. Where're you heading?"

"To answer your question, I'm on my way home. Just finished at the soup kitchen."

He gave her his widest grin. "When am I going to get another invitation for a cup of that great coffee you make?"

She tilted her head slightly. "When am I going to get invited to hear you play?"

"You like jazz?"

"I'd like to hear what you do with it."

He laughed. "My band's playing at Village Tavern in Manhattan tomorrow night. At nine. Think you'll make it?" Before she could respond he said, "Hold on." He pivoted and cleared his throat. "Sorry. I've got about a pound of soot caked in my nose, compliments of a two-story shithole in East New York."

Ellie shook her head. "I'll be there."

Cars behind the engine blasted their horns.

Kelvin Jordan stuck his head outside the cab and yelled, "Dog. How long is this gonna take?"

Coletti kept his gaze on Ellie but turned his head just enough to shout, "Yeah, yeah." To Ellie he said, "I'll look for you. Bring a friend."

Ellie watched him get back inside as the rig drove through the intersection and up the avenue. Tomorrow night, she'd learn something new about him, through his music.

CHAPTER 17

The Village bustled on a warm Friday night in May. Students, hucksters, and the Bohemian types that call MacDougal Street "the neighborhood" moved over to make room for the Bridge and Tunnel Crowd invading from the bedroom boroughs. It was a Friday night, and they got their hall pass to go "into the city" to get their hipster fix and feel artistic, not really knowing what they were seeking.

Those who filed into Village Tavern at the corner of West Third and MacDougal knew the fix they sought—good, straight-ahead jazz. The Tavern, as it was called by devotees, had etched its way into the fabric of jazz history by hosting nearly every impresario of this singular American art form, and had done so since 1935, when Stan Gottlieb used a hundred dollars and a forged cabaret license to open the doors.

Tonight, the Thad Rogers Septet was the headliner, their every-other-week session scheduled to start at 10:30 p.m. Aficionados flocked to the small basement lair, eager to hear the group known for clean, cool jazz issued through instruments from players out of well-known ensembles from decades past, equally eager to sip scotch and revel in the inevitable jousting between Thad Rogers's tenor saxophone and Mel Curtis's fluegelhorn.

Tonight, Rogers would introduce a young quintet—The Fabulous New Yorkers—having heard their CD, which prompted him to ask them to open for this regular gig. He had expressed particular appreciation for Phil Coletti's trumpet playing. If the quintet also impressed the sophisticated crowd of regulars, they'd have a shot at making extra bucks on the jazz and cocktail scene, which was what he'd told them.

Coletti arrived early for the gig around seven thirty. He took a seat at the beat-up, dingy bar, where more than one patron had experienced a wee-hours, alcohol-and jazz-induced personal epiphany on the state of his life. The Friday night bartender, an overweight fifty-something upstater named Pete, was setting up for the evening, a Pall Mall cigarette fuming in an ashtray behind the bar. It was Phil's customary practice on the night of a gig to arrive before anyone else did. It allowed him to get comfortable with the surroundings before others arrived, as if for a little while it was his place that everyone else was coming to.

"What's the profile tonight, Pete?" he asked, settling onto a barstool.

Pete wiped the bar top with a damp rag. "Usual scene. Nothing to write home about."

Coletti pulled a pack of Marlboro Lights from his pocket and lit one up.

"Unless it's your first time playing the Tavern."

Coletti exhaled smoke into the air. Pete nodded, still working the bar top.

"Let's hope it's not your last. You know this crowd—'demanding' isn't the right word for them."

Coletti took another drag and let it out. "I once heard them boo

Dizzy's sideman." He nodded.

Pete stopped what he was doing. He grinned and said, "Yeah. Dizzy busted out laughing."

Coletti flicked ash into the nearest ashtray. "Well, tonight they're gonna get as good as they give."

He wheeled around on the barstool and took another drag on his cigarette, surveying the room. The smoke-stained mahogany walls were dimly lit by tea candles at the tables. They barely illuminated the countless grainy black-and-white photos of jazz greats staring at him from everywhere he glanced. The flickering candlelight made the images seem as if they were conversing with each other, waiting for the next set to begin.

Damn. Who needs a live audience? Just playing in this room in front of these photos is intimidating enough. He had seen many of them play here in this very room. Davis, Baker, Konitz, Carter, and Evans. Many times, he'd listened to them work their craft deep and defiantly into the weekday nights, wondering what it would feel like to play on that tiny stage in this dingy pilgrimage site of jazz. Now, tonight, he was going to have his turn.

Coletti took another drag and then crushed the cigarette in the ashtray. He stood and picked up his gig bag. The silhouette of a middle-aged man carrying a saxophone case filled the doorway. His sideman, Willis White, resembled an accountant more than the municipal bus driver he was. Trailing in behind White were the band's drummer, string bass player, and piano man. Coletti waved and gestured for them to go to the stage.

It wouldn't be long before it was show time.

✦

Ellie and Samantha, her only friend from FIT, left the Indian restaurant in the Village, where they'd filled up on samosas followed by chicken vindaloo and a carafe of white wine. They found the Tavern and followed patrons down the steps to the basement jazz club. The place was filling fast. They stood inside, near the entrance. Ellie said, "This is like an unknown world to me."

Samantha nodded. "Same here."

A waitress approached them. "Two?"

They said yes at the same time and were led to a table near the back of the lounge, far from the stage and off to the side. Most tables were already filled. Every barstool was, and others crowded the bar.

They took their seats and gave their orders. Ellie turned her focus to the stage, set up with instruments, music stands, and microphones arranged in a line in front of a drum set and the piano. The room buzzed with palpable anticipation from patrons.

A few minutes later, Samantha squeezed the wedge of lime over her gimlet and then dropped it in, stirred, took a sip. "This guy we came to hear play—"

"Phil Coletti."

"Is he just a friend?"

"He's one of the good guys."

Samantha made eye contact with Ellie. "Any chance of him becoming more than just a friend?"

Ellie shrugged. "I don't know. Maybe."

"Uh-huh. You skittish about getting involved with a musician?"

"This is a side job for him. He's a fireman."

"So, a real hero rather than an imaginary one. Can't wait to meet him."

Ellie laughed. "Easy. I found him first."

The dim, recessed overhead lights blinked several times and then dimmed even more. A woman walked up to one of the microphones, stepping into the lone spotlight beam aimed at her. She smiled and nodded at the audience, who erupted into applause and cheers.

Samantha leaned toward Ellie and said, "What do you think? Is she like eighty or something?"

Ellie shrugged and sat up straighter as Coletti and the other band members took their spots on stage behind the woman.

The woman held up her hands for quiet. "Thank you. Thank you. My name is Muriel Gottlieb." The audience clapped and whistled. "Folks, tonight I have the privilege to introduce you to a group of young jazz musicians with a fabulous sound."

Someone at the bar yelled, "Hope you're right, Muriel."

"I know that voice. And don't you worry, Ben. They're not gonna disappoint you. They sound better than you ever did on this stage." Laughter rippled through the room. "Ladies and gentlemen, The Fabulous New Yorkers." She nodded to Coletti and White and exited the stage to tepid applause from all but Ellie, who sat forward in her chair.

The trumpet and saxophone players stepped up to their mikes slowly and reverently. Ellie could see them simultaneously inhale before placing their first breaths through their horns. The notes erupted in unison as the siren-like sound of "Blue Train"—the centerpiece of the Coltrane canon—reverberated off the basement ceiling, filling the air and ears of all in the room. The braided presentment of brass and reed—sans rhythm section—sounded a clarion call to even the most indifferent. After the first four measures, the rhythm section joined in, the walking bass leading the ensemble out of the head under the smoky sound of Willis White's tenor saxophone.

Ellie watched as the saxophonist bit hard on the reed and forced air through the woodwind's coiled chambers, pressing and opening levers to bend and mold the airstream into a deep, rich timbre that sounded like a wizened old fisherman weaving a tall fish tale. Willis took his time with his improvisation, begrudgingly offering riffs and runs like a big-league pitcher showing his stuff to a .300 hitter—sparingly and only as necessary. Behind the front men, the drummer kept a vigilant pace on his trap set, pinging his flat-ride cymbal along with his partner in crime, the string bass player, who plucked his axe in lockstep. The piano player, not to be overlooked, interjected chords under the saxman's solo, framing Willis's improvisation with Dorian harmonies.

Ellie broke her gaze, which she'd fixed on Coletti, to glance around the room. Some patrons tapped fingers on the tabletops, others nodded heads and sipped their cocktails, but all eyes were aimed at the stage. Even Samantha, whose eyes aimed at the candle on the table, was caught up in the music.

On stage, the saxman's solo was becoming more frenzied and louder. He worked his riffs all over the song's chords, wailing and soaring high in the upper registers and then plunging to the lower ranges with fervent intensity. Sweat beaded on his forehead, his eyes closed, like he was in a meditative trance. The man's fingers and lungs clicked in synchronization, urgently, so he could transmit the dispatch out of the instrument. After several measures, with its climax reached, the solo slowed and grew softer; his work was done. Willis retreated out of the spotlight to a spontaneous burst of grateful applause and cheers.

Now it was Coletti's turn. He stood before his microphone leaning forward, lips on mouthpiece with the raised horn in his hands. He tilted slightly down over the mike, like he was peering down into a ravine through a portable telescope. The sheen of the trumpet's brass bell and silver mouthpiece reflected smartly off the spotlight in front of him.

He began slowly, offering half notes over the driving rhythm section. His tone, rich and bright, demonstrated a disciplined embouchure and technique. As the solo picked up tempo, his notes rose from the horn smoothly, crisp in delivery, sprinkled over the audience like bright glitter. Coletti pressed the valves on the horn in rapid sequence, making his lines emerge faster and more precise through every chord change.

Coletti's demeanor was not like the sax player. He stood still behind the mike, playing almost effortlessly, eyes closed with a pious expression on his face. She thought how similar his playing was to his demeanor as she had come to know him: quietly understated, full of small surprises delivered with softness in a dimly lit room. It made her feel comfortable. Sitting there in the small basement listening to jazz with her friend, Ellie felt different, a little freer from the lingering pain.

Up on the stage, Coletti's playing remained steady. He didn't play over the rhythm section, just around it. His arpeggios and blues scales wrangled every last riff out of that ragged horn, bending the blue note with impunity the way it was meant to be played—righteously offensive. He brought the solo to an end with a growl and pop out of the horn, then lowered the instrument from his lips and nodded to the audience.

Applause was spontaneous. The bass player, who had a long, hillbilly beard, nodded knowingly to the piano player. They clearly enjoyed playing under Coletti's solo. The other players rotated through their solos and then returned to the melody before concluding their opening number.

The crowd responded appreciatively, almost with an air of relief in the room, as if they were an immigrant colony in a foreign land that had just received a radio transmission from their leader, raising in them a warm nostalgia for their distant, evanescent homeland.

Coletti stepped to the microphone, raised a hand, and repeated his thanks to the audience. When they settled down, he said, "We're happy to be here tonight. We're happy you decided to stay." Laughter ran like a wave through the room. "We're gonna slow the tempo a bit. Hope you like this one too. 'Every Time We Say Good-bye.'" Coletti raised the horn, turning to the band to cue the next song. The band softly played the slow-tempo ballad under his lead. His sound was much different on this number—plaintive and lyrical. The notes rose from the trumpet and swirled in the smokey room like feathers in a soft summer breeze.

Samantha shot a look to Ellie. "Oooh. If he can make love half as well as he plays trumpet, you would be a very lucky woman."

Ellie cleared her throat. "I think you're right about that." She returned her gaze to the stage, to Coletti. He had a pained look on his face. The sound coming from his horn, how he bent the notes, softly, gingerly, convinced her that he wasn't playing an instrument. He was telling his lover how distraught he was from her impending absence—with his notes, not words. The haunting sound coming from his trumpet sent chills up her arms to the nape of her neck. She shifted in her seat, slightly disturbed by the intensity of the reaction. She was glad her table was off to the side of the stage.

Phil continued his intimate dialogue on stage as the piano player gently placed chords under the melody and the drummer smartly swept his snare drum with his brushes. When the ballad ended, the room was quiet for a moment, almost churchlike, followed by soft, reverent applause. The Fabulous New Yorkers were living up to their name.

When the set ended, Coletti stored his trumpet in his gig bag, and bag in hand, stepped off the stage and wended his way through the crowded room, pausing to speak with patrons. He made it to Ellie's table, smiled broadly. "Glad you made it." He extended his hand to Samantha. "Phil Coletti."

She shook his hand and said, "I know. You guys are good. You sounded great up there."

"Thanks. Okay if I join you?" They both nodded, and he added, "As soon as I find a spare chair." He placed his bag between their chairs, said something to Pete, nodded, and disappeared down a hall. Moments later, he returned, carrying a folding chair, which he placed next to Ellie's.

Samantha pointed at him. "Your lip is swollen. That always happens?"

"Yeah. It goes down after a while."

"Playing the Tavern is a big deal."

Coletti nodded and grinned. "Yeah. It was good of Mel to give us a shot. Now we'll see where it goes, if it goes." He bumped Ellie gently with his elbow. “Sure beats the firehouse, huh, Ellie?”

“Well, there’s still the smell of smoke, just a different kind. But I’d think you’d miss the tar, gear, and trucks.”

“Not in here. This place is more, um, civilized.” He glanced at Samantha then back at Ellie. He draped an arm over the back of Ellie’s chair and kept eye contact with her. “What are you ladies doing the rest of the evening?”

Samantha smiled. “I have to get going. I’ve got an early shift at the coffee shop tomorrow.”

He smiled at her and then turned back to Ellie. “I’m starving. I know a good Italian place on Cornelia Street. Wanna join me?”

Ellie bit down on her bottom lip. “I promised to be at the kitchen by nine tomorrow morning. I—”

“A quick bite. Then I’ll put you in a cab.”

“Okay. But I can’t stay too late.”

Coletti grabbed his bag and rose to his feet. He shifted the bag to his left hand and held out his right. “Let’s go.”

Outside on the sidewalk, he thanked Samantha for coming to the gig and hailed a cab for her, before escorting Ellie to Cornelia Street.

In the dimly lit café, they took a table by a window. Ellie glanced up at the tin ceiling and the patterned wallpaper that, to her eyes, belonged to the 1940s. She sipped an espresso as he ate a dish of homemade pasta and let the server refill her small cup when Coletti ordered an espresso for himself. The conversation went back and forth between easy and strained. He paid the bill, and they exited onto the cobblestone street, walking past hundred-year-old townhouses.

Before they reached the corner, he stopped. “Ellie, give me your hand.”

She extended her right hand to him.

“Your left hand.” She positioned her hand behind her. “Please,” He said and kept his hand extended until she did as he asked. “This hand is part of your beauty."

Her expression of puzzlement was obvious.

"It makes you unique."

"That's one way to put it."

"Here's how I put it." He placed her hand against his cheek and moved closer, until their faces were mere inches apart.

When her body stiffened, he said, "Relax, Ellie. Don't think about anything."

Under the amber-tinged streetlight, he kissed her, letting his lips linger on hers until she let go of resistance. He slowly lowered her hand to her side. "I know this isn't easy for you. And I wish—I hope—you'll trust me." He wrapped his arms around her and flashed a smile. "This doesn't feel that bad. Or does it?"

She relaxed in his arms and shook her head. "No. It's not bad."

"I know we've just met, but how about we see where this might go?"

Ellie pushed away, wincing, and placed a hand over her stomach.

"What's wrong? You okay?"

"The thought of getting close to someone—anyone—makes me anxious. I wish it didn't, but it does. It's something I need to work through. I want to, more than you know, but I can't tell you when that may happen."

"I'm not going to rush you. I don't know everything that's happened in your life, but I hope that at some point, you'll feel comfortable enough with me to open up. That is, if you want to."

She turned away. "I do."

"Look at me." He waited for her to turn her eyes back to him. "You're stronger than *it* is. You can beat it. Promise me you'll go after it. I'll help you if you'll let me. So, what's it gonna be?"

"You're stubborn."

"Persistent."

"You're so … so—"

"Italian." He grinned. "It's my best and worst trait. Something else for you to get used to. Now what about that promise?"

She raised her hands. "Okay, I promise. Now can I go home?"

He planted a brief kiss on her forehead. "Yeah."

CHIEF

Treat your men as you would your beloved sons. And they will follow you into the deepest valley.

– Sun Tzu

CHAPTER 18

JUNE 22, 2001

FDNY Headquarters, Downtown Brooklyn. Bureau of Fire Investigations Hearing Room.

Chief Steven Brendan sat alone at the witness table. Dressed in his dress-blue uniform, wearing a starched white shirt fitted with collar brass, he sat erect. His white chief's hat rested on the table near the microphone in front of him. Seated across from him in swivel chairs on the dais were five chief officers, four of them gray-haired and ruddy-cheeked, carrying the extra weight of men who spent their careers behind a desk. In the center sat the fifth man, a younger, taller, slimmer, more handsome battalion chief, Lucius Knox. Cameras mounted on the ceiling videotaped the proceedings being held in front of a near-capacity audience of fire department brass, firefighters, press, and city officials.

Battalion Chief Knox kept eye contact with Brendan. "Chief Brendan, did you or did you not order Captain Boyle to remain outside the building when you concluded that interior conditions had deteriorated to a point to make an offensive attack untenable?" the young battalion chief asked, dryly, clinically. The leading question hung in the air like a noose ready to be placed around Brendan's neck.

Brendan stared at his inquisitor. *This prick Knox really has a hard-on for a promotion.*

"Captain Boyle had already reentered the building with Firefighter Andrews before I made the determination that interior operations should be terminated." After a brief pause, he added, "Sir."

Knox studied the file papers in front of him. "Once you made that determination, what did you do?" He kept his gaze fixed on the pages.

"I ordered all interior units to retreat from the building, so we could go to defensive."

Knox was not deterred. "And why did you let Boyle and Andrews reenter the building when interior conditions were not improving?" Knox's smooth, aristocratic tone conveyed a subtle air of detached superiority formed by his lineage as a descendant of one of the original New York families.

Brendan wanted to get up and walk out. *What the fuck does this guy know about incident command?* He cleared his throat, leaned forward in his chair, and looked straight at Knox. "As you know, Chief Knox, under department incident command priorities, life safety is the first priority objective. When a life is in jeopardy, we will risk a life to save a life. We will use considerable caution to protect savable property, and we will not risk a life to save what is lost. In my estimation, at the Avenue C fire, a life was in jeopardy, which necessitated Captain Boyle and Firefighter Andrews's reentry into the building to attempt a rescue of a civilian."

Knox lifted his head and faced Brendan. "How could you be certain about this?"

Under the table, Brendan knotted his hands into fists. "Captain

Boyle informed me that he heard someone calling for help from inside the building and that he was going in after them."

"So, you let Captain Boyle override your incident assessment. Are you certain he heard anything, or was it one of his gut reactions again?"

Brendan bit his lower lip.

"In my thirty-five years on the Job, in command of countless scenes, I've learned to trust the assessment of a veteran firefighter such as Captain Boyle when it comes to life-and-death decisions. At this job, Captain Boyle had heard a voice in the building when he and firefighter Andrews were making their first rescues, and they were told by one of the civilians that there was an elderly man still in the building. When Captain Boyle told me he was going back in, I did not order him to remain outside."

"Did you say anything to him before he reentered the building?" Knox asked.

"Yes."

"And?"

Brendan spoke slowly, clearly, at volume. "I told him the job was getting too hot. That he needed to get in and out real fast. That if it turned into a shit show, we'd be sitting in front of Knox, explaining Firefighting 101."

The room erupted into laughter. Knox pressed his lips into a thin line, grabbed the gavel with the manicured fingers of his right hand, and banged it on the table. His panel colleagues shifted in their chairs.

"That's enough. Quiet down," Knox bellowed into his microphone.

Knox placed the gavel down. Scowling, he said, "Chief Brendan, I expect someone of your experience and seniority to recognize the necessity and importance of this inquest. The department needs to discover how to avoid deficiencies in command decisions that may have been present at this fatal fire incident."

"I appreciate the important undertaking of this committee and look forward to reviewing the report it issues regarding the incident, *Chief*... Knox," Brendan responded, smirking almost imperceptibly.

There it was. The inflection used on the reference to rank emphasized what so many in the room already knew—that a dividing line existed between watchers and doers, dress blues versus bunker gear, Headquarters versus Hot LZ. And that Brendan, as many in the room did as well, perceived Knox as his inferior, unqualified to hold rank despite his pedigree or pay grade.

Knox, cheeks nearly as ruddy as his colleagues', turned his gaze to the file. "Thank you, Chief. That will be all." He moved the file out of the way and opened the one under it. "Captain Boyle, please approach the hearing table."

Boyle rose slowly from his seat a couple of rows behind the hearing table. Although it had been almost four months, his injuries still made walking painful. He took a seat at the table, removed his white captain's hat, and placed it in front of him. Pinned to his jacket were medals accompanied by a multitude of ribbons, awarded for his playing Russian roulette with the Red Devil, reluctantly or not, more times than anyone in the room. He positioned himself as comfortably as he could, fixed his gaze on Knox, and waited.

Knox shuffled a few papers, then said, "Please explain what happened at this incident that compelled you to take Firefighter Andrews back into the building, in order to conduct a secondary search after conditions deteriorated."

Boyle drew the microphone closer to him. "I believe Chief Brendan summed it up best—we took a calculated risk to save a life."

"But you didn't know, with any certainty, that someone was still inside the building."

"As the chief said, I heard someone, so I went back in. But that's irrelevant."

"Irrelevant? I don't understand how—"

"Chief, it's like this. Much as you want it, you can never get certainty on a fire scene. You work with the information you have, experience you've gained, and your gut—what you sense is going on in front of you. You make a split-second decision based on what you know, and you go with it."

"It appears your expertise wasn't enough to keep those under your command safe, was it?" Knox placed his elbows on the table, formed a pyramid with his fingers, and rested his chin atop the apex.

Boyle studied Knox.

"Was it, Captain Boyle?"

"As I was going to say, sometimes things happen on the scene that lead to unfortunate and tragic results. Like in this incident, where we had to go back in to pursue a rescue, even while conditions were deteriorating." He paused a moment, scratched the side of his mouth, and then added, "Truthfully, Chief, if I had to do it again, I wouldn't do anything different."

Knox dropped his hands and leaned forward. "You wouldn't? You don't think the results—the word you used was *tragic*—would warrant a change in tactics or approach?"

"No, I don't," Boyle continued. "I know you may find that hard to believe, Chief, but if you'd like to come down to our house sometime and ride out with us, you might get a sense of what we do and how we look at this very dangerous business we've chosen as our profession—Chief."

Murmurs emanated from the audience. Several heads nodded in agreement with the sentiment behind Boyle's invitation. The way Boyle said it carried just enough of a sneer to make the response disrespectful but not insubordinate.

Knox cleared his throat and adjusted his microphone. "I appreciate your invitation, though it isn't necessary. I think we have all the information we need in the files. Unless anyone else has questions, I think we can conclude this inquest." He glanced right and left. His colleagues nodded.

Voice volume increased as attendees filed out of the room. Boyle rose and made his way into the hallway. Brendan stood near a window where Boyle joined him.

"I think I may get it from the brass on this one," Boyle said, scanning the hallway.

Brendan unwrapped a stick of gum and popped it into his mouth. "Don't worry about it. What are they gonna do, put you on 323 Truck and send you on impossible rescues in the Lower East Side?"

Their laughter stopped as a red-faced Knox, gritting his teeth, approached them. He stopped two feet from them, stood in his pristine uniform and, with not one hair out of place, glared at them in turn. "You sons-a-bitches think this is a waste of time, don't you?" He waved the files in his hand. "Think you can waltz in there and show contempt for the brass because you're the big, swingin' dicks on the rigs, and we're just pencil-pushers downtown who don't know jack-shit about the Job." He struck Boyle's chest with the corner of the folders. "You push it. Always take chances." He tapped the medals on Boyle's chest with the folders. "These aren't for heroism. They're gambling winnings. Well, this time you gambled and lost. If you'd used your common sense—if you have any—Andrews would be alive."

Knox, veins bulging over his collar, glared at Brendan. "Both of you had better learn this is the *new* FDNY. The days of charging in balls-to-the-wall are over. No more of this cowboy shit. We'll finish this investigation. And if we conclude there was any negligence, any oversight or dereliction of duty by any company officer or incident commander that resulted in Andrews' death, you'll both spend the rest of your days testing hose lines and measuring gear for probies on the Rock. I'll make certain of it. Understood?"

Brendan leaned forward slightly. "I hear you, Lucius. You do what you think's best for the department. And we'll do the same. What comes of it, comes of it. Just remember one thing." He positioned his face a foot from Knox's. "Write whatever the fuck you want. Knock yourself out. But don't ever lecture me on how to do my job. I'll be judged by firemen greater than you could *ever* hope to be." He pointed to Boyle. "Like this guy. And guys like Denny Andrews."

Knox hissed, "You're out of line, Brendan." He pivoted and stormed off.

"That guy," Boyle said, "is the biggest prick on the Job."

"Fuckin' arrogant blueblood. Thinks the Job can be run like General Motors or IBM. He doesn't get it." He faced Boyle. "We'll see what Cianci does with the report."

CHAPTER 19

A warm June breeze, devoid of the stifling humidity prescribed to July and August, wafted past the open doors and into the bay of the Twelfth Street firehouse. It was not long after 8:00 a.m. Ladder 323's crew was busy cleaning the rigs after a warehouse fire on Fourteenth Street the night before. At the scene, the rig had been positioned in front of the burning building. All manner of debris had rained down on the apparatus. When the incoming shift lieutenant saw the rig backing into the house around 7:30 a.m., he scoffed that they should have taken the truck to the Department of Sanitation garage for cleaning.

The crew was working diligently to get the rig into top shape this morning. Not just because they took pride in their rig—which they did—but because their beloved captain, Paddy Boyle, was returning to work today after three months of recovery from the Avenue C hardware store fire.

Not much had changed at the house in the three months Boyle was laid up recovering from third-degree burns on his legs, except that the house had been assigned a new probie, who was on duty that morning, cleaning the chassis and aerial ladder with gusto. Kearns, the big, scrappy outside vent man, didn't waste a minute to seize the opportunity to take advantage of the circumstances the probie found himself in.

"C'mon, lad," the beefy Irishman called to the young probie, Reynolds. "This is a special day. Paddy Boyle is returning to work. Make him proud of his house! Those rigs have to be spotless. He'll have it no other way. You've heard of Paddy Boyle, I hope? The best fireman in the history of the department?"

The probie nodded earnestly.

"Yes," Kearns said, "a towering man. Stands close to seven feet tall. Can pry a door with a halligan in one hand and a two-and-a-half-inch line in the other. And with two children tucked into his turnout coat. If you're going to work with Paddy Boyle, you'd better—"

A voice called out from behind him. "Ken, I see you haven't changed one bit."

Kearns spun around and raised his hands. "It's himself. All five foot ten inches of him, though a few pounds shy of his usual one eighty, I'd say." He hurried forward and wrapped Boyle in a bear hug.

Boyle winced. "Easy. There's still some pain."

"Aye, lad. Sorry. But it's fine to see you again. I thought you were coming in for the overnight?"

"I am but I wanted to see the guys on today." Boyle adjusted the strap of his gear bag. A rolled-up yoga mat stuck out of it. "New guy?"

"We'll make a fireman out of him soon enough. Still, for now, I wouldn't trust him to save a cellar on a surround and drown."

Boyle smiled and made his way into the house. Others had seen him arrive and were quickly making their way up to him to welcome their captain back home to the Twelfth Street house.

✦

When he went on duty that evening, he received a visit from his old friend, Father Joe Kelly. The fire department chaplain found Boyle on the backstep of Ladder 323, cleaning his mask.

"Pat, it's good to see you."

"Thanks, Joe. At one point I wasn't sure I'd be seeing the inside of this place again," Boyle confided in his confessor of twenty-one years. He focused on the floor in front of him. "What do you think? You think I'm reckless?"

He raised his head to Kelly, who stared beyond the rig toward the open garage door. Boyle grew uneasy at the delayed response from his old friend and priest.

Kelly's shoulders went up briefly and then down. "I can't answer that. But I know what you're thinking by asking the question."

Boyle dribbled cleaning agent onto the rag and slowly wiped the plastic facepiece. "The whole thing spooks me. It's like this—when I'm at a fire, I go on autopilot. I know in here," he gestured toward his solar plexus, "what has to be done. I don't know where that knowing comes from or how to explain it. It's like I can see through the fire. I know what it's doing and will do." He paused his cleaning. "These guys look up to me. But I'm starting to feel uneasy about all of it. Like I've become some war lover or super-lifer fireman who feeds off the action more than he cares for his men."

Kelly put his hand on his friend's shoulder. "Do you remember that time you brought that kid out of that burning building on Seventh Street? When he died in your arms?"

Boyle nodded and stared back at the floor.

"You gave me that look of utter betrayal. God had let you down, I had let you down. I know you're hurting, like that time."

A silence followed. Boyle tightened the harness on the facepiece, staring down.

"Pat, listen to me. We all have our roles to play. You've chosen your path, and I've chosen mine. With it comes the likelihood that we will have days on the Job that will make us think we made the wrong decision, or worse, that we're failures. Don't let the doubt dig in. When it gets like this, don't think about. Just be stubborn and go about your business."

Kelly pointed out to the street in front of the house. "Out there are millions of people within reach of you and your rig, who rely on you to save them from danger and death every day. *Millions.* You know what lets them sleep at night? Knowing you're in this house, waiting for their call. That's it."

Boyle shook his head and smiled. "Where do you get this stuff from?"

"The Chief upstairs." Kelly smiled at Boyle.

The alarm tones cracked through the evening air, interrupting Kelly's counseling session followed by the dispatcher's voice.

"Get out. Truck. Box 2-8-5-3. 1-7-6 West Twenty-Ninth Street. Battalion 10. 10-75. Second Alarm. Everybody goes."

Boyle scrambled to get on his bunker pants and jacket next to the officer's compartment on 323. The other members of his crew converged on the truck from wherever they were in the house, donning gear as they got into the rig. Noah Beale, the burly Scottish chauffeur, fired up the six-cylinder, five-hundred-horsepower diesel engine and put the emergency flashers on to let the pedestrians know the truck was leaving the barn.

As the truck left the house, Boyle signed on the radio, confirming his response to the fire. The fact that the call came in as a 10-75 second alarm told everybody they were going to be working tonight. These were the call numbers for a non-fireproof building fire where the original assignment of four engines and four trucks wasn't enough, and incident command needed to call out more resources.

Over the radio in the cab, the crew listened as the incident commander communicated with an engine company inside the building. "Command, this is Six-Five Engine. We cannot, repeat, cannot knock the fire down. There's too much fire. We are retreating to the floor below."

Boyle turned to his crew in the cab. His demeanor was serious, businesslike. "Gear up, fellas. It's a hot LZ tonight," he said.

No one spoke in the cab as the truck made its way to the scene, taking Twenty-Third Street across town. Rush hour traffic had subsided, and Beale pushed the pedal hard to get to the fire scene as soon as possible. The crew listened intently to the radio traffic at the working job. Like stagehands or actors at a long-running Broadway play, the crew could envision and anticipate each operational action as it was reported on the radio. To the untrained ear, the transmissions themselves may have raised concern or even panic—'Fire exiting three apartments on 4 side of fourth floor. Initiating search of floor above the fire.' But to many of these men, having fought fires in New York City for years, the transmissions connected them to the emergency, removing the stress that arose from arriving at a fire scene with no knowledge of what to expect or do.

"Sixty-five Engine on the fifth floor. Heavy fire load on sixth floor. Start water," the lieutenant on 65 Engine reported to the incident commander, who promptly granted his request. Even though the transmissions from the IC were calm and deliberate, Boyle could tell the units were not getting ahead of the fire.

"Command to 14 Truck."

"Fourteen Truck, Go ahead."

"Have you located the civilian?"

The truck lieutenant responded, "Fourteen Truck, negative. We are continuing our search of the basement."

Boyle recognized the voice of Battalion Chief John "Jack" Seifert, the incident commander, as well as the voice of the truck's lieutenant and his friend—Andy Connolly. He didn't like what he was hearing. First due Engine 65 had to back down from the fire floor because the roof crew couldn't get the roof opened. Without the roof opened, the engine crew was down on their stomachs, "suckin' the nails," as they crawled on the floor under heat and flames, trying to get to the seat of the fire. No open roof meant heat, smoke, and gases couldn't vent the building. And that meant interior conditions couldn't improve enough to let the engine company reach the seat of the fire and knock it down.

Ladder 14, the second due truck company, had been assigned to search for a victim trapped in the basement. If interior conditions didn't improve, the fire would eat the building's insides, endangering the interior crew.

The incident commander was back on. "Command to 57 Truck. Status?"

"Chief, we're having trouble opening the roof. It's double tin-lined."

Boyle tapped the side door of the cab as he absorbed the distress in the 57 Truck lieutenant's voice. The guy was a rookie officer, only five or so years into his career. He knew this was likely the biggest fire he'd seen on the Job.

Seifert responded, "Lieutenant, this is command. If you can't get that roof opened, I'll get someone else to do it. Do you understand me?"

"Received, Chief."

Boyle put on his mask and harness, eyed Reynolds and said, "You stay close to me. Understand?"

"Yes, Cap."

"Roof to command. We have fire venting from the D side exposure, on the floor above the fire floor. I don't know how it got over there. We almost have the roof opened," the 57 truck lieutenant reported.

Boyle didn't like the fear in his roof lieutenant's voice. The man was still green on the Job. But he understood the fear. The fire had jumped to an adjoining building and to a higher floor with no visible means of transit. If the roof crew was in the right spot, they'd be atop the six-story apartment house and close to the front of the building. They'd cut a hole in the roof over the apartment where the fire had started. But the fire had managed to travel *laterally* to the adjoining building, an eight-story warehouse, Exposure 4, and had blown out a window on the eighth floor, two floors *above* the fire in the building it had originated from.

Boyle said to Beale, "It found a shaft."

As soon as he said this, Seifert's voice bellowed over the radio. "Command to Roof. It's in a shaft. Get the damn roof open. Now! And exit the roof."

"Fifty-seven Truck. Received."

Beale glanced at Boyle and shook his head.

✦

Bryan O'Rorke's 14 Truck had pulled up to the scene just under four minutes after the tones had gone off. On the way, O'Rorke had listened to Seifert's radio transmissions. He heard that a civilian was possibly trapped in the basement. His company officer, Lieutenant Andy Connolly, told him and the crew they'd be going in on a search and rescue.

O'Rorke muttered to himself, "Fuckin' idiot. Probably set himself on fire freebasing." He thought about the eternal question asked after every fire: How did it start? *I hate that question*, he thought. *Who the fuck cares how it started?* He didn't. *Trying to figure out how this thing started is not a mystery. People live with ignorance and carelessness, and fires start. Any mystery to this? No. Been happening since before the Flood. Leave that for the fire marshals. They'll figure it out after my crew and I knock it down and overhaul.* He scoffed to himself.

Chief Seifert met Connolly and his crew when they'd dismounted from the truck. The incident commander told the lieutenant to get his crew to the warehouse basement and search for the janitor.

Angry black smoke belched from the eighth-floor window of the warehouse. The chauffeur jacked the rig right in front, extending the hundred-foot Seagrave aerial ladder to the roof of the apartment building. O'Rorke and his crew masked up with protective hoods, gloves, helmets, and turnout gear. The crew grabbed their tools and followed their slender, blonde-haired lieutenant into the warehouse building. Inside, they took the interior stairs to the basement and stopped to listen.

Connolly shouted, "Anybody in here?"

A man cried out, "Over here. Help me!"

"Keep talking. We'll find you." Connolly shined his light ahead, into a corridor about two hundred feet long.

Lowell, the irons man, said, "This place is huge."

Roof man Larry Ruffalo nodded. "Gives me the creeps. And who knows what the hell's in these containers?"

The voice cried out again, sounding weaker this time. "Please help me."

Connolly said, "Bryan, you and Jay search the left side. We'll take the right." To the man he shouted, "Keep talking so we can find you."

As the man continued his pleas, O'Rorke pushed past storage lockers and vaults, shining his light down any crevice and notch he could find. The voice was coming across louder and stronger the farther they went in. About a hundred and fifty feet in, he found the janitor sitting in a folding chair near the oil burners.

The janitor had a rag pressed to a five-inch gash in his leg. "Lord have mercy. Please get me out of here."

Lowell called out that they'd located the civilian. O'Rorke pulled a baggie from his turnout coat. Inside was gauze and medical tape to dress the wound. Connolly and Ruffalo joined them moments later.

Connolly used his radio to notify command that they'd found the 10-45 and were bringing him out. He used his survivor light to survey the rest of the deep basement, which went on endlessly into a dark vault up ahead. "Bryan, get him bandaged ASAP. I want to get topside as soon as—"

A muffled *whomph came* from somewhere above them. The explosion rocked the basement. O'Rorke and Lowell pulled the janitor to the floor and covered him with their bodies as debris and flaming material cascaded down the freight elevator shaft behind them and blocked the corridor, the crew's only known means of escape from the basement. Burning debris scattered across the floor, igniting other materials and the corridor's walls.

Connolly had been thrown off his feet and against a wall by the blast, causing his handie-talkie and hand light to fly from his hands.

Smoke filled the air.

"Mask up!" O'Rorke shouted to the rest of the crew.

Connolly got to his feet, searched and found his radio, using it to mayday twice to the incident commander. He got no response.

All but O'Rorke put their masks on. He held his mask to the janitor's face, giving him a burst of fresh air.

Connolly said, "We've gotta find another way out." He grabbed Lowell's hand light, using it to scan ahead in the hallway, now illuminated by the fire rising behind them. To the janitor he said, "Is there another way outta here?"

"Not from here."

"Pick him up and follow me." Connolly led the crew down the corridor as he swept the ceiling for an opening and walls for a stairwell or shaft, anything that would lead them up and out of the basement. The corridor ended at a brick and masonry wall. He tried to raise the incident commander again, and again he got no response.

The smoke condition grew heavier. Heat from the fire behind them became more intense. Connolly could find no visible means of escape.

Lowell saw fear and despair etched on Connolly's face. He turned, lowered his head, and closed his eyes.

✦

The 323 crew sat in their rig, suited up in full bunker gear, with helmets and tools in their hands. Their truck was a block from the scene when Boyle keyed the handie-talkie. "Three-two-three Truck to command. Where do you want us?"

"Command to 323 Truck. Pull up in front of Exposure 4 and make the roof."

Boyle said to Beale, "He sounds annoyed."

Beale nodded and spun the rig wide onto Twenty-Ninth Street, where they were met with a sea of red, yellow, and white flashers, strobes, and oscillating lamps from fire apparatus already at the scene.

Flames were visible on the fifth and sixth floors of the apartment house. Glass had blown out of the windows of three apartments. Fire ate through the adjoining warehouse building, Exposure 4, with ferocity.

Beale pulled up behind Engine 65 and brought his rig to an abrupt halt.

Seifert stood behind the engine; his gaze fixed upward at the building. He turned his head, made eye contact with Boyle, and pointed to the roof of the warehouse.

Boyle opened the officer's door and said, "Let's go."

The crew made their way to the back of the rig. Boyle sized up the situation as Beale pulled the controls for the jacks and rear-mount aerial ladder from the chauffeur's compartment at the back of the thirty-seven-ton truck. The crew assembled around him.

"Kearns, get the second partner saw." To the others he said, "Everybody on the roof. And stay close." He turned to Reynolds. "You stay right behind me." He scanned the warehouse with a grimace on his face. "Stay loose. Let's go." He adjusted his radio harness and swung the regulator hose for his mask behind him like a draped sweater.

The roof man pulled the large circulating saw with its fourteen-inch graphite blade from the equipment compartment and then climbed up the ladder's turntable, now rotating, as Beale extended the hundred-foot ladder to the warehouse roof.

Kearns let the partner saw dangle from a shoulder strap at his side and held a six-foot hook in his left hand. Once the ladder fully extended to just over the roof, he climbed the rest of the way up.

Boyle was right behind him with the rest of the crew as they crawled past flames pumping out of windows to get to the roof. He glanced down. Spotted 98 Engine's crew enter the building while carrying standpipe kits of fifty-foot sections of hose and nozzle, knowing their mission was to climb the stairs that would take them to the fire floor. Their engine chauffeur had connected to the building's standpipe system, which was now pushing water from the pumper into the building's sprinkler system, enabling the interior crew to get water on the fire when they tapped the standpipe system inside the building.

Kearns reached the roof and grinned. The ladder was three feet over the parapet wall. "Beale never misses," he said. He leaned over the parapet and sounded the roof by thrusting the butt end of the hook onto the roof surface, which produced a thud and enough resistance to let him know he could stand on the roof, at least for a while. "Firm enough," he said to Boyle. He swung his legs over the parapet and onto the roof. Boyle and the crew followed.

Boyle keyed the handie-talkie. "Three-two-three Truck to Command."

Over sirens and static, Seifert said, "Go ahead, 323."

"We're on the roof. No vertical fire extension. Ready to ventilate."

"All right, Paddy. You've got about three minutes to get it open. Fire's moving fast and coming right at you."

Boyle grinned to himself. He loved roof work. Whoever had thought it up was an absolute genius. A madman who'd found a way to rationalize the irrational. The fact that someone paid him to do this work once again confirmed he was made for this profession.

When the brothers show up at a job where there's smoke and

heat but no visible flames exiting the building, there's a very good chance the fire is either smoldering, hungrily waiting for a fresh dose of air, or the flames are already working their way through the building, heating the combustible contents to an ignition point. Like a surgeon making an incision in the body for a pneumothorax to relieve a buildup of air in the lungs, the roof man is required to vent the building: make a cut to allow the combustible gases and heat to rise into the atmosphere, cooling the fire building and clearing the air. Many an engine crew inching down a blistering, darkened hallway toward the seat of the fire got needed relief when the roof was vented and the smoke and heat lifted off them, giving them a clear shot at knocking down the fire.

Boyle loved it. It was always a *Jack-be-nimble, Jack-be-quick* gamble against time on a sometimes deadly, unpredictable obstacle course: The Roof Man must pirouette by aerial ladder, bucket, fire escape, or extension ladder to the roof of a multistory building while lugging a twenty-pound circular saw, six-foot hook, and axe. Once on the roof—if it's still there— he makes a four-by-eight-foot cut through the tar, rubber, or shingle, avoiding the beams and rafters. Then, he takes a roof hook, louvers the cut roof section, and punches through the sheetrock and plaster, releasing the flames, heat, and gases into the air. If the Roof Man makes the cut and gets off the roof, he's beaten the clock and helped the engine crew get to work. But, if he's up there cutting, and the fire eats its way through the roof membrane, turning it into hot, porous sponge cake, then it's time's up. The trap door opens. It's into the inferno below, and there's an empty seat when the rig returns to quarters. And the purple-and-black bunting's going up tomorrow at the firehouse. *Whoever thought up roof work has to be the archbishop of adrenaline junkies.*

Heimboldt, the irons man, held one of the saws and an axe. "Forget the scuttles. Start cutting a hole," Boyle told him, before he walked off five steps from the parapet and pointed down. "Right here."

He faced Kearns. "Start on the other side with your saw."

Reynolds, six-foot-one and twenty-two years old, stood silently off to the side. Boyle told him, "Okay, kid, let's check for an extension."

Boyle and Reynolds walked to the back of the building to size up the roof and fire movement. At the end, Boyle surveyed the surrounding area. North were the skyscrapers of Midtown Manhattan, with the Empire State Building in the foreground. People watched from windows in nearby buildings that towered over the office-slash-warehouse. "What a city," he said to Reynolds. "It's almost peaceful up here."

Even in the biggest job—and this was not it—where people's lives were in danger, Boyle felt a sense of irony looking up at the surrounding buildings and the sky, unaffected by the emergency he was battling. He found it odd that, while he was in the middle of a life-and-death struggle to save a building and innocent lives, life was going on, business as usual, all around him. He thought it strange, almost like the rest of the world should show the same concern for the emergency that he did. He remembered a line from the novel *The Red Badge of Courage*, when the protagonist, Henry, glimpsed the clear blue sky in the heat of battle astonished at how "nature had gone tranquilly on with her golden process in the midst of such devilment." Boyle wanted to yell at those people to stop what they were doing and get down on the street and offer to help out rather than sit back like sleazy perverts watching a porn movie. That's what they were, social perverts, he thought, selfishly voyeuristic, as if they wanted to watch terrible things happen to other people.

The baritone whine of partner saws behind him drowned out the wail of sirens below. It was a comforting sound. Kearns and Heimboldt would open the roof in short order. Boyle leaned forward enough to look down, to survey the rear of the building. No smoke. No signs the fire had made its way to that side of the building. Still ... something didn't feel right.

Boyle pivoted. "Reynolds, that's your name, right"?

"Yessir," Reynolds shot back.

A muffled explosion knocked Boyle and Reynolds off their feet. He checked Kearns and Heimboldt, also down, then got to his feet, grabbed Reynolds's shoulder, and yanked him up. They hustled to the others, also back up.

Kearns said, "What the hell was that?"

Boyle shouted, "Get that roof open. Now!"

The two men resumed making the cuts as Seifert's voice blasted through Boyle's handie-talkie. "Command to 323 Roof."

"323 Roof. Go ahead."

"Explosion on the fifth floor. Get off the roof now."

"Chief, we just got it open. We're on our way." Boyle released the button on the mike and said to Reynolds, "Take your pike and push down the interior roof."

Reynolds held the handle end and thrust the hook down on the severed louvered section of roof. Boyle grabbed his arm. Keeping his voice calm, he said, "Wrong end."

Reynolds exhaled a shaky breath, reacting to the probie mistake, flipped the hook around, and thrust the butt end down, opening the roof section like a stove's hood vent.

Kearns and Heimboldt pried back the tar paper and wood with the pikes. Hot gases, heat, and top flickers of flames emerged like a geyser.

Boyle nodded. "Good. It's eaten through the interior roof. Okay, everybody off, pronto." He keyed the handie-talkie. "323 Roof to Command. Roof's open. Three-two-three exiting roof."

"Received. Report to command as soon as possible."

Despite their accomplishment, Boyle knew his crew's work was far from done. Flames now pushed defiantly through the newly cut hole. The roof team made its way to the parapet wall, where their ladder waited with their sole escape.

They made their way down the ladder, past the fifth floor now engulfed in flames. Radiant heat came off the building, so intense it singed Heimboldt's bushy eyebrows and scaled his ears. He and Kearns slipped on their hoods and masks to avoid further burns.

✦

Back on the ground, Boyle approached Seifert, who was spitting orders into his handie-talkie.

A battalion chief from Seventh Battalion radioed dispatch with a request to tone out a fourth alarm.

Seifert spoke into his radio. "Command to 14 Truck. What is your status?" He released the button and waited for a response. None came.

He repeated his request, which was met with silence. He swore like he just found out his car was totaled by his teenage son. He faced Boyle. "Some kind of chemical storage on fifth caused the explosion. Paddy, I need you and your crew to go get 14 out of the warehouse basement."

"Whatever you want, Chief." Boyle returned to his crew and told them to gear up. He smiled at Reynolds and said, "This is what you signed on with 323 for, kid. Time to earn your pay."

The crew masked up and grabbed their tools: a partner saw, two sets of irons, a halligan tool, axes, six-foot hooks, rescue ropes, and harnesses. They followed Boyle into the front of the warehouse, into the darkened entrance. Their sole light source came from their survivor lights hanging from the turnout coats or fastened on their helmets by rubber bicycle inner tubes.

Bulging two-and-a-half-inch hoses lined the stairwell to the upper floors. Boyle led his crew to the stairwell next to the bulkhead and headed down. Sounds of the raging inferno on the fifth floor diminished with each descending step. In the basement, the air was hazy and acrid. Boyle spotted a long corridor with doorways. He checked one of the rooms, about twenty-five feet square. In a building like this, it was likely most of the rooms along the corridor matched it. Toward the end of the corridor was a debris pile blocking whatever was behind it.

"That's where they'll be. Let's go," he said to Kearns.

Kearns and Heimboldt led the way. Visibility diminished with each step as the smoke condition intensified. The two men pulled away bricks, concrete, and wood, most of it still original from when the warehouse had been erected a century ago.

Boyle radioed the incident commander and announced his discovery, requesting an engine company join them and fast. To his crew he said, "Okay, guys. You see what's here. Debris from the elevator shaft probably has 14 Truck trapped on the other side, unless they found another way out. Since no one's heard from them, get busy."

What he didn't say, but they all knew, was if 14 Truck was there, they weren't only trapped, they were getting low on air and might even be closer to the fire.

The men worked at a frantic pace. Every second meant life or death for their trapped brothers.

✦

O'Rorke stood behind his crew. He held up the janitor, who had one arm around O'Rorke's shoulder. The man had a terrified expression on his face. O'Rorke thought, *No way this is it. I'm not going down like this. Not making the ten o'clock news as some poor, dead bastard lost in a basement job.* "What's on the other side of this wall?" he asked.

The janitor said, "A loft building. Used for fashion shows and stuff like that."

O'Rorke smiled and said, "That means we can breach it."

He called out to his irons man, "Hey, Jay. You're not gonna die today. Time to man up. Use your axe and take down that wall."

Lowell swung his flathead axe at the brick wall. There was no give with the first contact. Then brick, mortar, and concrete gave way with every shot the young truckie gave it.

They took turns with the axe, pounding the wall with it, prying the growing hole open with the halligan tool.

O'Rorke shared his mask with the janitor, who was coughing and heaving from the deteriorating air conditions.

The fire behind them grew with intensity. Connolly shouted, "Faster. We don't get outta here soon, we're gonna cook."

Two minutes later, a three-by-three hole had been made, big enough to crawl through while wearing their masks. Dim light shone into the corridor from the other side of the opening.

O'Rorke tapped Lowell's shoulder and said, "Go reduce profile. Remove your mask and get through that hole. I'll hand this guy through to you as soon as you're in."

Lowell removed his mask harness but kept the regulator attached. He sounded the floor on the other side, making sure it hadn't been compromised, then slid through, bringing his mask behind him.

O'Rorke held the janitor so that he could go through feet-first. He let go of him only once Lowell had him. He tossed the halligan and axe through the hole then went through it. The rest of the crew followed him through. Once each fireman and the janitor were on the other side of the basement wall, they pushed a large panel of lockers against the hole to stem the advancing, raging fire.

The five men rested where they were for a few moments, processing their very close call with the Red Devil.

Connolly glanced around at the room. He estimated its size at around ten-by-twenty; it housed lockers and benches. He shined his flashlight around. "Some kind of employee locker room. There's the stairwell." He keyed his handie-talkie. "Fourteen Truck to Command."

"Command. Go ahead."

"We breached the masonry wall on three side of the basement and escaped to the adjoining building. We're on our way to you with the 10-45 who requires medical assistance. All members accounted for."

Seifert's relief was pronounced in his voice. "Ten-four."

The crew moved up the stairs. Contemporary dance music grew louder as they ascended. O'Rorke said, "Jay, you're up on the trendy night spots. We in a disco?"

"Nah. Not here. The big joints are on Tenth Ave."

At the top of the stairs, the soot-stained, char-smelling crew and equipment emerged into the backstage of a theater.

A twenty-something male, dressed in jeans, black T-shirt, black shoes, and horn-rimmed glasses, a remote headset strapped to his head, stared at them with a stunned expression that shifted to relief. "There you are. All of you, come with me." He sauntered toward a room.

The crew followed him into a well-lit room filled with racks of clothes. Between the clothes racks were female models in various stages of dress and undress as they quickly changed their outfits. The crew members glanced at each other and smiled.

Lowell leaned toward O'Rorke, and with a lowered voice said, "You sure we didn't die and go to heaven?"

O'Rorke shook his head and chuckled, gestured for the young man to follow as they moved past the women who paid little or no attention to them.

They exited the dressing room and found themselves backstage and behind a curtain. On the other side of the curtain, a crowd applauded over background music and the voice of an announcer with a strong French accent. A stagehand parted the curtain, and several male models dressed in attire fit for hiking, fly-fishing, hunting, and other rugged activities passed through the opening. The crowd erupted in applause and shouts. The young man with the headset opened the curtain and gestured for the crew to pass through. When they didn't move, he pressed the back of his free hand against his hip and said, "What are you waiting for? Get out on the catwalk. Now, if you please."

O'Rorke glanced at his crew and shrugged. He deposited the janitor in the unused chair behind the stagehand and told him they'd be back. Single -file, they trailed the male models, the last one wearing mechanic overalls and a bandanna on his head. Filthy and tool-laden, their turnout coats still warm from the basement, they strode up the runway to boisterous applause and a torrent of flashbulbs attached to cameras.

The master of ceremonies' voice boomed his heavy accent and rolled *R* letters over the audio system. "And now, the *pièce de résistance* of the Marc Chevalier male autumn outdoor collection—Urban Gear de Rigueur!"

The audience leaped to their feet, clapping, cheering, whistling. The crew strode up the runway, waving at the crowd. Lowell said over his shoulder to O'Rorke, "This for real?"

"Just roll with it. You think the cops get this kind of reception?"

The emcee shouted over the clamor, "Truly, zis is fashion *vérité*!"

The crew played follow-the-leader, turned at the end of the runway and were heading back up the catwalk when a fire alarm split the air. Emergency lights flashed. The house lights came up. Attendees made an orderly exit from the space.

The stagehand, headset still in place, frowned as he listened to someone speaking through it. He approached the crew. "I'm afraid you'll have to exit immediately. No time to change. It seems there's a real fire next door."

The rescued janitor pulled the curtain aside and limped onto the catwalk. Connolly went to him and resumed his support. He did his best to imitate the stagehand's manner of speaking and said, "That sounds dreadful. C'mon, boys, we're leaving."

They moved behind the civilians, watching to make sure they all made their way out okay, then followed them out.

✦

Brendan and Department Chief Cianci had arrived on the scene of what was fast becoming a major fire. Twenty-five minutes had passed since the first alarm and the fire had expanded. It was starting to eat the warehouse and the upper floors of the apartment building. The fifth-floor explosion and interior collapse in the warehouse had triggered a third alarm. The call for additional resources also brought Special Operations Chief Rich Dougherty, an expert on building collapse, to the scene. Huddled on the south side of the street were battalion chiefs, aides, captains, and lieutenants. They waited for assignments behind High Rise Unit No. 11, a tactical operations truck.

Two ninety-five-foot Seagrave tower ladder trucks were positioned in front of the fire buildings, their tower ladders fully extended. Each tower was equipped with powerful mounted nozzles at the buckets. Supply hose lines attached to the nozzles were set and ready to throw 1,200 gallons of water per minute at the fire. The men in the buckets knelt inside, shielding themselves from radiant heat coming off the buildings.

Cianci and Brendan stood next to each other, surveying the fire in front of Chief Seifert.

Cianci spoke to Seifert. "Jack, any occupants left in the apartment building?"

Seifert pushed his helmet back. "All floors cleared except the fire floor."

"Any reason not to go defensive?" Brendan interjected, knowing where his good friend Cianci was going with his question.

"Three-two-three was in the warehouse basement, searching for 14 Truck trapped behind the collapse. We just got confirmation that 14, with an injured civilian, escaped into an adjoining basement."

Cianci faced the two buildings whose upper floors were fully involved in flames and gritted his teeth. He asked Seifert, "Who's left on the inside?"

"Sixty-five is on the fifth floor of the apartment building. Ninety-eight is on the fourth floor of the warehouse, trying to hit it off the standpipe."

Cianci grabbed Seifert's handie-talkie. "Command to 65. What's your status?"

The garbled response, shouted over crackling and other voices, responded. "Chief, we've got a two-and-a-half on it and can't get anywhere. We need another line up here to make some headway." Cianci's eyes darted to Brendan and back to the fire building.

Brendan knew, here, now, with the fire quickly burning through the building in front of him, Cianci's internal computer was working on overdrive at split-second speed. No man-made replica could match it. How could an artificial device replicate thirty years of experience and intuition when dealing with a capricious, mercurial opponent like fire? Brendan remembered something an old buffalo told him when he was a probie: The Beast has a mind of its own, sometimes not knowing where it wants to go itself. It makes a woman look reasonable, consistent, and predictable. Imagine that.

Brendan conducted his own analysis. His mind filed through the fires he had seen like this one: building size, construction, location of fire, location and condition of personnel and apparatus, inventory of resources, risk exposures. He listened to the fire, its intensity, watched the smoke, its color, behavior, and velocity of emission.

His thinking was interrupted by Cianci who had lobbed an essential question to his SOC chief. "Rich, what's your take on further collapse?"

Short of stature and white-haired, Dougherty said, "Depends. If it eats down to the next floor and triggers a secondary explosion, the load on that floor could cause a catastrophic collapse. As it looks now, it's headed that way. I'd say the collapse window is about thirty minutes away."

Cianci turned to Seifert. "Pull 'em out, Jack, and go defensive." He walked to the back of the command post, disappointment and disdain etched on his face. Brendan knew Cianci's expression was one of self-imposed judgment about professional failure very few chiefs would ever hold themselves to.

Seifert keyed his radio mike, ordering 65 and 98 out of the

building immediately. Told them to drop their lines where they were. He directed the tower ladders to open up their nozzles.

✦

Interior crews responded to Seifert's orders as quickly as they could. Inside the apartment building, 65's lieutenant told his crew to pull back. They did so seconds before one of the tower ladder's streams hit the fire floor with its master stream. The crew quickly descended the stairs, glancing back to watch the master stream hit the fire like a wet laser death ray. Clouds of white and gray steam rose from the burning fuels under the water assault. As fast as the crew retreated down the stairs, the fire pursued them, threatening to catch up.

Outside, the tower operators gave it all they had, manipulating their controls to spread the wet stuff over the hot mess that was once an attractive apartment building and a stocked warehouse. Flames lashed out in all directions, reaching for heat and oxygen away from clouds of white steam and gray smoke, the products of the relentless drowning the fire received from the pair of master streams. Almost seven minutes later, the conflagration had subsided, the innards of the high-rise structures transformed into charred embers, revealing the skeletal sections of the building where the fire had burned through the exteriors. The cost was borne on the structures themselves that received as much water damage as fire damage from the deluge.

✦

When Boyle heard on his radio that 14 Truck was safely out of the basement, he ordered his crew to stop digging and evacuate the basement even before the incident command ordered it. The exhausted crew of 323 Truck took a much-needed reprieve at the rig. The guys downed waters, smoked cigarettes, and watched the aerial platforms demolish the fire with their master streams one hundred feet above them.

Behind a police cordon, a throng of pedestrians had assembled at the east end of Sixth Avenue, to watch the crews in action. Fire alarms in the loft building had prompted attendees of the Marc Chevalier fashion show to exit and take their places on the sidewalk on the other side of the police tape, adding to the crowd of onlookers already there.

Boyle surveyed the civilians behind the tape. The crowd was well dressed in their finest evening wear and cocktail outfits. *A pretty swanky bunch*, he mused. He headed for the truck, just as he heard a woman's voice call his name. He recognized the voice and knew it was the kind of voice he would have expected to come from that direction.

Lauren Moore, dressed in a sleek black dress, wearing pearls and diamond stud earrings, stood just beyond the tape with a group of other women dressed just as exquisitely and a couple of guys in tuxedos. Her amber hair was pulled back to reveal her well-formed features and radiant blue eyes.

"Pat," she called out, just loud enough so he could hear her but not loud enough to call attention to her entourage. Boyle smiled the eager, boyish smile that made him look like a teenager. The guys on the crew took notice.

Kearns nudged Reynolds. "Watch and learn, probie. Tonight's lesson is about to continue."

The probie, his expression now slightly less than the deer-caught-in-headlights he had worn for most of the job, nodded.

Boyle moved with an easy stride only slightly affected by his injury from several months back. He and Lauren hadn't seen each other since she'd visited him at the hospital. She read his limp, he read her face—saw her concern about his altered gait.

He stopped a foot from the tape, facing her. "How's it going?"

"I'm good. How about you?"

"Better than the last time you saw me." He winked and quickly covered the gesture by rubbing his eye.

"When did you return to the Job?"

"Yesterday." He gestured toward the smoldering buildings. "They held off the Big One until I got back."

Lauren laughed. "Too true. You might say it was your welcome-back present.

Although she was flanked by so many of the *beautiful people*, she kept her gaze fixed on him. She leaned forward and whispered, "Pat, you look ... great."

Biting back the pleased grin he wanted to respond with, he cast his gaze toward her entourage, frowning at the hoi polloi and social circuit he didn't care for, though he'd never criticized them or her lifestyle to her.

She read his expression and smiled.

"You know," he said, "I never thanked you for stopping by to see me when I was laid up—that first night."

"You don't need to. It was the only thing I *could* do."

"It eased the pain."

He could read her as well. Her hazel eyes communicated genuine warmth and affection for him, along with fear that her feelings for him could lead her down a path she wasn't prepared to step onto. He saw in her eyes memories he dealt with as well—how it felt to hold each other—and more. He watched as she swallowed hard and her breaths came quicker. It was time to stop this. "I gotta get back. It was good to see you." He turned and started to walk away.

A little too fast, too eager, and too loud, she said, "Are you still doing yoga?"

Boyle pivoted and drank her in a few seconds longer. "Not yet. Maybe in a few weeks. You?"

Her laugh was forced. "I'm sort of a yoga junkie."

After a brief pause, he said, "Lotta worse things you could be addicted to. Maybe I'll see you around."

He'd taken one step toward his crew when he heard her say, "I hope so."

This time he didn't turn back.

CHAPTER 20

The firehouse on Williamsbridge Road in the Morris Park section of the Bronx was built in 1919, right after the First World War. The house was designed for horse-drawn fire carriages with broad, open doors and room for reshoeing horses. Occasionally, a probie would uncover an old horseshoe when he was cleaning the storage closet or behind the lockers. On the interior walls of the station hung old black-and-white photographs of the many pieces of apparatus that were housed there since the station opened. Next to the house watch just beyond the fire pole hung a plaque with the names of the six firefighters who had been lost in the line of duty in the past eighty-one years. Turnout gear and bunker pants hung in lockers along the rear wall behind the apparatus floor that 94 Truck and 181 Engine called home.

The living accommodations upstairs left much to be desired. Guys joked that the place had not been updated since 1919 and, except for the phone system, that wasn't too far from the truth. Most guys didn't care, though. They were so busy running to jobs that for anybody on duty, resting was not a major activity at this house. If a guy got an hour a night, he was living large.

On his way home from high school, Harry Sturgis approached the firehouse on Williamsbridge Road. Since the day of the fire on his street three weeks ago, when firefighter Murphy had enlisted his help, he'd wanted to stop in and thank him. He'd thought about doing it every single day. Some might have considered his involvement minor, but it was a big deal to him. For the first time in his life, he felt he'd made a contribution that mattered, was important. Like he'd made a difference. Murphy had relied on him, had believed in him. Wanted to believe that maybe, just maybe, the bullies and jocks at school would leave him alone if they saw him at the firehouse, mixing it up with firefighters.

The newspapers had included reports of varying lengths about the fire and the fact that the young boy, Jayden, had died. The descriptions didn't jibe with his memory of the event. He'd seen the firemen's expressions as they'd worked feverishly to save him—and fail. He'd kept this, and his part in the firefighting, to himself when his mother came home later that night. A neighbor told her about Harry's role. When asked if this was true, he'd nodded. Then he'd blushed when she told him how proud she was of him.

The firehouse hummed—from air ventilation units, guys talking to each other, and several men moving around and taking care of tasks. His own observations and research let him understand a shift change was taking place.

A firefighter he recognized from the fire scene entered the bay. Harry hurried to him and said, "Excuse me. I'm Harry Sturgis."

The man shifted the gear bag slung over his shoulder. "Hal Grimes."

"Is there a fireman named Murphy here?"

"Yeah. He should be here."

"Think I could talk to him?"

"Don't see why not." He glanced around. "Stay here. I'll check the kitchen and see what's what."

Harry kept his gaze fixed on Grimes, watched the firefighter place his gear bag down in front of a gray, metal locker, and then disappear down a hallway, returning several seconds later, waving for Harry to join him.

He followed Grimes, who held up a hand to stop him inside the doorway. Harry shoved his hands into his back pockets and leaned forward enough to peer in. Murphy was at the table with two others, each of them dressed in navy-blue FDNY T-shirts with their company name on them, matching work trousers, and black work boots. Coffee mugs were in front of each man. A pan filled with corned beef hash, potatoes, and green beans rested on the stovetop.

"Murph, someone here to see you." Grimes gestured toward Harry.

Murphy spotted Harry and said in a low voice, "It's the kid."

Kazmierski elbowed Leary who sat to his left. "Murph, you're in trouble now."

Murphy made a face and got up. Snickers from the men followed him. He approached Harry with his hand extended. "Hey, kid. How ya doin'?"

Harry stared at the outstretched hand as though it was the first time anyone had ever wanted to shake his. His return shake was awkward. His voice trembled as he said, "I'm okay. I've been wanted to thank you for letting me help out the other day."

"No problem. I was in a bind when that woman came over to me." He grinned and nudged Harry. "Thanks for covering for me with the lieutenant."

"Sure."

"What's your name, kid?"

"Harry Sturgis."

"How 'bout a tour of the house?"

Harry's eyes widened. "Yeah."

"First, let me introduce you." He gestured for Harry to follow him into the kitchen. He pointed to Grimes, who'd taken a seat at the table.

In front of Grimes was a plate filled with food. He gripped a steaming mug of coffee that displayed a picture of a bikini-clad model.

Murphy said, "You already met Grimes." He pointed. "That's Jimmy Leary."

Leary waved.

"And that's Kaz."

Kazmierski said, "I recognize you. You're the kid Murphy put on the hydrant when he decided to become a public-affairs officer."

The men at the table chuckled. Harry's face burned red.

"Don't mind him, kid. His father was the Missing Link," Murphy said. Seeing Harry's expression, he added, "Teasing each other is part of the job."

"Oh." Harry smiled, and his shoulders relaxed.

"I'm gonna give Harry a tour." He started forward, stopped abruptly. "We get a call, you'll have to leave. No civilians allowed in the house when we're out on a call."

Harry nodded, his expression earnest. "I understand."

Murphy did a show-and-tell about the apparatus and the engine, its compartment, and the equipment it carried. Let him handle the axe and halligan. Showed him the hose, deck gun, Hurst tool, and compressor. Explained the role of the truck company and its equipment. He put the mask breathing apparatus on Harry and demonstrated how it worked. Took him to the living quarters and lounge. Answered every question Harry had about what he'd seen at the fire.

"C'mon, Harry. I want to show you the Wall of Honor."

Before Harry could follow Murphy to the wall, the tones went off, followed by an announcement: "Fire Dispatch. Engine 181, Truck 94. Twelve forty-five Metropolitan Avenue. Apartment fire. Four-story walk-up. Get out."

Men walked smartly from the kitchen and bathroom, down the fire pole, making their way to gear lockers, kicked off boots and shoes, and donned turnout gear and helmets.

Murphy rested a hand on Harry's shoulder. "Sorry, kid. I gotta go, and so do you. But come by anytime." He grabbed his boots, coat, and helmet and stepped up and into the engine as it rolled out the wide doorway.

Harry ran out to the street to watch them drive down the street, lights on, siren wailing. The garage door closed behind him. He stayed fixed in place until the engine disappeared from view. Murphy had been so nice to him. Didn't treat him like a loser even once. This fire department, and firefighters especially, were the coolest thing he'd ever come across. It was big. Bigger than himself.

He couldn't explain it. He just knew he had to be a part of it. He was not "The Nothing" to these guys.

✦

Harry opened the door to his apartment and found his mother standing in the middle of the living room, arms crossed at her chest.

"You're late. Where were you?"

"At the firehouse."

Anita Sturgis relaxed her face and posture. "Oh. What were you doing there?"

Harry fiddled with a button on his shirt and shrugged. "I wanted to talk to the fireman from the other day. The one who let me help."

She walked to the kitchen. "Are you thinking of becoming a fireman?"

Harry followed her, remaining silent while she pulled a loaf of bread from the pantry.

She glanced at him. "Well?"

"I don't know. What do you think?"

"It's up to you. You turn eighteen in a couple of months. You graduate next month. You need to find something to do." She gestured toward the table. "Sit down, Harry."

He slid onto the wooden chair at the breakfast nook.

His mother sat next to him. "It's up to you to make something of yourself. That's something I can't do for you. It's been hard since your father left. You put up walls to hide the pain. You lose yourself in video games and TV. I'm glad it wasn't drugs or anything like that, but …"

He kept his eyes focused on the countertop.

"Harry?"

"Yeah. I know."

Anita rested a hand on his arm. "Son, do you have any idea about what you want to do?"

"I hate school. The kids suck. I can't wait to get out of there, away from them."

"What about your friends there?"

"I don't have any. I don't know how to make friends."

"I'm sure that's not true." When he didn't answer, she said, "What about girls?"

"They're just as bad." He reached for the twist tie on the bread bag and twisted it opened and closed.

Anita removed her hand from his arm and shifted her head to stare out the window. "Did you find the fireman you were looking for?"

He let go of the tie and sat up straighter. "Yeah. He gave me a tour. He let me handle some of the equipment. Even let me breathe through the mask."

She faced him and smiled. "Did he?"

Harry nodded and returned her smile. "He showed me the engine, the gear. Everything."

"That was nice. I'll bake some cookies and bring them to the firehouse to thank them."

He beamed at his mother. "The fireman's name is Murphy. He's totally cool. They all are."

His mother opened the refrigerator and stared inside. "What do you feel like eating?"

"Anything."

It was Harry's turn to stare out the window. To let his mind do a playback of his visit to the firehouse. Then he reminded himself that they'd headed out to a fire. He hoped they'd all be okay. He chided himself and said in his mind that of course they would be. They were pros. He'd seen them in action.

CHAPTER 21

FDNY Headquarters, Downtown Brooklyn

Chief of Department Paul Cianci entered the marble lobby of FDNY headquarters, located in the Metrotech Plaza in Brooklyn. As the highest-ranking uniformed officer in the eleven-thousand-member organization, he made it a point every day to pause in front of the large bronze plaque on the wall. The plaque displayed the names of every firefighter ever killed in the line of duty for the Fire Department of the City of New York. He did this to remind himself that his chosen profession carried a special burden few other occupations did. This pause, at this spot, served as an incentive to ask himself if he'd done everything possible to protect civilians and his troops when they battled the Beast, as well as how he might better protect them. This moment was always a somber one. And sobering. Especially when his gaze shifted to the blank space on the right, as it inevitably did, where the engravers had left room for additional names. Casualties, like Denny Andrews, whose names would be there for centuries to come.

He made his way to his office on the seventh floor of the

eight-story building. His other habit was to approach the window and take in the Manhattan skyline and New York Harbor before taking a seat at his desk. Having done so, he slapped the investigation report for the Avenue C fire against the sill and then dropped it atop a stack of papers and folders on his desk.

He was rereading segments of it and said, "Come in," when someone rapped on the door jamb. He lifted his gaze from the report and spotted Alice, his sixty-two-year-old secretary of three years, standing in the doorway. It was unlike her to disturb him because it was a rarity for him to be there instead of visiting firehouses or meeting with deputy chief at their offices. Seeing the worried expression on her face, he asked, "What is it?"

"Ellen came to me. In tears. The commissioner screamed at her for five minutes about a mix-up with his schedule. Said she's never been spoken to like that and wants to quit."

He resisted shaking his head. "I'll take care of it. Where is he?"

"His office."

As he passed her on his way out, she asked, "Should I tell Chief Knox to wait for you?"

"Yes. This shouldn't take more than five minutes."

Cianci took the stairs to the eighth floor, where the commissioner's office was located, and where his should have been. When he was appointed chief, he had asked that his office be relocated to the seventh floor with the rest of the senior uniformed officers. He never liked the way other chiefs of department had their offices on the eighth floor, close to the commissioner. He thought it created too cozy of a relationship between the brass and the civilian commissioners, and he always thought of himself as a blue-collar chief first—a fireman, not a civilian employee. Times like these made him glad he'd made that decision. Times like these were bullshit. Especially when there were more important matters to contend with.

He entered the commissioner's outer offices. Ellen, with red eyes and nose, sat with a tissue in hand at her desk. Standing next to her was Marie, the younger secretary, holding a cup of water. Cianci stopped in front of her desk. "What happened, El?"

Her chin quivered. She inhaled to compose herself and said, "The mayor's office called to find out if Bill was going to attend the ribbon-cutting at the renovated Bedford-Stuyvesant firehouse. I said it wasn't on his schedule, but I'd see if we could make it work. So, I talked to Bill about it, told him there was a commitment we'd have to move so he could make it. And he exploded. Called me an idiot. Kept cursing at me." She sniffed as tears welled. "Kept going on and on. Said a trained monkey could do a better job."

"Show me his schedule."

Ellen provided it, pointing to the appropriate time slot.

Cianci frowned. Anger flashed in his blue eyes. "Marie, take Ellen to the cafeteria for a break. I'll handle this."

Cianci rapped twice on the closed door and opened it without waiting for an invitation. He strode into the palatial office, where Commissioner William "Bill" Hollenbach sat behind his desk. His assistant, Edmund Gergels, sat in a chair across the desk from him.

"What is it, Paul?" Hollenbach asked.

Cianci studied the pudgy face framed by thinning blond hair. He kept his eyes fixed on the commissioner and said, "Ed, give us a minute."

Gergels glanced at Hollenbach, who gave one nod of his head. The aide got up and exited the office, closing the door behind him.

Cianci marched forward and rested his hands on the desk. In a voice deep and steady, he said, "I want to say this only once, and I want to make it clear. If you ever speak to anyone in this office or department the way you spoke to Ellen, we'll take this *discussion* somewhere and work it out, just the two of us. You understand what I'm saying?"

Hollenbach raised his eyebrows and sat back. "I can't work with—"

"Cut the bullshit. These women have served this department

since you pulled hose on 398 in Staten Island. They deserve better than listening to you acting like a fucking five-year-old who can't find his toy dump truck."

What both men knew—and Cianci knew Hollenbach not only knew, but sometimes resented it—was that despite the title of commissioner, it was Cianci who ran the show at headquarters, a position earned by the box filled with medals earned and kept in a footlocker under his desk. It was he who was treated with respect that bordered on reverence.

Cianci straightened up. "You and I know the only reason you're in that chair is because Pisani gave it to you as a reward because you can handle the press better than anybody in the department. Neither I nor anyone else here has the time to deal with your chicken-shit antics. So, cut it out. Am I clear?"

"Loud and clear."

"So, cancel your damn golf game and get your ass to Bed-Sty for the opening. You might even be able to convince some of the guys that you actually care about them."

Fuming, he stormed from the office.

Blunt, effective, and with no hidden agenda—that was Cianci's approach to almost everything. So often, when he was out of uniform, people mistook the blue-eyed Italian from Syosset, Long Island, for a prizefighter rather than a firefighter. The square jaw and nose obviously broken once upon a time, along with the no-nonsense expression he generally wore, led people to this perception.

What they didn't know, until they got to know him—if he allowed it—was that the Job was in his blood. He came from three generations of volunteer firefighters. As soon as he was discharged from the Eighty-Second Airborne, after two tours of duty in Vietnam, he joined the department, rising from lieutenant to battalion chief faster than anyone on the Job.

He possessed the ability to communicate with anyone, no matter their position or rank. He could convey what was important, distill even the most complicated matter to its essential aspect, whether talking to a probie when he was a truck lieutenant in Greenpoint or addressing the city council as department chief. This made him an easy pick for advancement but wasn't the primary door-opener for him. His years as a junior firefighter and company officer earned him the reputation as relentless, dedicated, concerned with doing the best job he could, whatever the job, and without concern for his own safety.

He yanked open the door to the stairwell and headed for the seventh floor. His words echoed in the enclosed space as he repeated, "A fucking golf game."

✦

Cianci nodded at Lucius Knox, who was seated in the waiting area. He spotted a copy of the Safety and Inspection Services Command Investigative Report on the Avenue C fire in the man's hand, told him to come in, and headed for his office. Knox followed him, taking a seat across from the chief's desk.

There were two things about his job Cianci didn't enjoy: dealing with pricks like Hollenbach and managing internal fire department politics. In this case, it was a matter of internal *and* external politics at play. Knox was an ambitious, reasonably capable safety battalion chief. He was also well connected in the city, and in Albany, through family connections, wealth, and family history in the state.

Cianci couldn't figure out why someone with Knox's pedigree and upbringing chose fire service with proletarians, like him and the rest of the guys on the Job. Knox could have any job he wanted, but for some reason, he chose to join the FDNY Safety Battalion. Still, with his background, he moved through the ranks at a rapid pace to chief officer.

Knox's motivations were unclear to Cianci, but not the man's ambitions. Knox wanted to be department chief someday, and he wouldn't let anything or anyone get in his way, including Cianci.

However, Cianci knew what Knox wanted—to make a name for himself by using a report on fires, where one or more firefighters were killed, to highlight perceived deficiencies, real or not, in department management or operations. Knox's tendency was to spin his reports so he could cast mildly constructive criticism toward top brass, point out "management shortcomings," while drawing attention to his contributions to improve department performance.

The Avenue C report was no different from any of the three others Knox had prepared regarding fires that involved line-of-duty deaths: self-serving and critical. Cianci had read the report at six this morning, before heading to work, and was not surprised by its conclusions. Knox and his committee had cited Battalion Chief Brendan and Captain Boyle with failure to follow proper fire department protocol regarding firefighter safety. The report raised "serious questions" regarding what the report called a "cowboy culture" in which veteran firefighters "are given wide latitude to engage in unorthodox practices on the fireground with no regard for incident command protocols and guidelines."

It was nothing more than a typical Monday-morning-quarterback attack on Brendan's and Boyle's actions at the fire scene, and done so to advance his own career as a self-appointed watchdog for firefighter safety within the department. Knox had probably already leaked his report to the press, making today's meeting a mere formality. A self-imposed delay holding him back from standing at a bank of microphones while pontificating to the press about firefighter safety and a need for greater accountability and emergency scene standards. He'd paste a somber expression on his face and add that his objective was to prevent firefighter fatalities.

Cianci couldn't be fooled, though. He rested back in his chair and linked his fingers behind his head. "I read your report, Lu. Can't really argue with anything in it."

"Thanks, Chief." He ran a finger around the brim of his white hat resting in his lap.

"It's well written and presents a conclusion we all agree on. That safety is of utmost importance and our greatest concern."

Knox crossed his legs and undid the last button on his pressed, navy-blue uniform jacket.

Cianci watched Knox strain to hold back a self-satisfied smile. He was sure the sheen on Knox's uniform brass was a result of the man rubbing them against his ass for an hour before getting dressed. He shifted his swivel chair to gaze out the window at the skyline and said, "However, it also raises a question, for me at least. One it doesn't answer."

"And what question might that be?"

"What is our primary objective at a fire scene?"

"Life safety. Obviously."

"Whose? The firefighter?"

"Of course. It's ..." Knox cleared his throat. "What I mean, of course, is that safety is paramount for both firefighters and civilians."

Cianci spun his chair back. "That's the problem with this report—and you. You've put firefighter safety equal with the public's. Your report indicts Brendan and Boyle because they took action that put Boyle and Andrews at risk in order to save lives. Andrews died. And to you, that's a failure. Isn't it?"

"Because it is."

"I don't see it that way. Not at all. It's part of the Job. I'm not alone on that." As angry red began to color Knox's cheeks, Cianci continued. "I'll give you a hypothetical. Say we train our people to put their safety first. They show up at fires, see it might be too risky for them, and despite hearing pleas for help, they stand down. What happens to our reputation in the eyes of the public then?"

Knox shifted his gaze out the window and remained silent.

Cianci jabbed a finger against the desktop. "We'll get the reputation—and deserve it—that public safety is less important than our own. Think they'll continue to look up to us, to respect and regard us as they do now? Not a chance. They'll stop calling us because we've broken trust with them."

Knox faced him, kept his lips pressed into a tight line for several seconds, and then said, "This report makes clear that Brendan and Boyle should never have gone back in."

"Why not?"

"You know why. Conditions were worse, and they should have known the building was compromised."

Cianci shook his head and made a sound of disgust. "You don't get it, Lu. You pull up to a job, a walk-up. Flames are pushing out a second-floor window. A woman comes up to you, screaming that her baby is stuck on the third floor. Do you go for the stairs and try to save the kid?"

"If you or a member of your crew can do so without getting harmed or killed, yes."

"That's not the way I learned the job." He shook his head. "Not at all how I was taught. We're all they have out there. You're forgetting that." He waved a hand.

Wearing a condescending smile, Knox said, "I'm certain, Chief, that you don't want me to quote that you don't value firefighter safety as a priority. How would that look?"

Cianci pursed his lips. "Say whatever the fuck you think is important." Cianci lifted the phone receiver, pushed a button, and said, "Alice, he here? Okay. Send him in." He cradled the receiver and said, "In light of your report and conclusions, I've asked Chief Brendan to join us. I'm sure you have no objections."

Knox fixed narrowed eyes on Cianci.

The office door opened. Steve Brendan entered. Cianci went around his desk and greeted Brendan with a firm handshake. He gestured toward the empty chair next to Knox.

Knox got to his feet and extended his hand. Greetings over, everyone took a seat.

Cianci glanced at Knox then made eye contact with Brendan. "Steve, having you here isn't standard, but I wanted you here to discuss the findings of the SISC report. Chief Knox concludes that you exercised poor judgment by letting Boyle and Denny reenter the building. That the continued search for victims led to Denny's death. And that such recklessness may warrant disciplinary action." Cianci hesitated, moved his gaze from Brendan to Knox, then continued.

"He and I disagree about goals and objectives at a fire scene. He thinks our primary objective is firefighter safety. What are your thoughts?"

Brendan kept his focus on Cianci. "Safety for the brothers is always a primary concern, but not at the expense of the Job."

"Which is?"

"To protect and save the public, the way we're trained to."

Cianci faced Knox. "Sounds like Deputy Chief Brendan agrees with my assessment. Lu, I'm going to give your report substantial consideration to determine how best we can implement your recommendations into our current… what were your words?" He opened the report to a specific page and placed his finger on a line of text. "Management culture. I appreciate all the work you and your committee put into the report. We'll study it carefully before implementing any changes."

Knox smoothed the knife-edge crease on one pant leg, rose to his feet, and placed his chief's hat under his arm. "Yes, well. Unless there's something further you wish to discuss, I should get back to work."

Cianci nodded. "Good idea."

Knox kept his eyes averted and made a hasty exit from the room.

"That guy," Cianci said, "is a dangerous threat to the brothers."

"Word is that he wants your job."

"Yeah, I know. And I don't give a fuck what he wants. He has no idea how to do this job. Doesn't know what it takes, 'cause he doesn't have what it takes."

CHAPTER 22

Coletti arrived at the firehouse and did the usual things before starting his shift. He went to the kitchen and got a cup of coffee. He greeted Les Ronkowski, who sat the table eating a hot dog and egg sandwich.

Ronkowski kept his eyes on his sandwich. "You didn't see it, did you?"

"See what?"

"The paper taped to the house watch door."

Coletti motioned with his hand for more information.

"The results of the lieutenant's exam."

Coletti didn't respond. Instead, he hurried to the house watch, found the paper, and read through the list of applicants who'd taken the test. He found his name. He'd passed but his name was midway on the list.

He went back over the list of names, placed in order of seniority. The name at the top would make lieutenant first, as soon as a slot became available. He continued to go through the list—something wasn't right. He couldn't understand how he placed so low on the test. He was sure he had aced the exam.

Lieutenant Rowan knelt on the apparatus floor, inspecting a tire on the engine. Coletti signaled to him. "Lieutenant, mind coming over here a sec?"

Rowan examined the list. "Glad you passed but where you are in the middle of the list, you're not making lieutenant anytime soon. The test is only given once every four years. Sorry about that, Phil."

"Thanks, but I think something's not right. How can I get a copy of my test?"

"You can call Citywide Administration—DCAS. They have the exams."

Coletti called DCAS and was connected to a secretary who told him he could stop by their office at the Municipal Building next to City Hall in Manhattan and he could obtain his test results and the correct answer for each question.

After his shift ended the next morning, Coletti headed directly to the DCAS office and got a copy of his test. He took it to his apartment and went through each question. He had gotten most of the questions right except for the high-detail curve-breaker questions that included details he had missed. When he reviewed where he was wrong and compared it to the books he studied with, he realized it was the books. In just a few instances, the information was wrong, indicating things like where to place knots on search ropes. It was the books his father had given him. Sal had given him books with some wrong information in them, and he had used them to study for the test. He realized that's what had happened, and it enraged him. *So much for him coming around to the idea of me making lieutenant. He just can't stand the idea of calling me "sir."*

✦

Later that day, Coletti rang the doorbell of his parents' home in the neighborhood of Bensonhurst, in the southern part of Brooklyn.

His mother, Angela, opened the door. She waved him in with the wooden spoon in her hand. "Follow me to the kitchen. I have to stir the gravy. It's Thursday."

"I know. Macaroni and meat sauce night. For three generations." He trailed her into the kitchen. "Is he home?"

"In the den. He's tired. Worked a mutual last night."

Coletti walked past the faded photographs of him and his brother, hung in nearly every room of his childhood home, right next to portraits of the Sacred Hearts of Jesus and Mary, and over the statues of Saint Anthony of Padua. He entered the small, dimly lit den, where midday sunlight had little impact. His father was prone on the couch, lit cigarette in hand, as he listened to news on the radio.

Sal Coletti smiled and said, "Philly-boy. What's doin'?"

Coletti kept his expression blank. "You tell me."

"Worked a mutual last night. This old bull still has some juice left in him." He sat up and smashed the cigarette out in the ashtray on the end table to his right.

"Still gotta prove you got it in you, don't you, Pop?"

"What's with the tone?" He studied his son's face. "What's eatin' you?"

"You know what. Cut the shit."

Sal lowered his head, linked his fingers together between his knees, and stared at them.

Coletti stood two feet from his dad. "When I was a kid, you didn't want me to play the piano. Said it was sissy. When I joined the fire department, you told me I couldn't hack it." He pulled the folded copy of his exam results from his back pocket and placed it on the coffee table directly in front of his father. "Now you can't stand the fuckin' idea that you'll have to call me lieutenant one day."

Sal exhaled hard and picked up the exam results. He unfolded the copy, scratched the back of his head. "C'mon, Philly. We both know the Job isn't for you. Making lieutenant doesn't mean anything. You know that."

Through lips curled into a snarl, Coletti said, "Maybe it doesn't mean a fucking rat's ass to you. But it means something to me. I don't know if you can get that through your thick skull, but you need to try." He pushed his father's shoulder, surprised that even at sixty-one, the old man's muscle tone was still there, that he was leaner and more fit than a lot of guys on the Job who were half his age.

Sal batted Coletti's hand away. "Easy, boy. And watch how you talk to me."

"I know who I'm talking to. An old man who doesn't know when to hang it up. A father who can't stand the idea that his kid got further up the ranks than he did."

Angela came to the door and said, "Phil, what's the matter?"

Coletti stayed focused on his father. "Go ahead. Tell your wife what you did."

Sal shrugged and remained silent.

"Yeah," Coletti said. "Didn't think you would." He faced his mother. "Pop here didn't want me to make lieutenant, so he gave me the wrong books to study from. They had just enough bad information so I'd score so far down on the list, it would take me four years or longer to get the job."

Angela glared at her husband. "Sal?"

Sal cocked his head. "Ang, the Job's not right for him."

"How could you do that to your son?"

Coletti threw his hands up. "You bastard. Forget seeing me around here anymore." He stormed from the room.

His mother hurried to follow him. "Phil. Please. Don't go. Don't listen to him."

Sal called out behind them, "Let him go. He's full of shit, anyway."

Angela said, "Son, wait up." She glared at Sal. "I've been your wife for thirty-one years. And sometimes you can be so impossible. How could you do something that terrible to our son?"

"You don't get it," he said. He pointed toward the now-empty hallway. "He doesn't get it. Hell, nobody gets it." Sal shook his head. She stood over him, staring at him.

"Can you explain why you did that?"

Sal grimaced, flicked cigarette ash into the ashtray on the coffee table. "There's only so much luck you can have on this job. When it runs out, it's gone. Why should he do this, this job? This job isn't for him."

Coletti had heard enough. He slammed the front door behind him.

✦

Coletti walked south on Eighteenth Avenue, past the Bensonhurst delicatessens and food shops prevalent in the predominantly Italian neighborhood. He boarded a city bus at Eighty-Sixth Street, continuing to head south, toward the bay. His mind raced with anger, resentment, and a deep sense of disillusionment about his father. He couldn't fathom how his own father could be so selfish and self-centered. His thoughts turned to Ellie, of her on the street corner that night after his gig, reminded him how much he liked her and how much she reminded him of a delicate bird searching for a safe place to land. If he could spend more time with her, maybe he could connect more deeply with her, and she with him. These thoughts calmed him some, but not enough. Anger flared again, and he wanted to go back to his parents' house and beat the crap out of the sonofabitch. But that would be pointless and would upset his mother.

He got off the bus at Cropsey Avenue and Fourteenth Street and walked the few remaining blocks to the bay. He stood at the shore and stared out at the shimmering blue expanse, letting the midday sun warm his face. He swiped at the sweat already beading on his face and forehead from humidity, worn like a second skin during a New York City July. He watched the gentle waves and sunlight sparkle on the water. His thoughts turned to memories of the seaside town in Italy from which his family came. How naturally beautiful and tranquil it was. He had been there a couple of times with his family and was struck by the established order and peace of the place, so different from the bedlam of living in Brooklyn. *I really need to get back there. That'll clear my head.* He headed toward the firehouse. For now, the only thing that would put him right was to be with his brothers. They'd center him and help him accept the hand he'd been dealt by his callous old man.

✦

Ellie and George had had their hands full at the soup kitchen for most of the day. It was as though every poor soul had decided to come in for a meal before heading to the beach for a respite from the heat and humidity. It was at the end of their day, while cleaning the fryer and putting away food, that the phone rang. Ellie answered, surprised and happy to hear Phil Coletti's voice.

"Hey, Ells. What are you doing right now?"

"Cleaning the kitchen. It was a madhouse here today. You sound—I don't know—happy or excited or something."

"I'll be there in fifteen minutes."

He ended the call before she could say another word. Twenty minutes later, Coletti stood in the doorway of the soup kitchen.

Ellie smiled. She was struck by how handsome he looked in jeans and a cream-colored, button-down dress shirt. The shirt was a nice contrast with his olive complexion and dark hair.

He motioned for her to join him, waited for her, and then led her to the alleyway on the side of the building. "I've got to go away for a little while, so I wanted to see you to say good-bye before I go."

"Oh." She studied his face. "Your eyes are sad. I've never seen that in you before. And what do you mean, you're going away? Why?"

He averted his gaze and hesitated.

"Now I know something's wrong. You always face me when you talk. You hardly even blink when you do. It's one of the things I like most about you. But now you're—I don't know—distant. Did I do something?"

He shook his head. "You didn't do anything, El. It's a long, screwed-up story. Maybe I'll tell you about it later. For now, I'm going to my family's town in Italy. I'll be gone a few weeks." He faced her. "And I wanted you to know."

She nodded, lowered her head. "I shouldn't feel disappointed, but I do. It's not like we're … I mean, I thought … Never mind." She forced a smile. "I hope you enjoy the trip. But I …"

She glanced away, then faced him. "It's just that I don't understand. It's so sudden. What happened? I mean, the other night … it was great. And now you're leaving town? For a couple of weeks?"

"Yeah. My father's being a pain in my ass about something. I think I should get away. Clear my head. You know? The town is a really calm, peaceful place, where people just accept you as you are, no questions, no preconceived notions." He studied her face. "I can see you're upset, but I need you to understand this."

"Oh, I understand. You got into a rough spot and decided to leave. That's your way to deal with him? With the situation?"

"You really don't get it. You don't know what you're talking about. Besides, it's not your damn business."

She glared at him past the tears welling in her eyes. "It's been my business since that day on the bridge. Maybe you don't see it that way, but I do."

"Ellie, I never know what the hell you're thinking. But if this is how you treat people you like, I'd hate to see what it's like for people you don't." He started to walk away.

"You're running."

Coletti halted his steps, wheeled around, and walked back. "What did you say?"

"You heard me. Your father knows which buttons to push, and you let him." She paused and said, "Is this about you becoming a lieutenant?"

He kicked a pebble, sending it down the alleyway. "Yeah."

"So you're going to take off. You're going to let him know he can get to you so bad that you run."

"It's not that simple. I'm not giving up. I just need to recharge. Besides, it's summer. I want to get out of town for a while. My time's saved up, and I want to use it. Now's as good a time as any."

Tears spilled onto her cheeks, and she wiped them away. "Then I hope you have a great time."

Coletti gazed into her eyes. "Can I say something?"

"Go ahead."

"I'm sorry. I shouldn't have said that."

She gestured toward the building. "We'll all be here. Maybe when you get back, you can come by and—"

He cupped his hand behind her head and pulled her to him, kissing her forcefully. After a few seconds, he eased up and kissed her with more tenderness. He pulled back and slid his hand to her waist. "I know this is crazy but, come with me."

"What?"

"Come with me. We need to be alone. I need this. So do you."

"I'm needed here. I can't just—"

"This place'll still be here when we get back. Come with me."

"For how long?"

"Three weeks. It's vacation time in Italy. We'll stay at my cousin's place. C'mon, Ells. I promise you'll have nothing to worry about."

She smiled. "That's so like you."

"Go home tonight and pack. We leave tomorrow night. I'll pick you up at two. One of the guys will drive us to the airport."

Ellie laughed. "I'll be ready. For what, I don't know."

Coletti gave her a quick kiss, then headed up the alleyway. When he reached the street, he turned, "No, you don't. But you'll find out. And you'll never forget it." He waved and disappeared.

"You're already unforgettable," she said to the empty space.

CHAPTER 23

Three months had passed since Harry Sturgis assisted firefighter Murphy by turning the hydrant wrench across from his home on Lurting Avenue in mid-December. He'd only recently learned that his mother had kept her promise about bringing cookies to the firehouse—and what else she'd done while there.

Anita had gone there, demanding to see the house captain. Captain O'Hara met with her, expecting to hear her complain about how his crew endangered her son—word had gotten back to him about the kid and the hydrant. Instead, she'd thanked him and told him what a good effect it'd had on Harry. She asked O'Hara to write a reference to help Harry get into the fire academy.

O'Hara responded coolly to her request. So, she gave him the whole story about Harry, ending it by saying training and being around the men would make a man out of him, and that's all any good mother wants for her son, especially a son who had no father around. O'Hara, a married man with no kids and nearing retirement age, was touched by her story. He told her he, too, had grown up in a broken home and knew what she was talking about. He said he would do what he could but made no guarantees. Now, two months after Harry filled out the applications to join the fire department, he received a letter from the FDNY that informed him he had been selected to join the next class of probationary firefighters at the FDNY training facility on Randall's Island, set to begin the last week of March.

When Anita told Harry what she did, he kissed his mother's cheek, lifted her a few inches off the floor, and spun around with her, as they both laughed.

✦

Drill instructor Ed Hodges scowled at the rows of probationary firefighters standing at attention ten deep and ten across. He shouted, "I don't believe what I'm looking at. A bigger pile of hopeless shit on two legs this sorry-ass fire instructor has never seen."

The probies, Harry Sturgis among them, remained motionless and silent.

Hodges was all business. The 5'10", 225-pound, crew-cut drill instructor with the ramrod posture moved slowly down the line of recruits, each dressed in navy-blue work pants, blue T-shirts, and black work boots. "Let me tell you something, you little shits. Someone in fire administration has got a perverse sense of humor to think any damn one of you could possibly join the ranks of the magnificent men and women who are members of the most elite, prestigious fire department on the face of the earth—the New York City Fire Department." The barrel-chested instructor stopped in front of Harry. "Good Lord. Is the recruitment office that desperate that they let you into this class?"

Harry kept his eyes forward and said, "Sir, yessir."

Hodges positioned his scarred face two inches from Harry's and barked, "What's your name, rubber?"

"Sturgis, sir."

"Stirrup? Did I hear right? What the fuck kind of name is that? You fucking with me, boy? You want to ride me like a horse?"

"Sir, no, sir."

The probie next to Harry tittered. Hodges stepped in front of the stocky, young African American man and yelled, "What are you laughing at, helmet?"

"Sir, nothing, sir." He bit down on the inside of his cheek.

"If you want laughs, go to the circus. I don't like chuckleheads in my class." He moved his face closer. "Looks to me like you're a chucklehead." Hodges wheeled around and shouted, "Rubbers, please say hello to Probie Chucklehead."

In unison, the probies barked, "Hello, Probie Chucklehead."

Hodges faced the young man. "I think they like the names. So do I." He leaned in, placing his face near the young man's, who swallowed hard. "Okay, Chucklehead *and* Stirrup, give me fifty push-ups. Now!"

Harry and the other probie dropped to the ground and complied with the order. Hodges returned to the front of the training ground. Standing at attention there was a fireman, lean but with an athletic build, thirtyish, hair worn in a crew cut. Dressed impeccably in his class-A uniform and bell cap, a row of medals hung from his neck. The name Grimes was engraved on his nameplate.

Hodges halted next to the man and faced the class, "All you sons-a-bitches, eyes at me. This, you maggots, is a New York City fireman. He's been through more working jobs, messy fire scenes, multiple-fatality car accidents, HazMat calls in one month than some cities experience in a whole year. He's made more grabs, resuscitated more dead souls, and saved more lives than a hospital full of doctors. To become this firefighter, gentlemen, is your mission, if you can complete it."

He raked his gaze over the class. "Now, you young punks may think you're invincible. Maybe you're all jacked up to be this man. I'm gonna let you in on a little secret, just between the two of us.

Turn and look at the man on your right or your left."

The probies did so, except for Harry and Chucklehead, still doing push-ups.

"Here's the secret," Hodges said. "Firefighter Grimes didn't get those medals for doing things his firefighter brothers *didn't* do. He got them for the things he did *for* his brothers. He didn't think of himself. He thought of his brothers and those he swore to protect and serve. That's what prompts his actions. That's what motivates him." He raised his volume to shout level. "Do you all understand me?"

Their unison, "Sir, yessir," reverberated off the brick façades of reconstructed brownstones at the other end of the training facility. The American flag flying above the school building behind the pavilion flapped in a brief but welcome breeze.

Hodges said, "Stirrup and Chucklehead, get up, you pissants." To the recruits he said, "See you all at six sharp in the morning. You're dismissed."

Hodges stood over Harry and the other probie as they slowly got to their feet.

"What's your name son?" Hodges asked the African-American probie.

"Reggie Small."

He eyed Harry. "And you?"

"Harry. You know the rest, sir."

"Go inside and get some food."

The two young men complied with his order. Hodges smiled listening to them head for the mess hall.

"Don't know why they gotta be so tight, but these dogs seem serious about this shit," Small said.

Harry nodded. "Maybe it's all an act. But I wouldn't want to swear to it.

✦

One of Hodges's assistants, dressed in bunker gear, held the handle of the wrought-iron door at the back end of the flashover simulator. Another assistant, similarly decked out, held a charged handline. Hodges barked to the fireman at the door, "Give me a three-second door."

The assistant opened the door for three seconds to let in clean air and the early May sunlight.

Hodges, in full personal protective gear, mask, facepiece, and helmet, stood in the middle of the corrugated sheet metal building that resembled a semi-trailer with a chimney. A fifty-five-gallon drum filled with burning combustibles composed of newspapers, wood, hay, and regular paper sat on a platform at the front end of the simulator. Flames raced upward from the drum and hit the ceiling, generating heat, smoke, and gases that filled the metal enclosure.

Harry, Reggie Small, and two other probies, also in full bunker gear, crouched behind Hodges along the side of one of the container walls. The paint on their helmets had bubbled and separated during each of the numerous cycles through the simulator.

The temperature rose as heat built around them from the burning combustibles. Hodges said, "Feel the heat, lads? This is how fire begins to eat up a room."

Harry glanced over at the assistant holding the door and then to the other one holding the hose. Both veterans shot comical looks at the probies. It was clear to Harry they were getting their kicks out of watching him and Reggie squirm during their first time in the simulator. He refocused his attention on the fire, now moving outward from the ceiling and spreading down and along the walls. Visibility diminished with each passing second and had reduced to no more than five feet in front of Harry's face. Through his mask, he could see the drum giving off some light, but it was mostly obscured by condensation fogging the inside of his mask, a result of nervous sweat he couldn't stop, on top of sweat from the building temperature.

As though reading Harry's mind, Hodges shouted, "You can expect these kinds of conditions in a fire. Can't see a fucking thing."

Harry had heard about these conditions from probies who'd been volunteer firefighters before joining the FDNY. He hadn't believed them. Had thought they were giving him a hard time for the fun of it. Now he was seeing it for himself. He literally could not see anything through his facepiece, just an orange glow ahead. The thought that he was supposed to go into a burning building, basically blind, find a fire that was out to kill him and put it out shot fear up his spine. *How the heck can I put out a fire if I can't even see it?* Eight weeks he'd been at the academy, and now, for the first time, he wondered if he'd made a mistake.

Hodges crouched until he was eye-level with the bottom of the drum. Over his shoulder, he said, "Stay low, lads. It's about to get a little hot in here."

Harry made himself as small as he could but kept his head up to watch what was going on. His bunker gear and hood got hotter, and he wondered how much more he and the others would be expected to take.

Hodges had explained ahead of time that the flashover simulator was designed to recreate conditions in an enclosed room, where a fire starts. If not extinguished or ventilated, the contents in the room burned, releasing gases and heat that could rise to 1,100 degrees Fahrenheit. At that temperature, every combustible surface in the room would auto-ignite. Anyone caught inside the room when it flashed wouldn't survive. "The simulator," Hodges had told them, "prepares firefighters to recognize the signs of an impending flashover, so they can either escape or extinguish the fire, depending on conditions."

Harry glanced behind him, at Small, who was pressed against his back and also staying as low as possible. "You're using me as a shield, you know."

"Damn straight. This shit scares the shit outta me. This is one fucked-up place to be. I hope I never get my ass in a room like this."

"Chucklehead," Hodges shouted, "shut up and listen." Thick, gray smoke and hot gases quickly filled the air around the instructor and trainees. "Don't any of you lads stand up, you hear me? Temperature three feet above your heads is nine hundred degrees. You won't survive."

Harry felt heat press against his coat with a vengeance, felt it working its way into the space between his Nomex hood and facemask, making its way toward his skin. He kept his eyes on Hodges, who knelt down and reached above his head, into the gassy mix seconds away from flashing. The instructor used his gloved hand to bat at the gases, creating tadpole-shaped streaks of flames that moved in different directions through the upper layer. Sweat streamed from Harry's brow, stinging his eyes. A nauseating feeling came over him.

"Feel the conditions?" Hodges said. "Look at the ceiling. Whenever you see what you see there now, you have two options: get out or hit it with the line."

He backed up and positioned himself next to Harry. Motioned to the fireman holding the line. "Busby, hit the fucking thing."

The nozzle man moved forward on his knees, pointed the hose nozzle at the ceiling, and pulled back on the handle quickly. A narrow stream of white water burst from the nozzle tip, hitting the ceiling. Smoke, gas, and heat moved in erratic patterns, as though in spasms. Interior temperature lessened and intensified in spurts, as water introduced into the upper heat layer reduced the heat built up inside the simulator.

Then, the nozzle man aimed the knob at the fifty-five-gallon drum, hit it with the stream, and within seconds, the fire was doused, the heat subsided. The other assistant opened the door, allowing deadly gases to dissipate into the open-air environment.

A shaft of midday sunlight hit the interior of the simulator. Harry was stunned at how peaceful, almost normal, the space became, when only seconds before, a raging inferno had pinned him to the floor, and made him feel like he was about to die in Hell. He glanced at Reggie, who wore a similar expression of shock on his face.

Reggie said, "That's some serious shit."

"I noticed."

"I love it!"

Harry nodded. They stood at the same time. "I feel the same."

They'd survived the first test. He, Harry Sturgis, former loser, had gotten close to fire, saw it up close and personal, felt its properties. Sure, it had made him a little queasy and anxious, but he hadn't panicked. He'd kept his cool. He'd followed instructions and learned what he needed to know to advance in the class.

He hadn't known he could feel like this—proud.

Damn proud.

✦

Over the next ten weeks, Harry rotated through all the training areas and classroom sections, and without difficulty, acing tabletop exercises and bookwork. Sections involving physical strength, however, were another story. He'd never been the athletic type, so when training drills involved significant physical exertion, the needed strength wasn't there; exercises like carrying a 150-pound dummy down a flight of stairs or trying to raise a twenty-four-foot extension ladder alone.

Harry's deficiency did not go unnoticed by his instructors, who recommended he start a conditioning and weight-training program. They were eager to help him, they'd said. His book smarts made him an asset to a department and probie class long on brawn but short on brains, they'd told him.

"I'll help you," Small said, as he tidied the contents of his locker. "I was all-city running back at Dewitt Clinton High School. I'll help you with this back-breaking stuff, you help me with the coursework, especially that hazardous materials shit."

"Deal."

"Come the end of the eighteen weeks, we gotta pass that written test, which you'll help me with, some kind of psychological exam, which, I guess, we on our own on that one."

"And the practical exam, where each of us is tested in twelve areas of firematic skills," Harry added.

"Almost as scary as fire itself."

Harry gave a light slap to Small's back. "We did all right there. We'll do all right with exams."

✦

Harry stood in front of his locker replacing the liner in his turnout coat, snap by snap. Next to him, Small shifted items around in his locker. Harry spotted a photo taped to the inside of Small's open locker door—the girlfriend, holding a baby. She looked no older than seventeen. "Look at you," Harry said. "Dressed in your new navy-blue work pants and work shirt. Lookin' sharp. Got a hot date tonight?"

"Negative. I'm just livin' the part. Took Hodges's advice."

"Which advice?"

"If I want to make it through this thing, I gotta eat, drink, and sleep this world. Said this wasn't a vacation, it's a *vocation*. Said I gotta treat it that way." Small checked his reflection in the mirror attached to the wall next to the lockers. He straightened his belt and evened up his work shirt. "This brother is serious. You're lookin' at a future FDNY battalion chief."

"Reg, I admire your enthusiasm, but we're not out of the woods yet."

"Three more days and we're done."

"We've still got the practical exam."

Small waved away the comment. "I'm not concerned about that. You saw what I did in the live burn. I had that shit down cold."

"If we both do as well on the practical as I did on the written and you did on the live burn, we'll make it." Harry watched Small admire his reflection for a few seconds and then continued with the liner.

Reggie had more than made it, Harry told himself. The guy was built for the work and had the right attitude. He'd entered the actual-fire scenario. Had acted on his assignment to enter the burning building, locate a trapped firefighter, and rescue him. He crawled through the burning room, following a hose line, until he located the 150-pound dummy, pulled it out and did CPR, as though he'd done both a hundred times before.

Instructors had been impressed with Reg's ability to follow orders and get the job done quickly and efficiently.

"All my football training," Small told Harry. "Told myself my team was down five points and I needed to run for a touchdown."

Yep, Harry thought, *Reg was born to be a real hard charger, as long as he passed the written exam.*

Small said, "You listenin' to me?"

"Sorry. What'd you say?"

"I said, do you remember what you told me about the written stuff?"

"No."

"You said, 'Reg, don't get frustrated with classroom work. You do that, you'll fail. You got to calm down and think.'"

"Yeah. I did say that."

"Look, dog, it's the same with muscle. You gotta calm down. Gotta tell yourself you can do it. Then just let your body take over." In his best Sunday-morning preacher voice, he bellowed, "I *know* you can do it!"

From the other end of the locker room, someone yelled, "Shut up, probie."

Small raised his eyebrows and returned to his locker.

"I hope you're right," Harry said. "I'll try to remember that. When I get to the search-and-rescue evolution, I'll do what we learned and not overthink it." He placed his turnout coat inside his locker, which was a few feet from Small's.

Small splashed aftershave into a palm, rubbed his hands together, patted his face, and then closed his locker. "Man, I can't wait to get my assignment. I hope it's an engine company in Bushwick. What do you want first, engine or truck?"

Harry hesitated. It was a loaded question; one he'd given a lot of thought to. An engine would place him at the heart of the action, putting fires out in tough situations and in rough circumstances. Over time, after pulling hose and backing up the nozzle man, he'd be able to work his way up the ranks, until he was the knob, the most coveted position on an engine crew, obtained only by merit. No one doubted how essential the role of engineman was at a fire scene. Without him, the fire didn't go out. But the truck had allure as well. It would let him attack the fire in a different way, doing outside ventilation, search and rescue, salvage. To him, the safer approach suggested the engine, where he could bide his time flaking uncharged lines down stairwells and out doorways. However, he had begun to develop upper-body strength, along with nimbleness he had never known he possessed, not until he went through the tenement fire simulator, where he'd shimmied up fire escapes and onto roofs as part of the outside vent team, discovering he was reliably good at what Hodges had called "the truck ballet."

Small stared at him, waiting for an answer. "I want the truck," he finally said.

"Not me. This brother does not want to go anywhere close to the Red Devil without a hose in his hand. I want to roll up on a working job in a Seagrave pumper, fire rippin' out of every window."

"Why?"

"I want to announce my presence, like, 'Brothers, the *Real* Brothers, are here to save you.'"

From a different section in the locker room, a voice boomed out, "Bottle it, probie."

Small said, "I'm gettin' outta here before they come for me."

"I'm right behind you."

As they stepped into the hallway, a nerf football whizzed past them. They broke into a run, zipping down the short hallway, out the doors and into the courtyard between the townhouse replica and classroom buildings.

Harry slowed to a walk and said, "That was close."

Small laughed. "Remember what Hodges said. 'Never run on a fire scene.'"

Harry smiled. "Yeah, but that don't apply to a locker room."

They chuckled and gave each other a fist pump.

✦

JULY 31, 2001

Harry Sturgis slid out of his mother's Toyota Camry, parked in the lot next to Queens College. Everywhere around him stood probies, attired as he was—dress-blue trousers and blouse with the red, white, and blue FDNY shoulder patch on the left shoulder, wearing black patent leather shoes, and bell caps, like the one Harry had in his right hand. Harry stood next to the car trunk as he waited for his mother to join him for the graduation ceremony, still moderately surprised that he'd made it at the Rock.

Walking through the gates on Randall's Island had changed him. On that first day, he hadn't known what to expect or whether he truly wanted to be a firefighter. Part of it was his own curiosity. The other part was to please his mother, who'd practically pleaded with him to take advantage of this opportunity she'd finagled for him. So many times, he'd questioned his decision once there, often surprised he'd stuck with it and got through the training. After all, some of the guys who were obvious candidates had flamed out. But he had always found a way to get through whatever was thrown at him.

Now, here he was, about to graduate, certain this was what he wanted to do, and he was good at it. Each week during training, that feeling he'd had after manning the hydrant that day on Lurting Avenue—the feeling of being an essential part of something bigger than himself—had grown exponentially. But he also came to realize that what he learned "on the Rock," as the veterans called the training academy, was only dress rehearsal to the real deal on the Job. If he could make it on the Job, then he would really know he had accomplished something.

Harry inhaled deeply and cast his gaze around the parking lot. Probies milled with their moms, dads, siblings, wives, girlfriends. Several waved to him as they made their way toward the training school auditorium. Their expressions said it all—happy, proud, and like him, dazed they were about to become members of the FDNY, receiving posts to assignments all over the five boroughs.

Anita Sturgis joined him and brushed a speck of lint from his shoulder. Harry thought to stop her maternal ministrations and then changed his mind. This was as much her day as it was his. All those kids at school, who'd thought they were so special and that he was the biggest nerd on the planet, wouldn't recognize him, not with his well-formed biceps and quads. He wondered if any of the high school jocks who'd taunted him could do half the things he'd learned at the Rock.

His mother raised her hand to brush the other shoulder. He grabbed her hand gently, smiled, and said, "We need to get inside."

"Just one more thing." She reached into her handbag, pulled out a handkerchief, and polished his badge. "You look so handsome in your uniform."

He stepped back. "Thanks. Now let's go in."

Anita sniffed, and dropped the handkerchief back into her handbag. "Probably best if I keep it handy."

"Are you going to sob through this whole thing?"

She linked her arm through his. "If I do, I have a right to."

He grinned. "Yeah. You do."

Harry took her arm. Together they walked toward the auditorium entrance. A Mazda sedan pulled up and stopped next to him. The driver, a large African-American woman, rolled down the car window.

"Excuse me. Are you Harry Sturgis?"

"Yes."

"Hold on, dear, my husband wants to talk to you," she said. The passenger car door opened. Instructor Hodges stepped out of the car and closed the door. He leaned back in the window.

"This won't take long, Lichelle," Hodges said in the meekest voice.

"It better not. I don't want to be late to dinner."

Hodges walked around the car, extending his hand to Harry.

"Harry, congratulations. Is this your mom?"

"Yes, sir."

"Mrs. Sturgis, you have a very good son. He is smart and capable. I know he will be an asset to the department." He shot a smile at Harry. "I put him through the paces a little because I had a gut feeling he needed it. But he took it like he should." He nodded to Harry. "Son, you stuck with it and made great strides. I know you got the bug for it, like we all do. Just stick with whatever gets thrown at you and you'll do fine."

Sturgis shook Hodges's hand. "Thank—"

The sound of the Mazda horn split the air. Hodges wheeled around.

"Okay, dear. I'm coming." Hodges hustled around the back of the car and slid into the front passenger seat. Lichelle gazed at Harry.

"I guess he likes you. He doesn't make me stop for anyone." She flashed an annoyed look at Hodges. "Can we go now?"

Harry heard Hodges mutter the words "yes, dear" as the Mazda pulled away. He gently took his mother's arm. "Let's go inside."

CHAPTER 24

The Alitalia DC-9 lurched as its tires connected with the runway. Coletti smiled at Ellie motioning to the window. "Welcome to Reggio di Calabria, Italy's southernmost city."

Ellie's first glimpse of the hard, ancient land surprised her. "Palm Trees? I didn't expect to see those here." She pointed. "And that mountain?"

"That's Aspromonte. Its jagged peaks go up to a thousand feet. Below it is the Tyrrhenian Sea. Prettiest aquamarine water you ever want to see."

"The water's so clear. It's unbelievable?"

"Down to two hundred feet."

"This is a long way from Ohio in more ways than one."

On the tarmac below, dark-haired, overall-clad crewmen wheeled mobile stairs toward the aircraft. Ellie held Coletti's hand when she exited the plane, met by a blast of midday heat. "Whoa. It's like a sauna."

"That's your first taste of the Mediterranean climate. Stifling summer heat always reminds me of Calabria."

Ellie cupped her free hand over her eyebrows to shield her eyes from the sun and stepped onto the narrow metal stairs.

They made their way across the worn tarmac, dodging the biggest chips or breaks. A cracked, weather-beaten wooden sign sat atop the small, beige Art Deco terminal, the words "*Benvenuti a Reggio di Calabria*" painted across it.

With their luggage in hand, the couple took a few steps toward the departure gate before Coletti stopped when someone called out, "Filippo!" He scanned faces until he spotted his cousin, mid-twenties, sporting thick, curly, black hair and an olive complexion just slightly darker than his own, and a pencil-thin mustache. "Enzo!"

Seconds after Coletti and Ellie passed through the gate, he put his luggage down and embraced Enzo, each kissing the other's cheeks, as was the custom. "*Cucino. Com'estai?*"

"*Bene.*" Enzo fixed his gaze on Ellie but said to Coletti, "*E questa tua amica?*"

"*Si, si. Questa e Elena.*"

Enzo straightened his posture, buttoned his jacket, and extended his hand.

Ellie blushed and put her normal hand into his.

Enzo lifted her hand and said more slowly, "Welcome to Italia. I am Enzo, Filippo's … uh … cousin. Anything I can do for you," he waved his free hand, "I will do."

She glanced at Coletti, raised her eyebrows, and said, "Um … thank you, Enzo. It's nice to meet you."

Enzo leaned forward and said, "*Piacere.*" He took her bags and told them to follow him.

The trio walked outside and got into a green late-model Renault Clio. Enzo lit up an American cigarette and spoke to Coletti in Italian. He drove the car with one hand, but not always the same hand. He held the wheel with his right hand and smoked the cigarette with his left. Or he held the wheel and the cigarette in his left hand

and gestured to his cousin sitting in the passenger seat with his right hand, which, Ellie concluded, was mandated accompaniment to his staccato-like Italian. Coletti sat back and listened, interjecting small remarks in Italian. Although she could not understand a word, Ellie enjoyed the show, observing both the animated conversation and journey up the winding A2 Autostrada that hugged the Calabrian coastline.

After twenty minutes, Enzo turned off the highway and made his way down a small local road toward the sea. Up ahead, a rock-encrusted promontory topped with a medieval castle rose boldly out of the sea beyond a small, ancient fishing village built into the Calabrian hillside. White-bleached stucco houses with tiled roofs and narrow windows lined a pristine beach, where sunbathers lazily lounged on beach chairs under umbrellas. A row of white and blue-bottomed fishing skiffs rested on the sands near the water's edge. The crystal-clear waters of the gentle Tyrrhenian Sea lapped listlessly against its shore in the late-day sun. A café stood next to the beach, filled with late-afternoon patrons arriving from their afternoon siesta hungry for panini and granita.

Enzo drove up narrow cobblestone streets, past women carrying produce back from the market and children riding Vespas in haphazard manners. After stopping on the road next to the medieval castle, he motioned for them to get out and said, "*Andiamo*."

Ellie walked around the car and stood next to Enzo. "I see why you stopped," she said. "That view—the sea, coastline."

Coletti moved up next to her. "Everything shimmers here." He pointed and said, "The rock outcroppings, inlets, grottoes, tidal pools."

"I've never seen water so clear."

The sun began its slow descent over the horizon, painting everything with hues of violet, lavender, indigo, and shades of pink.

Ellie sighed and touched Coletti's arm. "I'm awestruck. Never have I seen such natural beauty anywhere, not that I've been to a lot of places. What is this place?"

"This is the town of Scilla. This part of Italy is known as the Costa Viola—the Violet Coast."

"I can see why. If I lived here, I don't think I'd ever leave."

"Don't be so sure. Before my grandmother moved to America, she said, 'You can't eat the scenery.'"

A soft breeze wafted over them. Ellie inhaled deeply. "What is *that* scent?"

"Italian jasmine." He pointed to a cluster of plants nearby. "They're all over the hillside."

Enzo lit another cigarette, nodded, walked back to the car, and opened the trunk to pull their luggage from the car.

"*Andiamo alla casa.*"

"Where are we going?" Ellie asked.

Phil aimed his thumb over his shoulder. "That orange two-story stucco is Enzo's. Great view of the bay and beach. You'll love it."

"I already do."

They walked toward the house, through the wooden gate that opened to the courtyard and garden strewn with hanging vines. A dozen or so relatives came out to greet them with hugs, kisses, and a great deal of Italian verbiage. An older man broke into song.

Minutes later, Ellie told Coletti, "I've never felt so welcome before, especially by strangers. They're treating me like a relative they haven't seen in ages."

Various relatives grabbed pieces of the luggage and started indoors. Beyond the foyer was the kitchen. An older apron-clad woman stood at the stove.

Ellie whispered to Coletti, "Whatever she's cooking, it's making my stomach rumble."

He inhaled. "That's Enzo's mom. And if my nose is working right, that's pasta and *vongole*, with olive oil and garlic."

The woman, wearing a broad smile, left the kitchen to greet them. She barked something to Enzo, who picked up Ellie's bags, motioning for her to follow him up the stairs.

She followed him down a hallway lined with windows, providing a view of the sea below, then into a small bedroom that overlooked an interior courtyard. She studied the room. A single bed covered with a white bedspread was positioned against a wall. Across from the bed was an armoire. Next to it was a tiny desk with a water bowl and pitcher on top of it.

Enzo waved and said, "You like the room?"

"I like it very much. Thank you."

"I leave you to wash up." He closed the door behind him.

Strains of music filtered in from outside. Ellie returned to the window. Below her in the courtyard an elderly man sat under a vine-covered trellis softly playing a mandolin. A little dog lay at the man's feet. She felt ... calm. She couldn't recall the last time she felt so content, so accepted. A knock on the door interrupted her thought.

Coletti entered. He had two lemons and a paring knife in his hands. He smiled. "Can I come in?"

"Please. What are those for?"

"I'll show you." He checked the pitcher—it was filled with water. He cut the lemons into wedges and dropped them into the pitcher.

Ellie laughed and ran her eyes up and down him. "You changed clothes. Already."

"White cotton shirt. Beige khakis. Kind of my wardrobe here. So, what do you think of the place and my people?"

"It's all wonderful. I didn't know what to expect, but—"

"I know. It's a special place. This town's been here for three thousand years. Homer wrote about it in *The Odyssey*. 'The Scylla and Charybdis.' You ever hear of that?"

"No."

He grinned. "You have. You just don't know it. It means 'a rock and a hard place.'"

"I know a little about that."

"This is where that expression comes from. I'll explain more about that later." He dropped the last lemon wedge into the pitcher. "The bathroom is across the hall. My room's next door. Supper will be ready in a few minutes, so do whatever and meet me downstairs. I'm starving."

"So am I."

He kissed her on the forehead and left the room.

Ellie closed the door and sighed; she went to the pitcher and mused that she should have asked him if she was supposed to drink it or wash with it. Perhaps both. She opened the single desk drawer, found a hand towel, and took it out. Then she poured water into the bowl and rinsed her face, arms, and hands.

She changed clothes, grabbed her hairbrush, and stood in front of the mirror mounted to the back of the door.

As she studied her reflection, it occurred to her that ever since Phil had stepped into her life, she'd begun to feel reborn. And she found herself hoping it would last.

✦

Ellie woke before sunrise, to sounds of the sea gently lapping against the shore below. She put on her robe and walked to Phil's room—empty. Returning to her room, she went to the window to study the beach at dawn. As the sun rose, the outlines and details of twenty fishing skiffs became discernible. She could make out a figure leaning against one of them; it was Coletti, eating an orange and facing the sea.

She checked her reflection in the mirror, making sure that her robe was proper for venturing out, smoothed her hair, and then made her way to where he was.

He smiled as she approached the beach. "Ciao, Americana. Did you sleep well?" He moved his feet around a small satchel.

"*Si. Bene.*"

He nodded. "Nice. You're doing all right with picking up Italian."

"A little." She pointed to the satchel. "You going somewhere?"

"Yes. And you're coming with me."

"Where are we going?"

He jutted his chin toward the sea. "Across the water."

"What are we going to—?"

"Pack a bag with a few days' clothes, cover-ups, and sunblock." He tapped the satchel with his feet. "I've got the rest right here."

"No point in asking."

He popped the last orange section in his mouth. "Nope. Get going."

She saluted and returned to the house.

✦

Coletti held the tiller steady against a southerly breeze. He kept the eighteen-foot wooden sailboat northwesterly, still refusing to tell Ellie exactly where they were going.

Ellie, clad in summer slacks and cotton pullover, hair pulled back, peered over the bow to the waters ahead. To her right, Scilla's castle promontory cast its shadow onto the strait. She sat up straight. "Phil, are those holes in the water up ahead?"

"Yeah."

"We're getting closer to them."

"Yep."

She pointed. "There are more over there. But we're getting really close to the ones up ahead."

Coletti glanced over the bow. "The *Cariddi* are here."

"The what?"

"Homer wrote about two sea monsters that for centuries terrorized sailors in these straits. He named them the Scylla," he pointed to the coastline, "the rock promontory there, and Charybdis, the whirlpools. They could suck a ship down and into the deep."

She blinked. "Now I get it—a rock and a hard place."

"*Si.*"

A strong wind came off the Tyrrhenian Sea from the south, helping the sailboat to make good time. A few hours later, around two in the afternoon, Ellie scanned the horizon ahead and saw nothing but water shimmering under the bright sun.

Coletti said, “Can you see it?”

“I don’t see anything but water.”

“Keep looking.”

“Oh. I see something, like a silhouette of something large and dark sticking out of the water.”

“It’s an island. Strombolicchio.”

“What’s on it?”

“Nothing but a lighthouse.”

Coletti guided the boat to stone stairs that wrapped around of side of the rock. “They lead to the plateau and lighthouse.” He tied the boat up and stripped down to his swimming trunks. “I’m going to put you and our gear down here and then moor the boat about a hundred yards up.”

“And swim back?”

He beamed a smile. “That’s part of the fun.”

Coletti completed these tasks and swam back. He climbed up and said, “Follow me.”

They reached the plateau, and he paused. Pointing, he said, “That’s north. And that’s the island of Stromboli. That gray triangle, void of foliage, is an active volcano. That darker-gray streak running down from the cone into the sea is hardened ash, what they call *Sciara del Fuoco*, created by hundreds of years of eruptions.”

“Uh, Phil, it’s smoking. And rumbling.”

“Yeah. But we’re okay. So, what do you think?”

“I never thought I’d be this close to a volcano. It’s unbelievable.” The volcano belched another plume of gray smoke. “How long are we staying?”

“Overnight. We’ll sleep in the lighthouse.”

“How did you—?”

"Enzo arranged it. Let's get the gear inside."

He led her the rest of the way to the bleached-white lighthouse positioned atop a one-story bunker.

"I haven't been here since I was a kid," he said, as he placed a key in the door. He entered the room first, scanning the accommodations. "It's got a kitchen, bathroom, and bedroom. Not a lot of furniture, as you can see," he said, "but clean."

"How much room does a lighthouse keeper need?"

"I guess just the basics, when you think about it" He turned the tap on, water ran from it. Checked the stove, which worked. He carried the bags to the bedroom. "You might want to check this out," he called to her.

Ellie stood in the doorway. "Um … that's a single mattress."

"On a box spring at least. Better than the floor."

"And," she pointed, "there's a wall missing. Nice that they have a curtain there. It's flapping in the breeze."

He pointed. "That's a roll-up shutter. Like an overhead garage door. We can close it if the weather gets bad or cold or whatever. But check this out." He moved onto a terrace.

Ellie followed him out. "No railing. I'll have to remember to be careful if I get up during the night."

Coletti laughed. "You'll be fine. What a view."

"Really. Who gets a view of a volcano from their bedroom?"

"Leave it to Enzo to pull off something like this." He cheeked his watch. "Time to unpack some things."

With the supplies he had brought, that evening Coletti pulled together a meal of pancetta and provolone panini, red wine, fresh escarole salad, and Italian seasonings. The couple lay beside each other outside, drinking wine and watching the rose-colored sea swallow up the kneeling sun on the western horizon. As evening approached, Stromboli's volcano flickered against the slowly darkening sky to the south. The Tyrrhenian had become calmer, as if a flat desert surrounded the sharp volcanic island's rise.

In the fading light, Coletti tousled Ellie's dark-brown hair. She lay with her head against his chest, their breathing synchronized. The lighthouse's lantern had come on and cast its beam across the sea in a slow, silent, undulating motion.

"It's getting chilly. Let's go inside," he said, rubbing her temple.

They returned to the lighthouse and made their way to the bedroom. Coletti pulled back the curtain in front of the terrace to give them a clear view of the volcano's peak, a half mile away. It cast sparks of light and faint rumbles toward them like artillery bursts on some distant European battlefield.

He stood in front of her, took her hands, and held them by her side. "El, be still."

He cradled her legs with his left hand, lifted her up, and placed her on the soft bed, covered with the immaculate white sheets he had brought with them. She breathed deep, arched her back, and grabbed his shoulders. Their eyes met. In hers, he could see her affirmation of his advance. He gently removed her pullover and placed his weathered hands gingerly against her torso. She purred, guardedly.

"It's okay," he told her.

Slowly, she reached up and unbuttoned his white cotton shirt. Staring into his chestnut eyes, she removed the shirt and tossed it to the floor. She ran her hands over his firm pectorals and taut stomach, ending at his belt and then back up again.

"Phil, I don't know how—" She lowered her chin and closed her pained eyes.

Closing his eyes, he placed one hand behind her head and gently pressed his lips against her neck just below her right ear, giving her small, languorous kisses. He moved her head toward his until his kisses reached her lips. He could feel a wave of heat cascade through her upper torso. In the flickering orange light, she let out a thankful sigh.

He felt a sense of gratitude to be holding her in his arms. His blood stirred with unadulterated passion, but he checked it with the thought that she was, in a way, his ward. In his heart, he knew he was the only one on the bridge that day who could have rescued her, and the thought of that confirmed for him that their meeting was not chance, but destiny. Now, here, with her, in the middle of the vast Mediterranean on this speck of an island where he and his cousins, as children, had explored countless times, as his ancestors had done centuries earlier, he knew their meeting wasn't just happenstance. It was preordained, bound by the Calabrese traditions he knew not to ignore.

A sea breeze, warmed by the heat of Stromboli, entered from the terrace and enveloped their bodies. His lips held hers softly, without pressure, while he drew a line from her breasts to her pelvis with his index finger. She shifted slightly beneath him and squeezed his shoulders to steady herself.

It was not her stunning beauty that fueled his desire for her, but her honesty. Her self-recognition that the wounds she had suffered before they met had left her shy and vulnerable and hesitant to open up. This fact made him determined to bring her to a place where she would be comfortable with him, or with another. He wanted her to know that letting oneself love someone can sometimes bring with it a severe but necessary mercy.

He moved his head to her stomach and placed his hands on her torso, all the time planting kisses like rose petals on her stomach and lower abdomen. Her skin became warm, producing a bead of sweat that rolled down her side. In the orange light cast by the lava from the ancient island's top, he could see her extraordinary form, naked and febrile. Free of his clothes, he slid next to her, their legs pressing against each other.

She bit her lip and groaned, slowly, her eyes clouding over. Steadily, reverently, he took her. He breathed deeply, and prayerfully whispered her name as he led them both to that indescribable frisson.

He knew that there, at that moment, on that tiny island, the veil of pain had been torn from her eyes and she experienced that sweet, simple, redeeming joy.

✦

Ellie opened her eyes. Her pulse raced—she had no idea where she was. She lurched up in bed, glanced around at the white walls, white curtain billowing in a soft breeze, revealing the cobalt sea beyond the terrace. She smelled bacon. Footsteps came toward her.

Coletti entered the bedroom wearing gym shorts and carrying a plate. "Hey, sleepy. Hungry?"

"Wow. Room service with a view of a volcano. What's for breakfast?"

"Saffron and pancetta omelet." He placed the dish, which he'd adorned with a small posy of pink and yellow wildflowers, on the mattress in front of her.

She picked up the flowers and sniffed them. "What are these?"

"Mount Etna broom and Mediterranean spurge. They grow on most of the islands around here."

"They have a fresh scent, and something else, something different."

"That's because you can't find them growing anywhere else. Eat up."

Phil pulled the curtain to the side. He leaned against the wall and watched a sailboat on a heading for Stromboli. The small silver cross he wore on a sterling chain caught the sunlight and glinted against his chest.

"This is delicious," Ellie remarked. She pointed her fork at him. "You've gotten so tan. You look like Michelangelo's David, but with shorter hair."

He grinned. "You calling me buffed?"

Her cheeks flushed pink. "I guess I am." She cut into the omelet, placed the bite in her mouth, and chewed, kept her eyes on him. "Can I ask a question?"

"Ask away."

"What happened with your dad?" As his brow furrowed, she added, "Sorry. But what happened that caused you to bolt out of town?"

Coletti returned his gaze to the sea. "My old man is one of the best firemen in New York City. He's seen it all and done most of it." He rested against the wall. "He's in Rescue 22, one of the most elite companies in the department. Sixty-one, chain-smokes cigars, can outrun most of the guys on his crew, and has a chest full of medals to back up his talk. He's the real deal." He moved to the bed and stretched out at her side. "But he doesn't want his kids showing him up. He gave me bad advice on the test. With the score I got it'll be a few years before I make lieutenant."

"Why would he do that?"

"If I become an officer, he'd have to take orders from me, and show me respect on the Job, since I'd be a higher rank. He couldn't live with that."

Ellie shot him a quizzical look. "Why didn't your father become a lieutenant himself?

Coletti chuckled. "My old man? No way. He has no time for officers. He thinks they're a necessary nuisance that gets in the way of the guys who do the work. He's what's known as a 'senior' man—and that's a spot he likes quite enough."

She placed her hand on his chest and stroked the small cross. "You shouldn't let him get the best of you."

"Oh yeah?"

She nodded. "You tell him you're going to be a lieutenant whether he likes it or not. That he'd better get used to it."

Coletti grinned and ran his fingers through her hair. "He needs to mind his own business when it comes to what I do. However, that's my problem." He sat up. "Finish that. There's someplace special I want to take you to today."

Ellie stared at him and said, "What could top this?"

He leaned toward her and wiggled his eyebrows.

"Right. Don't ask."

✦

Late morning, their sailboat got underway. Coletti piloted it around Stromboli. The volcano was quiet, as though resting or inhaling before starting again. They cleared the island, revealing specks of land ahead.

Ellie adjusted the cover-up over her bikini top. "Is that where we're going?"

Coletti nodded. He steadied the tiller in his right hand and pointed the lit cigarette in his other hand. "It's a series of tiny islands, called Basiluzzo. They were formed by hardened lava thousands of years ago. The islands rise like fingers on a giant's hand, like he's trying to surface."

She squinted and said, "What's that? Are those ruins of a small fort or something?"

Coletti lowered the sails and nudged the boat against a stone pillar at the water's edge. He hopped from the boat and tied off a line.

Ellie stood. "The water's over the dock. Wow. The walls are covered with mosaics. Who built this place?"

"Romans. No one knows if they came here because it was strange or if they thought it was a great place to imprison slaves." He held out a hand. "C'mon. Let's explore a little."

He led her past the crumbling structure. "That," he said, pointing to something just under the surface of the water, "is a shelf of hardened lava and shoals. It extends well out beyond the island, like a quarter mile." Coletti placed his foot onto the jagged rocks. "Give me your hand."

They continued forward carefully, until they reached where the shelf began. He faced Ellie. "Here's the deal. You're gonna walk on this shelf, go as far as you can, and then walk back."

She backed away. "Uh-uh. I'm not going out there."

"Yes. You'll go and return. You have to."

"Why?"

"Look at me." He took her by the arms and turned her toward him. "Do you honestly think I'd do anything that put you in real danger? El, do you trust me?"

She stared at the shelf then back at him. "I trust you."

"Whew. You had me worried for a second." He sat on a nearby rock. "Better take your sandals off."

She slipped her sandals off and handed them to him, nodded once, and took a couple of short, tentative steps forward.

"The water is ankle-deep and warm. Stay in the center, El. The shelf varies from five feet to ten feet wide. Just watch your step."

Ellie continued, head lowered, eyes on what was below her feet. After what she thought was two hundred steps, she glanced back. In perspective, Coletti appeared like a toy figure. He waved; she waved back. He altered his wave to indicate she should keep going.

She inhaled and exhaled hard, then continued onward, until she saw the shelf's end five feet ahead of her. She inched toward the edge. Through the clear aquamarine water, she saw the bottom hundreds of feet below.

Ellie closed her eyes, imagined that she'd grown up here. Imagined that she'd always felt as she did now. That she'd never been desperate or had cause to feel that way.

She glanced back at Coletti, a mere speck in the distance. "I am different," she whispered, becoming more aware of this new feeling in her, another woman.

"I will go beyond this," she said. She looked up to the clear blue sky, and raised her hands, her eyes adjusting to her new sight.

"It is worth it. And I am worth it."

She knew, there, that day, that her life had extraordinary meaning. That her heart had the ability to feel things she never had known, and she now was eager to feel these things, all in their time and place. She turned and headed back to shore, taking her time, an expression of comfort and pleasure on her face, confident that she would get back to shore and go home to a new life.

CHAPTER 25

At 7:46 a.m., Harry Sturgis walked west on Thirty-Fifth Street. As he crossed Sixth Avenue, he used one hand to adjust the strap of his duffel bag and the other to keep a firm grip on the cardboard box filled with pastries and cookies his mother had made. At the Rock, a guy whose brother was on the Job, told him it was bad firehouse manners for a probie to show up the first day of work empty-handed. Harry wanted to make the best first impression possible, and it would take more than his brand-new navy-blue work shirt, navy utility pants, and shined black boots. He'd studied his reflection in the mirror before leaving home, concerned that the sharp creases in his pants screamed *probie*. Who was he kidding? It's not like he could fool anyone.

As he approached the firehouse, he sensed something was not right. The doors were up, and the truck bays were empty. The lights were on, but the place was deserted. He peered in the house watch next to the truck bays. No one was there. He could hear radio transmissions emanating from the house watch radio but could not understand what was being said.

He stepped inside. On the apparatus floor were shoes and work boots, discarded in a haphazard fashion. Harry continued toward a door marked "Kitchen" at the back of the bay, pausing in front of plaques mounted to the wall, each inscribed with the names of firehouse members killed in the line of duty.

Inside the kitchen, he put the box of pastries on the kitchen table and glanced around. There was no food on the stove or plates on the table. From the doorway, a baritone voice said, "Can I help you?"

Harry turned to see a fireman, about six feet tall, square-jawed and bushy-eyebrowed, watching him from the doorway. The fireman had on a navy-blue T-shirt, a Maltese Cross and the Ladder 14 logo on the front. "I'm probationary firefighter Harry Sturgis, sir. It's my first day."

"I know. And don't call me sir. I'm not a lieutenant. Name's Tim Reidy." He pointed to the box on the table. "What's that?"

"Homemade pastries and cookies my mom made."

Reidy picked up the box and threw it into the garbage can. He walked out of the room. "Get your bag and follow me. I'll show you your bunk."

Harry gaped at the garbage can, and then hoisted the duffel strap onto his shoulder. He caught up to Reidy and said, "Where is everybody?"

"They're at a job. A major worker. Three alarms. Came in around eleven last night. Fourteen and Forty-Eight have been there all night. Finally got it under control around three this morning."

The big truckie led Harry into the dusty municipal-gray tiled stair lobby. The wall was adorned with photographs of fire apparatus from generations ago. Laminated news clippings of major fires in the city hung on the wall under a red-and-orange banner with the words "Hellfighters" sewn on it in black letters over a silhouette of the Grim Reaper holding a six-foot hook and axe in his skeletal hands. Beyond the banner up the stairs hung four horseshoes around the word "Buster 1908–1913." Harry stopped for a moment to study the photos.

"It's an old place. This house. With a lot of history," the veteran said, heading up the stairs.

"I can see that."

"Some good. And some not so good," Reidy commented, the beveled wooden stairs creaking audibly with each step he took.

Harry kept pace with Reidy, who entered a room furnished with beat-up sofas and armchairs. Against the front wall and next to a window was a coffee table with a nineteen-inch TV on it. Toward the far-right corner was an alcove with a fire pole that ran down to the apparatus floor. He trailed his guide, who led him down a short hallway, past a bunk room, and then into a small bedroom containing a cot and a nightstand.

"This is you. No room left in the bunk room."

Harry nodded and smiled. He'd have his own room, at least for a while. He dropped his duffel bag onto the cot.

A faint rumbling came from outside and grew louder. "They're back," Reidy said. He left Harry without saying another word. The sound grew loud enough for Harry to realize it was the throaty engine and compressor on the J-brake of the massive ladder truck that was pulling up in front of the firehouse. Harry straightened his belt and then headed out the door a few steps behind Reidy.

When Harry got to the apparatus floor, he saw 14 Truck backing into the firehouse, the audible pinging of the truck's reverse-direction alarm echoing off the walls of the firehouse. Now, he was not alone. Other firemen who had arrived for the day shift were standing in the bays; two were in the street holding up traffic to allow the truck to back into the station. From Harry's vantage point on the apparatus floor, he could not see the faces of the crew on the truck, except for the turnout coat-covered arm of the lieutenant sticking out of the officer's compartment window.

When the truck came to a stop and the engine cut off, the rear door to the cab opened. A fireman, in his turnout coat and bunker pants, slowly emerged from the cab. His ruddy, char-covered face contrasted with the whites of his eyes, making him look like a coal miner who had just emerged from some dark cave. He stepped onto the floor lethargically, with a serious demeanor, making it clear the job he just worked was no milk run. He exchanged brief words with one of the guys standing on the floor holding a cup of coffee. The ashen-faced fireman nodded his head and frowned.

The lieutenant had still not yet emerged from the truck. Harry moved a little closer to get a better view of the rig. The officer sat in his seat, jotting something down on a clipboard with a pen. The atmosphere on the floor was quiet, punctuated by the sound of equipment and cab doors opening and closing over the quiet hum of the wall-mounted exhaust fans that had kicked on when the truck's exhaust fumes rose to the ceiling.

A twenty-ish fireman, ripped with muscles and slicked-back brown hair, wearing work clothes approached Harry. The softest thing on him was his teeth, Harry thought.

"Hey, you're the new probie, right?" he asked Harry, smiling and extending his hand. He spoke quickly, blurting out the words in chunks.

"Yes. I'm Harry Sturgis," Harry said, shaking his hand.

"Larry Ruffalo. They call me 'Truck Larry.'" Larry pointed over his shoulder to the ladder truck behind him. "You picked a busy day to start. We had a big job last night. These trucks are filthy. Did you get your gear stored upstairs?"

"Yes." Harry nodded. He peered in the kitchen. Several firemen were huddled around the TV monitor on the wall. Although he was curious about the fire last night, he thought it better to not ask any questions and just follow orders.

"Good. Go get the utility hose and wash down the ladders on 14, including the Little Giant. They reek," the cheery-faced body-builder said, before entering the kitchen.

Harry took up the detail in earnest, cleaning the worn, grimy ladders from 14 Truck. Some he could hose off. Others were so dirty, he had to use a wire brush to loosen the char and soot from the sections and dogs. While he was on his first firehouse detail, other guys in the house noticed him and stopped to watch, some holding cups of coffee, others eating the pastries he brought. He knew he was being sized up with every push of the wire brush. Out of the corner of his eye he could see the looks on these veterans' faces. It told him everything he needed to know: he may have graduated from the academy, but here, on the Job, it meant nothing. He was like a kid they took in off the street. They didn't know anything about him, whether they could trust him, how he would act in a fire, if he was reliable. Nothing.

He was a blank slate, a fuckin' new guy they would have to babysit and nurse along over the next few months to a year until they could determine if he were strong enough and smart enough to hold his own and execute orders smoothly when things got jamming. For now, Harry understood, all he had to do was clean the ground and roof ladders and return them to the compartment on the truck.

About ten or so minutes later, one of the old buffaloes said, "Probie, didn't anyone tell you it's rude to show up your first day empty-handed?" Snickers from other veterans around him followed the question.

Harry paused for half a second. "Yes, sir. It won't happen again." He picked up the hose and aimed it at the Little Giant, the collapsible ladder used in confined spaces like attics and basements.

"Just remember next time. And don't call me sir."

Harry nodded and sprayed water over the ladder. As he did so, he wondered if Truck Larry planned to help him put the twenty-four-foot extension ladder into the back of the truck or did he plan to see if Harry could handle it alone, as he'd been trained. He reminded himself of one lesson: *Don't expect help from anyone, and you won't be disappointed.*

He finished cleaning the ladders and replaced the roof ladder—a single-section ladder with hooks on the end, then replaced the Little Giant. He eyed the extension ladder.

Ruffalo approached him. "After you put away the extension ladder, Captain Hammonds wants to see you in his office." He nodded once and then headed for the kitchen, where the rest of the truck and engine crews had gathered.

"Will do." Harry hoisted the ladder onto his shoulder like a satchel, distributed his weight evenly along the length of the ladder, and maneuvered around a column so he could align the ladder with the runners in the storage compartment, which was behind a roll-down door in the rear of the truck.

He placed the end of the ladder against the runners, turned the ladder on its side, adjusting it until it fell into place on the runners. The ladder moved into place easily. He closed the metal roll-down door, feeling good about completing his first task without a hitch.

Harry wiped his hands on a rag and headed toward the captain's office. He passed the kitchen. Ten firemen stared at the TV, that broadcast a report on a fire. The men were subdued, serious, silent. It dawned on him that this was *their* fire being reported on. He paused to listen. The reporter stated a man and woman were rescued by firefighters, brought to the hospital, but had died from smoke inhalation.

A firefighter, tall, brown-eyed, and with a scar on his neck, shoved the chair he'd been leaning on across the floor. He stormed past Harry, briefly glancing at him, and then onto the apparatus floor.

But the expression he'd seen on the firefighter's face and in his eyes … Harry swallowed hard then headed to the captain's office.

✦

Captain Ray Hammonds sat in his cramped office on the second floor of the firehouse, working on an incident report for the fire from the night shift. A window-mounted air conditioner pumped semi-cool air overhead from the airshaft outside. On his desk sat a computer monitor and a keyboard that were unplugged, under a bookshelf containing logs, binders, and training manuals.

Harry rapped on the doorjamb and was told to enter. He took a seat in the empty chair across from Hammonds' desk and eyed the tropical fish tank against the wall. The captain kept his focus on the report. Harry glanced left and saw his duffel bag on the empty chair next to him.

Hammonds put his pen down, picked up a paper placed off to the side, and through smudged reading glasses, studied the paper. "Harry Sturgis?"

"Yessir."

"You scored high on the written exam. Quite high."

"Yessir."

"But not as well on the practical."

"No, sir. But I passed, sir."

Hammonds lowered his head an inch and studied Harry over his reading glasses. "Yes. You did." He put the paper down and leaned back. "How the hell did you end up in 14 Truck right out of the academy?"

"Sir, I like the truck. I believe I can contribute the greatest here, sir."

"How so?"

"The truck presents a greater degree of unknowns than the engine—rescue, ventilation, and search involve knowledge of more variables to ensure success. At least, that's my thinking, sir." Harry scratched the end of the metal chair arm. "I think my book strengths may be helpful once I learn the job."

Hammonds nodded. "Okay, fair enough. But this truck company isn't like any other in the city. Did you know that?"

Harry did, but decided not to admit it. He'd heard plenty about

Ladder 14's unorthodox reputation. "No, sir."

"They're a wild bunch. Castoffs. Misfits. Lunatics. Every last damn one of them, and on every shift." Hammonds lifted the phone receiver and hit a button. Static crackled over the intercom system. He brought the receiver close to his mouth and bellowed, "Whichever of you numbnuts thought it would be hilarious to put the probie's duffel on my bed will be written up the second I find out who you are. I'm not going to put up with that behavior in this house." Laughter erupted from all sections of the firehouse.

He pressed the receiver to his chest and asked, "Who brought you to your bunk, probie?"

"I think his name was Tim Reidy, sir." Thinking he might save the firefighter some grief, he added, "He explained about the bunk, sir."

"Explained what?"

"About there being no room. I'm fine about being in the room with the cot."

Hammonds brought the receiver to his mouth, hit the intercom button. "Reidy, this is Captain Hammonds, telling you to get to my office. Now!" He cradled the receiver and pointed to the duffel bag. "Take that out of here. We'll get to the bottom of this."

Harry sprang to his feet and grabbed the bag as a slender, blond fireman not more than a few years older than Harry stepped into the office.

"You called me, Captain?" He glanced at Harry.

"Reidy, did you put this probie's bag on my bed?"

He eyed the bag then Harry. "No, sir."

"You sure, after taking him to his bunk, you didn't decide to have a little joke at our expense?"

"Captain, this is the first time I laid eyes on this probie."

"He's right, sir," Harry interjected.

"That's what I thought. Some joker used your name, and I think I know who. I'll deal with him later. Reidy, show Sturgis his bunk.

The real one."

"Yes, sir."

Hammonds, jaw tight, picked up his pen, and returned his attention to the incident report.

Reidy exited the office with Harry trailing him to the bunk room. He motioned to a narrow top bunkbed against the wall under a ventilation chase that ran outside.

"Where's that ventilation come from?" Harry asked.

"The alleyway behind the firehouse."

"I'll have to remind myself not to bump my head."

"You've got a two-foot clearance between the bed and the chase. Should only take one knock on the head to remember to duck."

Harry sighed.

"What's that about, probie? What? You thought you'd been given a private suite or something?"

"Not exactly." Harry stuffed his bag at the end of the mattress, missing the ductwork by several inches.

"Hey, probie. Bet you can't guess the captain's nickname."

"Probably not."

"C'mon. Give it a shot."

"Um … Strawberries?"

"No. What kind of a fuckin' nickname is that? We call him 'Midol,' cause he's always on the rag."

Harry nodded. "Got it."

Reidy motioned with his hand. "C'mon downstairs."

Harry moved to follow him, sensing he was an inconvenience to the veterans rather than a new asset. It wasn't at all what he'd expected on his first day on the Job.

✦

Harry walked two steps behind the real Reidy as he headed for the lockers against the cinder block wall at the back of the apparatus floor. The Reidy imposter stood in front of an open locker, refastening the protective liner of his turnout coat. He caught sight of the real Reidy approaching, with Harry in tow, and grinned.

Reidy faced the imposter. "Hey, Lynch. Cute move, telling the kid you were me. Midol really appreciated the prank. Thanks a lot."

Lynch chuckled. "You engine guys need to lighten up. You're too serious." He smirked at Harry, held out his right hand. "Eddie Lynch. Welcome to 14 Truck. No offense intended, probie."

Harry gripped the man's hand. "None taken."

Reidy turned and walked away. He stopped halfway across the floor and said, "Lieu's looking for you, Lynch."

"Yeah? What for?"

"Lowell's on duty today. Lieu wants you to help bring him in."

"You cocksucker." Lynch slammed his locker door with his fist. "Where is he?"

"Truck Larry said Lowell told him last night that he was going on a stripper bender then taking a hotel room at the St. Regis."

Reidy gave Lynch what Harry read as a shit-eating grin.

Lynch flung his turnout coat into his locker and slammed the door shut. "Damn it to hell."

Harry stepped back, uncertain of what was going on and not wanting to get caught up in the exchange.

Lynch checked his watch. He pointed at Harry. "Probie, you stay here. I'm gonna need your help."

Lynch stormed toward the kitchen. Harry checked his watch periodically, wondering how long he was supposed to stand there or if this was another prank at his expense. Just under five minutes later, Lynch returned with a tall, slender, blonde-haired lieutenant flashing a concerned expression.

Lynch waved for Harry to join them. He broke into a jog to catch up as they exited the firehouse and got into a Chevy SUV painted with red, white, and orange markings and the FDNY emblem on the driver- and passenger-side doors. The lieutenant slid into the passenger's seat. Harry's door wasn't quite closed when Lynch cranked the engine, hit the gas, and got them to Sixth Avenue in no time, aiming the vehicle north.

No words were exchanged in the SUV until the lieutenant glanced at Harry in the rearview mirror. "Eddie, what's with bringing the probie?"

Lynch stared straight ahead and didn't answer.

The lieutenant glanced back at Harry and then aimed his eyes forward again. "I'm Lieutenant Connolly, your company officer. You're Sturgis, right?"

"Yessir."

"Well, Sturgis, you're probably wondering where Firefighter Lynch is taking us." He glanced at Lynch, whose eyes were fixed forward with a scowl on his face. "It's like this. Jay Lowell is Captain Midol's nephew. A trust fund kid. Ivy League graduate. Through a serious lack of judgment, Lowell decided to become a firefighter."

"Fuckin' pussy candy-ass," Lynch barked, his jaw clenched.

Connolly nodded. "Lowell's supposed to be on duty today. Without our assistance, he most likely wouldn't make it to the firehouse before 9 a.m." He glanced at Harry again. "Firefighter Lowell decided to treat himself last night to a visit to one of our city's finest exotic performing arts centers ... Ed, where'd he go?"

"Who the fuck knows? Or cares? I just hope the little shit gets the clap," Lynch retorted, turning the wheel to bring the SUV onto Fifty-Fourth Street. Harry checked his watch. The time was 8:29 a.m.

Connolly snickered. "I think he has a weakness for The Jiggle Room. So, as I was saying, after supporting the arts for the evening, he retired to a suite at the St. Regis, where I'm sure he dined on caviar and filet mignon, among other things." He glanced back with a smirking smile and then to Lynch. "Say what you want about the kid, he knows how to enjoy himself. So, Sturgis, we're the recovery crew who's going to bring him in, so he keeps his job, and we keep ours."

Lynch brought the car onto Madison Avenue, then left on Fifty-Fifth. He stopped the SUV in front of the St. Regis service entrance. He put the strap for his radio across his shoulder and opened his door. "C'mon, probie. Keep your mouth shut and do what Lieu tells you."

The lobby was bustling with well-dressed business executives on their way to meetings, as well as rich European tourists dining in the four-star restaurant when the trio entered.

Harry, wide-eyed, took in the cream-colored terrazzo marble, alabaster stairways, and polished guests, most of whom gave a moment's attention to the three firemen disrupting the ambiance.

Connolly strode to the front desk, smiled at the attractive Asian clerk, showed her his badge, and said, "Jay Lowell's room number, please. Official business."

She did well to act as though this was nothing extraordinary, moved the mouse and did a few clicks, then gave him the room number.

Once inside the mahogany and mirrored elevator, Connolly continued his taunt. "Hey, Eddie. Know what they charge for one night in a suite here?"

"No, Lieu. But I know you're dyin' to tell me."

"Something like fifteen hundred dollars. For you, that's one night here or two months' rent in your studio apartment in Bay Ridge."

Lynch smarted, his lips curled in contempt, just as the elevator door slid open. The trio traipsed down the hall toward a room at the end of the corridor. At the door, they could hear strains of music coming from the other side. Connolly knocked. From inside the room, a female voice spoke, answered by a male voice. The music was quickly shut off.

"Yes?" an accented female voice answered from behind the door.

"Excuse me, ma'am. Is Jay Lowell there?" Connolly asked through the door.

"Yes, he is," the female voice responded. Harry couldn't tell if the accent was Spanish or Russian.

"Miss, can you open the door? Please tell him Lieutenant Connolly is here to see him."

After a brief pause, the door opened. A twenty-year-old leggy brunette with waist-length hair wearing nothing but a white hotel spa bathrobe stood in the doorway. Her bright-red toenail polish accentuated her rose-colored skin. She was wearing hoop earrings the size of hockey pucks.

Connolly smiled at the raven-haired beauty. "Hi there. May we come in?" he asked.

"Please. He's in the bedroom," she answered. The accent was definitely Russian or Eastern European, Harry thought.

Harry trailed the two men across a spacious living room with baroque furnishings. The draperies were open, revealing a commanding view of Fifth Avenue. Off to the side was a room-service cart cluttered with dirty dinner dishes and two empty champagne bottles.

Connolly strolled into the bedroom, where Lowell, wearing only boxer shorts, lay sprawled face down on the king-size bed. Smoke from a lit cigarette drifted lazily upward from an ashtray on the nightstand. He punched Lowell's leg. "Rise and shine. I hope you slept well, Lowell."

Lowell groaned, rolled onto his side, and sat up. He scrubbed a hand through his brown hair, scratched one of his long sideburns, and yawned past the mustache that curled around his upper lip. He squinted at the three men. "What's the deal?"

All but Lowell turned at the sound of the TV in the living room coming on. Lowell's companion sat on the sofa, long legs crossed, scrolling through channels with the remote.

"Your uncle was afraid you might not make it into work today," Connolly explained.

Lowell flopped back on the bed. Eyes closed, he said, "You really didn't need to do this."

Lynch stomped to the window and pulled the drapes open. Brilliant sunlight blasted into the room.

Lowell flung an arm over his eyes. "Ed, did you have to do that? I've got a 747 landing on my head right now—and that … did … not … help."

Harry thought Lowell was a dead ringer for some beat jazz musician. His voice was smooth, possessing a dulcet, low tenor—a most unlikely specimen of a New York City firefighter.

Lynch said, "Harry, turn on the shower. Cold only."

Harry hustled to the bathroom. In seconds, the water was on full blast.

Lynch hoisted a loudly protesting Lowell into a fireman's carry and delivered him into the shower.

Lowell shrieked and cursed.

"Lowell, we'll wait for you in the hallway," Connolly barked. "You have one minute or we'll drag your wet, half-naked ass out of here."

✦

In the ride to the firehouse, Lowell sat in the back of the SUV with Harry, his gaze fixed out the window. No one spoke. Harry studied Lowell, figured he was aimless and could afford to be. Didn't need anything so had no drive to accomplish anything. How could anyone rely on him to respond in life-and-death emergencies? No wonder the guys were put out with him. Lowell's clothes were too large, as though he'd borrowed them from someone better built. Heck, if this guy had made it through the academy and onto 14 Truck, he, Harry Sturgis, had a shot at making it through his first year on the Job.

Lowell sighed and glanced at Harry. "Are you the new probationary firefighter assigned to the company?"

"Yeah."

"Allow me to welcome you to the best truck company in NYC." He shifted so that his body aimed more toward Harry. "Don't listen to anything you hear about us, including from my uncle. My uncle is Captain Hammonds."

"I know."

"Sounds as though you've met him."

"I have."

Connolly glanced at Lynch. "Someone stored Harry's duffel on your uncle's cot. He wasn't amused."

Lowell yawned, then said, "Couldn't resist, could you, Ed?"

"If it *was* me, and I'm not saying it was, Lieu here will take care of it, after this little recovery detail."

Connolly pulled up in front of the station. Harry checked his watch. They'd made it back with two minutes to spare.

Cheers erupted when the four men entered the firehouse. One of the guys called out, "Cover your bet, Reidy."

Lowell smirked and confided to Harry, "They should never doubt me or my brother truckies."

Harry nodded. His attention was drawn to a chalkboard hung on the wall next to the house watch window. Written at the top were the titles Engine 48 and Ladder 14. Underneath was written the riding assignments and responsibilities for the members of the engine and ladder companies on day-tour duty. He stopped in front of the board, already knowing what his assignment would be. He read the list.

OFFICER: CONNOLLY
CHAUFFEUR: LYNCH
OVM: O'RORKE
ROOF: RUFFALO
IRONS: LOWELL
CAN: STURGIS

Low man on the totem pole, he thought. But he knew from the academy there is no "I" in the words *company* or *brotherhood*, and he knew his role, although not as demanding as the other members of the company, was an essential one.

As the junior member on the crew, he was assigned the "can," the portable water fire extinguisher, a job that does not require as much skill as other assignments on the rig but is still vital. At a fire scene, along with a six-foot hook, the can man is required to lug a pressurized water fire extinguisher and use it to douse small fires and contain larger ones. A truck company does not carry hoses and water, so the can man is the only guy who can suppress flames and give the interior crew enough time to conduct a search of a room for occupants.

A good can man knows how to use his extinguisher to buy just enough time to get a primary search done of the fire room before conditions go to shit. If he needs to hold back flames, he dumps the can on the fire to slow it down. If the fire is smoldering, he sprinkles the water like he's watering the garden, to cool the heated fire load so it won't ignite again. Knowing how much water is left in the can and measuring that against what is needed only comes with experience. It's not uncommon that more than one jittery probie has been known to dump the can on the first sign of flames without thinking to conserve the precious wet stuff.

When the can man is a probie, he's attached to the company officer everywhere on the scene and goes only where the company officer orders him. The department had found the life expectancy of probies, or "Johnnies," goes up when they aren't assigned to ventilate a roof on their first assignment. That's because a good case of "probieitis," that combination of youth, a feeling of invincibility, and a rush of adrenaline, will make even the most self-reflective person ignore even the most logical danger, like knowing not to step out on a roof that has more holes in it than a target at a shotgun tournament. No, probies need to take the can and stay right next to their company officers until they're cured of their rookie condition and can function on the fire scene with an unclouded head for business and a nose for danger.

Harry inhaled down to his toes and let it out through his nose.

All he needed to do was follow orders and keep his head.

And he needed a chance to prove himself.

✦

Larry Ruffalo, aka "Truck Larry," wasted no time loading Harry with chores as soon as he returned from the St. Regis Hotel. But Truck Larry made it clear Harry wasn't to do them alone. Engine 48 also had a probie fresh out the academy—Hector Leon, built like a fireplug, short and stout, but with rippling biceps and Popeye forearms, perfect for someone who'd need to wield a two-and-a-half-inch hose, and short enough to stay low when he had to get below the fire and heat.

Harry and Leon cleaned the kitchen, toilets, apparatus floor, house watch, and the day room. They helped to peel potatoes and prepare food under the direction of a senior man who knew little about cooking. At lunchtime, they served the brothers, cleaned up after them, sat down last at meals and got up first to clean up. People at the Rock had prepared him for this. It was all part of the ritual used to break in probies. The brothers put probies through their paces to see how they reacted to orders, no matter how mundane or demeaning. Harry, as it was with Leon, maybe didn't tackle the tasks with a smile, but did so without complaint.

One day while serving lunch, Harry heard some of the guys talk about someone called the Wart. Kept busy, he caught only bits and pieces but got the impression the guy stood out in some way. This impression was boosted when Lowell asked Harry if he'd met the Wart yet.

Harry shook his head.

Lowell smirked. "You won't forget it when you do."

"Is he here?"

"He's on short-term disability. He'll be back in a couple of weeks."

After lunch, Harry was taking care of yet another chore, which led him near the firehouse apron. He stopped what he was doing to watch a man he recognized from the fire in his neighborhood talking to Lieutenant Connolly. It was the fireman who'd done CPR on the kid who hadn't made it. The tall fireman raised one of his tattooed arms, bringing a cigarette to his lips for a drag as he spoke with Connolly. The man wasn't an officer, but he moved with ease, carried himself as though he was the man in charge. When he spoke, he surveyed the street rather than facing Connolly, like he was searching for someone or something, as if speaking with the lieutenant was an inconvenience he had to tolerate. Harry chided himself for imagining this, right until the moment Connolly walked away wearing an annoyed, flustered expression.

Harry began to ask Hector who the fireman was but was cut off when the tones went off. A pang of fear ran up his spine. This was it. The first run. Guys in the house moved toward the rigs, kicked off shoes, threw on turnout coats and bunker pants. Others slid down the pole from the second floor. The veterans' movements were deliberate and swift but not frenzied. Every movement brought them to the rig—engine or ladder—as quickly as possible.

Harry fought the desire to race to the truck, but he knew he had to get his gear in his locker first. He smartly walked to his locker and jumped into his boots and bunker pants. The boots were brand new and hadn't been broken in, so they were difficult to get into. He put on his coat and helmet with his pumpkin-orange helmet shield—standard issue for all probationary firefighters.

He made it into the cab just before the truck started to roll and closed the door behind him. As can man, he sat on the right side of the cab, facing backward toward the hundred-foot rear-mount aerial ladder, which also put him directly behind the officer's seat. He was surprised his hands shook when he fumbled with his turnout coat, trying to adjust it so it would be easy to put on his SCBA, if needed.

Lowell, assigned the irons, sat facing forward across from Harry. He gave a light kick to one of Harry's boots to get his attention.

"Take a breath, Harry. You'll have enough time to gear up."

Harry nodded and swallowed hard. He inhaled through his nose and blew out a breath. He, Harry Sturgis, former nerd king, was on an FDNY truck, responding to an emergency, the piercing sound of the truck's siren ricocheting all over the cab. He glanced at Ruffalo, the outside vent man, who sat in the left front-facing seat, then at the tall fireman who sat laterally across from him.

The tall fireman nodded to Harry. "Do me a favor, probie. Stay close to the lieutenant and follow orders. Okay?"

"Will do." He assessed this guy as someone who fit into the category Hodges at the Rock called *a combat stud with a big swingin' dick*, and someone who could barely tolerate Harry's existence.

In his race to get on the truck without making any mistakes, he'd neglected to listen to the type of alarm Dispatch had toned out. He had no idea if it was a major fire or an automatic alarm. He watched the other guys inside the cab. They didn't seem concerned, which could mean they were the coolest crew in the city or knew the call was minor. His SCBA was located in the recessed hollow of his seat, held there by a metal fastener. He wondered if he should put it on. None of the other guys had theirs on or were so much as considering it. He decided it was best to do what they did and avoid standing out in a negative way.

A transmission from dispatch crackled over the radio. It was meant for the battalion chief who was the assigned incident commander. He was in the SUV traveling ahead of the ladder truck. Harry strained to listen.

The dispatcher said the condo owner had called 911 back. The smoke condition had lifted. Said all it took was for them to take the bread out of the toaster. The battalion chief ordered all units to return to quarters, except Engine 48 and Ladder 14, who were to continue in with the battalion chief to investigate.

The tall, tattooed fireman, still frowning, said, "What a bunch of numbnuts."

Ruffalo and Lowell laughed. Lowell made eye contact with Harry and said, "O'Rorke," he motioned toward the fireman, "our most distinguished member, has no time for the shortcomings of the species. You'll see people do a lot of stupid things in this job."

Harry stared with wide eyes at O'Rorke, recalling how impressive he'd been that day, and how upset when he couldn't save the kid.

So that's his name.

Ruffalo guffawed, glancing to Lowell. "Hey, Jay, how was your evening out?"

Lowell cocked his head and stared out the cab window. "Tatiana. What a young vixen. A true enchantress."

"That means she's hot?"

Lowell turned to Harry. "You saw her. What's your assessment?"

Harry nodded. "She had really pretty eyes."

The rest of the crew groaned.

"Geez, I'm not interested in her eyes," Ruffalo chided.

Harry's cheeks grew warm. "She had a hot body."

Lowell said, "'She walks in beauty, like the night of cloudless climes and starry skies; and all that's best of dark and bright meet in her aspect and her eyes.' And so on."

Harry interjected, "Um ... Byron?"

Lowell's surprise was evident. "Yes. Very good."

Ruffalo gleamed. "Whatever. But you've got the life, eh, Jay? Fancy hotels. Hot broads. Ain't that right, Bryan?

"He's a regular *bon vivant*," O'Rorke replied, adjusting the hose to his SCBA. The guys all shared a chuckle at his smart comeback, including Lowell.

Harry glanced at O'Rorke. He now knew the man's first and last name. All he needed now was to be accepted as one of them, though they were including him in their conversation rather than ignoring him. That was an improvement. If it lasted.

CHAPTER 26

Harry stood on the firehouse apron with a wet mop in his hands, washing 14 Truck. A few feet away Lowell stood, wearing small sunglasses and smoking a cigarette, watching the probie complete yet another chore.

"What is it with civilians and fire trucks?" Harry asked Lowell.

Lowell took a long drag on his cigarette, exhaled, and leaned against the firehouse wall.

"To the civilian," Lowell said, "the fire truck is just another annoying part of the fabric of life, to be tolerated as long as it's needed and no more, gone from the mind once it races past with lights flashing and sirens blaring. It leaves those in its wake happy that it's not stopping anywhere near them, tying up traffic or detouring them from their important daily business."

The irons man flicked ash on the water-soaked apron. Harry continued to douse the side of the truck with soap.

"What they don't like is that it's designed to not let itself be ignored, even by the sneering public. Could you ignore the spectacle of a thirty-seven-ton, rear-mount aerial ladder truck careening around Midtown corners, emitting blinding strobes, alternating red and white flashers, and screeching high-frequency air horns?" Lowell peered over his sunglasses at Harry and pointed to the engine that sat on the apron next to the truck.

"I remember one automatic alarm we got at Tavern on the Green. This very polished septuagenarian asked the truck captain, 'Why do you have to show up in front of a building with the sirens wailing and lights flashing? There's no fire here.' His response was priceless: 'Perhaps you'd want us to send the F.A.R.T. team, ma'am, the False Alarm Response Team? And if we find the flames shooting out of your daughter's bedroom window, then we'll call for the trucks? Would that be a more ... polite way to arrive?' The old biddy bristled in a huff and got into her chauffeured limousine."

Harry laughed. "It seems like some people just don't get it."

Lowell nodded and took off his sunglasses, revealing a suddenly serious demeanor. "Listen, to a lot of guys, the truck is something more, a lot more. It's like it's part of your family. It's your old, reliable father, who's there to have the right tool ready at the right time and never let you down. It's your best friend, who pulls up with you on the scene of something that you know is going to taste like shit, ready to back you up. You wax it to a radiant sheen and show it off to countless generations of children who always come down to the house on Saturday mornings to admire your little bundle of joy. And it's your mother, ready to take you in on those silent trips back to your house, when things went bad on the scene, when you couldn't make the grab, or worse, when you had to return to quarters with an empty seat because one of your brothers got injured or jammed up."

Harry stopped soaping the truck, glanced at Lowell, who was leaning in toward him to press his point, then smiled.

"And the house mechanics. They treat these trucks the way a Kentucky Derby trainer treats his thoroughbreds: with tender care, gentle hands, and a soft word. They fix the engines, chassis, pumping manifolds, and hydraulics with zealous dedication. And sometimes you'll see those guys here at the house, waiting vigilantly for the rigs to return from bad calls, like the ground crew at an English airfield waiting for the returning flights of B-17s in World War II. It's really something else. Nothing like it."

Harry nodded to Lowell and resumed mopping. "Jay, you have a great way of explaining things."

Lowell pressed his lips. "You gotta understand, for a lot of guys, the truck is a refuge away from the house. It's like a chapel where you could collect your thoughts and say your Hail Marys when you're listening to radio transmissions from the incident commander at the scene you're heading to. I know I start praying—and I am not religious—when I hear the IC say those words, 'flames showing, occupants trapped on floors above the fire floor.'"

Harry tensed up a little, grabbed the mop handle a little more firmly, and stared at the truck. "I hope I don't have to hear those words."

Lowell shot Harry a knowing smile. "You will."

✦

Harry's feeling of inclusion into the firehouse culture was short-lived. Being a probie, he was mostly given the silent treatment. Unless someone ordered him to do menial chores around the house or on the fire scene. The guys talked with each other but excluded him and Leon. Only Ruffalo had anything to do with them, because he had to, as he was in charge of "breaking them in," as he'd told them. Otherwise, the probies might as well be invisible to the house veterans. At first, it annoyed and concerned Harry. Then he figured it out—it was up to him to earn their respect. And until that time, he could forget about sitting at the kitchen table to share stories or bullshit with them.

The silent treatment didn't include exclusion from the rituals many new probies got when they first get on the job. On Harry's first night shift, 6 p.m. to 9 a.m., the whine of a partner saw next to his ear woke him up cold. He bolted upright out from his cot and slammed his head into the ventilation duct above his bunk. The perpetrator wore a ski mask and goggles, making identification impossible—not that he was going to do anything about it anyway. On his second night shift, when he got up after rest, he found his face and hair ash white. Someone had put talcum power in his bed before he lay down. He looked like a floured chicken ready for the fryer.

On his second day shift, Harry arrived at the house by seven forty-five. He wanted to get a head start on tasks. He checked the riding assignments, more out of habit than necessity, because he figured he'd be assigned as can man for the foreseeable future. Instead of Ruffalo's name chalked in next to OVM, the outside vent man would be someone named Mangold. He wracked his brain, matching names to faces. Then it struck him—they'd told him the Wart was scheduled to return in the near future. Today was obviously that day.

He went to his locker, put away his personal items, and changed into his navy-blue work clothes. First on his list was to clean the house watch. While inside, the phone rang. He answered and listened to a woman's sultry voice ask to speak to Jim Mangold. Harry told her to hold on a moment, stuck his head out and said, "Reidy, is Mangold here?"

"Should be here any minute."

Harry asked if he could take a message and scribbled the information onto a piece of paper, which he left on the house watch desk. He was on his way back from the utility closet with the mop and soap pail when he spotted a middle-aged man with male-pattern baldness and beady eyes enter the firehouse. He had on civilian clothes and clutched a green-and-black gear bag in one of his hands.

Harry approached him. "Excuse me, are you Jim Mangold?"

"Yeah. Who are you?"

"Probationary firefighter Harry Sturgis. You got a call. I took a message. From Laura. She wants you to call her back." He returned to the house watch. "I wrote down her number." He scooped up the piece of paper and handed it to Mangold.

Mangold scowled at him. "You fuckin' with me, probie?"

Harry's eyes opened wide. "I don't understand."

"Who told you to tell me she called?"

"No one. I took the call when I was cleaning the house watch."

Mangold studied the message. "She say anything else?"

Harry's cheeks flushed. "Yeah. I didn't think I should write it down."

"Well?"

"She said she's sorry about everything and wants to talk to you."

Mangold thrust his fist into the air. "Hot damn. I knew she'd come back. Probie, you just made my day." He grabbed Harry's hand and shook it hard, and then walked away, whistling the theme tune from the old movie *Laura*.

Harry released the tension in his shoulders and dipped the mop into the pail of soapy water.

Mangold stowed his gear and followed the aroma of bacon, eggs, corned beef hash, and fresh coffee to the kitchen where he found Exxon Valdez at the stove. O'Rorke was leaning against a wall, with a cup of coffee in his hands. Lowell sat at the table watching Lynch inhale his breakfast next to Connolly who had the *Daily News* propped in front of his face.

O'Rorke saw him first and walked to him with his hand extended. "Look who's back."

Greetings came from around the room. Mangold grabbed a cup and poured coffee into it. "Couldn't help but hear. You guys had a job last night?"

Connolly said, "A good-size one. Warehouse on Twelfth Street. Just doing the usual blow-by-blow war stories."

Lynch swallowed a sip of coffee. "Jim, you're jacked. You that happy to be back on the job?"

Mangold shrugged. "Truth is, I had mixed feelings about getting back to work." He grinned. "But I got some good news the second I walked in. My day's off to a beautiful start."

O'Rorke arched his eyebrows. "What's up?"

"I got a call I never thought I'd get."

Lowell leaned back. "Not Laura?"

Mangold took a sip and nodded. "Yes, my Ivy League friend. She called to say she was sorry and wants me to call her back."

Connolly lowered the newspaper. "Congratulations." He put the paper down and picked up a Kaiser roll stuffed with an egg, hash, and melted cheddar cheese. He took a bite, ketchup and mustard oozed from its sides.

Mangold put his empty cup in the sink and announced, "I knew she'd come back." He nodded once and exited the room.

Lynch said, "I wonder how long he'll wait to call her back."

Lowell checked his watch. "It's 8:15 now. I give him till 9:05."

✦

Harry glimpsed Mangold shuffle past him and head up the stairs. Hector appeared on the apparatus floor, struggling with three large plastic bags filled with garbage. Harry asked, "How's the committee work going?"

Leon shifted the bags in his arms. "It's going."

Faint music wafted down from the upstairs lounge. Harry stopped to listen, recognizing it as what his mother called big band music. He dipped the mop into the bucket and resumed swabbing the floor. He was near the kitchen when he heard a cell phone ring.

Lowell answered and said hello in a sexy, decidedly *non-male* voice.

Harry swallowed hard, uttered a silent expletive, and moved to the doorway. The guys watched Lowell.

Lowell kept his voice altered and said, "Jim, I'm so glad you called. I wanted you to know how much I miss our times together."

The guys strained to hold back their laughter. Harry strained in a different way, especially as Mangold practically purred in response.

Lowell said, "I hear you. You as the outside vent man, me as the irons man. I feel we have a certain something between us. You feel it too, don't you?"

The line went quiet—followed by a crash upstairs.

Mangold's voice boomed through the phone and from above. "Jay Lowell, you piece of shit!"

Everyone in the kitchen scattered like roaches. Harry flung himself against the wall to avoid being mowed down by the exodus.

Mangold thumped down the stairs, saw Harry, and said, "Where is he? Well, probie?"

"Who?"

Veins throbbed on the side of Mangold's neck. "Lowell is who. I'm gonna kill that little ferret when I get my hands on him."

Snickers came from the other side of the ladder truck. Lynch called out, "Lighten up, Jim. Can't you take a joke?" Voices tittered from unseen places.

Mangold eyed the floor. "Where is that pussy shit?" He aimed a finger at Harry, and said, "You'd better not be in on this, probie."

Lowell stepped out from behind the truck. "Leave the kid alone. He didn't know anything."

Mangold, red-faced and shaking, stopped behind the engine. "I oughta wring your neck."

The crew stepped out from their hiding places.

Lowell assumed a pose that would allow him to flee if needed and said, "C'mon, brother. You have to admit—I got you good."

Mangold blew out a breath and dropped his shoulders and his fists. "Jay, you know how I feel about the girl." He jabbed his head with a finger. "She's in here, you know? It's damn hard to let go. I just hope she's okay."

"I know, and I'm sure she's fine. C'mon, get some breakfast. I'll fill you in on what's been going on around here."

Mangold nodded. "The big job last night. Know what that means, don't you? We'll catch an ever bigger one soon."

"That's how it goes."

"Yeah." Mangold halted his steps. "What worries me is how big and how bad it could be. I got this feeling, you know?"

They approached Harry, who hadn't budged. Lowell said to him, "And that's why we call him the Wart."

"I don't get it."

Lowell lowered his voice and leaned in. "He's a worrywart. Get it now?"

"Oh. Yeah."

"Worries about every damn thing. But wait until you see him at a fire."

✦

Over the course of the next two shifts, Harry got a full dosage of the Wart and found the name completely appropriate for this strange guy. He worried about everything. If he saw a news program about medicines, he told the guys in the house a story about some kid who got paralyzed from his neck down from some bad prescription drug. If he saw a newspaper article about an asteroid passing the Earth, he would launch into a speech about how the world doesn't even know what's headed for it and one day the Earth is going to be hit catastrophically by a meteor.

No event was too small for the Wart to brood over. He sometimes paced nervously around the floor, inspecting gear compartments and hose lines. The guys in the house had gotten so used to his antics, they did not pay him or his behavior any attention. Harry kept his distance from the Wart and wondered why a guy with his disposition would ever choose to become a fireman, where he had to put himself at risk on every shift. To Harry, it made no sense. But then again, he thought, if you're in a profession where your job is to run into a burning building when people are running out, you have to have a screw loose somewhere.

Harry shoved these thoughts to the back of his mind and returned his focus to earning the crew's respect. So far, all he'd been on were jerk jobs or minor emergencies. Seven in total, during his two shifts. He was referred to as a *white cloud*—a probie who catches no real work on the job, as opposed to a *black cloud* probie, who shows up and all hell breaks loose. Feelings about both were mixed in the minds of veterans: quiet shift versus work, no action versus heavy shit.

His next shift was a night one. He arrived and came face to face with O'Rorke, who stood on the house ramp, smoking a cigarette, in front of the ladder truck. He nodded at Harry.

Harry returned the nod and continued to his locker. Taped to the locker was a piece of paper listing a full roster of chores. It wasn't written in Ruffalo's scrawl, who had worked the day shift. Had to be by whoever was doing probie management in his place.

He ran his finger down the list of tasks. He'd been busy for three shifts straight, cleaning the ass-end of everything in the house, including toilets, lockers, floors, drains, sinks. He let out a sigh and went to the kitchen.

Guys from the day and night shifts had all sat down to eat dinner. Harry waited until all the other guys were seated then he grabbed a sandwich and ate it sitting at the corner of the table, not speaking, not being spoken to.

He was mopping the house watch floor when Lowell arrived and gave Harry a thumbs-up before continuing on. After all his training, he'd come here ready to prove himself, only to become a damn firehouse janitor. He swished the mop back and forth, going deeper and deeper into self-imposed misery. He'd reached the point of contemplating whether all his hard effort had been worth it when the alarm ripped through the house, shredding his qualms and self-pity.

"Box 4587. Engine 48. Ladder 14. Respond 231 West Eighteenth

Street. Multiple calls. Fire on sixth floor. Occupants trapped. Everybody goes. Get out."

Whatever doubts Harry had about joining the department disappeared with that transmission from dispatch. He could tell from the serious expression on the guys' faces who were now moving briskly that this was the real deal. No bullshit. It was on in a big way.

He dropped his mop, walked across the floor, jumped into his bunker pants and grabbed his coat and helmet. He kept telling himself, *Fuck them, I can live up to this.* He was surprised that he felt that way. He had never had such an urge to think like this. It was as if he wanted to get even with the guys in his crew, at his house, and anyone else in the whole fucking department who thought he couldn't measure up.

Out of the corner of his eye, Harry saw the Wart, in full bunker gear, standing by the door to the cab. He had a serene look on his face, utterly calm, with the demeanor of a devout catholic who had just left Sunday mass. He was clearly in a different place. Harry thought this guy must be on drugs or something.

Mere seconds later, the Cummins 450-horsepower truck engine fired up, sending a burst of gray smoke from the side exhaust. Harry wondered how Lynch had gotten behind the wheel so fast. He'd just seen him in the kitchen, stuffing his face.

Mangold opened the cab door, calmly climbed inside, and sat in the outside vent man seat. Harry followed him. Lowell entered the cab from the other side where he found O'Rorke, already in his seat, affixing his facepiece to his regulator.

Engine 48 led the way out of the firehouse ahead of Truck 14 that Lynch eased out of its bay with an empty officer's seat. The truck was on the concrete ramp when Connolly flung open the officer's compartment door and jumped in. Before Connolly could get his backside in the seat, Lynch had the Whelen sirens wailing and accelerated up the street to shorten the distance between the truck and the engine.

It was a Sunday night and traffic was nonexistent on Seventh Avenue. This gave the engine and truck chauffeurs an advantage they wasted no time taking. Both apparatuses raced down the avenue like stock cars at a NASCAR junior circuit race. In Truck 14's cab, the crew heard borough dispatch report that a second source reported fire on the sixth floor. Lynch pushed the rear mount almost up the backside of Engine 48, the handheld radio pressed to his ear with his right hand.

"Battalion just banged a 10-75. Called for a full assignment—four engines, two trucks, rescue, squad, and another battalion chief," Lynch shouted to those in the cab. "Major working fire, bros."

"Mangold, you'll come inside with us. We're gonna need more help in there," Connolly told his outside vent man.

Harry drew his eyebrows together. "I thought the outside vent man on the first due rig was supposed to work on the exterior of the building with the roof man?" he asked Lowell.

"Unless the lieutenant needs more help on the inside. This is one of those times. Better gear up, probie," Lowell answered.

Mangold sat in his seat, a smile on his face. Harry shook off what he considered an inexplicable disposition given the apparent circumstances and donned his SCBA, then fastened his facemask to the regulator and hose. He reached for the knob to open the airflow on the tank.

Lowell waved a hand in front of Harry's face. Over the nearly deafening siren wail, he yelled, "Not yet. Wait until we get inside. Otherwise, you'll set off the mask's PASS alarm."

Harry lowered his head to hide his warmed cheeks. He'd nearly committed a stupid probie move, and at the worst time. He didn't dare eye the others, especially O'Rorke. Any expression of derision they might aim at him was too much to deal with at the moment, even if he did deserve it.

Lynch swung the thirty-seven-ton Seagrave right onto Eighteenth Street, giving Harry a visual on the fire building, a fourteen-story concrete apartment house, located midway between Seventh and Sixth Avenues. Thick, dark smoke belched from a window about halfway up from the street.

The engine pulled ahead of the building to let 14 Truck set up directly in front of the structure. Lynch eased the truck into the space left by the engine. The second he set the brake, the crew dismounted from the cab, grabbed their tools, and opened their SCBAs.

Lowell grabbed the irons next to his seat and hopped down.

Harry was right behind him. As soon as his feet touched ground, he went to the side compartment to get the can.

Mangold pulled a six-foot hook from the side of the truck, as well as a halligan tool.

O'Rorke went to the rear of the truck, ascended the stairs to the turntable, and waited for Lynch, who was pulling the controls for the aerial ladder.

A white-haired, black-mustached battalion chief approached Connolly and his interior crew at the building entrance, handie-talkie pressed to his ear. "Get your crew up there. I've got reports of trapped civilians on the sixth floor." He pressed the button on his handie-talkie and barked, "Battalion to 28 Truck. You've got outside vent. Fourteen is going in for a grab."

Connolly nodded and walked into the building, followed by Mangold, Lowell, and Harry. Civilians made their way down the stairs past the crew en route to the fire floor. Even in the cement-encased stairwell, the smell of smoke got stronger with each floor the crew passed. When they reached the landing of the sixth floor, they came upon a middle-aged guy in sweats, coughing, trying to gain his composure. Connolly asked him if he could make it down the stairs on his own. He nodded and staggered past the crew. Harry heard familiar voices a few stories below and realized 48 Engine's crew was making their way up the stairs.

The metal door to the sixth-floor hallway had a small wire-mesh window in it that Connolly tried to peer through without success.

The floor was filled with smoke, making visibility challenging.

"Mask up," he told the crew, who complied and removed their helmets to don their SCBA facemasks.

Once headbands were tightened, seals formed between their heads and the masks, the crew crouched down behind their lieutenant. As he opened the door, smoke spilled out into the stairwell. The sound of demand valves releasing clean air into the SCBA masks could be heard, followed by the eerie hiss of air filling the mask and the lungs of the crew.

Connolly crouched and moved into the public hallway, followed in line by Harry, Mangold, and Lowell. The crew encountered a grayish haze with clean air along the floor and dense smoke at the end of the hallway. They quickly moved down the hallway until they came upon a locked apartment door with heavy smoke pushing from around it and fire shooting through the peephole.

"How rude," Lowell said, his voice muffled through his facemask. Connolly scanned the door and the doorframe. He took a position on the right side of the door and knelt down.

"Take the door," Connolly said. "48 should be up here in a minute."

✦

Mangold knew what to expect once that door was popped. He knelt behind Connolly, very still, to conserve the strength and energy he knew he was going to need as soon as Lowell and the probie took the door. Once that door opened, the Beast would be all over him, if it hadn't already vented out the window. Connolly had enough sense on this job to ask for more help on the interior search—which is why Mangold was there and not outside pulling windows. Rescue work—it was never easy and sometimes fruitless. And the outside vent man found himself on that assignment more times than he wanted. The outside vent man worked alone at a fire. He was responsible for ventilating—finding ways to enable the smoke, flame, and heat to escape and cool the fire building. If he didn't do his job quickly, the interior search team would be chewing on smoke and heat, jabbing around looking for victims in the hazy darkness as the building got hotter. Only a veteran firefighter would be given the outside vent assignment. Someone who had enough years on the Job, after having worked the other truck company assignments, that he knew the role of every fireman on the fire scene the way a choreographer knows every dancer's role in a ballet. On immediate rescues, he would be pulled inside to help the forcible entry team locate victims, like today. And he was usually the first one into the fire room when the door opened. If someone was going to be lost searching for victims, it would likely be him. He was like an infantryman walking point into an ambush that was arranged just for him, but without the element of surprise. He knew what he was crawling into but not whether he could get out. The outside vent man always ended up in the most desperate situations. The hapless bastard thrown into the volcano to be immolated searching for the hapless victim.

Mangold knew it was pointless to even think about what he was doing. Just let muscle memory and experience take over and put a good thought on it. Hopefully, he'd survive.

✦

Lowell moved to the left side of the door and leaned the flathead axe against the hallway wall. He took the halligan tool and jammed the claw end into the doorjamb, just above the lock at a forty-five-degree angle, leaving the adze end of the tool ready for striking. Harry put his can down and picked up the eight-pound flathead axe. He now had a very simple but important job. He had to take the flathead side of the axe and strike the halligan tool with enough force to push the claw end into the doorjamb. Too much force and he could miss and clock Jay. Too little and the strikes would be useless. *Stay focused*, he thought.

"Hit," Lowell commanded.

Harry gave the axe a swing with moderate force, making a direct hit against the adze. The clank of metal on metal broke the still silence in the deserted hallway.

Lowell moved the halligan, wedging it farther into the jamb. "Hit."

Harry gave the tool a second strike. He could feel the halligan inching slightly deeper into the jamb. Jay moved the halligan up and down, causing the door to bend back.

"Hit," Lowell said. He gave the halligan another shot. The halligan was deep into the jamb, so that now the doorframe's outline was clearly demarcated in orange from the fire on the other side.

"Stop," Lowell said, waving for Harry to stand behind him. Lowell worked the halligan tool around the lock like he was back at Princeton rowing crew until the door gave way. Without wasting a moment, Connolly took Mangold's halligan, violently shoved open the apartment door, and spun back against the wall and lowered his head.

The inferno that shot out of the door shocked Harry. Flames, smoke, and heat erupted into the hallway with a vengeance and spilled burning material onto the floor around the four men. Harry watched in awe. At that moment, he realized he was up against a living, breathing enemy that was out to kill him and anybody else that got in its way. Full-throated flames blasted out the upper two-thirds of the doorway. No one could enter that room, and whoever was in there was surely dead, he thought.

He thought wrong. And he couldn't believe what he saw next.

Mangold crawled past Lieutenant Connolly, deftly grabbed his halligan tool, and disappeared under the flames into the room. Lowell followed him with his halligan. In that instant, whatever doubts Harry had about either of these two brothers were dispelled as he watched them crawl into that furnace.

Connolly shouted, "Use the can."

Harry grabbed the extinguisher, pointed the nozzle at the fire, and squeezed the handle, keeping his thumb over the nozzle to fan the stream onto the fire. *Like throwing a snowball at a volcano*, he thought.

Connolly said, "Stay here. I've got to bring forty-eight up here." He crawled down the darkened hallway, toward the stairwell door.

Harry watched the lieutenant's progress for a moment, until his attention was drawn back to sounds inside the apartment. Mangold and Lowell were pushing furniture around as they conducted their search.

Harry felt beads of sweat roll down his back. Over his head, the fire that had vented into the hallway was working its way to the ceiling, burning wallpaper, paint, wood, and anything else that would melt at fifteen hundred degrees.

✦

Crushing heat came down on Mangold, as though someone had pressed a clothes iron on his bunker gear with him in it. He lay prone on the ground with his right hand on the wall, feeling his way into the room. Holding the halligan tool in his left hand, he swept the floor, hoping to hit something that might resemble a body part. Lowell followed and entered the room. He went to the left, using his left hand to guide him into the room and sweeping with his halligan in his right hand.

"Jay, where are you?" Mangold called out calmly, unable to see through his facemask other than an orange glow and the contours of dark pieces of furniture.

"I've found a doorway on the left, going in," Lowell responded.

Mangold was now under a windowsill against the wall opposite the door. He still had not located anyone in the room. He swung his halligan methodically but hit nothing. From the hallway, he heard what sounded like a thump.

"I got one," Lowell called out. "Near the hallway on the left side of the room."

The outside vent man quickened his search of the final corner of the room. The flames were now banking down toward the sofa that he was crawling next to, and it was just a matter of time before that piece went up like a roman candle at Mardi Gras, he thought. It was really hot, punishing heat, and the sweat on his body now made him feel like he could swim in his gear. He moved along the sofa and found the opening to the interior hallway. Out of his now fogging-up mask, he could see Jay's boots lying next to the pants legs and bare feet of an unconscious woman. She was face down. Lowell tugged her arm, but she didn't move. She was a large woman, about two hundred pounds. This was going to be no easy carry.

Lowell turned back to Mangold. "Jim, gimme some help."

Mangold grabbed hold of her shoulders and turned her over on her back. When he did so, they saw the baby, no more than a year old, she was cradling in her arms, also unconscious.

"Shit, there's a baby," Lowell shouted.

Mangold keyed his handie-talkie and pulled the mike up to his mask. "Fourteen inside team to Command. We've got two 10-45s. Adult female and infant inside the fire apartment. Will attempt to remove to public hallway. We need a line up here." His voice remained calm and clear, like a radio announcer for a classical music station.

The incident commander responded, "Copy that, fourteen. Forty-eight should be at your location momentarily."

Mangold scanned the living room. "This place is gonna go fast."

"You're telling me," Lowell responded.

Mangold peered toward the door but couldn't see anything except a large volume of fire starting to bank down again through the door to the hallway. He pondered his options. He could try to make the door with only the baby and leave the mother. Not a good long-term family solution, he thought. He could find a spot in another room to buy some time so the engine crew could get into operation and hopefully hold this thing back. Well, the room was hot enough already, and he may run out of time. That would be good headline for the tabloids: two firemen and two civilians perish in a Lower West Side blaze. Not the best option, but it may the only one. Lowell struggled to get the woman into a position to pull her out the front door, the baby lying motionless on the floor next to her. The solution finally dawned on Mangold. He needed the kid in here. *Man up time for the probie.*

"Harry?" Mangold called out.

"Yeah, Jim."

"We need you in here. Come in on the left and feel your way along the wall to us," he said calmly.

"Jim, there's too much fire in the doorway. I can't get in," Harry responded.

"Probie, you gotta trust me, get in here now."

"Jim, the heat's—"

"Tell him to hold on," Connolly's voice bellowed from down the hall.

Harry peered down the hall to see the silhouette of a fireman, followed by three more, dragging a limp hose line toward him. It was Connolly and 48 Engine's crew. Connolly got to the doorway and leaned in, pushing Harry back out of the doorway.

"Jim, get down, I've got 48 setting up to knock it down."

"Okay," Mangold responded. He scanned the room and spotted a coffee table a few feet away from him. He pulled it next to the hallway door. The flames moved closer to banking down onto the top of it.

"Jay, put the baby next to her and lay on top of the mother." Mangold leaned the coffee table on its side and placed it between the four of them and the doorway. He then lay next to Lowell over the baby.

"Get small," Mangold said as he pushed his head down toward the ground. Lowell did the same.

"Jim, sit tight, 48 will be on it in thirty seconds. Is Lowell with you?" Connolly called into the room.

There was no answer. Connolly put his head down and quietly cursed. The line rose off the hallway floor, taut, filled up with water. The nozzle man knelt in the doorway with his backup man right behind him. PASS alerts began to chirp from Mangold and Lowell's masks, a sign they weren't moving.

The nozzle man wasted no time bleeding the line for air. He knelt down at the doorway and pulled back hard on the smooth bore's handle. The straight stream went right at the combustible gases at the ceiling and disrupted the thermal balance immediately. After ten seconds of painting the ceiling, he banked the stream down and shot straight for the window which had been blown out. Water, heat, and flame shot out of the window like the discharge from a field cannon.

Mangold peered back toward the apartment door. He could tell the guy on the knob knew what he was doing. If he left the stream on the ceiling, he would only thwart the possibility of a flashover and would have only held the fire at bay. The nozzle man knew he had to get to its source on the floor as soon as he could. But there were people in the room he needed to protect. So he shot for the window to drive the heat and flame away from the rescue crew and their victims. In doing so, the stream entrained flame, heat, and air with the water, drawing the flames away from Lowell and him lying in their prone position, protecting the mother and child. Then, he would bring the stream down to the floor and knock out the burning room and contents.

It lasted only twenty seconds, but it felt like an eternity to Mangold. The punishing heat had finally saturated Mangold's bunker gear to a point where he could really feel the heat on his skin. Lowell coughed in his mask, taking in big gulps of air. It had been twenty minutes since he turned on his mask, and his low-pressure alert started ticking audibly.

Mangold tensed his muscles and clenched his jaw. *It should let up soon*, he thought, *one way or another.* He thought, *you know, when I die, I know I'm going to heaven because I've already been to hell.* The ironic thought made him smile. He had sweated to the point that perspiration had filled up his facepiece like he was a skin diver with a leaky mask. The flames pressed onto the back of his bunker coat like steak knives.

Then, a little bit at first and more soon after, it eased. The crackling and popping of burning materials gave way to the friendly, beautiful drone of cascading water hitting hard surfaces and ricocheting in all directions. The air became lighter, and the temperature cooled. Visibility improved. The macabre orange glow that had enveloped him was replaced by a grayish pallor that reminded him how beautiful the mundane could be. He and Lowell had, once again, passed through that portal that only they could, and came out on the other side with, hopefully, two hearts that would go on ticking long after he and Lowell left this earth. *God*, Mangold thought, *can there be anything more beautiful than the perfection of this moment?* It was righteously humbling.

"Jim, can you hear me?" The voice of Connolly rose over the chutes of water now turning the room into a backyard kiddie pool.

Mangold sat up. "Lieu, we've got a mother and baby in here. Get Bryan to the window, now."

He picked up the baby and took her to the window, pushing charred furniture out of the way. To his relief, when he reached the window, he saw Bryan O'Rorke perched at the end of the aerial ladder, right up against the window to the adjoining apartment. He held up his open palms as if to say *What took you so long?*

"Hold on," O'Rorke told Mangold. He motioned to Lynch on the turntable fifty feet below him to move the ladder to the right. In one motion, Lynch directed the aerial ladder off the fire escape for the adjoining apartment and placed the top of the ladder right against the windowsill in front of Mangold.

Mangold handed the baby to O'Rorke, who descended

one-handed backward down the ladder, all the while pushing clean air in the baby's lungs. He watched O'Rorke hand the baby to the EMT crew waiting at the foot of the turntable.

In the fire apartment, Harry crawled in along the left wall to Lowell, who had gotten the unconscious mother into an upright sitting position and placed his shoulder underneath her armpit. Harry helped Lowell drag the unconscious victim out of the apartment behind the hose team that had now advanced ten feet into the fire room and knocked down lingering pockets of fire.

In the hallway, Lowell laid the woman down on her back, took off his mask, and gave her mouth-to-mouth resuscitation. Harry was about to straddle the victim and begin compressions on her chest when he felt a tap on his shoulder. Mangold stood over him and waved him off. The outside vent man had taken off his helmet and gloves, and his mask sat on his forehead like the Tin Man's funnel hat in *The Wizard of Oz*. His face was bright red, his hair matted down and pasted to his forehead.

"Get the irons," Mangold ordered Harry dismissively.

Harry stood up and made his way into the fire apartment while Mangold assisted Lowell in administering CPR. Harry gathered up the two halligan tools and the flathead axe. When he returned to the hallway, an EMT crew had arrived with a gurney and placed a backboard under the mother as Jay and Mangold continued CPR. The EMT crew lifted the gurney to waist level and wheeled it to the elevator. Jay and Mangold were relieved at the elevator by a second EMT crew. The interior crew and Lieutenant Connolly watched the elevator's doors close as the EMTs continued CPR. The woman had not regained consciousness.

Mangold said, "What took you guys so long?"

Connolly faced the crew. "The standpipe connection at the street was fucked. The clapper valve on the Siamese was jammed shut. Took 48 time to run a line up the stairs."

Mangold bristled. "That was close, in there."

Lowell slapped Mangold on the back and said, "You weren't worried, were you?"

"Let's just say there were a few things that concerned me."

◆

On the rig heading back to the house, Lowell sat in his jump seat, totally spent from the grab. Mangold sat on the other side of the cab, staring out the window, running a piece of insulated wire through his fingers. O'Rorke occasionally eyed Harry askance from his seat. No one said anything to the probie. They didn't have to. It was clear to Harry they were not happy with how he acquitted himself at the job. Lowell flashed two fingers to Harry to get his attention, then shifted in his seat.

"You know, Mangold, there's no reason to deny it."

Mangold kept his gaze out the window. "Deny what?"

"If you want to curl up next to me, I understand."

Mangold, brow fully furrowed, pulled his arm inside. "I saw something on the news yesterday about a new strain of flu they got no cure for—bird flu. Said if it spreads, it could kill thousands of people every day. If it comes here, we're all goners. I'm worried that—"

Lowell chuckled. "The Wart's back."

The other crew members cackled, all but Harry, who felt he'd given the Wart and the rest of the crew something else to worry about. He was sure of it.

CHAPTER 27

O'Rorke closed his eyes while the truck backed into the firehouse and thought about what Harry needed.

There is, among firemen, a rarely spoken truth. It is raised only in the quiet, at the house, away from the action, usually when the guys are looking back at some job and what went down there. It does not show itself at every job, but it exists and reveals itself usually at the most inopportune times, when things are turning to shit quickly. It has different names—courage, guts, balls. Whatever it's called, it sets some firemen apart from others. Many times, the question of whether someone will live or die depends on whether or not a fireman has the Trait. The Trait is the behavior, either intentional or subconscious, to not withdraw from perceived, imminent danger—but to face it, engage it, and subdue it. Some call it courage, but it's not as conspicuous.

Some firemen don't have the Trait. They will talk a good talk, get on the rig, follow the routine of the Job, perform the most menial tasks, and avoid assignments that could put them at risk. If they happen to end up at a job where they might actually need to put themselves in harm's way, their danger antenna goes up, and they hang back a little and wait for a real combat stud to step up and take the assignment; the pretenders quietly fade into the background and make themselves as inconspicuous as possible. Many times, on the Job, life or death is determined by those guys who exhibit the Trait.

O'Rorke loved to find out who had the Trait, but more importantly, who didn't. When a new guy was assigned to his crew, he'd watch to see how the guy reacted to a dicey situation. He would give a new guy a somewhat dangerous task and observe how he handled it. If the guy embraced the assignment without hesitation, he was a candidate for more dangerous work. If he dawdled or slowed down, O'Rorke flagged him for greater observation or more direct attention. Such guys, more times than not, put in for a transfer to a slower house. Sometimes a guy surprised O'Rorke by passing his little tests. In O'Rorke's mind these tests were the only way to determine if the guy could bring "it" when he needed to.

O'Rorke knew he had to find out if Harry had the Trait.

✦

After 14 Truck was parked in the bay at the firehouse, Harry got to work cleaning the tools used for the fire, salvaging, and overhauling the building. He kept his eyes aimed at whatever he was doing, deliberately avoiding the expressions of contempt on the faces of the others, and certain there would be a consequence for not complying with Mangold's request. He'd had a knot in his stomach since Mangold had taken over the CPR Harry never got a chance to start. As he cleaned, he replayed events over and over in his mind.

A voice crackled through the intercom. "Sturgis, report to the kitchen."

In no way did it sound like a friendly request.

Harry stowed the axe he'd been cleaning and headed for the

kitchen. He stopped in the doorway to survey the scene, to see if he could determine anything about what might be about to happen.

Mangold, still in his bunker pants, and Lowell were at the table, stuffing pot roast and stewed vegetables into their mouths. O'Rorke stood at the far wall, studying the picture of Miss August on the *Playboy* calendar tacked up inside the door to the broom closet.

Lynch made eye contact with Harry and pointed to the one empty chair at the table.

Harry moved forward, glancing at the faces of his crew. No one returned the glance. He took the seat and stared at the sugar bowl at the center of the table.

Silence hung in the air until Mangold, his eyes aimed at his food, said, "Harry, would you mind getting me and Jay some beers?"

Harry didn't hesitate. He went out the back door, grabbed two Millers from the cooler in the backyard, and placed them on the table in front of Mangold and Lowell.

Mangold said, "Thanks," and continued eating.

Harry remained standing, unsure whether or not he was supposed to sit again. Feeling awkward, he decided to sit, elbows pressed to his sides, linked hands in his lap.

"Probie, you want a beer?" O'Rorke asked.

"Nah, I'm good."

O'Rorke walked to the table, picked up the beer in front of Mangold, and walked to where Harry sat. "I think you could use one." He popped the tab, raised his hand, and slowly poured the whole beer onto Harry's head.

Beer cascaded over Harry, down his shirt, into his lap, and onto the table. He aimed his gaze at the far wall and kept silent.

Lynch, Mangold, Lowell, and the others laughed at the ritual they appeared to know so well.

Leon walked in and saw what was happening. He joined the laughter, caught himself, and stopped.

O'Rorke put the empty can on the table and said, "What are you laughing at, you puke?" He grabbed the other beer, pulled the tab, and poured it over Harry.

The guys laughed even harder.

Leon, jaw dropped, stood like a stone.

"Probie, you can thank that shit-for-brains against the wall for this one," O'Rorke said. "Do you have any idea why we called you in here?" he asked, returning to his examination of the buxom Miss August on the calendar.

"Yeah," Harry said, his words muffled from the beer dripping down his face. "I didn't follow orders."

"Okay. That's a good start. If you're gonna make it in this job, you have to learn to follow orders. Doesn't matter what you think about them. You understand what I'm saying?"

Harry lowered his head. "Yes."

"Never question an order from one of these guys, even if you think it's crazy. Follow it. Mangold's been on this job since before you were crapping your diaper. He's seen enough shit to know what the fuck is going on in a fire."

Harry nodded to Mangold, who didn't look at him.

O'Rorke stood over Harry. "You want to make it in this house, you need to grow a pair. Were you raised by two women or something?"

Harry's tone was flat. "Only one."

"Let me make this clear. This is 14 Truck. The best damn truck company in the city. I don't know how you got assigned here, nor do I care. What I care about is that you're gonna be there when me or one of these guys need you. Understood?"

Harry sat up straight. "It won't happen again."

O'Rorke fixed a smirk on his face. "We're gonna make sure it doesn't. From now on, when you're done with your shift, you report to me for additional training. Got it?"

Harry eyed the other firemen in the kitchen. Only O'Rorke and Leon focused on him. He swallowed hard. He'd let the men down. And that outweighed any sense of danger he'd perceived while kneeling inside the fiery doorway two hours ago. He met O'Rorke's eyes and said, "Yes, sir."

"All right. Get out of here and back to work."

Harry, head down, left the kitchen, carrying his shame with him.

Halfway across the apparatus floor, some of the darkness began to lift—they were giving him another chance.

✦

Harry asked some of the guys what O'Rorke's extra training might involve. They stayed tight-lipped. He figured he'd just have to go with it and take whatever came. Two night shifts later, 14 Truck caught a motor vehicle accident on the West Side Highway and a small kitchen fire at a restaurant in the West Twenties. At the end of the shift, O'Rorke, staying true to his word, laid out a "highrise pack" on the apparatus floor—a coiled fifty-foot section of hose with a smooth-bore nozzle attached, used for fighting fire on upper floors.

O'Rorke lit a Winston, inhaled, and while exhaling said, "Pick up the pack. Walk up the stairs to the third floor, then back down. Do it until I tell you to stop."

Harry, dressed in bunker gear and gloves, picked up the pack and started up the stairs. An hour and thirty round trips later, O'Rorke told him to stop. The pack felt like it weighed five hundred pounds. His gear was soaked with sweat.

"Get changed," O'Rorke told him. "Meet me after the next shift."

The training grew more rigorous with each session. One time, Harry did a hundred push-ups with a section of an inch and three-quarter hose on his back. Another time, he unpacked and repacked hydraulic tools and equipment on the ladder truck. It didn't take him long to figure out the drills were designed to get him to act on orders and not think. He realized the repetitiveness was meant to be painful so when he was ordered to do something, he should just do it, get it done, and get it behind him so he could be rewarded by not having to do it over and over again.

Most of the guys were usually heading home after their tour when the training sessions began. The guys on the next shift got a big kick out of watching O'Rorke put him through the paces. The officers on duty turned a blind eye, knowing that sometimes a little "close-in treatment" had to be applied to turn a reluctant probie into a reliable asset for the company.

✦

The basement of the hundred-year-old firehouse had a warren of rooms and storage areas, built when coal burners heated the house and steam engines were pulled by horse-drawn carriages. Horseshoes, nails, bridles, and brass nozzles were sometimes found under a century's worth of debris and crud. The few people who went down there did so just for a moment or to take a brief trip through history. Plus, there was the enticement of the ghosts of the original owners reported to haunt the space.

Harry, following orders, had on his full bunker gear, facepiece, and mask. He followed O'Rorke to the basement.

O'Rorke handed Harry an axe and turned on his mask. Then, he covered Harry's facepiece with his Nomex hood so he couldn't see anything, spun him around, and faced him to a wall. "Okay, rubber, find your way out of here before your thirty minutes of air runs out."

Harry knelt against the wall in the darkness of the basement and the interior darkness of his mask. He told himself to relax and use his head, or he would never get through this. He paced his breathing to avoid unnecessarily using up air. He tried to construct an image of the layout of the basement in his mind's eye.

Harry moved a gloved hand along the wall as he crawled forward. He found a corner. Followed the connecting wall until he reached another corner. Followed the new wall, found another corner, and repeated this process. Four walls in total, but he couldn't find the door.

Exhaustion crept into his body. He'd put in a full day's work responding to a car accident and a chimney fire, where he'd carried equipment up eleven flights of stairs.

Where's the door?

In the absolute blackness, he continued to feel along the wall, pacing himself. He decided that this time around the room, he'd push on the flat surface to see if he could find a door. First wall—nothing moved. Second wall—the planking creaked, bent, but had no real give. Third wall—movement. He pushed hard. The wall swung back until it hit something. He'd found the door. He shoved the butt end of the axe against it, pushing it farther out. A second shove caused it to give way completely. Harry crawled through the doorway, praying it really was one.

Now what?

He caught himself breathing too fast, slowed his breaths, and kept going. He felt around on the ground, searching for a wall, unable to find one. He backed up to the doorway he'd just crawled through. He reoriented himself by finding the wall to the side. He moved along the wall to the right, imagined he was in a hallway. Moved about twenty feet and found a corner, turned right, and continued his search for another door, stairs, anything.

A sound he'd heard before came from somewhere ahead of him—running water. Like when a fire hose is dousing flames and hits a wall. He moved toward the noise. It sounded close and in a direction where there was no wall. Simulation or not, he needed to take a chance if he wanted to get out. He told himself he'd die undiscovered in here if he didn't find that hose line.

He steadied his breathing and crawled away from the wall, keeping contact with the wall with his right foot. He moved slowly, swept the axe ahead of him, trying to connect with the line. He moved forward by two feet. Three feet. Six feet. Nothing.

He stretched his left arm out as far as it could reach, moving it in an arc, the sound of the water getting louder with his slow progress.

Anxious to get out, his breaths quickened. Crushing darkness began to play tricks with his mind. Even the sound of his bunker gear scraping against the floor got to him, disoriented him. He paused, chided himself for giving in to panic.

It was time to move away from the wall. If he didn't find the line within five feet, he'd go back to the wall and try something else, with whatever air he had left in his tank.

He fixated on the sound and moved in that direction, still swinging the axe ahead of him, still making no contact. Until he'd gone four feet forward and hit something. He stopped moving and crawled toward the obstruction. He grabbed hold of it, his gloved fingers curling around the nylon fabric of an attack line that pulsated with water flowing through it.

"Yes!" He let go of the axe, grabbed the line and ran his hands along it, crawling, until he came upon the coupling connecting it with the next section. He hands first touched the smooth aluminum metal mouth of the coupling's female end. On the other side of the connection, he felt the raised rocker lugs of the coupling's male shank. He breathed a sigh of relief. He knew he could follow the hose line in the direction of the smooth ends and work his way out of this wretched basement.

Before he could focus his thoughts fully, the low-air alert sounded. He had ten minutes of air left. Harry stayed low, crawled along the line, followed its every turn, bend, and coil for, he calculated, about thirty feet, when the line lifted off the floor. He was going to get out of this black abyss.

His hand found stairs. He crawled upward, spilled onto the sidewalk, and stayed there on his back. Evening light seeped under his hood through the edges of his facemask. He removed the mask and hood. Eyes closed, he drank in the fresh air. He opened his eyes. O'Rorke, cigarette in hand, leaned against a car parked on the street.

Harry's eyes went to the hose line connected to the hydrant. A hydrant wrench was atop the screw above the bonnet.

"You lost your axe, probie."

Harry sucked in a few more deep breaths and then rolled onto his knees, totally spent.

O'Rorke stepped away from the car. "Get up, rubber. We're not done." He walked into the firehouse.

Harry sighed, got to his feet, and went inside.

O'Rorke said, "Take off your gear." He let a few seconds pass and said, "Then run in place."

Harry removed his bunker gear and got into his work boots.

"Heads up." O'Rorke tossed a halligan tool to Harry.

This guy gets off on this shit. Guess he thinks he needs to show me he's a real badass and I'm just a punk. He started running in place, holding the halligan tool in front of him.

O'Rorke walked away. As he did this he said, "Hold it over your head and get over here." He got onto the ramp and took the small, 1¾ -inch line with fog nozzle and handle into his hands.

Halligan over his head, Harry jogged toward O'Rorke. Fatigue was setting in. His energy faltered.

"C'mon, pussy," O'Rorke shouted. "Keep going." Still holding the attack line, he said, "I checked around. You grew up in a broken home. Your father was a loser. Well?"

"Yes, Firefighter O'Rorke." All he had to do was get through this. Then he'd collapse, sleep, and prepare for more of the same. He wondered how long this *training* would go on then decided to put that out of his mind. It was out of his control unless he quit altogether.

O'Rorke pulled back lightly on the nozzle, sprayed Harry and said, "What makes you think you can be a fireman?"

Harry tilted his head up a few degrees. The spray was refreshing, needed. He told himself not to take the bait and quickened his pace. Told himself if he bit on that hook, he'd be done. And if that's what O'Rorke wanted, he could forget it.

"I asked you a question, probie."

"I can do this, sir."

O'Rorke shut down the stream. "This is a man's job, not some teenage girl's. That's what you acted like. How am I supposed to believe you're gonna back me up when I need you inside on a grab? Maybe you want to stay at the curb with the rest of the char babies."

Harry raised the halligan higher over his head and sped his pace.

O'Rorke came toward him, stood to the side, leaning in until his face was six inches from Harry's.

Harry stared ahead, knees bouncing.

"Probie, we both know you're not cut out for the Job. You should be in college with the rest of the smart guys, somewhere where you can feel special, not where men can live or die any day of the week." He softened his tone. "It's okay to admit it. You know you want to."

"No, sir. I'm a firefighter, sir."

O'Rorke backed up a yard and hit Harry with another blast of water, harder than the first time.

The stream knocked Harry to the side, but he stayed upright, halligan high, feet pumping. He shook water from his face and ignored the several brothers who'd gathered to watch.

"Ready to quit, rubber?"

"No, sir."

"Fuck you, probie."

"I'm not gonna quit."

"Fuck you. Quit, damn it. I want you out of my crew."

"No way, sir. Never."

O'Rorke moved around to the front and hit Harry dead-center on the chest with a stronger blast of water.

The blast knocked Harry back. He slipped and spun in an attempt to regain his balance. His head hit the brick encased column between the two bays. Blood spurted from the cut on his forehead. The halligan tool hit the concrete apron. Harry lay next to it, dazed. After a few seconds, blood streaming down his wet face, he rolled onto his knees, grabbed the halligan and got up, slowly, to his feet. He raised the halligan over his head and ran in place.

The brothers watching him applauded.

Harry shook his head in an attempt to clear his blurred vision. He pumped his legs as best he could, determined not to give that bastard O'Rorke the satisfaction of forcing him out. "Do it again, sir."

The corners of O'Rorke's lips turned up slightly.

Captain Hammonds's voice boomed, "O'Rorke. Cut this crap out!"

O'Rorke leaned over Harry. "Next time you're in the shit, remember what you learned here," he said tightly.

Hammonds grabbed the line from O'Rorke. A vein throbbed at the middle of his forehead. "I'm sick and tired of your cowboy bullshit. You're way out of line. I'm writing you up for this. When Legal Affairs is done with you, you'll be filing medical reports at headquarters. If you're lucky." He turned to Ruffalo. "Clean Sturgis up and check him out."

He shoved the line to O'Rorke, who took it and said, "Better call your union rep. You're done."

The brothers, shock clear on their faces, dispersed. Harry's blood swirled and thinned in the water spreading across the concrete apron.

Harry raised his head to the sky and took in a deep breath. A wave of relief washed over him blanketing the pain. For the first time, he started to think he could make it on the Job.

CHAPTER 28

Boyle sat at one of the tables positioned on the sidewalk outside the Two Crows Café at the corner of West Broadway and Thomas Street. He liked this place, especially the vantage point it gave him to people watch, and there was no time better to do this than a lazy Sunday afternoon in the city. Because of the Job, he viewed civilians differently than most. While others might see people walking down the street, their minds obviously on what they needed to do or family or work issues, giving little notice to their surroundings, he saw them as people in his charge. He alone knew how, in an instant, their lives could turn to shit. A moment when they found themselves in the desperate place Chief Brendan spoke about at Denny's funeral, one when he'd have to do something to help them.

This was one of the reasons he loved the Job as much as he did. Making a lot of money didn't jack him up. Doing so would never give him the satisfaction rescue work did. The Job completed him.

As he waited, memories came to him of when he was a young

probie at his first job—a tenement fire in Brooklyn. When the engine arrived at the front of the building, the captain saw nothing and called in a false alarm, a 10-92. But when Boyle's truck pulled up behind the building, flames were ripping out the back. The captain was old school and too proud to reverse his false alarm report to dispatch, so no backup was called in. The two companies had to eat that job alone. Boyle remembered his company fought it all night long. Twice they'd thought they had it under control, only to discover it continued to roar. Guys did everything that night, truckies helping enginemen. Enginemen on the roof. It was sunrise before they finally got it under control.

That fire had sealed his love for the work, with all its dangers and the exhilaration that resulted from it. He emerged from the fire with what he described as *better sight*, literally. Everything appeared different, clearer, brighter—the old lady on the corner, the panhandler, the sidewalk trees. The fact that his life had hung in the balance had made even the mundane more beautiful. That feeling remained and was bolstered by moments such as these, when he watched people, saw them with different eyes. Adding to his gratification during the afternoon heat of this late August day was the fact he was waiting for Lauren.

She arrived a few minutes after two. She had told him she'd see him only after her yoga class.

He watched her approach. Enjoyed how her toned body effortlessly carried the creme slacks and powder-blue button-down blouse. Her hair brushed her shoulders with each step. Except for lip gloss, her face was untouched, revealing the natural beauty she was.

They sat and talked about everything and nothing—his injury, her work, yoga, how they usually weren't chatty people but had no problem filling an afternoon, or any other time, with conversation.

The waiter placed a second cappuccino in front of each of them and removed the used cups and saucers.

Boyle rested his elbows on the table. "So. Why'd you do it?"

Lauren went still. "I'm sorry, Pat," she said finally.

"I didn't expect that. Not from someone like you."

Lauren furrowed her brow. "I suppose I realized I couldn't let what we had lead me to where I thought it was going."

He fixed his gaze on her. "Why not?"

She ran a hand through her hair and cleared her throat. "I grew up without the closeness you have with your buddies. My father was older. My mother wasn't the most expressive person." She ran a fingertip around the rim of her cup. "I don't think she was a happy person. I suppose this made me jaded practically from the crib."

Lauren gazed across West Broadway. Two children chased each other, their mother just behind them. "When I met you, as I got to know you, I began to feel different. Rather than proprieties and expectations, I had a feeling of unconditional—what word am I looking for?"

"Acceptance?"

She tilted her head slightly, toward him. "Yes. Acceptance. With you, I didn't have to act a certain way. And when we were together, I didn't seem to need anything else. I'm not explaining it very well. I don't know how to. But it frightened me, in a way. It was unfamiliar ground. I didn't know what to expect next."

Boyle leaned back. He shifted his gaze from her to the passersby and back.

"Then," she continued, "Ross showed up, and from a world I know well—smart, savvy, a businessman intent on advancing socially and professionally. He can be quite sweet, and I think he truly loves me. With him, I could see what life would be like. It's familiar. With him, I'm clear about the kind of person I'm supposed to be. It's all so—easy."

"Okay, I hear what you're saying. But you should've told me."

"You're right. I guess I'm not as strong as I thought."

"I had to hear about it from Kearns's wife, who read it in the society pages."

"How could I face you when I couldn't face myself?"

Lauren stared at her coffee, her finely manicured fingers covering the cup. Boyle sat back and studied the amber-haired beauty across the table from him.

"Why'd you agree to come today?"

"Because you called and asked me to."

"Even though you're about to be married? You didn't need to meet with me. Maybe you don't know yourself all that well, but I know you. You've got a fair amount of pride. It makes you do things you regret later, like shippin' me out the way you did." Boyle sipped his coffee and studied her as she watched the kids on the sidewalk. "You're here because your head is still in it. So you can spare me the psychobabble about being jaded from the crib. Face it. You've got nowhere to go, emotionally speaking, except right here."

A silence followed. "You're right, of course," she said, with moist eyes. A small smile formed on her lips. "And it's so like you to say all you did, to be blunt, but without anger or deprecation in your voice."

He stood, pulled a twenty from his wallet, and tucked it under his saucer. "Let's walk."

✦

The sun was beginning to set as clouds collected overhead, a portent of a thunderstorm later, though it would do nothing to cool the heat and humidity. They walked south on West Broadway to the plaza of the World Trade Center. They made their way past Fritz Koenig's sculpture, *The Sphere.*

Lauren said, "Where are we going?"

He opened the glass door to Tower One and said, "You'll see."

Aside from the skeletal assignment of security and cleaning staff on duty, the monstrous north tower was virtually empty. The security guard rose halfway to greet the visitors, saw it was Boyle, grinned, and returned to his seat. From his side of the counter was heard announcers discussing the baseball game over the miniature TV he kept there.

Boyle said hello to the guard and added, "How's the game?"

"Them Mets. They're getting blown away at Shea."

"Maybe next time."

"One can hope."

Boyle placed his hand at the small of Lauren's back and guided her to a waiting elevator, which took them to the Sky Lobby on the seventy-eighth floor. A couple of quick elevator rides got them to floor 101. He took a key from his pocket and opened a door to a mechanical room that housed the tower's ventilation and heating equipment. Compressors and chiller units hummed and whirred.

He led her past the equipment, to an office with windows facing west, with a clear view of the Hudson River below, and across the river, New Jersey.

From a westward distance the dark pewter clouds bore down on the city and cast the ground and skyline in coral-colored shadows.

Boyle turned the desk lamp on.

"The view is remarkable," Lauren said.

Boyle nodded, opened a desk drawer, and pulled out a bottle of Jameson's Irish Whiskey and two paper cups. He poured two fingers' worth into each cup and handed her one.

"Captain Boyle, are you trying to get me intoxicated?"

"Wouldn't be the first time."

She smiled. "True."

He rested half on, half off the desk, sipped from his cup, and stared out the window. "Sky's churning."

Lauren sipped. "Mmm … this is quite good." She took another sip. "Is this your lair? Do you bring unsuspecting young ladies here to impress them with the view, feed them liquor, then seduce them?"

He didn't smile. "I've never taken anyone up here. I found this place on a run here a couple of years ago. I love the view. It makes me comfortable. Plus, it's cheaper to drink here than at Windows on the World upstairs."

The light in the room was dimmed by dark clouds that blotted out the remaining sunlight. The sound of thunder filtered through the triple-paned windows. A thunderhead continued its gradual progression toward them.

"My goodness, at this height," Lauren said, "we're practically eye to eye with the clouds."

"Only way to watch a thunderstorm." He stretched his arm and turned off the desk lamp.

He stood at her side a moment, then took her cup and placed it beside his on the desk. He pulled her into his arms, happy she offered no resistance.

"Pat, what you said earlier, about me—you're right. I needed to see you."

"I know." He moved his hand up her arm and rested his fingertips against her collarbone. She gasped at his touch so familiar.

"It doesn't make—"

Boyle took the back of her head with his hand and pulled her him as their lips clenched. She placed her hand on his forearm as if to pull it down away from her, and began to do so, but she stopped, the energy in her arm rushing to other parts of her body. He took his other hand, put it around her waist, and rotated her so she was now up against the window, a quarter of a mile off the earth. They kissed passionately and quickly. She could not resist him and wanted him with an indescribable desire, fueled by her need to redeem herself from the eighteen-month absence she had imposed on their romance.

Outside, the thunderstorm had begun to punish the horizon. Shards of lightning pierced the evening sky, rocketing down to lower buildings far below the towers. The illumination from the strikes cast them both in an eerie, flickering glow. She had started to unbutton her blouse but stopped, frozen by the crashing thunder and lightning that she feared was about to enter the room. The hair on the back of her neck began to rise and, for a moment, frightened her. The storm, and here with Pat, at the top of the city, made her feel a little unsafe. She settled down as the unwavering firmness of his grasp around her waist gave her that familiar sense of security she remembered from the many nights they had spent together. His arms, one around her head and the other around her waist, cradled her in such a way that her fear subsided quickly. *I don't feel this way with anyone else*, she admitted to herself.

The relentless thunderstorm was now below, over, next to, and around the towers. With every lightning strike, she could feel the kinetic energy reverberating through the building and its infrastructure. The light cast from the strikes sporadically illuminated them like two lonely moviegoers in an empty theater.

She kissed him incessantly, trying to catch up for their months apart, trying to erase the stultifying memories of their romance she had contrived for herself. *God, I almost convinced myself it wasn't like this.*

Her back was against the glass, with her hands on his shoulders. The rain mercilessly pounded the window and the towers; his body pressed against her elegant, statuesque frame. She moved her hands to his chest and slowly unbuttoned his shirt, revealing the wounds and injuries received from twenty-five years fighting the Beast in the cauldrons of New York. He interrupted her efforts, taking a more efficient route of his own and raised her button-down blouse over her head in one movement. She smiled as he broke her lips' embrace and kissed her bare neck and shoulder.

"You've never been tentative, Pat," she said.

"I don't have time to be tentative," he shot back.

"No, I guess you don't," she responded knowingly.

She finished unbuttoning his shirt and pulled it down around his back as he lowered his arms to let the shirt drop to the floor. In the fitful bursts of illumination, she saw the latest injuries on his torso—the permanent bruises and scars from the burn injuries he had just recovered from. She wrapped her arms around his back and gently placed her fingers on the scars, which felt like coarse sandpaper.

"Oh, Pat. It's too much," she said, her voice distressed and beginning to falter. "These wounds. They're so deep." She lowered her head and wept.

He said nothing. She knew there was nothing to say. What was done was done. She knew he could not escape it. His body was broken and battered by the incessant pounding the Job inflicted on him; and she knew he accepted it. He continued to slowly kiss her shoulder, one hand on her waist, their bodies pressed against each other and a pane of glass.

She wept quietly. There was nothing she could do for herself or for him. It was pointless for her to fight it. He owned her soul. She had fallen for a man who was married to a passion that she knew would kill him someday and take her heart with him—and she knew she couldn't do anything about it. *I guess this is what they call destiny*, she thought to herself.

Pat abruptly stopped kissing her shoulder, took her head in both hands, and firmly kissed her on the lips.

"Don't cry. Do you hear me?" he said sternly. She nodded, holding back a sob. "I don't need it. It doesn't matter," he added.

With a firm gentleness, he lifted her up against the glass on top of him. She closed her eyes as her wrists lost any ability to control her hands that fell on his shoulders. She found his lips and kissed him repeatedly, the strength of his body against her, in her, affirmed the fateful conclusion that she now knew was all too true: she loved Pat Boyle—and no other.

Slowly, she felt a sense of relief. They made love. She could tell this was not just sex to him. This was oceans deeper than that. And the sensation she felt as she held him against that glass high in the sky, with the storm breaking around them with angry prejudice, transported her to a place she could only describe as metaphysical.

"I love you, Pat," she confessed.

He did not respond. She hesitated to open her eyes, not knowing if she could face his reaction to her confession, no matter what it was. They continued to make love quietly. When she did open her eyes, his demeanor was now serious, but his eyes had welled, if only slightly. She knew, even without words, how he felt about her. And she was sure, as sure as the sun would rise the next day, that he knew she knew it also.

✦

Lauren stared out the cab window as she pondered the impossible situation she found herself in. Her head told her it would be so easy to put Pat in the past, even after today, and tell him she really couldn't share the kind of life he lived. But that's not what her heart said. She knew they loved each other but, that may just not be enough. She remembered the last thing he'd said as he held the cab door for her. "Don't overthink this. Follow your heart. It'll sort things out."

Easier said than done, she thought. Yet, here she was, on her way back to Ross, knowing that with him, all she was doing was marking time.

Many minutes and many mental machinations later, the cab pulled up to the Fifth Avenue apartment. The doorman hurried to the cab and opened the door.

Lauren paid the driver, accepted the doorman's hand, and stepped onto the curb. "Thank you, Bert. Is Ross home?"

"Yes. He called down a little while ago asking if we knew where you were."

She pasted a smile on her face. "Okay if I use the lobby restroom to freshen up?"

"Of course."

Lauren locked the bathroom door and tidied her appearance. As she brushed her hair, she remembered something her father had told her while engaged with the acquisition of a large company. "If this deal is completed, it will seal my fate as the preeminent shipping tycoon in the states." He'd tweaked her chin and added, "Life is measured by what you do in a few instances, not in years. Remember that."

This was one of those instances.

She rechecked herself in the mirror, then made her way to the elevator. Inside the apartment, Ross stood at the window, highball glass in hand. He didn't break his stare when she entered. "I suppose I'd come across as pathetic if I asked where you've been. After all, what you do in your spare time is your business. Isn't it? Certainly not the business of your fiancé."

Lauren moved to the Lexington Salon sofa and sat down.

Ross turned, leaned against the sill, and kept his eyes fixed on her. "Want to tell me why your cell phone was off? Why you were unreachable most of the day?"

She checked her hands for a tremor—there was none. Lauren returned her gaze to him. "I'm sorry, Ross. This can't go on."

He tilted his head slightly. "Excuse me?"

"For the past six months, I've been trying to work through something. I thought I could resolve it on my own and in a way that would let us move forward in life together."

He moved to the armchair across from her and sat. "What are you talking about?"

"There's someone else."

Eyes aimed at her, he took a large swig of vodka from the tumbler, swallowed, and said, "You're serious?"

"Yes."

"Let me get this straight. Are you telling me you're having an affair?"

"It's not like that."

Ross rested his elbows on his knees and leaned forward. "Exactly what is it like?"

"I thought I was over him but I'm not."

"Who is it?"

"Pat Boyle."

"The fireman?"

She nodded.

Ross flopped back in the chair and stared at the ceiling. "You have got to be kidding me."

Lauren was not surprised by his reaction. She knew that to him, anybody who was not a force to be reckoned with in the business world was a nonentity, an inferior of no consequence. And for her to betray their relationship for a civil servant and a blue collar one at that was as if she possessed some great character flaw or had lost her senses.

"Well, that's going to run great in the tabloids, isn't it? I can see the headlines in the *Post* right now: One Less Vote: Challinor fiancée ditches him for Bravest."

"Ross, please. I know the timing on this is not good but I—"

"Timing? It couldn't be worse. The election is eight weeks away, and the wedding is right after that. Did you think about that?"

He stood up and paced around the room. Lauren stared at the floor. He came over to her and knelt in front of her.

"Have you given this any thought? Any real thought?" His voice was very composed, almost businesslike. "Have you thought about what your life will be with him—with his life?" He smiled wryly. "I mean, what are you going to do? Move in with him in his one-bedroom apartment in Bayside and clean his clothes when he comes off shift? Is that really you, L? Is it?"

His demeaning remark insulted her and confirmed for her his total inability to understand her on a fundamental level.

"What I do with my life is my business. The fact that you cannot fathom these feelings or how I came to this place confirms for me that any affections I ever had for you were grossly misplaced."

Ross closed his eyes, his jaw tightening at her upbraiding response.

"L, please. I'm sorry. Put yourself in my spot. How would you react to this?" He placed his hands on her knees, his eyes welling up with tears.

She turned away from him, toward the window. For a moment, she felt as if a huge weight had been lifted off her shoulders, tempering the remorse she felt for having told him her feelings so directly.

"L, I know I haven't been focused on us as much as I could. This campaign has been all-consuming. But I thought you understood it was for a greater good, a greater purpose. I guess I misread both you and our relationship, or what I thought was our relationship." He stared toward the window over the treetops in Central Park.

"I don't know how you came to this decision. For all I know, this could be a fling that passes, and you'll come back to me in a week, telling me you were wrong. It's clear I don't understand you or how you think. That's for sure."

He got to his feet and adjusted his shirtsleeves. "So, I'm going to ask you to do one thing for me."

Lauren now eyed him warily. She knew he was treating her as an attractive business deal that was going south.

"Hold off on saying anything about this for a couple of weeks. If you really feel this way after that time, we can make it official. If you want to move out, go ahead. I think we can both agree that you owe me that much."

She pondered his request. *He was right*, she thought. Her timing was horrible, but such is it with love and the inconvenient results it produces.

"Ross, I'm quite sure I won't change my mind, but I don't want to make this any more difficult for you than I have."

She slowly slid the five-carat diamond engagement ring from her finger and placed it on the couch.

"I won't say anything about this to anyone for that time."

She got to her feet. "I'll get a few things now. I'll be staying at the Princeton Club for a few days. I'll get the rest of my things next weekend. I realize we had a number of commitments on the calendar. Make any excuse you want about why I'm not with you."

She left Ross sitting in stunned silence and went to the bedroom. Fifteen minutes later, overnight bag in hand, she returned to the living room.

Ross was at the window, cell phone pressed to his ear. He turned to her, covered the phone with his hand, and said, "No matter what you think at this time, I love you."

"I know. At another time and place, things could be different. I'm sorry. Truly."

She opened the door, stepped out, and quietly closed the door behind her.

CHAPTER 29

SEPTEMBER 10, 2001

Ocean City, New Jersey.

O'Rorke stared at the vast, vacant expanse of ocean, watching the first rays of sunlight creep over the hazy, gray horizon. The shore was deserted with the exception of seagulls bobbing on the surf. He brought the Winston to his lips, took a deep drag, and glanced back at the dunes and the top of the small, ramshackle beach cottage where he and Melanie had taken shelter for the night. He'd ridden his bike here with the sole purpose of getting away from the craziness of the past week, and to sort through what he wanted to do about the Job, and about her. He wanted to convince himself that he didn't want to be around her, but he couldn't understand why he felt that way. This was one reason he stood outside alone at this hour. That and the fact that alone as he was, with seagulls and sunrise and surf, he could think, as well as feel like master of the world, especially with no one there to steal that feeling from him.

Hammonds had leveled charges against him—reckless endangerment of a subordinate firefighter, and assault. Facing that, he now seriously questioned how he could go on with the Job. He loved the work. It was part of him, blood, pith, and marrow. He'd sworn that his last breath would be taken as a fireman. But maybe it was better to just pack it in and move on. Better to do that than be subjected to ridicule and abuse that would be part of answering the charges.

He took another drag and exhaled. This wasn't his father's fire department. That was for damn sure.

His thoughts turned to Melanie. He liked her, she liked him, even though he was a rank fireman, for now at least. She couldn't have been more supportive of him this past week, which had scored big points in her favor. But it puzzled him why she wanted to be with him. He cursed at himself under his breath for overthinking this. That path would lead him to screwing it up, if there was anything there to screw up.

You don't need any more screw-ups.

The sun was fully over the horizon, warming the shore with its light. O'Rorke headed back to the cottage, located at the end of a sorry street of bungalows built in the 1940s for veterans and Pennsylvania workers who wanted a vacation spot on the coast. Many cottages had either been shuttered or abandoned. The once-happy days there had come and gone. He was starting to relate.

He pulled back the screen door, which was missing the screen, and turned the rusted knob on the second door, letting himself in. They'd gotten there last night, tired and hungry from the long ride from the city. Too tired to deal with the filthy living room pockmarked with water stains and rat droppings. They went to Fat Rippy's just outside of town to pick up burgers, which they'd eaten by candlelight at the busted kitchen table, before crawling into their sleeping bags and calling it a night.

O'Rorke peeked into the bedroom. Melanie was out like a light. He had to give her credit. When he told her yesterday that he was riding down to the shore to get away for a few days, she'd asked if he wanted company. He had been about to say no and then changed his mind.

He smiled, closed the door, grabbed the small radio from his overnight bag, and went to the front porch. He tested one of the dilapidated wicker chairs, sat in it, and tuned the radio to the FM station that played oldies. He lit another Winston and scanned the horizon, letting himself be soothed by the sound of the music and ocean waves rolling onto the shore fifty yards from the house.

The sun was higher in the sky when the screen door creaked behind him. Melanie, barefoot and wearing a pale-yellow nightgown under a University of Tennessee hooded, unzipped sweat jacket, stood in the doorway. She smiled at him, stretched her arms over her head. "It's a nice morning," she said.

"Beautiful."

She ran her hands through her messy hair. "How'd you find this place?"

"One of the guys at the house told me about it."

"Does the owner know we're here?"

O'Rorke shrugged. "I've been down around here before. A local told me some family owns the house and are fighting about who gets it. None of them want to pay for the upkeep. Pretty stupid if you ask me."

"Well, it isn't going to waste this weekend."

He grinned. "That's a fact."

"All I Have to Do Is Dream" by the Everly Brothers came on the radio.

Melanie walked to where O'Rorke sat, stood next to the chair, and placed her hand on his shoulder. "I've been thinking about your situation. I know it's bothering you."

He shrugged. "It's a pretty shitty rap."

"How they're treating you isn't fair. Sounds to me like a misunderstanding that got blown out of proportion."

"Well, the brass downtown don't see it that way. They have to cover their asses."

"Can't you get them to see what you were doing? You told me the guy had to be taught to follow orders so you and the others could rely on him. I don't see what's so wrong about that."

"At least someone sees it that way." He leaned forward. "Problem is, they think I went too hard on the kid."

"Why would they think that?"

"I put the kid through some pretty tough paces."

"Don't they understand what it takes to do the job?"

O'Rorke picked at a loose strand of wicker on the chair arm. "It's like this. The brass downtown—not the big chief, but the chiefs hungry for promotion—want people to see the fire department as modernized from the old days, when they fought fifty fires a weekend and drank beer in the basement during down time. They have to act like they can't ignore the treatment I gave the kid to get him in line. If they don't take action, it'll look like they're protecting their own."

"Okay. I can see that. But isn't it a bigger disservice to the kid if no one helps him become a better fireman? What you did might save his life or the other guys one day. Right?"

He turned one palm up. "That's how I learned, and where I was coming from. But they don't want to hear that." He gazed back to the shore. He traced a finger on a spindle on the porch railing, hoping she wouldn't see him purse his lips.

She let her hand run down his short sleeve shirt over the tattoo of a Celtic Cross with the date July 2, 1863 below it.

"Why do you have the date of the Battle of Gettysburg on your arm?" she asked.

"You know that date?" O'Rorke responded, surprised.

Melanie shook her head. "Duh, I am from the South, you know."

"My great-great-grandfather was killed at Little Round Top on the second day of the battle."

Melanie's turned away, then her eyes widened. "No. Your great-great-grandfather isn't Pa—"

"—Paddy O'Rorke. Yes, the one and only. County Cavan's finest."

"He's got the biggest monument on that hill. Have you been there?"

"I'm embarrassed to say I have not," O'Rorke responded sheepishly. "Have you?"

"Yeah, I have. Wanna know why?"

O'Rorke shrugged his shoulders. "Okay, try me."

Melanie put her arms across her chest. "My great-great-grandfather was in the Fifteenth Alabamans and charged up Little Round Top."

"What are the odds?" O'Rorke asked wide-eyed.

"Did you know that if it wasn't for Paddy O'Rorke, those Alabamans would have taken that hill?" Melanie asked, in her best schoolteacher voice.

"No. But I was told he died with the flag in his hands."

"Yeah, the line was giving way. The flag bearer had fallen, shot. And your great-great-granddaddy grabbed the flag and held the line. The Yankees rallied around him and closed ranks."

She spoke as if O'Rorke's ancestor had committed some heinous crime against her family.

"And to think here we are." She touched her chin with her index finger. "Crazy." She pointed to the Maltese Cross tattoo on his other bicep. "And that date. August 2, 1978. What's that for?"

"That's the date my father died. He was killed with five other firemen when a roof over a supermarket collapsed in Brooklyn."

"Oh, Bryan. Wow. I didn't know. I'm so sorry."

"Nah. It was a long time ago. It was a truss roof, gave out pretty quick. The department didn't know much about them back then and learned the hard way—with six coffins lining the center aisle of Saint Patrick's Cathedral."

Melanie scanned the ocean. "It's not easy losing a parent ...

when you're a kid," she said distantly.

"You got that right," O'Rorke replied. "It's a big hole that never gets filled in. No matter how many probies you run into the ground."

They both laughed at his observation.

"How long is your suspension?" she asked.

"Until the department finishes its investigation." He stubbed out his cigarette on the deck railing. "If they have to reprimand me, I'll be done. I'll have to quit."

Melanie moved until she was on her knees between his. "Listen, buster. You're a fireman through and through. Anyone who knows you knows that. You're scared they're going to fire you. Okay, it's worth being scared about that. But if it happens, you'll deal with it. You're trained to deal with sticky situations. Got that?" She shook his shoulders. "We'll deal with it. Okay?"

The corners of his lips turned up. "We will?"

"You bet. Because I know you've got the potential to be a superstar, whatever you do."

"You really mean that, don't you?"

"You bet."

"You're talking about some other guy. When I meet him, I'll let you know."

O'Rorke could see she was totally serious. He realized she was far stronger than he was. For all that talk that men were the stronger sex, to him it was total bullshit once you left the physical part out, and with Melanie, the emotional part also. She was a lot stronger than he was, and he knew it. The thought gave him a sense of assurance. He wanted to believe her; he had always believed the notion she had just mentioned but never thought anyone else had come to the same conclusion. He wanted to continue believing what she said, but the cynical, stoic side of him took over.

Melanie stood, crossed her arms at her chest, and said, "Oh, please. You throw out so much bullshit, you're starting to believe your own."

O'Rorke's head snapped back, and he laughed. "Can't fool you."

Melanie moved to the rail, arched her back and stretched. O'Rorke studied her shape, smirked until she caught his leer.

"Easy, Cowboy. I see that look. We can get more mileage out of this place before we leave," she said.

"I'm not so sure."

Her smile faltered. "What do you mean?"

"We're leaving today."

"We're going home? Already?"

O'Rorke shook his head. "Gettys—"

His cell phone vibrated on the porch railing, bouncing off and onto the deck. Melanie and O'Rorke just stared at it, startled by its abrupt movement. He slowly picked it up and flipped it open.

"Hello."

Larry Ruffalo's thick Bronx accent was crystal clear in the receiver. "Bry, you've been cleared of all charges."

O'Rorke sat forward. "What? What are you talkin' about?"

"Sturgis told downtown he refused to testify against you. Said you were doing the right thing. He refused to cooperate with any investigation. Hammonds is supposed to call you, or maybe he's tried. He's gonna ask you to come in tomorrow to cover a mutual."

O'Rorke gripped the phone. "Listen, jerk-wad, if you're fucking with me, when I get a hold of you, I'm gonna shove your head so far up your ass, it'll take a Hurst tool to get it out."

"Nah, man, I'm totally serious." Alarm tones wailed over the phone. "I gotta go."

O'Rorke ended the call and stared at the phone, firmly in his grasp. Neither of them said anything.

The phone vibrated. He hit the call button.

"O'Rorke, it's Captain Hammonds."

"Yes, Cap."

"Bryan, you've been given a reprieve. That pecker Sturgis has more balls than I thought. He told Legal Affairs he won't testify.

Doesn't think you did a damn thing wrong. Headquarters dropped all charges."

O'Rorke leaped to his feet. "Captain, are you shitting me?"

"You're cleared to start work again. It's your lucky day. Erskine has appendicitis. I need someone to cover for him tomorrow. Someone told me you took off out of town with your shack-job. If you get your ass back here for the day shift, you can work a mutual."

He glanced at Melanie to see if she'd heard Hammonds' insult. If she had, she was pretending not to. *That's Hammonds*, he thought, *a miserable, judgmental motherfucker.*

"Put me down, Cap. I'll be there."

"Do me a favor, Bryan. Just do your job, and we'll all be fine."

"Got it, Cap."

The call ended, he grinned.

Melanie smiled and said, "Sounds like we have something to celebrate."

"You bet." He explained the situation.

"Bryan, that's fantastic!" She jumped into his arms and wrapped her legs around his torso.

"Yes, it is," he responded, grabbing her thighs. "Yes, it is."

She took his head between her hands and kissed him firmly on the lips.

"Let's go inside. I think we've got some unfinished business, and we've got to get up real early in the morning," she said, flickering her eyelids.

Holding her where she was, he opened the screen door and carried her inside and up the stairs.

CHAPTER 30

Coletti and Jordan sat in their jump seats with their masks still strapped to their backs, ready to dismount from the rig and hit the next worker. On that last Saturday night in August, the boys at the Big House in Brooklyn had run all over their district, chasing arson fires started by innocent, heat-crazed kids condemned to stifling boredom on simmering streets. What better way to relieve the pressure than burning a vacant tenement, abandoned car, or garbage-bloated dumpster and waiting for the guys in the funny helmets to show up?

By 4:30 a.m., things had quieted down, and the number of runs had ebbed. The torrid pace of calls had taken its toll on the borough dispatcher. "Fire Alarm Box 2278 Kings Plaza for a car fire."

The control man leaned his head to one side, exhausted. "Man, do you hear that guy? He sounds like a zombie."

Jordan nodded. "I wouldn't want his job for anything."

Coletti stared out the window as the rig drove past a brick tenement, its inhabitants cluttered on the front stoop.

"Livin' the dream in the Big Apple once again. Can you believe two weeks ago I was lying on a beach in Southern Italy with a beautiful woman, eating pasta and drinking wine, and now here I am in Southern Brooklyn, chasing fires in the projects set by kids who don't give a shit about anything?"

"What did the old guys call these buildings?"

"Widowmakers," Coletti responded. "Because more than a few guys bought it in these things."

Coletti thought about Ellie and her transformation on the trip. He was quite surprised at how well she had embraced Italy and the impact it had on her. By the end of the trip, she was outgoing, smiling, almost effervescent, a far cry from her disposition when she arrived: withdrawn and guarded. But something bothered him. Since they had gotten back to New York, she hadn't called him once. When he stopped by the soup kitchen to check in on her, George told him she got a job at a store in the Financial District as a graphic designer's assistant and stopped working at the soup kitchen. He was happy to hear this, but he couldn't understand why she didn't call him or return his calls. He thought she would have at least called him to give him the good news.

He checked the gauge on his mask. He was down to his last tank of air after using the rest of the spares chasing fires all night.

Jordan focused on Coletti. "Dog, I can tell when you're not right," he said. "What's up? Since you got back, something's been up."

"Nothing's up."

"Bullshit. Wanna know what I think?"

"No."

"I think that dip you partied with in It'ly got your number, and you don't know what to do about it."

Coletti gave him a half-smile. "Very observant for a dumbass engineman."

"So? What happened?"

"I don't know. Maybe she wasn't as into it as I thought."

Jordan rubbed his forehead between his thumb and forefinger, "What she tell you?"

"We haven't spoken since we got back."

"Damn."

"Yeah."

"If it were me, I'd want to know. Only one thing to do, bro."

Coletti nodded and exhaled hard. "Yeah."

✦

Coletti stood in front of Ellie's apartment and checked his watch. It was 5:37 p.m. It was possible Ellie hadn't made it home from work yet, but he rang her buzzer anyway. And got no response. He went down the steps to the sidewalk, lit a cigarette, and waited. He smoked it down to the filter when he spotted her walking in his direction. Her hesitant gait and stooped posture had disappeared.

She approached him, smiling. "Hi, Phil. What a surprise. I've been meaning to—"

He gestured toward the entrance door. "Let's talk inside."

Ellie's smile faded. She descended the stairs in silence, opened the entrance door and the door to her apartment. Once inside, she said, "Have a seat. I'll put on some coffee."

"None for me." Coletti went to the sofa and turned around. He leveled his eyes at Ellie. "I don't get it. I thought we had a phenomenal trip, for both of us. We got back and you act like you don't know me. What gives?"

"I can explain. When I got back, a girl I used to work with in SoHo told me about a job on Wall Street. A graphic design firm needed entry-level help. She knew about my courses at FIT and thought I could get the job. I went for the interview and they hired me on the spot. That's what I've been doing since then. It's been really good for me." She returned to the kitchen. "Coffee's ready," she said, over her shoulder.

Coletti followed her, waited until she poured coffee into a cup and returned the pot to the stove. He took her hands and turned her to face him. "Work with me here. It's really great to see the new you. It's like you've been transformed. To see where you were when we first met and now, it's unbelievable. Let me ask you a question. Was there a time, when you were a little girl, that you remember being with your mom and dad?"

She paused then nodded.

"Is it a good memory?"

Ellie nodded and cast her gaze to the floor.

"Maybe they played chase with you and let you think you were running away. Let you get far enough away to make you think you'd eluded them?"

"Yes."

"Then they'd swoop down, picked you up and tossed you into the air. Right?"

"Please stop."

"Do you remember how it felt? How safe they made you feel? Like you knew nothing could or would hurt you as long as they were there, holding you?"

"Yes, but that doesn't last."

"You're right. It doesn't. But that's part of growing up. You remember the good. You keep it with you, and let the bad go. You have to let the good experiences prevail in your mind. How else can you go on in life?"

Ellie slid her hands from his and walked into the living room. "I can't let myself think about it. It's too much for me right now." She crossed her arms in a protective embrace. "I need you to understand."

"I know what I know. I don't see what we've experienced as some kind of coincidence. I've also seen enough darkness to know that when something good comes along, you need to go in the direction of that light. You have to have the courage to follow wherever it leads." He approached her. "Do you know what I mean? Ellie, talk to me."

She didn't answer, eyes cast to the floor.

"I've never taken anyone with me to Italy before. Never shared that part of me with anyone. I didn't do it to impress you."

Ellie extended a hand toward him, then pulled it back. "Phil, I can't really come to grips with everything that's happened to me over the past few months. The good and the bad. I can't even begin to think about where this can lead. But please know I don't have the words to thank you for all you've done."

"I don't want or need your thanks."

"I owe you my life. But you want something from me I'm not ready to give yet."

Coletti jerked his head as if she slapped him. At his expression, her eyes filled, and she said, "Please don't look at me like that."

Coletti backed away, his jaw tight. "Unbelievable."

"I'm sorry."

"Yeah. Me too." He went to the door, opened it, and turned back. "I hope you find someone who you can love as much as he loves you, and that you'll recognize it when it comes around. Sometimes you don't get second chances."

He exited and closed the door, cutting off the sound of her sobs, and trekked back to the firehouse, his own chest tight with ache.

✦

Coletti sat on a barstool in the Nightingale Lounge, one of the saddest, beat-gone dive joints in Brooklyn. He nursed a tall glass of whiskey and flicked cigarette ash into the butt-filled ashtray in front of him. Jordan nursed a beer to his left. Sean Hurley from 218 Truck sat on the other side of him, swizzled a rock glass filled with bourbon. Sinatra crooned from the jukebox in the corner.

Hurley winked at Jordan and nodded to Coletti. "So, let me see if I got this straight. Back in March, you walk this smokin'-hot jumper-babe—who's got a crippled hand, I might add—off the bridge. You help her glue all the pieces of shitty, pathetic, little

I'm-the-new-girl-in-New-York-woe-is-me life back together. You romance the ass out of her, take her to Italy, turn on that Dago charm and abuse her G-spot with all of your ample resources, bring her psyche to places it's never been, blah, blah, blah. And then, when you get her back to New York, she runs from you like you've got the HIV. Is that right?"

"That's pretty much it." Coletti took a swig from his glass. "The naked truth, with no sugar coating. You've got the gift of being succinct, Sean."

"You poor bastard." Hurley put his arm around Coletti's neck and gave him a bear hug.

Jordan laughed.

Coletti nodded, chuckled. "There's an old saying that goes, 'A man isn't a man until a woman shits all over him.'"

Jordan said, "Bro, she didn't shit on you. She shit-hemorrhaged on you. Long as I'm breathing, I'll never figure the babes out."

Coletti took a drag on his cigarette, inhaled, and said, "One of life's eternal mysteries." He exhaled. "Probably for the best. She's got a lot of shit to work out." He doused his cigarette. "But I sure thought she could have been the one."

He checked his watch. "Eleven forty, September 10, and so it goes." He elbowed Hurley. "You workin' tomorrow?"

"Yeah. I've got a mutual."

"Then I'll see you at the house around eight."

Hurley held up his glass and waited for Coletti and Jordan to do the same. "To another day slugging it out in Brooklyn South."

They downed their drinks.

Coletti slid from his stool. "One thing we can look forward to."

Hurley stretched. "What's that, Phil?"

"Weather's supposed to be perfect."

MANHATTAN

BOX 55 - 8087

SEPTEMBER 11, 2001

I heard the voice of the Lord, saying,
Whom shall I send, and who will go for us?
Then said I, Here am I; send me.

—Isaiah 6:8

CHAPTER 31

0800–0846 HOURS

Division 10 Headquarters, Crosby Street, SoHo, Engine 264, Ladder 86

Brendan sat in his office. He had continued on from the overnight shift and was completing incident reports. Morning rush hour traffic limped up Lafayette Street in front of the house. Honks of horns and growl of car engines rang in another Tuesday morning in September in Manhattan, the listlessness of late summer now a distant memory.

The phone rang and he picked it up.

"Steve?" He relaxed a little when he heard his wife Peggy's voice. "Tonight it's open house at the girls' school."

"I know. I plan to be there."

"I know you're working a double, so just go directly to the school. There won't be enough time to come home first."

"Okay."

"And Steve," Peg added, "don't break your neck to get there. It starts at seven o'clock, so when you get there, you get there."

"I wouldn't miss it."

"I know you know it means a lot to the girls that you never miss these things."

Brendan grunted affirmatively and hung up the phone. In front of him stood the lieutenant on Ladder 86 holding his departmental radio.

"Chief, we're still having problems with the new radios."

"How so?"

"They don't work in basements. Last night in that subbasement on Elizabeth Street, I could barely hear you. I had to walk up two flights of stairs to get to a spot where we could transmit from the repeater in the building."

Brendan frowned. "I'm hearing it from a lot of guys. The best I can do is report it up. I know they're considering returning to the analog system."

The lieutenant stared at the radio as if he wanted to throw it out the open garage bay.

"Until then, we've gotta deal with it," Brendan added.

The junior officer nodded and headed to a group of guys from the night shift bragging to the incoming guys about the big job they caught last night. Brendan returned to his reports. It wasn't long before he heard a commotion in the kitchen. The thick Brooklyn accent of Guy Ricicci rose above everything else. From the sound of it, Ricicci was challenging a guy or busting his chops. Brendan put down the report and listened. The voices were clearly audible from the kitchen next to his office.

"So what house are you at?" Ricicci asked.

"397 in Staten Island," a guy's voice responded.

"397? I heard that's a pussy house. You're there?"

"Yeah. We have our share of jobs. As many as you get here."

"Really? Dumpster fires don't count."

Brendan enjoyed listening to Ricicci. He was a master at

ball-busting. He knew how to take someone from a pleasant disposition to a simmering boil to out-and-out rage in a matter of minutes. Brendan understood Ricicci's MO: if you can't handle the heat in the kitchen, how the hell are you going to handle the shit on the scene? Ricicci was in rare form this morning. He was talking to a Staten Islander who was detailed to the house for one of the guys on vacation. This guy had never been to the house before and didn't know anybody there. From the sound of his voice, Brendan thought the newcomer was in his twenties, junior to Ricicci by about twenty-five years.

"Fuck dumpster fires. I'm talking about house fires," the younger fireman responded.

"House fires? Whoa. That's some serious stuff. Like a two-story colonial home in Tottenville? Excuse me. I thought you guys just drove around going to pizza joints," Ricicci shot back.

Chuckles emanated from the kitchen.

"Listen. I've seen enough work to not have to explain anything to you. From the looks of it, you've had one too many pizzas yourself."

The putdown elicited jeers from the other guys in the kitchen. The visitor's retort was a major breach of unspoken protocol for someone who hadn't been at the house not even fifteen minutes.

"Yeah, I figured you were checking me out. Just like I thought. You come from a pussy house," Ricicci growled.

"I don't have to take this shit. Let's go!" The sound of a chair pushing away from the kitchen table accompanied the challenge from the newcomer.

"Hold on. We have a rule in this house," Ricicci explained. "No fighting inside the house. Let's take it outside."

"You're on. Let's go. I'm gonna fix you."

Brendan got up from his chair and walked to his office doorway just in time to see Ricicci and the Staten Islander emerge from the kitchen. Ricicci walked the guy to the doorway to the backyard, a fenced-in parking lot with no means of access except through the rear door to the firehouse. The young guy was totally jacked up, chest out and hands curled into fists. He stared down Ricicci's neck. Ricicci opened the back door to the rear yard.

"After you. You're the big shot, tough guy," Ricicci said, holding the door open. The visitor took the bait and barged out the door ready to brawl. Ricicci closed the door behind him and locked it, leaving the guy outside alone in the fenced-in parking lot. The guys on the floor howled at the gullibility of the Staten Islander. Ricicci saw Brendan, shrugged his shoulders and put out his palms, then headed back to the kitchen as the guy outside banged on the door.

It was a good fifteen minutes before Ricicci let him back in the house. By then, he had calmed down and realized he had been a prick and apologized for his rude behavior. Brendan could hear all this from his office. He returned to his desk and his reports. "Nothing like the social dynamic in a New York City firehouse," he said to himself.

He had just completed an incident report when he heard something. It started like a low roar, almost like the rumble from the subway two stories below. It was muted, muffled. At first, he didn't think anything of it, but then it grew louder, stronger, and sharper. The tinny whine of a jet engine forcing air through its compressors permeated the house, even in the latrine where a couple of guys were shaving.

Brendan listened. He knew what it was, and he expected to hear the impact any moment. He got up from his chair and went out to the street. The sound of the engines was now a little fainter but no less clear. Several guys stood nearby glancing up. A pedestrian stood near them.

"It was real low. Its wings were rocking back and forth," she remarked.

Even before she could finish her sentence, a splintering crash split the air.

The brothers bolted for the rigs. Brendan headed for the battalion

SUV where he met his aide, Tommy Enright, who was already in the driver's seat. On the command channel, he could hear the familiar voice of one of his battalion chiefs, Jack Seifert.

"Battalion 10 to Manhattan."

"Battalion 10."

"We just had … a plane just crashed into the upper floors of the World Trade Center. Transmit a second alarm and start relocating companies into the area."

Enright gaped at Brendan, mouthing a "holy shit".

"Take Broadway," Brendan said.

Enright pulled the SUV out onto Lafayette Street, followed by 86 Truck and Engine 264 not far behind. The chauffeurs didn't waste any time getting downtown. For some reason, the traffic on Broadway was uncannily light. It gave the crews a straight shot to the Trade Center. Up ahead, thick, dark grayish smoke rose from the top of the tower. *The jet fuel is starting fires*, Brendan thought.

Out on Broadway, pedestrians peered south. Some pointed to the towers. Many glanced toward the street distracted by the fire apparatus moving at breakneck speed, something not commonly seen by jaded New Yorkers.

The dispatch crackled, "Engine 1-0 to Manhattan. Engine 1-0 World Trade Center. 10-60. Send every available ambulance. Everything you got to the World Trade Center now."

Seifert's voice came up on the command channel, calm but terse. "We have a number of floors on fire. It looked like the plane was aiming toward the building. Transmit a third alarm. We'll have the staging area at Vesey and West Street. Have the third alarm go into that area. Second alarm assignment report to the building. K."

When Brendan's car got to Canal Street, the towers came into crystal-clear view. The spectacular late-summer cloudless sky was stained with smoke rising from the North Tower. About ten floors below the top of the building, an enormous almond-shaped gash cut directly across the façade. Inside the gash, a man stood in shirt sleeves, peering out over the city. Behind him, inside the building, flames illuminated the darkened space.

"Will you look at that," Enright remarked, in disbelief.

"Keep your eyes on the road," Brendan said.

Enright gunned the SUV past City Hall and made a sharp right on Barclay Street and then turned left onto West Street, pulling up close behind the first two engines on the scene. Brendan got out of the car, his eyes rising upward. *The loss of life today is gonna be tremendous.*

✦

Eastbound Lane, Pulaski Skyway, New Jersey

It was 6:05 a.m. when O'Rorke and Melanie had left Ocean City. They figured they'd be able to make the Holland Tunnel by eight fifteen so Bryan could get to the house before the day shift started at 9 a.m. Melanie had told him to not worry about getting her home. She would take a cab home from the firehouse. But the traffic on Interstate 78 was badly congested because of a jackknifed tractor-trailer. After weaving in and out of cars and making up time on the open road where he could, it was eight forty and the couple found themselves on the Pulaski Skyway approaching the city.

The couple had just crossed the bridge over the Hackensack River, where the highway bridges give eastbound motorists a close, unobstructed view of the New York skyline. O'Rorke was so focused on the road ahead he paid no attention to the horizon beyond. It was the tug on his jacket from behind by Melanie and her right hand pointing ahead that focused his view on the city.

The tracer smoke from the tower laced the sky ahead of them. He grabbed the handlebars tightly and hit the accelerator. The Harley roared and took off, passing cars and buses that had stopped in the middle of the highway to observe the ominous spectacle far in front of them.

As traffic slowed, O'Rorke found he had an open lane to the tunnel. With his left hand, he pointed to his right pocket. Melanie reached into it, pulled out his threefold wallet, and stuck it in her own pocket. O'Rorke leaned the bike into the turn on the approach to the entrance to the Holland Tunnel.

At the mouth of the tunnel, two Port Authority police cruisers had blocked off the New York-bound lanes. Three Port Authority police officers and a police sergeant stood in front of the cars.

O'Rorke took the badge from Melanie and slowed the bike just enough so he could flash his FDNY badge and identification without stopping. The cops saw the familiar badge and waved him through.

✦

Twelfth Street Firehouse, East Village, Ladder 323

The guys on the overnight shift, all five of them, were wrapping up their assignments for the night, talking with the guys coming in for the day shift, all five of them, who, as usual, had arrived early. As he did most mornings before his tour began, Captain Patrick Boyle stood in front of the house, coffee cup in hand ready to greet both the incoming shift and any passersby on their way to work. The mood in the house was upbeat. Boyle could hear guys talking about the Giants, the Jets, and the Yankees. One of the guys was getting married in a couple of weeks, and there was a lot of talk about the bachelor party scheduled for this coming Saturday night. From up the street, Boyle saw the discernible form of a young man approaching, clad in his FDNY regulation work blues. It was the probie, Kevin Reynolds, who was assigned to Boyle's house in June. The kid, a tall and slender jock, had run cross-country in college at SUNY-Binghamton. Boyle liked the kid. He had an unflappable demeanor. He thought the kid would work out well on the Job.

Boyle checked his watch. It was eight forty-four. He made sure Reynolds could see him doing so. "Cutting it close, troop," Boyle remarked as the probie approached.

"I'm sorry, Cap. The subway was running late."

Boyle smiled. "Then you gotta leave earlier."

"It won't happen again."

"One day, when I hang it up, I won't be here to show you the way," Boyle said, raising the cup to his lips.

"I hope it's no time soon, Cap," the probie responded.

"May be sooner than you think. Go check the tool fuel and the partner saw blades. The guys caught a job last night in a storefront and had to use the saws."

Reynolds nodded and headed into the open bay. Boyle turned to enter the house when he heard a roar overhead. The shadow of a commercial jet briefly darkened the street and the firehouse façade. A couple of guys heard the sound and ran out into the street.

"That plane's going down," Boyle said. "Let's go."

Both shifts of brothers scrambled for their gear. It was 8:46 a.m.

"Cap, it's the night shift's run, right? Kearns asked his captain.

Boyle glanced at the guys in front of him, the outgoing shift and the incoming shift, including Reynolds.

"Everybody goes," he ordered finally.

And with that, seven brothers piled into the cab built for six. The remaining four climbed onto the aerial truck's turntable like their fathers and grandfathers did decades earlier—riding a convertible with their coats flying like pennants. Ladder 323 responded to Box 8087 at the World Trade Center "heavy" with eleven brothers.

The truck made its way westward on Thirteenth Street. The repetitive "plink" of sideview mirrors being knocked off parked cars punctuated Noah Beale's decision to take a less trafficked approach down a narrow street before turning onto Broadway. Over his radio, Boyle heard Battalion 10 transmit a second alarm assignment for a plane crash into the World Trade Center. Boyle keyed the radio.

"323 Truck to Manhattan."

"Go ahead, 323 Truck," dispatch responded.

"Early reports from up here are a plane just crashed into the World Trade Center. 323 Truck is available."

"Ten-four, 323Truck."

Beale pushed the truck down Broadway against traffic.

"Watch it. We're a convertible with those guys on the turntable."

Beale nodded.

"Take Houston to West Broadway; that's a straight shot to the towers."

Beale eased the wheel right, bringing the Seagrave rear mount smoothly onto Houston Street, a crosstown thoroughfare as wide as an avenue. Boyle had the command radio against his ear. Initial transmissions were not promising. Ladder 101 reported fire on twenty floors of the World Trade Center. When the truck made its turn onto West Broadway, the towers rose ahead, clearly. Boyle keyed the mike on the dispatch frequency.

"323 Truck to Manhattan."

"323 Truck, go," the dispatcher responded.

"We're at Houston and West Broadway. We can see this from here. We've been directed by numerous civilians. You want us to take this in, or you want us to stand fast?"

The dispatcher, as well as everyone listening to those transmissions, knew who was talking. From the urgent tone in his voice, it was clear Boyle was going to the World Trade Center, with or without orders. After a short pause, the response was given.

"Take that in, K," the dispatcher said, with a slight tone of resignation.

In short order, 323 Truck pulled up on West Street. The truck was the fourth on the scene. Boyle's instinct to get on the rig and just go without waiting in quarters to be dispatched had paid off. Ladder 323 beat other companies to the scene who were on the second alarm.

The crew piled out and pulled hooks, cans, ropes, harnesses, and irons. Boyle signaled for all of them to gather around him. When they assembled, he looked into their eyes, the eyes of his veterans, his senior guys, three-year men, and his probies. They all didn't look the same, but they all listened the same.

"This is gonna be the biggest job of our lives. We're gonna see things and do things today that we'll talk about for the rest of our lives. Keep your eyes and ears open and listen to what I say. Got it?"

The brothers nodded, the younger ones more earnestly than the older ones. The sound of debris crashing into the ground drowned out some of Boyle's words, as did the wail of sirens from police and fire apparatus around them.

"All right. Follow me and stay close."

The rig was parked next to the entrance to the North Tower on West Street, a short walk into the tower. The brothers picked up their gear and followed Boyle. When the crew came through the revolving doors, they immediately came upon a startling sight: a man and woman on fire and alive, flailing and spinning. Civilians scurried away in horror. Reynolds paused for a second, himself shocked, and then dumped his water extinguisher on them.

"Don't move," Boyle told the middle-aged woman.

"It burns!" she shrieked. The skin on the back of her head and shoulder was burned to a leathery feel. Boyle clutched her and lowered her to the floor.

"Easy, ma'am. Please sit down," Boyle pleaded with her, but she kept repeating herself.

"Noah, get EMS over here," Boyle told Beale, who flagged down two EMTs in the lobby. Reynolds and Heimboldt helped the man sit down. The two paramedics rushed over and began working on them immediately.

The crew waited for Reynolds and Heimboldt before they continued past the elevators toward three chiefs in white helmets huddled at the other end of the lobby. In front of the elevators was a security desk. It was completely incinerated. A burnt corpse of a security guard was fused to the chair and desk in front of an open elevator that itself was charred and melted. A strong odor of kerosene, one of the base chemicals in JP-8, permeated the lobby. Boyle stopped to analyze what happened.

"The jet fuel shot down that elevator shaft and caught this guy right where he sat," He said to Reynolds who was right next to him. "Poor bastard."

Boyle told the crew to wait on the other side of the elevators and headed to Chief Seifert and Chief Brendan at the building engineer's station now the FDNY command post. The white-marbled lobby echoed with the din of stressed voices, sporadic shouts, and men talking in strained, desperate tones on portable radios.

The chiefs were receiving several calls from dispatch informing them of 911 calls from people trapped on floors above the fire. Seifert keyed the mike and told dispatch to tell the callers the fire department was coming for them. He raised his head, saw Boyle standing there.

"Paddy, we've got calls of people trapped on the eighty-first floor. Take your crew upstairs and do what you can," Seifert said.

"Will do, Chief."

Boyle returned to his crew, who were on their feet, leaning against the wall. He made a circular motion with his hand and pointed up. The crew collected their equipment, tightened gear, and gathered water bottles, cans, and hooks. A familiar voice cut through the air.

"Pat, don't go in. There's nothing you can do."

Boyle pivoted to see Gordy Ryan standing a few feet away. He initially smiled upon seeing his old friend, but then frowned and leaned into him, close to Ryan's face.

Boyle spoke quietly, firmly. "Gordy, there's *people* up there." Ryan said nothing. Boyle pulled away, heading back to his crew.

"People," he said, over his shoulder.

The crew followed Boyle into Stairwell B. They moved slowly and deliberately.

"Guys, pace yourself. Conserve your energy," Boyle told them.

Hundreds of people moved down the stairs calmly. Some of them tapped the truck crew on the shoulders, others wished them good luck. The crew reached the twentieth floor and stopped to take a break.

"Keep moving. We're not gonna know what we got until we get there, and we gotta get there. No one stops until we get to fifty. If you stop, as soon as you catch your breath, start up again and catch up. We've got to get up there."

The brothers marched up the stairs against the tide of civilians descending from the upper floors. Their captain picked up the pace, and his crew followed. Every flight of stairs made their sixty pounds of gear feel a little bit more than that. The younger guys initially stayed close to Boyle; the veterans behind them moved at their own pace. But as they climbed higher, it was the middle-aged men, in their thirties and forties, men whose muscles had memories of countless, all-night, back-breaking jobs fighting the Beast in concrete crevices and far-flung, misbegotten firetraps throughout Gotham, who had the stamina to keep up with Boyle.

✦

Brendan had made it into the North Tower just as he saw Paddy Boyle's crew dousing two civilians on fire. He pushed it out of his mind. He realized he needed to get a situational size-up from the incident commander, Seifert, as soon as possible to get the situation under control. At the far end of the lobby, he saw Chief Jack Seifert surrounded by building personnel. Port Authority staff manned the building desk. They called elevators to determine which ones were out and called down the operational ones. Screams emanated from the desk's radio sets from people trapped in elevators high in the building. Those sounds cut through the din of men's voices talking on their radios. When Seifert saw Brendan approaching, he put down his handie-talkie. He wasted no words addressing his superior officer.

"Chief, it looks like the plane hit the building around the ninetieth floor. Multiple 911 calls from floors close to or above the fire, many burn victims. We've got several people trapped in elevators. Jet fuel shot down the shaft and caught some people in the lobby. I'm sending crews up no higher than the eighty-first floor. I want to set up operations on that floor."

"Okay. Any idea if the standpipe is working?" Brendan asked.

"I don't know. I gotta believe the standpipe system up there is shot. I saw the plane hit the building. It was dead on, as if it was aiming for it." The sound of a shuddering thud almost drowned out Seifert's response. Brendan turned to see where the sound came from.

"Jumpers," Seifert said.

Brendan sized up the command post. He saw that his boss, Chief of Division 10, and Citywide Tour Commander Bernie Cullen, in his turnout coat and helmet, had arrived. Behind him was Special Operations Chief Rich Dougherty. *Man, this is bad, but we've got the best guys on duty today.*

Cullen asked as he approached the two chiefs, "Any thought on a collapse?"

"You think there could be one?" Brendan asked skeptically.

"A partial one. Maybe in a couple of hours. You've got a lot of fire on that steel," Cullen responded.

"We've established stairwell B as the attack stairs, and we're sending crews up with fifty-foot sections," Seifert interjected.

"I think what we gotta do is get as many people as possible out of the building. We let it burn. We ain't puttin' this fire out," Cullen said.

Dougherty shook his head to Brendan. "We can't put this fire out."

"That's the priority," Cullen said.

"But we gotta get those people down," Brendan said.

Brendan listened to both chiefs, while he took in the scene. The lobby was filling up with crews that had now lined up to get assignments. An elevator opened, and people exited it, some oblivious to what was going on. A Port Authority police officer directed them toward the doors on the West Street side of the building. Firemen had gathered around the trio of chiefs as they contemplated a plan, listening. Others didn't even check in with the command post and just headed for the stairwells.

Brendan sensed that order was fracturing in the lobby. He needed to get better control of the scene. The Port Authority building engineers and staff at the command post were becoming inundated with distress calls from the upper floors. They wrote them down on pieces of paper and placed them on the counter by the chiefs like they were short orders at a coffee shop.

"Have your aide tell the guys they've gotta check in before going upstairs," Brendan ordered Seifert.

Seifert waved a young battalion chief toward him. "Take two companies and clear floors thirty-one to thirty-five." The battalion chief flicked a nervous glance, then took an engine company and a truck company toward the B stairwell. The fire safety director for the North Tower approached Brendan and Seifert, a radio in his hand.

"Chief, should we evacuate the other tower?" he asked.

"Yes, get 'em out of the other building. Evacuate it," Brendan said, before Seifert could respond. The director keyed his mike and relayed the order to his counterpart in the South Tower.

"323 Truck to Command." Brendan heard the familiar voice of Paddy Boyle on his radio.

"Go ahead, 323."

"We're on forty. We've got a couple of burn victims here; 12 Truck will take them. We're heading up."

"Ten-four."

✦

FDNY Headquarters, Downtown Brooklyn

Cianci knew it when he heard it. The explosion, detonating impact, and shattering steel could only mean one thing. A plane had gone down somewhere in the city. He heard the "Dear Lord" Alice, his secretary, uttered just as Cal Bruno, one of his deputy chiefs, entered his office.

Cianci bolted from his chair and headed for the elevator. "Get the car," he told his aide, Scott Rusello, who was talking with Deputy Commissioner Tom Sheehan in his outer office.

Both men stared back at the chief with unknowing looks on their faces.

"A plane just crashed into the World Trade Center," Cianci said, pointing over his shoulder. "Look out my window."

Bruno gave an affirming nod to Rusello and Sheehan, as he followed Cianci. The aide and deputy commissioner made a quick stop in the chief's office before hastily joining Cianci by the elevator.

"Tom, ride with me," Cianci said to Sheehan.

There was very little talk on the quick ride over the Brooklyn Bridge. The North Tower was directly ahead; its smoke streamed in their direction high overhead. Cianci studied it closely.

"Twenty floors of fire? That's unbelievable. Scott, issue a fifth alarm." Rusello did so over his departmental radio. The command from Manhattan cackled on the radio in the SUV repeating the assignment that would bring two hundred and fifty firemen and their apparatus to the World Trade Center.

The SUV got onto Pearl Street, then made a turn onto Fulton Street. Cianci checked his watch. It was 8:55 a.m. Right behind them was Cianci's deputy chiefs and two staff chiefs in the other SUVs. Cianci got out of the car and peered toward the East face of the North Tower, which was covered in swirling smoke. He walked north toward the Customs House to get a better view. When he glanced up, he couldn't believe the volume of fire he saw. The top of the building was being broiled. Fire spat out from every window about fifteen stories below the roof.

"Jesus Christ. Have you ever seen anything like that?" he said, more to himself than to Sheehan. Sheehan said nothing and shook his head. The staff chiefs had gathered around him and studied the sight also.

In Cianci's mind, the operational command wheels began to spin. *Okay, I've got a high-rise fire. I know what to do with that. But no, I've got an airplane crash. That presents a totally different set of priorities. But no, I've got a large commercial airliner that crashed into a commercial high rise a quarter of a mile in the sky and sent jet fuel, JP 8—shit, that's fucking napalm—down the elevator shafts and throughout the structural supports and around the flame-retardant innards of the building. What's the fucking priorities on that? That one's outside the field manual I learned from.*

This incident involved more than he could comprehend. *Break it down into small parts,* he told himself. *Handle this one piece at a time. Just use the book you have, improvise and adapt as needed, and pray for the best.*

"Let's go," he said, heading for the North Tower, past civilians walking north on West Street.

Inside the tower, Cianci and the staff chiefs passed several companies near the elevator banks waiting for assignments. Chief Dougherty has already gotten to the scene and was involved in an animated discussion with Chiefs Brendan and Seifert about the fire and the structural integrity of the building.

"I tell ya, at some point this building becomes compromised. The integrity of the steel will fail," Dougherty argued.

"In how long?" Brendan shot back.

"I don't know. Eight, ten hours, maybe a little longer," Dougherty answered matter-of-factly, scratching the back of his neck under his white chief's helmet.

"C'mon, Rich."

"Expect a partial collapse—guaranteed."

Brendan frowned.

"Steve, give me an update." a voice interjected.

Brendan turned to see Cianci and the staff chiefs in front of him.

"Chief, we've got civilians trapped on the upper floors. People trapped in elevators; some are working. Radios are working sporadically. The building repeater's out. I'm assigning crews to blocks of floors and sending them up." Brendan put the radio to his ear to capture a transmission. It was from dispatch, telling him of civilians trapped on the ninety-eighth floor.

"The standpipe system?" Cianci asked.

"We don't know. Up there? It's probably shot," Brendan responded.

Cianci listened to the bleak assessment of what was becoming a surreal situation. A plane crash into a skyscraper at seven hundred feet altitude started a five-alarm fire where thousands were trapped causing people to jump to their death. Seifert, radio to his ear, stood behind Brendan, at the command post. Company officers were lined up in front of him to receive assignments. Cianci liked Seifert. He knew the guy from a house they were both assigned to back in the late eighties. Seifert was a by-the-book guy and a good fireman. Cianci remembered a tenement fire in East Harlem one night, and Seifert was the lieutenant on the first engine on the scene; the truck was delayed. Terrified tenants had crowded on the fourth-floor fire escape with the fire ripping on the first floor. Seifert saw the people were getting ready to jump but he didn't lose his composure. He ordered his crew to knock the fire down immediately with the five-hundred-gallon tank on the engine; then he yelled for the people to stay where they were. He then climbed the fire escape. By the time he got to the fourth-floor railing, his crew had the fire out, and the tenants had calmed down and backed away from the railing. He probably saved a half-dozen people, Cianci thought. He was glad Seifert was on duty this morning.

"I think we better establish a command post outside the building," Dougherty interrupted. A jumper had just hit the pavement, and the sound of impact echoed through the lobby.

Cianci nodded. "We'll do that."

He faced Brendan. "Okay, good chief," Cianci said in response to Brendan's grim report. "Forget about anyone above the fire. They're gone or they're gonna be gone. We can't do anything about that. Evacuate everyone from below the fire. Let the thing burn off, and we'll set up a collapse zone. We'll set up a command post out on West Street." He then headed for the automatic doors. The staff chiefs, Dougherty, and Sheehan, followed. He could sense their eyes were still trained on him as he walked away, trying to absorb the order he just gave.

"That's why he has the five stars, and we don't," he heard one of them say, quietly.

CHAPTER 32

0847–0915 HOURS

Incident Command Post, Corner of West and Vesey Streets

At the corner of West and Vesey, Cianci and Dougherty stood among a handful of staff chiefs and some lower-ranking officers. Chauffeurs in bunker gear stood by their rigs in the long line of trucks and engines that had staged on West Street. Police units had set up wooden horses along Vesey Street, pushing civilians north on West Street away from the towers.

The cell phone vibrated in Cianci's pocket. He pulled it out. It was the mayor.

"Paul, can you give me an update?" Pisani asked the chief with urgency in his voice. Cianci knew Pisani could be a cool customer, but today was different.

"Mr. Mayor, I can't save anybody above the fire. There's no way we can make a rescue on the roof and there's too much fire. We're evacuating everybody below the fire, but I can't do anything about anyone above it," Cianci said.

"Nothing?" Pisani asked.

"Fire's too big. Unreachable. Standpipe system is compromised," Cianci said almost dismissively, as if he were telling the mayor to let him do his job.

"That bad?" Pisani asked.

"Yes. We're throwing everything at this. If we're lucky, we can get most everybody out of the building. Then we'll set up a collapse zone and let the fire burn itself out."

Cianci shoved the cell phone into his pocket. His mind went to that night his rifle company was almost overrun at Ripcord in '70. How he was getting ready to go to hand-to-hand with the NVA before the Huey gunships showed up and evaporated the enemy. He remembered he just wanted to get into it and not think about it and let God write the ending.

Movement in front of him brought his mind back to the fire scene. He clenched his jaw and glared at Dougherty, like he wanted to beat somebody with a truncheon tool. About fifteen chief officers had assembled at the command post. Company officers, just dismounted from their rigs, approached the post to check in and get assignments, while other companies headed straight for the towers. The staff chiefs, glued to their radios, received updates from their respective battalions.

Dougherty stared at the North Tower and leaned toward Cianci. "Paul, all we gotta do is get everybody out of the building. I think we have—"

The sound came from out in the harbor, starting as a rumble and then turned into a deafening roar. Everyone in the command post turned south toward the towers. The wings and fuselage of a commercial jet momentarily darkened the space between the towers before it slammed into the untouched South Tower. Dougherty stood motionless, watching the impact and the resulting fire explosion, itself about thirty stories in diameter. Explosive debris shot away from the South Tower, flying past the North Tower and slamming into the earth in every direction.

"Mother of God," Dougherty whispered. "They're trying to kill us."

"Those fucking sons of bitches," Cianci cursed, turning to Bruno. "Transmit a fifth alarm assignment now."

Bruno keyed his radio and ordered the new assignment. The sound of dispatch transmitting the call to the 31st Battalion in Brooklyn for a complement of 250 brothers, twenty engines, eleven trucks, and five battalion chiefs echoed from the stationary radios in the cabs of the rigs that had staged on West Street. Radio traffic erupted on the tactical channel with reports of another plane making impact with the South Tower.

Cianci stared up at the sight of two populated skyscrapers burning out of control. He could see the fire in the North Tower was now burning heavy fuel loads. The smoke had turned from a light gray to a dirty black color and increased noticeably in quantity. At the edge of the command post, Knox stared up at the sight, his hands in his pockets.

What a curb captain, Cianci thought to himself. *He's fucking useless.*

"I give it about four hours before we get a partial collapse," Dougherty said. "Paul, I think we should move the command post down the block to get a better view of both towers." Sheehan said.

"Yeah, let's go."

Cianci led the assembled command to a spot on West Street across from the Trident Hotel. It was between the North and South Passageways on the west side of West Street, in front of a parking garage.

At the new command post, Cianci and Dougherty could see both towers with aggressive fires burning on the upper floors. Jumpers came down at such a frequent pace that Cianci would only glance up when he wanted to check on the advance of the fire. Every time he saw a jumper fall, a feeling of visceral anger collected in his stomach and moved into his chest. He commanded the largest, most effective, most well-equipped fire department on the planet, populated with men with hundreds of collective years of clinical and intangible experience in how to fight the Beast in all its permutations, and now he felt completely impotent. On this day, hundreds of people in his charge chose to jump from mountainous heights to avoid burning to death, and his fire department could not save them. Cianci wanted to get a hold of whoever did this, take a bowie knife, and gut him like a fish. He took it as a personal affront to his ability to command the department.

Cianci reacted by doing what he always did at big jobs: he paced around a little to help him think his way out of the problem in front of him. He knew the rescue and truck companies had made their way up into the towers. From his brief observations in the North Tower lobby, he knew civilians were making their way out of the buildings, but there would be those who would not evacuate or could not evacuate. And he knew the window on getting those people out was closing. How fast, he could only guess.

But something else gnawed at his instincts. This event was getting beyond his span of control. With the impact of the second plane, Cianci knew this was a deliberate act, well planned and well-coordinated. He wondered if there were more planes headed for the towers. Or maybe another target in the city. He thought about doing the unthinkable: pulling guys out. With civilians still in the building the thought was beyond his comprehension, but the thought was compelling.

Cianci gazed south down West Street. Engines and trucks pulled up just south of the South Tower in response to the new assignment. The crews emerged from the rigs and entered the building. Others pulled onto Liberty Street at the base of the South Tower. Ladder 208—a hook-and-ladder crew from Red Hook that called themselves the Happy Hookers—had parked in front of the Trident

Hotel at the base of the South Tower. Their nickname always made him laugh. Civilians exited the hotel in every direction. Some approached the command post, where they were met by cops who directed them north.

On the command channel, he heard the familiar voice of Assistant Chief Ron Turner, the citywide tour commander, telling dispatch that he was taking command of the South Tower.

"I think I better get over there," Dougherty replied.

"Okay. But make your way back here as soon as you can. I want to monitor the North Tower."

✦

252 Engine, Brooklyn-Queens Expressway

"Ronk, what are you looking at?" Rowan asked his chauffeur.

"There's a plane heading over the harbor, see it?"

"Yeah, what's that guy doing?" Rowan turned his head left and leaned forward.

A large commercial airliner accelerated in a burst of speed over the harbor in the direction of the towers. It stayed on course and slammed into the south face of the South Tower, which shockingly swallowed the plane completely. A fireball erupted from the skyscraper's north face.

"Did you fuckin' see that?" Ronkowski said.

"Un-fuckin-believable."

Coletti craned his neck to peer across the cab through the window on the side that faced Manhattan. Smoke banked down from the towers, staining a gloriously blue, cloudless sky.

"The chiefs are going to have their hands full today," Coletti said to Rodriguez.

Rodriguez's mouth was shut, but his lips and tongue were moving, praying. The engine was now at the mouth of the Brooklyn-Battery Tunnel. The Manhattan-bound traffic was backed up at the toll plaza, where two police cruisers had blocked off traffic from entering the tunnel.

Ronkowski slowed the rig so he could swing around the toll plaza and avoid the traffic. People turned to watch the engine approach the tunnel. Coletti glanced out the cab window at the civilians. The look those people gave him said it all. It was one of part bewilderment, part concern, and complete disbelief. *These people are looking at us like we're fuckin' nuts.*

Rowan pointed to the entrance as Ronkowski careened the rig around the toll plaza and into the tunnel's mouth.

"Go. Get through this thing as fast as you can," Rowan told Ronkowski. "I don't want to be caught in here if they blow it up."

Ronkowski leaned heavily on the gas pedal, giving the Seagrave all of the five hundred horsepower from its Cummins engine. The deafening high whine of the engine bounced off the sides of the tunnel and entered the cab. Coletti rolled up his window to deaden the noise.

Ronkowski eased his foot off the gas when the end of the tunnel came into sight. The engine exited the tunnel underpass onto West Street into an almost surreal environment. The sky was awash in paper, as if a ticker tape parade was marching down the nearby Canyon of Heroes. Near and distant sirens split the air amid airplane and building wreckage was strewn all over the roadway. Jordan reached out of his window and grabbed a piece of paper that wafted by.

"Marsh McLennan. Ninety-Fourth Floor, 1 World Trade Center," he said out loud. "Shit, this came out of the Trade Center."

The rig slowed down as it got closer to the World Trade Center. The street was covered in debris. Ronkowski maneuvered the rig around the larger pieces, so as not to damage the truck's undercarriage. It was Rowan who realized it wasn't debris that littered their path to the towers.

"Ronk, those are body parts. Just go straight as fast as you can,"

Rowan ordered the chauffeur, who nodded and complied.

"God, please forgive me," Ronk whispered.

Ronkowski steadied the wheel and headed straight up West Street. As the rig got closer to the towers, shards of metal, plastic, glass, and aircraft wreckage hit the roof of the cab and the side of the truck. Debris landed everywhere.

Rowan rolled up the window on the officer's door. He leaned forward and craned his neck to get a good view of the top of the towers as building debris careened down. Ahead, other engines had staged just north of the towers, out of the way of the falling material.

"Get up there," Rowan ordered. Ronkowski swung the truck into the opposite, vacant lane of traffic, to avoid a roaring car fire in the middle of the street. The car was at a traffic light, its door open as if the driver had fled the car. A piece of a jet engine had landed in its back seat, fiercely burning the car. *Lucky bastard.* Out of the corner of his eye, Coletti saw the Rescue 22 rig parked right under the South Overpass near the South Tower. He was pretty sure his dad was working today. *He's probably knocking the thing down by now.*

The engine entered the staging area on West Street just south of Albany Street and came to a stop right behind a row of other engines. To the left, the eight Manhattan ladder trucks staged on the other side of the concrete divider, their chauffeurs congregated near the traffic-directing battalion chief.

"Everybody grab an extra bottle along with a roll-up and a flashlight. Coletti take the rope," Rowan said, putting on his turnout coat. He got down from his riding compartment and strapped his radio harness across his shoulder.

"Come around," Rowan ordered his crew.

The crew gathered their gear and equipment and closed in around Rowan.

"Okay, stay with me and do not, I repeat, do not get split up."

Now outside the cab, Coletti finally got a good visual of the towers. He couldn't believe the volume of fire. About forty stories below the top of the South Tower, a large body of fire burned throughout the floor and around the exterior of the tower at its southeast corner. It gave off dark-black smoke that gushed heavily from the opening in the tower's south face.

Instinctively, the training he received at the academy on building construction came to mind. *For every thousand degrees, steel will expand one inch in an hour. In doing so, the structural integrity of a building will likely be compromised by a fire that burns that long.* He could hear the words from the crusty old buffalo who taught building construction and structural collapse at the Rock. Coletti figured the upper floors of the building could be in danger of a partial collapse if the fire burned out of control. *We're gonna have to make a stand somewhere below this thing if they can get us water.*

Ronkowski stayed at the rig as the 252 crew followed their lieutenant north on West Street. Thunderous crashes reverberated from around the towers where the debris hit the ground. The amount coming down was tremendous. Alternating between glancing skyward and ahead, the crew shimmied along the east side of West Street, stopping to take shelter under the South Bridge, a short thirty yards from the entrance to the South Tower. The firemen knelt on the sidewalk against the supporting column for the South Bridge.

Coletti sized up the approach to the South Tower. The massive tower's revolving doors were straight ahead. An easy approach on any day. But today the sidewalk was littered with debris. The windows to the lobby were all blown out. That was the only way in. He studied the obstacle course in front of the building when he was distracted by another piece of debris that hit the plaza between the crew and the building and exploded on impact. It didn't really explode. It burst.

At that point, it registered to Coletti and the other firemen huddled under the South Bridge that the debris coming down, that hit the ground with thunderous impact, was not building materials.

It was people.

Rowan gazed up toward the tower. A huge amount of smoke pushed out of the gaping hole in upper midsection of the tower.

"Okay. When I say *go*, we make a run for the revolving doors. You got it?" Each nodded quickly. Rowan stared upward and then waved his right hand forward.

"Go."

The crew, heads down, scampered toward the tower, each fireman carrying sixty pounds of bunker gear, masks, and rolled sections of hose.

Once inside, they dropped their roll-ups and took stock of the lobby. Dozens of firemen lined the walls, waiting for orders. Civilians emerged from stairwells onto the mezzanine level above the lobby and exited the building. Several Port Authority workers walked around, radios held to their ears. The elevator panel had been turned into a small command post manned by chiefs, a couple of Port Authority police officers, three building engineers. A departmental chaplain, wearing a chief's helmet with "FDNY Chaplain" emblazoned on the front piece, paced the floor, watching, praying to himself, his Roman collar visible under his turnout coat.

Rowan reported to the command post and stood in line behind a couple of officers. When he got to the desk, he asked Chief Turner what he needed.

"Just take your crew upstairs and do what you can," Turner answered numbly.

Rowan nodded and signaled to his crew to head to the stairs. The crew, now standing in line with the other companies, gathered their gear and equipment. Out of the corner of his eye, Coletti saw one of the brothers talking with the chaplain. The priest nodded, and the fireman turned and walked back to a group of firemen assembled near the elevator bank wall. They all turned and knelt down in front of the chaplain. Other brothers realized what was going on, knelt also, joined by Coletti and the crew of 252. The priest raised his hand over his head and recited the prayer of general absolution.

"God the Father does not wish the sinner to die but to turn back to him and live. He loves us first and sent his Son into the world to be its Savior. May he show you his merciful love and give you peace."

Coletti felt like he was in confession back at Saint Agatha's Parochial School in Bensonhurst. The priest continued each incantation followed by a hushed "Amen" from the kneeling brothers, eyes all cast to the floor.

"And I absolve you from your sins in the name of the Father, and of the Son, and of the Holy Spirit."

The priest made the sign of the cross over the sixty firemen, lieutenants, and captains that knelt before him.

The brothers stood up. Rowan motioned to his crew to follow him to the stairwell next to the elevator banks from which civilians had just emerged. Coletti spotted Sammy Gaddis, one of the guys he knew from a Manhattan truck company, walk past him, an eight-foot hook in his hand.

"Hey Sammy, did you see my father?"

"He went up about ten minutes ago," Gaddis replied.

The answer triggered conflicting emotions in Coletti. Part of him didn't want his father to be here. The other part was a little relieved he was here. If Sal Coletti, the best, most experienced rescue guy on the Job was here, they had a good chance of beating this thing.

✦

14 Truck, Corner of West and Vesey Streets

"There goes another one," Lowell said, dryly. The deafening thud of the jumper's impact made Lowell turn toward Mangold, who could only frown nonchalantly.

The rest of the crew of 14 Truck stood motionless next to the rig, gear in hand, waiting for direction from Lieutenant Connolly.

"C'mon. Follow me," Connolly said tightly. He headed to the

opposite side of West Street. "We'll go down the street and come up from the south."

The crew followed him past the staging engines and trucks. When they got to the hotel at the base of the South Tower, they crossed back over the street and headed toward the South Tower entrance on Liberty Street. They hugged the wall of the hotel, which had an overhang of about twenty-four inches. It gave them some protection from the people falling from the sky. After a good five minutes inching along the wall, the crew made it to the sliding doors of South Tower doorway. By then, Mangold and Lowell's turnout coats were laced in a deep crimson.

Once inside, the crew regrouped by the marbled wall of the lobby nearest the plaza between the two towers. Connolly headed to the command post, where the battalion chiefs had assembled.

Lowell tried to gain some perspective but found it hard to collect his thoughts. Every time a jumper hit the ground, the sliding glass doors would open and close, triggered by the reverberations of the impacts. He slouched down against the wall, next to Mangold, and tried to quell the pangs of fear and resignation rising in him.

He breathed deeply, sighed, and focused his eyes at his feet. The sliding door continued to open and close.

"Jay, take it easy," Mangold told his junior partner.

Lowell pursed his lips. "Jim, this is fucked."

"Don't think about it," Mangold responded calmly. "I know this looks bad. But we don't know what'll happen today."

Lowell nodded. Mangold put his hand on Lowell's shoulder. "All we can do is play the hand we're dealt. That's it, okay?"

"Yeah."

Truck Larry stood over his two crewmates. He eyed the lobby closely. "Man, this is a fucked-up scene. How are the chiefs gonna get us out of this one?" he remarked.

"Did I ever tell you guys when I was young, I went on a date with Cheryl Ladd, one of Charlie's Angels?" Mangold said, quietly, almost as if to himself.

"What? You're shitting us," Truck Larry responded.

Mangold smiled. "Yeah, I did. She was great. No bullshit."

"How the hell did you pull that off?" Lowell asked.

"I'll tell you when we we're back at the house."

"Hey, look. It's Sturgis." Truck Larry stood up and motioned to the courtyard outside the building.

Lowell and Mangold turned and saw an encouraging sight: Harry Sturgis, in his bunker gear, was walking across the plaza toward the building, followed by Hector Leon, the stocky probie on Engine 48. The crew scampered through the revolving doors to meet the probies. Truck Larry waved to Sturgis, who saw him and headed in his direction. Mangold, eyes cast upward, waved his hands vigorously.

"C'mon you guys, run!" Mangold implored them.

Harry glanced up and saw a jumper diving down right over them.

"Hector, c'mon, run!" Harry yelled.

The two probies broke into a sprint. Mangold continued to wave them in, both he and Truck Larry shouted to them to go faster.

"Don't look up, just run," Lowell yelled.

Harry opened up some distance between himself and Hector, who wasn't as fast. About ten feet from the door, Sturgis stumbled and fell. His knees buckled, and he tumbled to the ground. A loud *boom* ricocheted off the tower. He cast a bewildered look at the crew whose faces said it all.

The jumper had landed on Hector, crushing and killing him instantly. Truck Larry threw his hands up in disgust. Mangold and Lowell ran out, grabbed Harry, and dragged him through the revolving door. Once inside the doors, his brothers helped Harry to his feet. Six guys from an engine company ran out onto the plaza, picked up the body of Hector, and carried him across the plaza. Harry turned to help Hector but was stopped by Mangold.

"He's gone. Don't even think about it."

Harry gaped at Mangold, who delivered that information without a hint of emotion. The automatic doors continued their death cadence at the other end of the building. Catching his breath, he saw people streaming out of the stairwells and then out onto the plaza.

"How'd you get here?" Truck Larry asked a gasping, disoriented Sturgis.

"I took a bus. "Where's Lieu?"

"He's over at the command post, checking in," Truck Larry responded.

Connolly approach the crew briskly.

"They just transmitted a third alarm," Connolly said.

"They want us to head over to the Trident Hotel. They've got reports of people trapped in an elevator." He noticed Sturgis. "Nice to see you made the party, Sturgis." Connolly rubbed his eyebrows and adjusted his radio harness. "Let's go."

"Aye, aye, Lieu," Sturgis responded, numbly.

CHAPTER 33

0916–0959 HOURS

Engine 252, South Tower

Coletti followed Rowan steadily up the stairs, the high-rise kit digging farther into his shoulder with every flight up. The crew stayed to the right to let civilians move down to their left. Every once in a while, a quiet "thank you" was passed from civilian to fireman in the narrow walkway.

Eight flights up, the crew came upon a man in shirtsleeves and slacks with blood on his shirt. He was wheezing.

"What floor did you come from?' Rowan asked the man.

"Seventy-nine," he responded.

"Did you see fire there?"

He nodded. Rowan asked a civilian—a young guy in a shirt and tie—to help the wheezing man down the stairs. The young civilian took the man's arm, slung it over his shoulder and continued down. Transmissions barked from Rowan's radio as the crew continued its ascent.

"Rescue 22 to Command."

"Go ahead, Rescue 22."

"Were on twenty-five. We have multiple burn victims and are taking them down Stairway A from this location."

"10-4," Command responded.

Coletti eyed the fire doors above on the next stairway landing and saw a "19" stenciled in white paint on the door. He realized his father was six floors above him. At the twentieth floor, Rowan entered the stairwell, followed by the crew. Rodriguez and Jordan leaned against the wall, catching their breath. The climb with gear and hose was taking its toll on them. Other engine and truck crews had stopped there also. Down the hall an engineman broke into a vending machine and returned with five bottles of water for the crew, who downed them quickly.

Coletti inspected the roll-up he was carrying, all thirty pounds of it, and wondered if he could carry it up to the seventy-ninth floor on top of the sixty pounds of gear he was already carrying, but he knew he was going to find out. He caught Rowan sizing up the crew.

"Let's go. We'll stop every ten floors," Rowan said.

The crew got on their feet and marched up Stairwell A. When the crew got to the twenty-seventh floor, they were alone. No more civilians on the stairs. The crew continued up and stepped into the thirtieth floor to take another break. They took off their gear to try to cool down a little bit. Jordan slumped down next to Coletti.

"Phil, this is the shit. What do you—"

Before he could finish speaking, the building jerked abruptly. It faintly thudded, making Jordan reach for the wall. Then it got quiet. The overhead lights went out, and the emergency lighting came on. Rowan's radio went completely silent.

"What was that?" Jordan asked.

Rowan got up, walked to an office door, jacked it open with his officer's halligan tool and peered down the hallway. "The building is compromised," he said. The look of disbelief on his face sent a pang of fear through Coletti.

"I think we better head down. Leave the equipment," Rowan said.

Jordan, Rodriguez, and Coletti got to their feet and quickly followed Rowan to the stairwell and down the stairs. When they got to the twenty-third floor, the conditions in the stairwell had deteriorated. Ash and smoke filled the air. The door to floor twenty-three was open. Coletti peered into the hallway. He saw a couple of truckies from Ladder 57 standing over an older fireman who leaned against the wall, holding his knee. The shock of thick white hair gave the injured fireman away immediately.

It was Sal Coletti.

Phil peeled off from his company and entered the floor. The rest of his company didn't break stride and continued down the stairwell. The two Ladder 57 guys tried to help Sal up, but he didn't want to go.

"Guys, you can go. I'll take him," Phil said.

"Okay, but his knee is hurt pretty bad," one of the truckies said.

Phil knelt down next to his father. "I got it. You better go," he said. The truckies nodded and headed down the stairwell.

"Pop, what happened?"

"Big lady fell into me on the stairwell. She caught my knee in just the right place," Sal said. He turned away in disgust.

"Pop, it's okay. I'll get you out," Phil said as he took off his bunker coat. "Can you put any pressure on it?"

"Nah, I'm shot. You better go. This building's coming down."

Phil didn't know what to say. Sal pulled a cigarette out of his turnout coat, put it in his mouth, and lit it with the Zippo lighter he got from his dad, who carried it with him from Normandy to the Rhine in World War II.

"Your mother won't be able to handle it if both of us buy it today." He closed the lighter and stuck it in his pocket.

"Pop, c'mon. I'm not gonna leave you here."

He put his father's arm around his shoulder and lifted him up. Sal winced from the pain but steadied himself. He limped to the doorway, his arm around his son's shoulder. The father and son were able to negotiate the first flight of stairs, but it was slow going. When they got to the next floor down, Sal leaned against the recess in the wall of the stairwell, next to the standpipe.

"Pop, we can do this. Let's keep going," Phil said with no sense of urgency in his voice.

Sal eyed his son.

"Philly, I need to tell you something." He took a long drag on his cigarette.

"Yeah, Pop?"

"When you were born, I was at work. You came in a little early, so Uncle Vincent had to drive mom to the hospital. That night, we had a big job. Big apartment house in Bed-Sty. A lot of guys got hurt. People died. A really holy mess. When I got back to the firehouse, Uncle Vincent was waiting for me. We jumped in his car and went right to the hospital."

Sal took a drag on his cigarette, eyes glistened.

"When I got to the hospital, Mom was sleeping. So the nurses brought you over to me. You were so perfect. Your skin was so soft, but you were bawling your head off. I was so banged up from the worker we just came from. I reeked of smoke, and my hands were sooty black. They didn't want to let me hold you, but I told them to give me my boy, and they did."

The elder Coletti paused. A couple of guys from 94 Truck came down the stairs and stopped when they saw Sal. Phil waved them down the stairs; they resumed their descent.

"As soon as they put you in my arms, you stopped crying. The nurses were even surprised. Did you know that?"

Phil shook his head. "No. I didn't."

"That's when it hit me that I wanted you to be better than me.

I knew it. I could feel it when I held you that you *were* better than me."

Sal propped himself up against the wall a little.

"Look at you. So calm. The way you carry yourself. It's something I can't do. You're a born leader. I know you can make lieutenant, but you could go do something else. Be a teacher, professor, something like that."

"Pop, I hear you, but you never asked me why I wanted to get on the Job. Maybe if you did, you'd understand.

Sal grinned. "It was the telephone company fire, when you were eight. When I got hurt and laid up in the hospital, right?"

Phil's eyes widened. "Yeah, how'd you know?

"Mom told me you were scared I would die, and you wanted to help me. She said you wouldn't go to sleep every night until I came home from the hospital. She said you told her you were gonna be a fireman to help me."

Phil nodded. "Yeah, that was it."

Sal tried to move his leg. He winced in pain. Ash filled the air in the stairwell.

"Look at this shit. Philly, please. This is why I didn't want you to stay on the Job—shit like this. Get out of here. You gotta go. I'll be okay."

Phil took his father's head in his right hand and kissed him on the forehead.

"Pop. I'm with you. I'm not—"

It started as a low rumble. Sal looked up. The ceiling shook. Coletti knelt over his father to shield him from the falling concrete and metal. He breathed in, closed his eyes, and forced a memory of Ellie's rapturous scent to his mind. He hoped death would come quickly.

CHAPTER 34

14 TRUCK, TRIDENT HOTEL, WEST STREET

Connolly led his crew out of the South Tower and down the sidewalk to the lobby of the Trident Hotel; they stayed close to the building to avoid the metal and debris raining down. Once inside the lobby, they encountered a battalion chief, Joe Gannon, at the front desk. There were about forty firemen there. Gannon was combining companies into large detachments and sending them upstairs to search and evacuate the building. A steady stream of civilians came down the stairs. Gannon ordered Connolly and the crew of 14 Truck to assist people out of the building through the south entrance of the hotel, which was farther away from the towers than the entrance on West Street.

Connolly set up his crew to form a cordon, to prevent people from exiting out the West Street entrance, which was littered with twisted steel girders and bodies like Omaha Beach on D-Day. He waved the evacuees toward the south entrance.

"C'mon, everybody out. This way. Don't go onto West Street. C'mon," Connolly shouted.

The unsuspecting evacuees of the nine-hundred-room hotel moved quickly. They kept their heads down and followed the fire lieutenant's orders, all but one. A young woman, in her twenties, wearing a corporate suit, stopped as others passed.

"Aren't you guys going to get out of here too?" she asked Lowell.

Lowell stared into her eyes.

"Ma'am, you have to keep going. This building may come down," Lowell said. The resignation in his voice caused the woman to gasp before catching herself from being rude. She exited the building with a bewildered expression on her face. Minutes later, one of the lobby elevators opened, and two businessmen exited, just as a muffled explosion broke over their heads. Connolly raised his eyebrows.

"That's not good," Truck Larry said. The explosion was followed by a vibration that got louder, followed by successive sounds of popping. Mangold figured it out first.

"The building's coming down," he said.

Connolly took one of the businessmen and pushed him to the ground and got on top of him when the full impact of the collapse hit them. Cement and building materials started flying through the lobby. The sound was deafening. Sturgis saw Truck Larry get laid out by a piece of metal. Lowell dove for an alcove space as parts of the ceiling came down on top of him.

Sturgis was motionless. He hunched in a crouched position, transfixed by what he was witnessing. He was paralyzed, gripped with fear that he was about to lose his life. His hearing diminished to almost nothing. The booming sounds became muffled, like he was underwater. That was, until he felt a hand on the back of his jacket jerk him violently to the ground. He looked up to see Mangold, helmetless, standing over him. The veteran took Sturgis's arm and stretched it out on the floor. Then, he picked up his leg and stomped on Sturgis's hand with his leather boot, repeatedly.

Sturgis was surprised that at first he didn't feel anything, then the sensation of pain shot up his arm and into his brain. He recoiled from the pain, staring at Mangold, dumbfounded, as the booming sounds returned in full volume in his ears, and he realized he was able to move after all.

"Follow me," Mangold shouted. He grabbed Sturgis by his turn-out coat and pushed him toward a large column near the center of the lobby.

"Hold onto this, and don't let go," Mangold told him.

Sturgis grabbed the column with both hands and curled around it in the fetal position just before debris hit him. He closed his eyes and felt something heavy hit him in the side. The floor shuddered. Large pieces of concrete, electrical cable, and sheetrock rained down and plowed into the main doors to the lobby, followed by a black cloud that enveloped everything around him.

When he opened his eyes, it was pitch black. He opened his mouth and coughed. A thick, pasty film coated his throat. He tried to spit but couldn't, so he stuck his finger down his throat. Voices could be heard close by, but he didn't recognize any of them. He heard a voice on a radio giving a mayday call. Someone said they had a flashlight. He scanned the blackness for a beam of light but didn't see anything. The complete darkness gave him no frame of reference.

He tried to move and felt dull pains in his knee and side. He shook his hips to get debris off of him, which hurt even more. He yelled out for the guys but heard nothing. No Jay, no Larry, no Connolly, no Jim. Slowly, he pulled himself up, leaning against the column. He still had his mask on but no helmet. He felt all alone and didn't want to leave his spot. He was alive because Jim Mangold had told him to stay in that spot, and he listened to him.

The darkness was cut by a beam of light, followed by a voice. "Can you see my flashlight?" the voice said.

"Yeah, I can," Sturgis responded.

"Okay. Just try to come closer to it," the voice commanded.

Sturgis used his hands to pick himself up. The beam of light revealed a pile of debris about four feet high in front of him. He crawled over the pile and down the other side, where he was met by a fireman holding a flashlight. Sturgis could see the outline of a doorway opening to the street outside, dim light entering through the dust. He saw figures moving through the dust out in the street.

"Was anybody else with you?" the flashlight-toting fireman asked. He had a "235" on his helmet shield. He was covered in dust but otherwise uninjured.

"My whole crew. I'm from 14 Truck," Sturgis said, standing up. He called out the names of each of the guys in his crew. There was no answer. He leaned against a block of cement to steady himself.

"I can't find my crew either," the 235 fireman said.

The fireman studied Sturgis. "Brother, you look pretty banged up. Come with me." He put his arm around Sturgis's shoulder. They both made their way over the rubble to the outside, where they encountered a truck lieutenant from a Brooklyn company who was spitting up phlegm, holding his hands on his knees. When he saw Sturgis and the 235 engineman, he stood up, slowly regaining his composure.

"Let's get out of here," the lieutenant said, coughing and spitting. Sturgis and the 235 engineman glanced around for a path away from the building. A five-story-high debris field blocked their way north on West Street. South of them, the South Pedestrian Bridge had collapsed across West Street, cutting a southward escape. It was clear to Sturgis the only way to go was to head west on Liberty Street into Battery Park City.

"We gotta go that way," Sturgis said, motioning with his hand. The lieutenant nodded.

The trio slowly evacuated the demolished Trident Hotel. They gingerly walked down Liberty Street, as if they were walking through a wartime minefield, then turned right and moved north where they were able to enter an office building at the end of South End Avenue in the World Financial Center. From there they were able to get back out to West Street just south of the burning North Tower.

✦

Hudson Street, Lower Manhattan

O'Rorke and Melanie had ridden to the police checkpoint at the corner of West and Chambers where they parked the motorcycle. O'Rorke had told Melanie to go to her apartment and get out of the area. Melanie had objected and told him he should go to his firehouse. O'Rorke assured her he would call her when he got back to the firehouse then hustled down West Street toward the towers.

Just north of Vesey Street O'Rorke came upon a truck chauffeur standing next to his rig. He asked about a spare set of gear, which the chauffeur was more than happy to give to him along with a set of irons. With bunker gear and tools, he headed south toward the towers to get to work.

It was then that he heard it. The rumbling high above him. He raised his eyes and saw the top half of the South Tower heave forward and cascade down. He froze, in a state of shock, until the sound of a familiar voice pierced his ears.

"Bryan!" It was Melanie, about ten yards from him. O'Rorke dropped his irons and sprinted toward her as the building raced toward them. Debris rained down with such velocity it forced O'Rorke to crouch down and crawl. He grabbed his helmet with his hands and tried to move forward but the showering debris stopped him. He needed shelter and curled up at the street curb under a light pole.

Melanie knelt down facing him. A piece of concrete hit her in the torso and slammed her to the ground just as the dust cloud enveloped them both.

"No! Mel, no!" he yelled.

He was pummeled by pieces of concrete and glass; a blast of heat rushed by him. He lay prone and waited.

It was a good five minutes before O'Rorke opened his eyes. When he did, the dust crept into his eyes, forcing him to rub them. He raised his head slowly, scanning for Melanie. Nowhere. Slowly, he crawled across the rubble to where she had been; the rough edges of glass and metal scratched and scoured his thighs and his hands in the process. The fog of dust lifted slowly. It took him a couple of minutes to close the twenty feet to where he had last seen her. When he got there, he wildly pushed away pieces of concrete and glass, rummaging through the rubble for her, until he found something soft. It was her arm. He cleared away more debris until she was freed from the rubble. Her shoulder was crushed, and her left arm was twisted, broken. She had a three-inch laceration on the back of her head.

"C'mon, Mel, c'mon. Stay with me," he desperately pleaded. He checked her pulse. She still had one, but barely.

"C'mon, Mel. I know you can hear me. You've got to fight. C'mon. You're tougher than this," he said to her, his voice choking up.

Her face was still as pristine and beautiful as the night he met her on Saint Patrick's Day, six months earlier. Her eyes were shut. He cradled her in his arm and got that feeling he only had once before, on that hot summer night in 1978. It ricocheted through him, bringing back the pain of that day when he realized his father was dead and never coming back. He was surprised his body had the memory of that day in it, but here, holding Melanie, he felt it again. He held her to his chest, leaned close to her face, and started to cry.

"Don't leave me, Mel," he said softly. "Please don't leave."

Then, his reflexes took over. He stood up, holding her in his arms, and glanced around. Red lights pulsed faintly through the fog north on West Street. O'Rorke carried the unconscious Melanie past crushed and burning fire trucks toward the lights, past the dead and injured—brothers and civilians alike. He could not believe the carnage—1945 Berlin carnage. Injured reached up, pleading for aid, writhing in pain. He followed the pulsing red lights to an ambulance with its compartment doors open where two emergency medical technicians were giving a middle-aged woman oxygen.

"Guys, you gotta help me. She's in really bad shape," he said.

The EMT examined Melanie, rendered a half-second triage decision. "Okay. Give her to us. We've got one packaged already. We'll take her to Saint Vincent's."

O'Rorke handed Melanie over to them. They placed her on her back on the stretcher, her lifeless arms dangled from its sides. O'Rorke lifted up her extremities and placed her hands on her stomach on the stretcher as one EMT fastened her to the stretcher. The other one quickly wrapped a bandage around her head while O'Rorke helped lift the stretcher into the back of the ambulance. He watched it pull north on West Street, weaving around cars until it disappeared in the dust-driven fog.

✦

323 Truck, North Tower

Boyle took the flight of stairs between forty-three and forty-four in three steps; Kearns followed a floor below him at the same pace. The truck captain felt good knowing his senior man was staying close. The flow of civilians had now ebbed to a trickle, with only one or two passing the firemen as they moved up the stairs.

The captain's mind was racing. He kept reviewing what he saw of the building from the outside, trying to envision the conditions they would experience when they got to the fire floor. He could feel the weight of the gear on his back and a sting in his legs from the burn injury. He blocked out the pain and kept climbing. Kearns was now a good two floors below him, followed closely behind by Reynolds. Boyle stopped for a moment to catch his breath; he heard Kearns say something to Reynolds.

"I don't know how he does it," Kearns said to the probie, between gasps for air. "He got back on the job two months ago, and it's like he's your age."

Boyle smiled at the compliment. The descent of civilians had stopped; he looked up and saw the number 50 on the door. He pulled the door and propped it open before entering, then took off his helmet and checked his watch. It read 9:24 a.m. He stood against the wall and waited for the rest of the crew, each member making his way onto the floor. Some sat down immediately. Others put their hands on their knees and sucked in air. Boyle straightened out and sized up the crew.

"Okay, we're more than halfway there. No stopping until you get to the scene. We gotta get up there." He stood in the doorway to Staircase B and keyed his radio mike. "323 Truck to Command. We're on fifty and heading up."

Some of the guys gave him a look like they wanted to quit, like they couldn't give it any more, but none of them said anything. Between catching their breath and resting their legs, they pulled up their gear and marched forward behind the only guy they would follow anywhere on earth.

The boys climbed. Now, past the lower floors and into the fifties, they never saw a civilian. Like whale hunters sailing north into the Arctic Ocean in search of their prey beyond the habitable southern regions, the brothers climbed the stairs alone, cut off from the rest of the world, into the sky for another engagement with the Red Devil.

With sixty floors below them, it was clear all they had to do was to get to the seat of the fire. Just get there. Don't think about anything else. Not the pain, the weight, the sweat, the fatigue, and slow disorientation that was creeping into each ponderous step up against gravity. The veterans had zoned themselves into a steady pace—partly to conserve energy, partly to steel themselves for what they expected would be a long struggle against their ardent foe—knowing full well that when they got into the shit, adrenaline they never knew existed would kick in.

At the seventy-fifth floor, a slight haze filled the stairwell. Boyle heard popping and crackling sounds. *Not too much more. Probably another ten floors.* Reynolds was right behind him, sweating. His gear was wearing him down.

"Leave your gear on the next floor," Boyle told the probie. "We gotta get to this thing to see what is going on."

"Really?"

"Yeah. The rest of the crew is heading up. We can come back and get it later."

Reynolds stripped off his mask and put down the fire extinguisher and six-foot hook on the seventy-seventh floors. Boyle waited and then together they picked up the pace, without any sound of the rest of the crew well below them. With every passing floor, the smoke condition intensified; the sound of fire burning and eating everything in its path grew louder. Boyle thought about where they would first find the fire. He figured having seen twenty floors of fire en route to the scene, the thing had to be eating up the fuel package on lower floors as well as the floors above it.

It was Reynolds who got to the fire floor first, or what would pass as the first floor where fire was encountered, the eighty-first. Boyle came up a few seconds later. He was surprised by what he saw or, more accurately what he didn't see. As the two firemen entered the eighty-first floor, they were met with a significant pocket of fire right in front of them. The windows on the floor had blown out. Smoke and heat rose through an enormous hole in the ceiling. He could see a huge mass of fire above them, eating its way up into the core of the building and rippling out to the building's superstructure.

The truck captain knew, as only a hunter and killer of the Beast would know, that the heat above that fire was terrific, making life unlivable for anyone up there. Because the fire had breached the windows, he had a clear view to the outside. He caught sight of a shadow darkening the window, intermittently, the shadow of people falling.

"Cap, those are people jumping," Reynolds said incredulously.

Boyle never broke his stare. "I know. You would too if you were going to burn," he said.

Boyle pulled the radio mike on his bunker jacket and keyed it. "323 Truck to Command."

"Go ahead, 323."

"I am on the eighty-first floor. We have three pockets of fire and multiple 10-65s. I need two engine companies and EMS to my location."

"Ten-four, 323."

Boyle took off his bunker coat and placed in on the floor next to a severely burned unconscious woman. "Turn her over," he said to Reynolds.

Reynolds rolled her onto Boyle's bunker coat. Boyle felt her pulse. Her face was grotesquely burned. "She's gone. Leave her there."

Boyle surveyed the scene. There was no one alive on the floor. In his head, he formulated a plan to contain the fire. He knew if he could get some water on the fire, he could try to knock it down enough and stop any further compromise to the building. Maybe they could even rescue people from above the fire, who knows? A disconcerting sound interrupted his thought process. It was a slow rumble that got louder, like an approaching subway train when it pulls into a station. The floor shook, and the doorway to the stairwell crimped like it wanted to blow off its setting. Air rushed past them with a fierce, whooshing sound.

"Get into the stairwell," Boyle shouted.

Reynolds dove for the doorway, followed by Boyle, who fell on top of him. The two truck firemen lay prone on the floor of the stairwell, riding out the shaking and rush of air that rolled over their backs. The shaking grew more violent. Boyle could feel his teeth chatter and his toes separate. He thought to himself, *This must be it. This is how it goes.* He clutched Reynolds's bunker gear, covered him, and closed his eyes. After about ten seconds, it stopped. Boyle got up slowly and glanced around. The stairwell had gone dark. The emergency alarm began to beep incessantly, and the emergency lights lit up, casting a dim glow down the stairway.

On the landing below Boyle, Kearns slumped against the wall. Men called to each other throughout the stairwell.

"What the fuck was that?" Kearns yelled up to Boyle.

"I don't know," Boyle responded.

Boyle got his bearings and stepped back onto the floor. He looked through the window and couldn't believe what he saw. The other tower wasn't there. Bright daylight shone through the window, tinged with a grayish haze.

"Shit, the other tower just fell," he said. In front of him, the fire was advancing across the floor toward him.

"We gotta get out of here. Back it down. Now," the captain ordered his crew.

Reynolds and Kearns got to their feet and headed down the stairs. Boyle followed them until they got to the seventy-second floor, where they found their irons man, Heimboldt, leaning up against the wall, holding his thigh. Blood slowly oozed between his fingers.

"What happened?" Boyle asked his irons man.

"Cap, the doorway blew out and caught me in the side," he said, wincing.

"Help him," Boyle ordered Reynolds.

Reynolds and Boyle put their arms around Heimboldt's shoulder and helped him down the stairs. On the sixty-first floor, they were met by the six guys from the 323 nightshift crew who had waited for them. The combined crew made it down one more flight when Heimboldt told them he was feeling dizzy.

"Bring him in here," Boyle said, opening the door to the floor. The brothers moved Heimboldt onto the floor and propped him up against the wall.

"We gotta get a tourniquet on him. Kevin, go find something we can use around here—an extension cord, rope. Something."

Reynolds moved down the hall, trying doors, all locked. At the end of the hallway, he found an open door and went in.

It was only a minute before Reynolds returned with an extension cord. He gave it to Boyle. The probie had a strange look on his face.

"What's the matter?" Boyle asked.

"Cap, you've got to see this. Come with me." Reynolds gave the extension cord to one of the guys who was working on Heimboldt and headed back to the office from which he'd emerged. Boyle stood up and followed him.

When Reynolds opened the door to the office, Boyle couldn't believe what he saw. In front of him sat about fifteen people, staring at him, peacefully, quietly, casting expressions of fear and bewilderment.

They said nothing. They just sat there—in wheelchairs.

"It's okay," an older woman said to one of the others calmly. "The fire department is here."

Boyle felt his hands get clammy and took a short breath. For the first time in his career, he really felt the odds were stacked against him. A mountain of fire was burning over his head where he was standing sixty-one floors above ground level with no elevators, with an injured, exhausted crew. A 110-story building had collapsed next to him, and now he had handicapped civilians to get out of the building. And he knew, as sure as night follows day, that once he came upon these people, he had to get them out. That was all he knew, because in all of his days of making grabs, in basements, tenements, hardware stores, and motor vehicle accidents, as soon as he came upon a living soul that needed help, they owned him. He was committed to them like they were his own flesh and blood. He knew no other way.

"Okay," he said to Reynolds. "Go get the guys."

Reynolds headed back to the stairwell doorway, where he

corralled Kearns, the six guys from the night shift and Heimboldt. He leaned against the wall, on his feet, his leg now bandaged. Reynolds led the assembled crew back to Boyle, who now stood outside the office, its door closed.

"Listen, guys. I'm going to give you a choice. We've got about fifteen handicapped people behind this door who need to be evacuated. You can stay with me and help me get them out, or you can head down by yourselves. It's up to you. You heard the order to evacuate." He spoke calmly, like they were in the kitchen back in the house, discussing what to cook for dinner.

After a short silence, it was Reynolds who spoke first. "Cap, I'm staying. Let me know what your pleasure is," he said.

The other guys nodded. Boyle gazed at each of them, cocking his chin slightly. For the first time in his life, Boyle felt that he was truly not alone.

"You guys are sure?" he said.

They all nodded.

"All right, let's go," he said, opening the door.

The brothers filtered in behind their captain and fanned out among the wheelchairs, where they were met with "thank yous" and "thank God."

"Please listen to me," Boyle said to the group. "These firemen will take you one at a time down two floors at a time. There's ten of us and fifteen of you so some of us will make multiple trips to get everyone out and down the stairs. For now, guys, just wheel everybody to the stairwell."

Reynolds approached an older woman in a wheelchair. She was sitting next to a younger man who had an emaciated arm.

"Sir, why don't you help him first? He's younger than me. I can wait," she said.

Reynolds paused. She nodded with a determined look on her face. "Go ahead. It's okay."

Reynolds took the chair of the younger man and wheeled him

into the hallway. In a few minutes, there were fifteen wheelchairs lined up down the hall by the stairwell. Boyle led the way, pushing a wheelchair occupied by a slender, middle-aged woman with straight brown hair.

"What's your name?" he asked the woman.

"Helen."

"Pretty name. My grandmother was named Helen."

The woman smiled. Boyle came around in front of her.

"I'm gonna have to pick you up and carry you down two flights of stairs. I'm then gonna leave you there and come back for the others. That's how we're going down. Okay?"

"Okay," Helen responded.

Boyle picked her up and carried her down the two flights of stairs. Behind him followed Reynolds with an older man and then Kearns with the younger guy. The others trailed behind. When they got to the fifty-ninth floor, Boyle entered the doorway to the hall and placed Helen against a wall. He headed back up the stairs past the rest of the crew who completed the same detail with their civilians.

Truck 323's captain picked up a middle-aged man in a polyester shirt with a pocket square and put him over his shoulder and carried him down the two flights. He took a head count that confirmed that the crew had gotten everybody to the fifty-ninth floor before he picked up Helen again and carried her into the stairway, this time in his arms. Boyle's radio cackled with a transmission from command that was audibly clear to everyone within earshot.

"Command to all units in the North Tower. Evacuate the building. Evacuate immediately."

Helen squeezed Boyle's turnout coat.

"Why don't you go? Just leave me here," she said, her eyes tearing up.

"Nah, I can't do that," he said, clearing his throat. "That's not me."

Helen stared at him, her eyes gleamed with what Boyle thought was admiration and disbelief. She grabbed onto the survivor light on Boyle's coat to steady herself as they entered the fifty-seventh floor hallway. He placed her against the wall and was about to get up when it started. The slow rumble got louder and louder and would not stop. Helen clutched his shoulder and started crying.

"Don't cry," he said.

The rumbling grew louder, stronger, as the floor heaved and sagged. Boyle pressed her face into his bunker jacket and thought of those days when he was ten, chasing Engine 371 on his bike down Third Avenue in Bay Ridge. How he never stopped chasing that engine and caught up to it just when it pulled up to a bad job at a shopping center that was rippin'. For some reason, this time his mom was there, next to the building, wearing a summer dress holding out her hand to her ten-year-old son.

CHAPTER 35

Incident Command Post, Corner of West and Vesey Streets

When the South Tower fell, sections of the collapsing structure hit West Street in thunderous bursts, causing every fireman at the command post to run toward the parking garage under the American Express building. Cianci was last in line right behind Knox. When they had gotten within five feet of the entrance, Cianci stopped and turned to witness the collapse. Knox stood inside the garage entrance and saw structural material falling in a trajectory headed right for the entrance. Instinctively, he left the garage, grabbed Cianci by the arms, and pushed him into the garage as a shard of concrete five feet across fell on Knox's legs. The concrete, glass, steel, and plastic slid down the ramp in a mélange of dust and powder that enveloped everyone inside.

The rubble that slid into the garage created a chest-high obstacle for the officers who had taken shelter there. Like a biblical scourge, a fine dust permeated the air, reaching every exposed crevice within the garage. Some brothers knelt, and put their heads in their jackets, while others pushed their faces into corners of the garage to avoid suffocating in the ensuing dust-driven darkness.

It was the familiar voice of the chief that brought them to orientation.

"Who's hurt?" Cianci asked, between coughs.

"I am. Meisel," a voice called out from the darkness.

"Dermot, are you okay?"

"Yes, Chief," Dermot Cusack responded from farther back in the garage.

"Okay. Follow the sound of my voice and come to me. Chief Knox is hurt badly. I'm near the entrance to the garage. Everybody else sound off. Rusello, find Meisel and help him."

One by one, the officers assigned to the command post called out, all accounted for. By now, some light was coming in over the top of the rubble pile blocking the garage entrance.

"Anybody's radio working?"

The sound of radios rattling against bunker gear echoed off the walls of the garage followed by attempts by division chiefs to reach dispatch on their departmental radios.

"Nothing"

"Negative."

"No."

"Fuck these fucking radios," a voice cursed.

Cianci rubbed his eyes, trying to clear the dust that had encased his eye sockets and nostrils.

"Anybody got any water?" he asked.

"Yeah, I got a couple of bottles," someone said.

"Okay, pass them around. Clean out your eyes and nose."

"We gotta dig out."

Cianci knelt next to Knox. The safety chief was ashen white, lying face down on the entrance ramp. His breathing was labored. His face grimaced in pain; his legs pinned under concrete. Cusack knelt next to him. Cianci leaned close to Knox's ear.

"Lu, that took big balls, brass ones. We're gonna get you out of here real fast. Just hang in there, stay with us."

Knox, gritting his teeth, nodded, writhing.

"Get EMS over here as soon as you can. Do not leave him. Do you understand?" Cianci instructed Cusack.

"Yes, Chief."

When the dust cloud subsided, Cianci threw chunks of concrete from the top of the rubble pile to make the escape opening larger. The battalion chiefs each took a section of the pile and moved away rubble until an opening appeared big enough to climb through. Cianci was first out of the garage, followed by the rest of the trapped inhabitants.

Cianci gazed south where the South Tower once stood. In its place was a dust cloud fifty stories tall above a debris pile ten stories high. The debris field completely covered West Street and impacted the office buildings on its west side. Through the haze, he could make out the crushed, mangled frames of engines and trucks underneath the steel and concrete. Building dust gagged him. Sheehan handed him a plastic water bottle that he used to douse his eyes. When he could finally see, he grabbed his radio.

"Car 3 to South Tower Command."

Silence. He repeated the transmission, but there still was no answer. The debris field was so high, it blocked his view of downtown. He inspected himself. He had a laceration in the top of his hand. Around him, his officers stood, taking a moment to get their bearings and shake the dust and debris from their turnout coats.

"Everybody head north. Bruno, establish the command post three blocks north of the towers, okay?"

Bruno nodded. Cianci stayed where he was, next to Sheehan, his eyes cast south. Of the assembled officers, the chief and deputy commissioner were standing the farthest south.

"Scott, I need two trucks," Cianci said to his battalion aide, as he started to walk south.

"Chief, aren't you coming with us?" Rusello asked.

"Get me two trucks," Cianci responded over his shoulder, now a few feet away, as he made his way to the South Tower. Sheehan followed him. Bruno and the other officers moved north.

What may have been hard to grasp for others was patently clear to Cianci. It was an idea he never thought was possible, at least in the context of firefighting. It raised in him a distant memory that was accompanied by a feeling he had only experienced years before, and then only vicariously, when he was a captain in the Eighty-Second Airborne in Vietnam. He had stopped into his commanding officer's tent after the six-week Battle of Ripcord, after the unit had received heavy casualties. Cianci remembered the look of resignation and regret on the colonel's face. He recalled thinking how tough it had to have been to have to send men to their deaths and then write dozens of letters home to their parents, wives, and children.

Cianci glanced at Sheehan, who now was next to him, as they headed south. Sheehan didn't say anything. *No*, Cianci thought. *He would have to face it alone*, and the painful conclusion was becoming clearer to him, just like the improving visibility: within the span of fifty-nine minutes, he had just sent two hundred firemen to their deaths.

These men were not nameless faces or names on a page. They were lifelong friends, brothers, people he had played softball with, drank beer with, and attended their kids' weddings and First Holy Communions. Men he had fought the Beast next to, in front of, behind, under, and over, in sunshine, snow, and rain. These were men he led, men he learned the trade from, men who rescued him and whom he rescued. But most of all, these were men for whom he had an indescribable brotherly love that knew no earthly bounds.

These men were not colleagues—such a word does not exist in the fire service—these men were family. And now they were dead. How could he look their wives in their eyes? Or their children? He tried to push the thought out of his mind with every step, as he and Sheehan passed the severely crippled North Tower, until a sight ahead of him grabbed his attention.

Three firemen approached from the World Financial Center on the west side of West Street; a Brooklyn truck lieutenant, a guy from 235 Engine, and a young johnnie from 14 Truck who had the name "Sturgis" sewn on the back of his turnout coat. They were absolutely filthy, covered in dust. Sturgis' hair was matted down with cement. The lieutenant recognized the chief of department and saluted him.

"Where did you guys come from?" Cianci asked.

"We were in the Trident Hotel, Chief."

"Really? Anybody else make it out?" Cianci asked.

"I don't know," the lieutenant wheezed.

"All right. Keep heading north on West Street. There's a command post being set up farther north." The three survivors nodded and continued up West Street.

"We've got to find the guys," Cianci said to Sheehan, as he quickened his steps. He could sense Sheehan was staring at him, puzzled, but he didn't say a word.

Cianci stopped at the beginning of the massive field of debris just south of the North Tower. The front end of Engine 218 protruded from the pile, its cab fully involved in fire. The air was heavy and very still. The fallen debris muffled nearby sounds, making the wail of a nearby police car's siren sound very distant. He pulled his radio to his mouth.

"Car 3 to South Tower Command," he said. After a few moments, he repeated the call, with the same unsuccessful result.

Sheehan put his hand on Cianci's shoulder, who was about to repeat the call a third time but stopped. "Chief, I don't think the radios are working."

"Yeah, I guess I shouldn't rely on them." He faced the enormous rubble pile in front of him and studied it. Sheehan stood behind him and focused on the North Tower, its peak lost in a swirling, smoky inferno. Cianci got down on his knees and began to pull debris from the pile.

Sheehan leaned over and put his hand on Cianci's shoulder. "Chief, I think we better pull back. I don't think the other one's gonna last much longer."

"You go. I'm gonna stay here," Cianci said, continuing to dig.

"Paul, we've got to go. That building is—"

The sound was now familiar to them. This time, they didn't hesitate. Cianci got up, and both men hustled up the street as the North Tower made its descent as furiously as its twin. Cianci knew it would be quick. When the glass and steel took him, his only thought was that he would be with his brothers.

CHAPTER 36

1000–1030 HOURS

North Tower Command Post, North Tower Lobby

Total darkness. Just-before-the-dawn, dark-side-of-the-moon blackness enveloped Brendan, and he couldn't believe it.

The air around him was filled with fine, granular dust that reduced visibility to a few feet. When he breathed in, the particles entered his respiratory system and made him gag. When he got to the lobby it was almost unrecognizable. The ubiquitous dust caked the floor about six inches in depth. Rubble and building materials had plowed through the glass atrium and entered the lobby, which now was virtually empty except for the bodies of a fireman and a civilian lying face down on the floor near the elevators. An eerie stillness intensified its ghost-town feeling.

Brendan approached the corpse of the fireman. It was Father Kelly, his Roman collar clearly visible under his turnout coat. Brendan checked his pulse. Nothing. A couple of Port Authority officers and a fireman who had followed Brendan into the lobby helped him put their chaplain's body in a chair and carried him out of the building. Outside, Brendan flagged down a civilian to take his place and returned to the lobby.

Once back inside, he came upon Jack Seifert on his handie-talkie, giving repeated orders for all North Tower units to get out of the building.

"Jack, we gotta get out of here," Brendan said to Seifert, who gave him an expression Brendan interpreted to mean: "I know but I'm fucking busy right now."

Brendan couldn't understand what happened. Was it a partial collapse of the top of the building or a bomb? All he could see was rubble and dust. The doorway to West Street was unobstructed. He motioned to Seifert to head toward the doorway and gently grabbed his arm, pushing him in that direction. Seifert moved but did not stop the ritual of repeating the evacuation order into the handie-talkie radio—with virtually no response from the other end.

Once outside the tower, Brendan took refuge under the bridge just north of the fifteen-story high wall of rubble.

"Let's go. We can't stay here," Brendan said, pointing north.

The two chiefs trudged north along a deserted West Street. Cars burned wildly, followed by their gas tanks exploding with violent pops. The soft film of dust had blanketed the entire streetscape. At Vesey Street, they came upon Chief of Operations Sal Toscano, one of the staff chiefs who had accompanied Chief Cianci when he visited the lobby of the North Tower.

"Steve, head up a couple of blocks and set up a command post," Toscano told Brendan between coughs, his hands on his knees. Behind him, an EMS crew packaged Chief Knox into an ambulance.

"I've gotta find Paul. He went toward the South Tower after it collapsed," Toscano said.

"It collapsed? On what floor?" Brendan asked.

Toscano glared up at him.

"The whole thing." Toscano said, pointing south over his shoulder. Brendan gazed south past the burning North Tower to the dust and mist beyond it. He had seen the smoke and vapor rising when he left the North Tower, but his mind did not—could not—register what had happened. Not until Chief Toscano had told him did he realize the whole building had collapsed.

"Okay," he responded and headed north.

"There goes the other one," someone shouted. Brendan looked up and saw the top of the North Tower disintegrate. The vertical drop snuffed out the fires above the eighty-fifth floor and caused the chain reaction of floor plate slamming into floor plate without the benefit of a load distribution. The weight of each floor caused the floor beneath to collapse onto itself in a macabre accordion effect.

Brendan turned north and ran up Vesey Street. In the confusion, he lost Seifert. He made it twenty yards and realized he wasn't going to outrun this thing. He threw himself under a ladder truck. He saw the legs of firemen run past, others fell near him, covered with debris and dust. He lay with his face pressed to the pavement under the twenty-five-ton ladder truck. He knew his time was short and it would be quick, and he wanted his last thoughts to be of his children, his two girls. A memory of his daughter, Brigid, when she was five came to mind. She was sitting on the front steps to their house, drawing in a coloring book. She was so engrossed in coloring she did not hear him coming up the front path. When she finally saw him, she threw aside the book and raced up to him. The memory calmed him, provided him with a content fatalism, burnished by the thought he had helped and saved so many in his career. He hoped he would leave this life with a surplus in the "made a difference" column. *God, I hope I've done more good than harm with the time you've given me.*

He waited for the inevitable sound of concrete hitting the chassis of the ladder truck and compressing it like a tin can. The sound of the building and its materials slamming into the ground reverberated all around him. A wave of intense heat hit him, as if he'd opened a door to a blast furnace. The ashen death powder collected under the truck, forming a berm that blocked out the sunlight. The air around him was so thick with dust, he coughed and gagged blindly, offended by the thought that he and his brothers, really good men, would have to die in a dark, hot place away from the company of family and friends.

The unimaginable circumstances he found himself in, on duty in command, about to be crushed by a falling skyscraper, made him angry. He could accept a death in the line of duty made during a daring rescue attempt of an innocent civilian or a fellow brother. That was within his realm of reality. But here, lying prone under a rig, was such an undignified way to get jammed up. He felt like some small mammal vulnerable to lethal predators, naked and exposed, awaiting an embarrassing, humiliating fate. *What a way to go*, he told himself.

Then, the avalanche stopped almost as quickly as it began. He lay there, not knowing if he was alive or dead. The air was still. It was as dark as the wee hours of the morning. He heard voices. Men calling to each other. Some calling for help. Others saying they were okay, coughing, swearing, trying to collect themselves. But around the voices was a stillness that almost drowned out the outbursts. It was the silence that told Brendan Death had come and was on the scene, patiently, methodically working his harvest.

He moved his leg and didn't feel pain. Keeping his eyes closed, he heaved sputum and phlegm from his throat and nostrils. The dust was everywhere. He could even feel it under his armpits beneath his turnout coat. He was surprised that he was not seriously injured. He scraped the dust away from the edge of the truck and peered out toward the street. Visibility was zero. A thick, brownish-orange atmosphere heavy with dust was all he could see, as if he had plunged into a murky lake and opened his eyes underwater.

Slowly, he crawled out from under the ladder truck and knelt against a tire rim. He was covered in ash and clay. He wondered if there would be a follow-up event, an explosion, another collapse that would be the *coup de grace* and really finish him and the rest of them off. He checked his radio. It was still on, but he couldn't tell if it was working. For the past ten minutes since the collapse, there was nothing but a deafening silence on the command channel. His eyes stung; he felt shards of glass and kernels of concrete that loosened and fell from the hair on his head.

The landscape had changed, dramatically. Thirty-five minutes earlier, at the height of the emergency, Brendan could gauge the situation with some degree of comprehension. At least, at that time, he was presented with a scenario that permitted him to apply his thirty-five years of firematic expertise to it, even if the impact of such expertise could not be measured: two towers rising from the streets of Manhattan were burning out of control at their apexes.

But now, after the collapses of the monstrous structures in such a violent and precipitous way, he could not begin to size up the situation. He may be a deputy chief in the Tenth Division of the Fire Department of the City of New York, and he may have the white hat and generate the modicum of respect that comes with the bird-colonel chief rank, but he was just another fire officer trying to grasp what he had just experienced. Rank, and the semblance of order that accompanied it, had vanished. He thought about the extraordinary loss of life that had occurred and forced himself to put that thought out of his mind.

Through dust-caked eyes he tried to get his bearings. He thought he was trapped in a Ray Bradbury science-fiction thriller. Nothing had been spared from the tsunamic deluge of dust and ash. The street signs, light poles and streets in every direction were covered like a heavy snow on a February morning.

He stood still and listened. The distressing rhythmic chirping of PASS alarms filled the air. The alarm was a component of a fireman's mask and only sounded when a fireman was motionless for more than thirty seconds or when manually activated in a life-threatening situation. At any given emergency, when the alarm sounded without interruption for more than a minute, it was a good sign a fireman was down and in need of assistance.

This morning, it sounded like a symphony of PASS alarms had gathered for a performance in southern Manhattan. Brendan listened somberly. He knew this was Death's concerto, a requiem played for fallen brothers that, right now, he sadly could not enumerate.

Brendan waited. He couldn't do anything until the darkness lifted. Slowly, over the next ten minutes, conditions improved. He could make out other figures on the street—firemen—coughing and heaving. Some were hunched over. Others held their extremities or clutched their more wounded brethren. And still others lay on the street, motionless, their helmets nearby or still on their heads.

There was light in the darkness though. Nearby, an engine and a squad burned out of control, fire spewed from their cabs as if they were car bombed on a street in Beirut. They cast an evil glow over the field, illuminating the contorted landscape. From the west, daylight seeped in from beyond the dark haze that surrounded Brendan. The light reflecting off the Hudson River gave him a good picture of the extent of the carnage and destruction.

And when he beheld it, his mind could not grasp what his eyes saw.

The remains of the towers had collected in piles fifteen stories high on the buildings' footprints. Dust and ash, puréed from the collapse of concrete, steel, plastics, wires, glass, and filament, had crawled down the streets in every direction around the towers. Now, with the towers down, Brendan had a clear view south to the buildings on the other side of the World Trade Center. The void in the sky where the towers had stood minutes earlier glared at him. His eyes strained to process the sight until the gory damage to buildings still standing distracted him. A huge gash ran up the façade of a building on Liberty Street, as if someone had taken a giant axe and wantonly hacked out a portion of the building. Tons of debris had crashed into the glass-encased Winter Garden Atrium and shattered hundreds of panels of glass.

Brendan surveyed the dark and bloody battlefield that southern Manhattan had become. He could now make out dozens and dozens of firemen who had emerged from their sheltering places in the rubble. He placed his helmet on the ground next to him and picked up his handie-talkie, turned it to the command channel, and keyed the mike.

"Division Ten to Command."

No answer. He tried it again. The same response.

"Division Ten to Manhattan." No response.

Shit, did they wipe out dispatch also? He eyed the firemen around him. He didn't see anyone he recognized—all strangers. No battalion chiefs, division chiefs. It was as if he had entered a portal into a strange, foreign land. To his right, a rescue rig stood crushed, completely gray, no sign of red paint anywhere. Debris piled up against its driver-side window. He could make out a street sign behind it: Liberty and West: a block from the North Tower. He felt a sense of bewilderment and uncertainty. He reminded himself he was a chief, and from the looks of it, the only chief alive. He realized what he had to do, and it was the only thing he honestly thought he could do at that moment. So, he did it.

A young truckie from 438 Truck staggered by him. He held out his arm and stopped him.

"Son, can you give me a hand?"

"Sure, Chief," the truckie said dazedly.

"Help me up to the roof of that truck."

The young fireman helped the deputy chief climb the debris pile until he was able to place his shoe on the plate next to the chauffeur's compartment and pull himself up onto the mangled roof of the rig. He knelt, then reached down toward the truckie.

"Son, hand me my helmet," Brendan asked.

The truckie complied. Brendan put his helmet on his head and stood on the roof of the cab—still.

CHAPTER 37

West Street, South of the North Pedestrian Bridge

When the top floors of the North Tower began to collapse, O'Rorke threw down his tools and ran up West Street. The crew from Ladder 213 did the same. Above them, they heard what sounded like a half a dozen freight trains coming at them. One of the guys from 213 darted off to the south and headed for the South Pedestrian Overpass.

Debris hit O'Rorke and the ground around him. Out of the corner of his eye, he glimpsed other guys falling, the dust cloud gaining on them. Ahead, he saw two engines. He took two steps, made a flying dive onto the street, and crawled under the closest engine. Under the other engine, another guy had taken shelter. The guy, wide-eyed in fear and shock, stared at O'Rorke as pieces of the buildings hit the trucks. At first it sounded like BBs, and then rocks, and then safes. A gust of wind passed over him. He heard the scream of the guy under the engine ahead of him being crushed by steel beams and girders that hit the earth from unfathomable heights.

He waited for the inevitable final moment. The dust cloud had overtaken him and the engine and blocked out his view of everything. He heard firemen around him calling out they were being hit. He lay prone with his eyes closed. He was startled when he felt water rise up around his face. He opened his eyes and realized the steel and concrete had hit the ground with such ferocity, the mains under the street ruptured, causing water to rise to the surface.

The image of his father, the last time he saw him, came to mind. He was in the kitchen of their home, in his blue work shirt, about to head off to work, drinking a cup of coffee. He was smiling at him. O'Rorke remembered he said, "Hey, gunner, how about we go to the Ozone Lanes when I get home from work tonight?" He remembered he nodded and gave his dad a high-five. Now, he thought he'd be able to keep that date with him after all these years.

But then he was overcome by a warmth he had never experienced before. He could not describe it, but it made him feel, in some strange way, that he was not going to die today.

He waited. And nothing happened. The final blow was not delivered. The rush of air subsided, the water receded. The sound of collapse ended, replaced by an eerie, overwhelming silence. He opened his eyes and received another dosage of dust that collected in the back of his mouth. He peered out from under the truck. It was pitch black. *They must have dropped a bomb on us*, he thought. He slowly crawled out from under the engine and tried to stand up. A spasm of pain raced up his back. Squatting, he put his hands on his thighs and pushed up. That straightened him out. He shook the dust from his hair and found a helmet in the engine's cab. The helmet's shield displayed 101 Engine. Above him the sky was a gray black. It had to be 10:30 a.m., but it was as dark as just before dawn. And the silence was so eerie, it frightened him. The air was still, bereft of any sound but PASS alarms.

O'Rorke asked himself if he were dead. He thought, *Maybe they're gonna do something else and finish off the rest of us*. A shaft of opaque, ferrous-laden light appeared above him that he hoped would presage a lifting of the darkness. Around him, brothers just as banged up as him, lurched, stumbled, inhibited by the dead who littered the lunar landscape they now occupied.

He saw a body lying on the ground nearby, face down, dressed in the fluorescent-striped turnout coat of the FDNY with a radio harness around his neck. He lifted the radio off the body and keyed the mike.

"14-Roof to Command." It was the only thing he could think of saying. He knew he was a member of Ladder Company 14, and his last assignment was as the roof man, and there must be a command post somewhere. He listened. No answer. He repeated his transmission, again with no response. *Damn*, he thought, *we don't have a command post?* South of him visibility was now at about a thousand feet. He could see street signs and parked vehicles, and he could now make out the staging engines and trucks on both sides of the divider running along West Street.

He wasn't sure about which way to go. He felt a little scared, really, for the first time since the day his father died. He'd never been at a fire scene where he felt alone—no crew and no command. His only instinct was to get to where he could perform his job.

Out of the corner of his eye, far down West Street, a familiar shape took form in the lifting fog. It was the figure of a firefighter in a turnout coat wearing a white chief's helmet. The figure stood on a crushed rescue rig. He just stood there, still. O'Rorke rubbed his eyes to make sure he wasn't seeing things. Brothers were slowly making their way toward the figure. So he did the same.

✦

West Street, US Customs House

Sturgis, the 235 engineman, and the Brooklyn truck lieutenant had made their way between the two buildings when they heard that terrible sound again: tearing steel and glass. This time, none of them raised their heads. They knew what it meant. The lieutenant and the 235 engineman picked up their pace and ran up the alleyway. Sturgis stopped and faced the glass window panel in 6 World Trade. With both hands he took the axe and hurled it as hard as he could at the window. The axe shattered the large glass pane, creating an eight-by-ten-foot opening. Sturgis took three steps toward the opening and jumped through as the rushing air behind him catapulted him to the back of the hallway. He landed on his side and slammed into the wall. A crippling spasm of pain shot through his legs into his hips. He would have remained motionless if it weren't for a burst of adrenaline wrought from a visceral fear of being crushed that deadened the pain. He got to one knee just as the warm, falling debris of the North Tower came piling into the hallway and pushed him back down against the lobby wall. He buried his head in his turnout coat and stuck his fingers in his ears, trying to muffle what sounded like a meteor crashing next to him. His body shuddered from the force of energy violently hitting the earth. *This time*, he thought, *this is it. At least it will be over.*

Sturgis stopped shaking when the ground did. He could feel weight pressing against his legs but was afraid to try to move. His nostrils were clogged with dust. He opened his mouth and took in a dose of ash that made him gag. He reached behind and turned on his air tank. The sound of air rushing through the regulator and the hose to his facemask comforted him. He fumbled for his mask and discovered it was filled with dust. He shook it out and put the mask on, taking in the clean air. He lay there in the suffocating darkness. *If I have to go now, at least I have clean air to breathe.*

Sturgis waited for the second black interregnum to end and realized he wasn't dead. Somewhere inside of him, he got the idea to ignore any feelings that might come on. He told himself to just push forward; don't think about anything other than staying alive and doing whatever it took to do so.

The air was again very still, more so than the first time. After a couple of minutes, he lifted the mask from his face and called out to the lieutenant and the 235 engineman. His voice carried in the silence but received no response other than the sound of distant explosions and car alarms from the streets nearby. He realized he was alone again for the second time today.

He sat up slowly and shook off the cover of papers, concrete, and metal sheathing that had fallen on him. He spotted a patch of daylight to his right at the end of the hall and crawled to it, realizing his legs were functioning. He climbed over the cragged debris pile down to a street.

He clawed and meandered over the undulant rubble, moving like a crippled rodent seeking shelter. The torn and ripped remains of his brothers' bodies, in their bunker gear, lay in the streets nearby. Dark pools surrounded each of them. These were men who had controlled any fire scene through their brawn and agility, honed from decades of fighting the Beast with unrelenting, patient tenacity. Now, they lay dead, gone; Sturgis felt orphaned. In no small way, he felt guilty, ashamed, leaving these men where they lay, as if Death's capricious generosity in sparing him—the undeserving, one-month-old probie—was the cruelest injustice of all.

Back toward the Trade Center, it was all smoke and darkness. Up the street the other way, the sun rose in the sky, its light cascading between the office buildings like a lamplight shining between outstretched fingers. It illuminated the street and gave him a path to follow through the no man's land in front of him.

The street was desolate. Abandoned. He spotted a ladder truck and tried to focus on it; he hoped to see a fireman, any fireman, near it, or in it—but there was no one around. The living had fled. *Maybe they know something I don't know*, he thought.

He took his time and took a slow walk through the apocalyptic landscape toward the sunlight. He passed flattened rigs and burning cars parked in front of ruptured buildings, vomiting smoldering ruin. His knees and left side hurt with every step. He stopped at an intersection, and peered at the street signs, trying to figure where he was. The dust had covered everything: street signs, building cornices, the tops of streetlights, power lines. Sturgis lowered his head and plodded up the middle of the deserted street toward the sunlight, still disoriented and light-headed.

He passed a coffee shop and jumped back when the door opened. A paunchy, swarthy, middle-aged man in a cook's apron emerged from the shop and waved him in. For a second, Sturgis didn't want to move closer to any building. He harbored the irrational belief that it would fall on him. The man waved earnestly to Sturgis to come toward him.

Sturgis approached the man cautiously, not knowing what to expect.

"Come in. You are hurt," the man said to him.

Sturgis shook his head.

"I will help you. Come into my shop. Come in," the man said, in a thick Greek accent. Sturgis followed the man into the shop. It felt strange to be near a living person. Inside the shop, the man handed him a plastic bottle of water and a towel that he used to wash his face, eyes, nostrils, and mouth. Once he could see, he got an arresting glimpse of himself from his reflection in the door to the soda case: a black right eye, cuts on the left side of his neck, his forehead, and his right hand stared back at him.

"Can I get you something else?" the store owner asked.

Sturgis shook his head again. "I've got to get to a command post and … you should come with me."

"No. I stay here."

Sturgis held up his hand, closed fingers with the thumb up, pointing outside. "You've got to come with me. No civilians are supposed to be here. This could get worse."

The shop owner opened his mouth, like he was going to say something. Then, he took off his apron. "Okay. We go."

The two exited the coffeeshop and walked up the block,

eastward toward Broadway. On their right, 5 World Trade Center, an eight-story building, coughed out flame and smoke from three floors. Just beyond it, through the smoke and dust, a barricaded checkpoint appeared, manned by police. Next to it sat two ninety-five-foot tower ladders, with jacks planted against the curb, pouring nine hundred gallons of water per minute at the flames in 5 World Trade, the throaty groan of the trucks' diesel engines drowning out all sounds in the near vicinity.

One of the cops at the checkpoint came forward and put his arm around Sturgis and helped him to walk the last few yards to the barricade. Two medics rushed to help the shop owner, who waved them off.

"Where's the command post?" Sturgis asked, leaning on the wooden horse. The cop pointed to a Tactical Support Unit parked next to one of the tower ladders.

"Brother, take it easy. You're in rough shape," the cop responded.

"I'm all right. Let me go check in." Sturgis worked his way through the collected crowd of EMS, ESU cops, and civilians. A chief stood next to the TSU, his gold-colored leather helmet shield flashing in the sunlight. He was on a field telephone. When Sturgis hobbled toward him, the chief abruptly hung up the phone and signaled his aide to help the probie.

"Chief, I'm probationary firefighter Harry Sturgis, Ladder 14. Two buildings collapsed. I was with my company in the lobby of the Trident Hotel, but I can't find any of my guys."

"Son, thank you for that report. You need medical attention." He turned to his battalion aide. "Get him to an ambulance."

The battalion aide grabbed Sturgis's arm and escorted him to an ambulance, where he was examined by an EMT.

Sturgis sat on the back step of the ambulance and took a deep breath. His mind raced with questions, images, and the memory of sounds and smells he just experienced overwhelmed him. He could see the EMT's mouth moving, but he could not hear anything. The

EMT flashed a light in his eyes. He blinked—and finally returned him to his senses.

"You've had a concussion," the EMT said.

"Nah, I'm all right. I just got pushed around a little bit," Sturgis answered, almost brazenly.

"I think you better get to the hospital."

"I'm not going anywhere. Just let me rest here for a while. I can't leave." Sturgis stared straight at the EMT, a middle-aged woman with salty hair.

"Okay."

Loud noises drew his attention from the EMT to a remarkable sight. Behind the barricade back up Vesey Street past Broadway, a throng of firemen, hundreds of brothers, all in clean gear, milled and waited for orders. Fresh troops. Dozens of officers stood in line near the chief he had checked in with. A battalion chief walked up the line and collected BF-4 riding lists from the companies. Sturgis could tell they were eager to move; they were jacked to get into the Red Zone.

Sturgis had mixed emotions about this. It gave him a sense of pride and encouragement to see all these guys here. But he also felt a little different than these guys. He couldn't put his finger on it. He didn't feel older, just *wiser*, like he had lived a few more years in a few hours. He sat back down on the step, loosened the shoulder strap on his mask, and took off the harness.

Out of the corner of his eye he saw a fireman's turnout coat lying on the ground in front of an ambulance across the street. Its back doors were open. The name "SMALL" was stitched on the outside of the coat—*Reggie*. Sturgis stood up. The EMT tried to restrain him.

"Let me go. My buddy's in that ambulance." The salty-haired EMT saw the ambulance and released him. Sturgis made his way across the street. Two Engine 90 firemen stood next to an EMT who was leaning into the ambulance.

Reggie sat on a gurney in the ambulance. His right arm was in a sling and a bandage was wrapped around his head, an oxygen mask across his face. He stared ahead as if he was looking at something a thousand yards away. Harry leaned over the EMT.

"Reg, it's me, Harry. Reg, it's Harry." Reggie showed no emotion. His eyes didn't even blink.

Sturgis turned to one of the Engine 90 firemen. "What happened to him?"

"Don't know," the engineman said. "When we pulled up on Washington near Liberty Street, he was limping up the street, mumbling to himself. He's got a bad head injury and broke an arm." The EMT stood up and pushed Harry back. "We gotta get him to Beekman. Please move out of the way."

Harry took a step back. The EMT got into the ambulance and swung the door closed as the ambulance left, carrying his friend.

CHAPTER 38

1031–1100 HOURS

Acting Incident Command, Corner of Liberty and West Streets

On the roof of the crushed rescue rig, Brendan stood and waited. His black turnout coat was now a dull gray pallor. He kicked away the dust that had settled around his patent-leather work shoes and turned his navy dress pants into white painter's pants. He said nothing as the brothers approached from all directions. He knew they'd come if he just stood there, wearing his white helmet. *They're firemen; they know what to do.*

It was a desperate, solemn scene. He saw about a hundred to a hundred-fifty guys, all covered in dust, assembled at his location, drawn there by the sight of the helmeted chief standing on the crushed rig. Some were clothed in their turnout coats and helmets, others just their bunker pants and workshirts. Many didn't have their helmets on. They were quiet, beaten-down. Some had minor cuts, some with bandages on their arm covering bruises and wounds. Most eyed the chief, but some just stared at the ground, still in a state of shock. One guy leaned against the back of the rig, out of sight from the group, vomiting. Another couple of guys had found a working rig. They opened the gate to the booster tank and cleaned their eyes out. All of these guys should have been on their way to a hospital to get checked out, but Brendan knew they weren't going anywhere.

This must be it. The survivors. He tried to work his mind around the number of companies that should have responded to a call like this. *For an airplane crash, that's a five-alarm assignment and two hundred and fifty guys. Two airplane crashes – Gotta be five hundred guys*, he thought. He guessed maybe he saw a hundred and fifty guys around him. *We lost four hundred guys.* The thought made his stomach turn. He realized there was a good chance a lot of his friends would not be meeting him back at the house. *And maybe this wasn't the only place they were hit. This has gotta be war.*

He scanned the immense debris field where the towers stood only minutes before. It reminded him of a John Pitre poster one of the guys had put up in the TV room at a house he worked at in Bed-Sty in the seventies. The poster showed an urban landscape after a nuclear attack, with a caveman standing on a pile of rubble holding a plumbing pipe in front of bombed-out, smoldering buildings. The guy had put it up to welcome new probies to what he called the "End of the World"—the neighborhood that was burning itself to the ground faster than the enginemen could put out the fires.

That poster was no match for what he now observed. In every direction he faced, fires burned out of control, in buildings, in cars, fire trucks, ambulances, on the debris pile. The debris field was now fifteen stories high riddled with pieces of concrete and rebar steel the size of semis. The side of 6 World Trade, an eight-story structure, was shorn from the rest of the building, revealing the interior floors and furnishings like a giant dollhouse set out for viewing.

Smoke of all colors swirled in the sky above the debris field.

Thick and heavy black, sooty smoke rolled over the streetscape, contrasted by white wisps emitted from burning light combustibles. Iridescent sparks punctuated the smoke where flames touched live power lines. The rubble banked and meandered in every direction, partially shrouding him from the brothers congregated on the ground in front of him. Beyond the assembled ground, he could see other brothers, lying in the street where they were felled by the collapses—a chaotic, holy mess.

So, this must be what Hell looks like.

Brendan beheld the hundred or so men in front of him. He didn't think about himself, what he was doing there, or maybe that he should just get down off that rig and walk to the Battery and find a way home to his neighborhood. He couldn't do that; it was not in his DNA. He didn't know how to think of himself. He had an allergic reaction to using the word "I," feeling uncomfortable in any place where he was the center of attention. He remembered when he made chief, one of his uncles, who was a hard-charging nozzle man from Engine 383 in Highbridge, told him, "Now that you're a chief, don't let those bugles on your label go to your head. You're only as effective as the guys who agree to follow you. If you make it about you and not them, they'll know it, and when the time is right, they'll let you know they don't respect you—not a bit. If you get there, you might as well hang it up."

Brendan never forgot what his uncle told him. Now, on top of the rig, he knew the brothers needed to see that there was still some order, that a chief was in charge, and that command would continue. His decision to stand there was a reflexive action, mirrored by the men facing him who chose to do the same. They didn't know anything else. They were just being firemen. Brendan cleared his throat.

"Men, let's have a moment of silence," he said to them as he removed his helmet from his head. The brothers slowly did the same.

With his head bowed, the thought of his friends and whether he would see them again came to him. He asked God to spare them, but he knew, for some, God was not answering that prayer today. He asked God for strength, and told Him, when he got home—if he got home—he would make a good and forthright confession of his sins.

The quietness of the moment was punctuated by the PASS alarms chirping close by and in the distance. The air was so heavy, he was reminded of what Paul Cianci had told him about Vietnam, after the bloodiest night, when the living had to retrieve the countless dead from the battlefield. *It must have been like this*, he thought, and wondered if he'd ever see his good friend alive again.

Brendan raised his head, opened his eyes, and spoke.

"We need to get some accountability. So I want all officers over there." He pointed to his left toward the west side of West Street. His voice carried over the hushed debris field. Men stepped forward from the withered, broken ranks, their white helmets and white frontpieces emerging from a sea of ash. They filed over to Brendan's left, about forty of them.

"And all firefighters over here," he motioned to his right. The rank firemen, a little over a hundred, shifted to his right.

"We're going to form companies. Give your names and units to the chiefs." Brendan turned to the chiefs.

"Chiefs, make up lists and give them to me."

The brothers in the ranks slowly approached the officers. A lieutenant grabbed a clipboard and pen from the officer's compartment of a severed rig and stood next to six chiefs. He wrote down names of the first five firemen on a piece of paper. Then he handed the list to the first officer in line. The newly formed company, spawned by necessity and desperation, moved away from the queue to await their assignment.

Brendan needed to prioritize assignments. He counted at least fifteen fires burning around or near him—cars, apparatus fires, apartment fires in Battery Park City—everywhere he turned. Flaming steel beams had rained down from the South Tower onto a twenty-story prewar office building at 90 West Street, gouged the façade, and lodged in the building's infrastructure. Fire ate at the building voraciously. He counted seven floors fully involved. And he couldn't even start to think about where the hell he could find water.

Captain Hammonds had joined him on the top of the rig. His turnout coat was ripped down the side, as if someone had sliced it with an X-Acto knife, and he had a cut on his cheek. He had a bull-horn in his hand. *Say what you want about the cranky captain of 14 Truck*, Brendan thought. *This guy was one tough son of a bitch you could rely on.*

"Ray, we need to get a water source established," Brendan said.

Hammonds nodded and put the bullhorn to his mouth. "O'Rorke, over here, now." Hammonds bellowed into the bullhorn. O'Rorke approached the rig. His new company officer, a captain from Engine 22, and the other guys followed him.

"Bryan, I need you to take your crew and get a line set up from the river to West Street. We've got to get water to the scene fast. The mains are all cut," Brendan said.

"You got it, Chief," O'Rorke responded.

"Will do, Chief," the 22 Engine captain added.

The assignment lieutenant handed the list of companies to Hammonds, who gave them to Brendan. Brendan scanned the list and found the name Jenkins, his academy buddy. He spotted him next to a ladder truck, its aerial ladder was twisted like a Krazy Straw. Brendan took the bullhorn from Hammonds.

"Chief Jenkins."

Brendan studied the fire in 90 West. From his estimate, the fire going there was a four-alarm assignment. On any other day, dispatch would have sent sixteen engines, nine trucks, five battalion chiefs, one deputy chief, and a staff chief to fight a fire of this magnitude. The department would have devoted over a hundred and thirty firemen and their relief companies to work a job of this size.

But this wasn't any other day. Today, Brendan estimated he had only that many men in total to work with and an unknown quantity of working apparatus—and he had two other fires of similar size going in other buildings nearby.

Jenkins appeared in front of the new command post on the collapsed rescue rig. Brendan knelt to talk in confidence to his old friend of thirty-three years.

"Hugh, I need you to take four companies and hold that fire over there in 90 West. It looks like it's gonna extend into the hotel."

Jenkins studied the building, sullenness etched onto his face. "Those flames are the size of dump trucks." He pointed. "The internal conditions have gone to shit."

Brendan strained to keep his frustration from his voice. "Just do what you can to contain it. I'll get you water as soon as I can."

"Okay, Steve, we'll do it," Jenkins responded. Brendan could tell Jenkins realized how surreal the command he had just been given sounded. Jenkins waved over two captains to gather the limited resources available to him.

Brendan turned west to tackle his next objective. He saw a fire burning out of two windows on the sixteenth floor of one of the residential high-rises in Battery Park City. He scanned the list and uttered the next name to Hammonds, who called it out on the bullhorn.

"McBride."

Chief McBride, a young battalion chief from Brooklyn, stepped up to the rig.

"Chief, take two companies and put out that fire over there in Battery Park City. Don't radio me. Don't give me a report. Just put the fire out and report back here."

"Yes, Chief," the young battalion chief responded.

Beyond his immediate area of operation, another command post had formed up West Street near Vesey. Forms of firemen congregated beyond the North Pedestrian Bridge that had collapsed down on Rescue 22. A speck of flickering color caught Brendan's eye. It stood out in stark contrast in the gray, monochromatic streetscape. Brendan trained his eye toward the top of one of the piles just east of the pedestrian bridge.

"Well, I'll be damned," he said, under his breath.

On a jagged pile just east of the pedestrian bridge, three brothers had gerry-rigged a flagpole from a severed pipe and were raising an American flag over the scene. For a moment, Brendan could feel a weakness in his chest as he choked up. He was surprised he had such a reaction. He watched one of the brothers slowly pull the improvised lanyard raising Old Glory from the hands of his fellow fireman as the third stood by, inspecting the presentation of the colors. When they completed their task, one of them took off his helmet and rubbed his lowered forehead. Then, the trio stepped off the pile, saluted the colors, then moved on to other duties. The flag swayed gently in the morning sun, now marking hallowed ground.

You gotta love this city.

CHAPTER 39

1101–1230 HOURS

Sector Command, Corner of Vesey and Church Streets

Behind the barricades on Vesey Street, Battalion Chief Donald Thalheimer stood, with a stack of riding assignments in his hand and an army of adrenaline-jacked, angry firemen in front of him. He had come into Manhattan over the Brooklyn Bridge and made his way through the throngs of fleeing civilians as far as Church and Barclay before the North Tower collapsed. By that time, the police had closed off the streets around the World Trade Center, so he parked his SUV, donned his turnout gear, and headed down Church Street on foot with his battalion aide through the blinding maelstrom of dust and papers. His attempt to raise Chief Cianci on his departmental radio got no response. He cursed—no one was in charge at his location. He gathered the officers standing nearby and said, "Get riding assignments from every company checking in." By 11:00 a.m., when Sturgis stumbled into his makeshift command post, Thalheimer had assembled four battalions, thirty-five companies, and over two hundred and forty guys, that had massed like a medieval army on the border between Scotland and England. Battalion chiefs, captains, and lieutenants stood in line waiting for assignments.

Thalheimer, desperate for current information of the fire scene, could get it solely from those who'd survived the collapse. He sent his aide back to the row of ambulances to find the probie from 14 Truck and any other guys who had been inside the Red Zone. He told his aide to bring them back to the command post. His aide returned with Sturgis and a shell-shocked engineman from 454 Engine in tow. Sturgis took a seat on the riding board of the TCU rig.

"Stay here. I'll get to you in a minute," Thalheimer told them. He had a radio in one hand and the stack of riding lists in the other. A battalion chief and a captain stood next to him.

"Take five engines and four trucks. Head west on Vesey. If you see any trucks, take anything you can find—masks, hoses, hooks. Gather whatever you can find and find a way to put out the fire in 6 World Trade. Get in operation. Make one of your guys a runner and have him report back here with anything you find. You got it?"

The chief and the captains nodded in unison and headed off to gather their companies.

Out of the corner of his eye, he spotted a burly battalion chief and five officers approaching him. He heard the familiar, melodic baritone voice of Staff Chief Leo Santucci carry over the din of commotion.

"Don, I heard you might need some help." Santucci delivered his words smoothly, with an undertone of confidence, almost optimism, that made Thalheimer smile when he heard them come from his friend's large, imposing frame.

"Leo. I thought you didn't make it."

"Nah, I'm good. What do you need?"

"We've got three, maybe four buildings with multiple floors on fire. Seven World Trade is fully involved. I haven't heard from Paul's command post, and everybody's missing."

Santucci's face stiffened at hearing his old friend's name. He grabbed Thalheimer by the biceps. "We gotta find Paul!"

Thalheimer thought Santucci was going to throw him out of the way and just march forward. "Okay. Okay. I'll send somebody."

"No, I'll go. Let me do it," Santucci insisted. Thalheimer knew he better say yes, or he might need an ambulance himself.

"Okay. But I don't know where the command post was. Last we heard, Cianci was on West Street across from the South Tower."

"I saw him," Sturgis interrupted. The two chiefs wheeled and eyed the beat-up probie, still sitting on the riding board. "I saw him. Just after we left the Trident Hotel, before the second tower came down."

"Okay. Do you think you know where the command post was?"

Sturgis stood up. "Yeah, I think so. I know where I last saw him."

"Okay. You go with Chief Santucci here and go find the chief of department."

Sturgis finished his water bottle and put on his turnout coat. He sized up the chief and five officers in front of him stoically, like they were from some rear echelon part of the fire service and he was about to take them on a tour of a war zone. He could sense they were almost sneering at him because he, a probie, had just been through the Biggest of the Big Ones.

"Okay, probie. Let's go," Santucci said.

Sturgis nodded and shambled ahead of the chief toward the barricades, looking like he didn't give a flying fuck if the entourage followed him.

✦

Inside the perimeter, things were quieter. Sturgis followed the turgid, five-inch supply lines that ran up the street from the working hydrants back on Broadway. He led the search party west on Vesey toward 5 World Trade. The fires in that building were still blowing hard and hot. Guys scrambled to put handlines into operation. Two engine companies had set up next to the two tower ladders and raked the flames at six hundred gallons per minute from their 1½-inch smooth-bore deck guns.

Sturgis led the detail back down a deserted and obliterated Vesey Street until they came upon 7 World Trade Center. Flames and smoke poured out of a twenty-story gash in the south face of the forty-seven-story office building. As they passed the engulfed office building, they encountered a lone engine company at the corner of West Broadway and Vesey. The crew had a line in operation, but it couldn't reach the fire. It was clear they had tapped a hydrant with no water pressure. Santucci flagged down the company lieutenant.

"Lieu, you better find a stronger hydrant or pull back. You're doing nothing with that line. Who knows how long that one is gonna stand up?"

The lieutenant studied the building. The volume of fire on one side was tremendous.

"I think we better pull back," the lieutenant told his crew.

Sturgis took the search party north around 7 World Trade onto Barclay Street and headed west. When they got to West Street, they headed south. At the corner of West and Vesey, they came upon a staging area where dozens of firemen had collected around a group of chiefs who were giving out assignments. Santucci stopped the detail and went over to the command post. Sturgis could see him talking to the chief who Sturgis assumed was in charge. The command chief motioned to a group of about twenty firemen, directing them toward Santucci.

"These guys are gonna help us," Santucci told his junior officers. "Probie, where was the command post?"

Sturgis pointed. "It was farther down on West Street." The collapse of the North Tower had sent a towering, rubbled debris pile onto West Street, blocking any advance in that direction.

"How we gonna get down there?" a lieutenant asked.

"C'mon. I came out through the Winter Garden," Sturgis replied.

Sturgis led the party into the World Financial Center and down North End Avenue. The group entered the Winter Garden from the west. The firemen followed Sturgis down the escalators and out onto West Street, right in front of where the North Tower once stood.

"Where was the command post, probie?" Santucci asked. He sounded a little impatient.

Sturgis pivoted. He tried to get his bearings. The dust cloud swirling over the debris field where the towers stood was no help. Nor were the pock-marked buildings in the World Financial Center. South of where he stood, he spotted the building he had walked through after he had evacuated from the Trident Hotel.

"Over there," Sturgis said. He pointed to the building. "I came out over there and saw the chief standing in the street."

Santucci addressed the group. "Okay, everybody fan out and move south. Slowly work your way down the street. If you come upon anyone, call out, and an officer will come over and check it out."

The thirty firemen dispersed into a line and slowly walked south over the pile of rubbled debris, pushing pieces of steel and concrete out of their way. The only sound in earshot was a mayday call from a company trapped somewhere in the pile that emanated from one of the officers' radios. Sturgis walked behind Santucci. He spotted the door to an engine buried in debris about ten yards in front of them. It took them about ten minutes, but they were able to make their way up to the door. The engine was mangled and crushed. They peered inside the compartment, but it was empty.

"I've found somebody," someone called from down the line.

Santucci and Sturgis retreated from the crushed engine and made their way with all the other guys to where two guys from 317 Truck stood.

"Are they alive?" Santucci called to them as he approached.

The 317 guys shook their heads, lowering them, not saying a word. The guys who had rushed over stood around now, dejected looks on their faces. Sturgis stopped where he was when he saw what they found, more out of a sense of decency than anything else.

The 317 truckies had recovered the crushed and mangled body of a boy, no older than about eight years old. His face was twisted in a horrible grimace, and his arms were contorted in unnatural ways. The sight of a child victim of the collapse made Sturgis nauseous. It wasn't the sight of the body but the fact that a child had been killed. He thought that was the most barbaric thing he had seen. One of the guys had a tarp and spread it out over the boy's body.

Santucci eyed one of the lieutenants in the detail; he was rubbing his eyes, as if to rub it out of his mind, the image of the kid.

"Gerry, head back north, and radio for a chaplain." Santucci turned to the search party. "When you find something, call out if you think they're alive. If they're gone, just let us know. Now let's keep going."

The brothers dispersed and continued working over the debris field. Sturgis focused on an area near the North Pedestrian Bridge that had collapsed on Rescue 22. He pushed away concrete and ash, poking and probing, for what he did not know. In the back of his mind, he was sure everyone was dead. He harbored no hope of finding anybody alive. His knees were killing him, but he didn't care. He felt glad to be among the living and was innately pleased with the idea that he could walk and breathe and was responsible for searching the ground in front of him and nothing more. How little it took him to be happy at that moment, he thought.

"I found something," a guy four men down from him called out. "It's somebody, their leg, dress pants."

The firemen again descended on the guy's location. He was pushing debris away and uncovering more of the body. It was a man's body with dress shoes. Sturgis and two guys pulled away a section of rebarred concrete, revealing a black turnout coat.

"I think it's the chief," Sturgis called out to the approaching officers. In the mid-morning sun, they could make out the name "CIANCI" on the back of the turnout coat. The body lay face down. Santucci knelt and placed his arms under Cianci's chest and gently turned him over on his back to see his friend's face one last time. The rest of the guys were now all around him. After a short while, he stood up.

"Everybody take off your helmets. We'll have a moment of silence." The brothers removed their helmets and lowered their heads. Some guys made the sign of the cross. After about a minute, a captain approached Santucci with a stokes basket and a tarp. Santucci and the captain placed their chief's body in the basket, covered it with the tarp, and turned to carry their friend back home. Sturgis and the thirty brothers instinctively had assembled in two rows as an honor guard between which Santucci, the captain, and two truckies stoically walked the basket off the pile.

Faster than the internet, the word had made its way up the line all the way back to Barclay Street: they had found the body of Chief of Department Paul Cianci and they were bringing it out. As the cortege of beaten-up, dispirited firemen escorted the stokes basket up West Street, guys stood at attention, saluting their fallen chief, while others knelt, blessing themselves as the basket passed them, with the recovery detail following as an honor guard. Sturgis remained at the site where the chief was located and watched the procession move up the street. When he lost sight of it, he headed south toward the raging inferno in the building at 90 West Street.

✦

World Financial Center, Battery Park City

As O'Rorke walked to the river, all he could think about was how to get water to the scene. He counted at least sixteen fires in plain sight, including the one in 90 West that was ripping wildly. If the mains were shot, like Hammonds said, the only place they could get water was to try to draft from the Hudson River. When he and his makeshift crew got to North Avenue in Battery Park City, they came upon Engine 595 from the Bronx, that was creeping slowly down the street. The 22 Engine captain flagged down the chauffeur.

"Where are you guys headed?" he asked.

"We're trying to find a working main. Everything up the street is shot," the chauffeur replied.

"Okay, follow us." The engine captain walked south on North Avenue toward the North Cove Marina. The Bronx engine puttered behind them.

At the marina, the crew came upon a jarring sight. The esplanade around the marina teemed with civilians, ten deep. Some were ash-white, like ghosts. Others leaned on the railings, over the water. A commuter ferry, packed with people end to end, idled at the dock. The deckhands had cordoned off the hatch and had to push people back as the boat eased away from the pier. O'Rorke eyed the scene in disbelief. It reminded him of the TV shots of Saigon in April 1975, just before the city fell to the communists. Some people had stripped down to their T-shirts and socks. Some had jumped in the water and swam to recreational boats moored just off dockside.

"Shit, this is a pretty bad scene," the engine captain said. "How are we going to start a drafting operation?"

O'Rorke gazed out across the river to contemplate the problem when something caught his eye. It was the *John J. Carver*, the fireboat he had served on eight years earlier, steaming toward the marina.

"Son of a bitch," O'Rorke remarked.

"What?" the engine captain asked.

"It's the *Carver*," O'Rorke said. "It was decommissioned and turned into a floating museum. I used to crew on it."

"Really? Okay, wave it down and have it tie up next to the esplanade just north of the marina. We'll draft from over there."

O'Rorke walked to the esplanade and waved toward the 130-foot vessel out in the harbor. The fireboat was about a half mile away. The pilot saw O'Rorke's gestures and altered course to head in his direction. The other guys stretched two supply lines from 595 Engine to the esplanade.

The arrival of the *Carver* at the esplanade did not go unnoticed by the throng of escaping civilians at the nearby marina. People ran north toward the esplanade and the approaching vessel. The 22 Engine captain saw what was happening and asked the chauffeur in the 595 cab next to him to turn the apparatus radio to public address and hand him the mic. After several announcements that the fireboat was not taking passengers and was being used in firefighting operations, the crowds dispersed and returned to the marina.

When the *Carver* pulled up next to the bulkhead, its deckhand threw a line to O'Rorke, who tethered it to the railing running along the esplanade. The ship's captain stuck his head out of the pilot house.

"We received a call you guys need water pressure," the boat's captain called out.

"Yeah, we do. I used to crew on this boat."

The captain stuck his arm out of the pilothouse and waved to him. "C'mon on board."

O'Rorke jumped over the railing onto the deck of the 268-ton vessel. The deckhand sized him up. He was a mid-thirties engineer with a ruddy complexion and wore an oil-stained New York Rangers cap on his head.

"Man, you're filthy. You okay?" the engineer said.

"I'm good. We gotta get water pressure up fast."

O'Rorke took a supply line from one of the firemen on the esplanade and ran it aft.

"What are you doing?" the engineer asked.

"Last time I checked, these motors can pump four thousand gallons of water per minute at a hundred and fifty psi."

The deckhand grabbed his arm. "Hold it. That ain't gonna work. You can't hook in."

"Why not?"

"The valves to the deck pipes are all stuck on open. We can't close 'em. Won't be able to bypass them and pump water."

O'Rorke looked skyward. *What else could go wrong today?*

He waved to the engineman on the esplanade. "Get me an axe, halligan, anything."

The engineman pulled a flathead axe from a compartment on the engine and handed it to O'Rorke.

"What are you gonna do there?" the engineer asked wide-eyed.

"We'll stopper the fuckin' deck pipes and force the water into the hoses," O'Rorke responded as he headed for the deck pipes that could send three thousand gallons of water per minute into the air.

"Get me anything to clog the guns. Wood, soda cans, metal pipes. Any fucking thing. You guys, go get some of that crap and bring it over here. Go," O'Rorke barked.

The two enginemen on the esplanade headed out on their scavenger hunt. The engineer gaped as if a light bulb went off in his brain, realizing that O'Rorke's plan would work.

"I'll connect the lines in," he said, as he returned to the original detail O'Rorke had started.

After ten minutes of clogging the deck pipes with wooden blocks, bottles, soda cans, and cement, the improvised solution allowed water to flow from the four centrifugal pumps through the valve connections into the large supply lines. The engineer watched in amazement as O'Rorke got the pumps to drive a total of eighteen thousand gallons of saltwater per minute, equal to the pumping capacity of twenty engines, through supply lines to Engine 595 and another engine on North End Avenue. O'Rorke stood proudly near the engineer's compartment on 595. He surveyed the operation he had devised. For the first time he felt they had caught a break.

"Now that's a beautiful thing," he remarked.

✦

On the corner of West and Liberty, things were not going well. The fires in 90 West ripped furiously through floor after floor of the ninety-four-year-old concrete structure encased in scaffolding. Flames and blistering heat impinged on the hotel across the street. Chief Jenkins had taken the four companies assigned to him—twenty men in all—and had them forage for fire extinguishers, handlines, tools, and working engines. After twenty minutes of improvising and searching, they had gotten a couple of handlines in operation off of a pumper that was being supplied by relay from a squad about five blocks north of the site. But the water pressure was a joke. One of the hose teams hit the second floor with a stream that arced like water from a garden hose. To further complicate the attack, a ladder truck burned on the street in front of the building, creating a smoke screen and raising the possibility of a heat-induced collapse of the scaffolding.

Amazingly, the hose teams had knocked down the fire on most of the first floor and had pushed their way to the front doorway of the building. Knowing the lads would instinctively start to make an interior attack, Jenkins stopped the team at the front door to let him "read" the fire—discern its behavior and stage of development—in order to determine how to subdue it.

Jenkins spotted a side door. It smoked and radiated heat. He stepped into the side doorway. The smoke on the ceiling crawled back into the building as if it were being sucked in.

"That's not a good sign," he said to the guys. "This fire has got a sustained source somewhere in the building." The ceiling buckled over Jenkins's head. He waved the hose team away.

"Okay, back it up. I don't like the looks of this," he said, retreating from the building. The hose team backed up into the street and shut down their anemic stream.

"Guys, we're gonna have to make a move on this building from the outside," Jenkins said to the nozzle man.

"Chief, we've got no pressure. What do you want us to do? Piss at it?"

"We're working on boosting pressure. Keep at it."

The backup man on the line bit his lip, smiled, and mumbled to the nozzle man, "I like getting kissed when I'm getting fucked."

Jenkins took a couple of steps back. He didn't want the young guys to see the desperation in his eyes. His battalion aide, a young college graduate named Bennett, stood nearby. An engine had pulled up behind him.

"Bennie, tell that engine to go down the street and try to find a working hydrant."

"Yes, Chief."

Jenkins surveyed the fire. It was burning unchecked, mostly on the north side of the building facing the Trident Hotel. The fifty-two-year-old chief from Pelham Bay wanted to scratch his head, literally. If this were any other day, he'd put two tower ladders in place and have them rip the shit out of this thing with their blistering Stang nozzles. They'd go to defensive for the rest of the day, sit back, and play hearts with the chauffeurs until the thing was done. But not today. Today he just stood there, feeling useless. He stared at the guys around him; they held their lifeless handlines, while they stared back at him with a look he read to say, *Chief, what do you want us to do? You're the chief, tell us.* Here they were, he thought, twenty-one firemen alone and isolated on a desolate, bombed-out street, with no means to put out a major fire. *If it weren't so pathetic, it would be comical,* he thought.

Jenkins cleared his throat. The smoke swirled around the rubble pile that once was the twenty-two-story Trident Hotel. The collapse had severed the building in two, obliterated the northern half closest to the North Tower and left the southern portion relatively intact. He told himself to go back to basics. *How would the old buffaloes handle this?* He took a moment to collect his thoughts. *Maybe we should just let this thing burn down and come back later, if the city is still here.*

It was the faint sound of distant voices that drew Jenkins's attention away from his encroaching despair. And he couldn't believe the sight. About twenty guys were dragging supply lines toward him. The guys on the hose lines raised their arms in celebration. One of them whistled through his fingers.

In no time, the twenty guys had stretched three supply lines to the supply engine and hooked in. The officer leading the party, a captain from 22 Engine, approached Jenkins, followed by O'Rorke.

"Chief, we're drafting saltwater from the Hudson off of a fireboat. We can pump all day if you like. What's your pleasure?"

Jenkins smiled and squinted to squeeze the tear out of his right eye.

"Cap, if you were a big blonde, I'd kiss you right now," the chief responded.

"Glad I'm not, Chief."

"Let's see if we can supply the standpipe in the hotel. I want to take that deck gun off of the engine and set it up on the terrace. We'll get more lines into the building. We're gonna hit this thing like we would in the old days."

"Roger that, Chief," the captain responded. O'Rorke, acting on the order, had already climbed the rig to collect the deck gun. From up the street a fireman approached the chief and O'Rorke slowly, his turnout coat and bunker pants covered in white ash.

It was Sturgis. He stopped about twenty feet from the engine and looked at O'Rorke up on the hosebed, knelt over the deck gun. O'Rorke smiled.

"Harry, would you grab the toolbox in the chauffeur's compartment and come up here and help me?"

"Sure."

In short order, the two firemen from 14 Truck unbolted the deck gun from the engine, removed it, and put it in operation.

CHAPTER 40

6:00 P.M.

Midtown

Lauren had first become aware of what was happening downtown a little after 9:15 a.m., when the sound of sirens wailing down Midtown avenues distracted her from her morning tea. She had watched the events unfold on the television with everyone else not in the vicinity of the towers. Transfixed by what she saw, she had tried to reach Pat, praying that he was off duty and would pick up her calls. Deep inside, she knew, even before she heard the dial tone in her ear, as sure as she was standing in the Princeton Club, that Pat was down there. When his answering machine had picked up, she hung up. The images on the television of the towers burning pained her. The last time she had been with Pat was there, in one of those buildings, that had now become the site of unspeakable and immeasurable carnage. After a while, she had closed her eyes and stared out the window. It was such a glorious late-summer day. She could not comprehend what had happened.

Around ten o'clock her cell phone rang. It was Amy.

"Don't ask. I think so," was all she could say.

Lauren had just put down the phone when the gasp from the television reporter made her turn toward the TV to witness the first tower fall. In that moment, she knew she would never see Pat again. She came to feel as if a large, imposing door was closing for good in front of her. She knew her path ahead would be one alone, without Pat. No one had to tell her. She didn't need a phone call, a photo, or a visit. The tight, small feeling of emptiness in her torso was all she needed. She had lowered her head into her arms and sobbed quietly, feeling both ashamed that she had let herself love someone so completely and, at the same time, strangely grateful, almost proud, that she had done so.

It was around six in the evening when she finally brought herself to leave her room and take a taxi downtown.

The cab was only able to get as far as Seventh Avenue and Fourteenth Street, where the police had set up barricades to keep out vehicular traffic. She got out of the cab and made her way on foot down Seventh Avenue to Varick Street and then to West Broadway. She took her time. In her mind, she had nowhere else on earth to go, except to the World Trade Center. She was a little taken aback at the quietness on the streets of Lower Manhattan. On any other night, she would have blocked out the inexorable bustle of the traffic that was the pulse of New York. But tonight, the streets were eerily quiet, almost lifeless. People she passed on the street displayed a distressed reverence and stupefied state of shock in reaction to the day's unimaginable events.

When she got closer to the World Trade Center, she detected the pungent smell of burned polychlorides that got stronger with every step. At Barclay Street, she was stopped at a police checkpoint. She told the cop at the barricade that she was looking for her fiancé who was a fireman, and she hadn't heard from him all day. The cop told her he couldn't let her in. He told her that family members were being directed to City Hall Park, and she should see if she could get information over there.

When Lauren got to City Hall Park, the wrought-iron fence around the park was already covered with handmade flyers—hundreds of them—of loved ones who were missing from the World Trade Center. She entered the park from the West Gate at Park Place and realized others had the same idea as she did. About fifty people had congregated around a fire officer dressed in a white dress shirt with captain's brass, black tie, and navy dress pants. He told the assembled group that they didn't have any information yet, but they would get it out as soon as they could. He said something about the mayor holding a press conference in an hour.

Lauren studied the faces of the people around her. Sullen, knotty faces weathered by hard work. These were good, working-class people, young and middle age. One woman had two young children in tow. There was an older guy talking to her. Lauren overheard him saying something about not jumping to conclusions, that it'll be best to wait until the mayor speaks. The woman nodded and walked away, a blank stare on her face. Two middle-aged women stood in front of her, talking in almost hushed tones.

"He's gone. I know it. Widowed at forty-one with three teenagers and a mortgage." She clasped her hands at her waist.

"Eileen, we don't know that yet," the other one responded, trying to fix her focus on the fire officer talking to the group.

On the perimeter of the group, Lauren spotted a young, attractive brunette in her early twenties, near a park bench. She was wearing jeans, a pastel-blue T-shirt, and flats. She held a photo in her right hand, close to her thigh. Her facial features and carriage gave Lauren the impression she could be a model, but the distressed look on her face made her seem awkward and withdrawn. She also noticed her left hand was missing fingers. She got the sense this woman was there for the same reason Lauren was. She moved closer to the young brunette and caught her glance.

"Excuse me. Are you looking for someone?" Lauren asked.

The young woman nodded and looked at Lauren. Her perfectly exquisite facial features were in no way impaired by her pained expression. Lauren had never seen such radiant green eyes in her life. She thought they were almost feline in origin.

"Yes," she said, running her deformed hand through her shoulder-length, raven-black hair. "He's a fireman." She rubbed the photo between her index finger and thumb.

"What's his name?"

"Phil Coletti," she said. "I've tried calling him, but he's not answering his cell phone."

"Is he your—"

"He's a friend," she interjected, eyeing the willow oak trees in the park, their leaves rocking gently in the evening breeze. "And from the looks of it, I'll probably never see him again." The dryness in Lauren's throat made her swallow.

"Now, you don't know that yet," Lauren responded, not knowing what to say. The young woman cast her a slight glare that told Lauren she found her response almost insulting. Lauren extended her hand.

"I'm Lauren." The young woman shifted the photo to her left hand and took Lauren's hand.

"Ellie."

"Would you like to sit down?" Lauren asked. She moved toward the bench behind them. The park was beginning to fill up with more people.

"Thank you," Her response gave Lauren the impression the young woman did not often find herself on the receiving end of courtesies. Lauren pointed to the photo.

"Is that a picture of him?"

"Yes." She handed the photo to Lauren, who took it and studied it. Two people sitting at a dinner table. The man in the photo was in his twenties, smiling easily, virile and confident. He has his arm around Ellie, who was also smiling.

"He's seems like a really nice guy." Lauren handed the photo back to Ellie.

"Yeah." Ellie took the photo and stared at her shoes. "He loved me more than I deserved, and now he's gone. I can feel it. He was too good for this world. Too good." The resignation in Ellie's voice was overpowering. Lauren didn't know whether to get up and walk away or continue to listen, nursing her own stress empathetically.

"I'm sorry," Ellie said. "I just feel terrible right now. You must be here waiting for someone also."

"I am."

"Who is he?"

"He's a fireman too."

"Oh. I'm sorry. I was so rude."

"No, no. Don't say that. We're both here looking for someone. How could you know?" Lauren realized her life was veering, changing course, and she and this young woman were now following the same heading.

"Ellie, listen to me. Forgive me for being forward, but I sense he was a little more than a friend to you."

Ellie nodded, her eyes welling.

"You may be right," Lauren continued. "What you said before. Both of us may have lost someone who meant the world to us. And I think you recognize that that is pretty hard to come by—that kind of love. Many people don't ever experience that. But I know how you feel. You can't believe you let it slip away from you. I know what you mean. I do."

Lauren watched the still-gathering crowd pensively. "You can't beat yourself up about it. I would rather be grateful for the brief moments I had with him in the sun than to regret the fact that he's gone—or what could have been. I believe Fate gives us the chance to find love. Sometimes we do. Sometimes we don't. But you have to go on, either way."

Ellie wiped her eyes. "Lauren, I hear you. But before today, was it wrong for me to think that I would see him tomorrow or maybe next week?"

Lauren smiled. "What line of work was he in? Aren't we sitting here, right now, trying to find out where they are exactly because of what they do?"

Ellie bit her lip.

"Ellie, you don't have to answer this question, but be honest with yourself. Didn't you think deep down, when you were with him, that he was never completely yours? That being a fireman was his passion, mistress, whatever you want to call it? And he was on loan to you?"

Ellie shot a knowing glance at Lauren. Lauren sat up on the bench, breathing in. It eased the heaviness in her chest. Lauren smiled.

"I thought so. I don't know if it's the profession that makes them who they are to us or if the profession attracts a certain type of person to it, but—" Lauren's voice broke. "I think you'd agree, it's who they are and part of why we love them."

Lauren lowered her head. She could hear Ellie weeping quietly next to her. She placed her left hand over Ellie's hands.

"I think our lives are going to change in a big way." Lauren said. "All we can do is face it—just like they did."

✦

In downtown Brooklyn, on the ninth floor at FDNY headquarters, after the first tower fell, Alice Comstock decided she had to call her boss, Chief Cianci, whom she had not heard from since he left for southern Manhattan after the first plane hit. She had been monitoring the command channel on the scanner in her office and had heard all the radio traffic from the call, which came to a standstill when the first tower fell. Cianci didn't pick up his cell phone. Commissioner Sheehan's secretary, Marie, did the same, also getting no answer. Assistant Chief Turner's secretary was next, followed by the other five secretaries in the office, all making repeated attempts to reach their bosses. It was only when the chief of dispatch called to tell Alice that they had found Chief Cianci's body that the secretaries closed the door to the outer office, sat together in disbelief, and realized they would never again see the men they had worked with, collectively, for over two hundred years. It was around eleven o'clock at night when the secretaries, still at their desks fielding phone calls from family members of their bosses and working the phones to track down some good news, which never came, finally closed the outer doors to their offices, sat down, and cried for well over an hour.

KEEP

SEPTEMBER 12, 2001. 3:00 A.M.

In a modest, single-family row house in Woodside, Queens, the Brendan girls, thirteen-year-old Brigid and twelve-year-old Catherine, slept quietly in their beds. Their father, Steve, sat in a chair in the corner of the room, watching them.

This ritual was the good chief's therapy. No matter how many fatal car accidents, failed rescue attempts, or child burn victims he had to deal with on the Job, watching his daughters sleep peacefully in their beds when he got home was the only way he could put himself back together and get ready for the next shift.

Some nights he'd sit in the chair for ten minutes, other nights for three hours, depending on how much punishment the day's work inflicted on him. This night, Brendan planned to sit in the chair for a year, maybe two.

GLOSSARY OF APPARATUS, EQUIPMENT, TECHNICAL TERMS, SLANG AND JARGON

10-45 FDNY radio signal for a fire-related civilian death or serious injury

10-60 FDNY radio signal for a major emergency

10-75 FDNY radio signal for a working fire

10-76 FDNY radio signal for a working fire in a high-rise office

10-77 FDNY radio signal for a working fire in a high-rise multiple dwelling

10-92 FDNY radio signal for a malicious false alarm

alarm The emergency alert sent to fire personnel ordering their response to an emergency. Alarms are categorized sequentially (i.e., first, second, third, etc.). Each assignment activates a response by a pre-determined complement of fire apparatus and personnel with smallest responding to a first alarm and largest to a fifth alarm.

all hands The notification an incident commander would provide to dispatch to indicate what units are working. For example, if all units assigned on the first alarm to a fire are working, the chief would notify dispatch that "We are using all hands for a fire in a three-story tenement."

backdraft An event which occurs when oxygen is introduced into an oxygen-starved atmosphere during the smoldering phase of a fire. Associated with confined spaces, when oxygen is introduced, combustion is almost instantaneous and can occur with explosive force.

backup man The firefighter on an interior attack team assigned to flake out the line on the fire floor and assist the nozzle man in advancing the line.

brunt man A reference to firefighters who fought fires during the 1970s when thousands of fires occurred across all five boroughs of New York City during a time of social unrest, upheaval and displacement. These firefighters bore the "brunt" of the action.

bunker gear Informal reference to personal protective gear worn by a firefighter in fire operations consisting of turnout coat and pants, boots, helmet, eye protection, hood, and gloves.

chauffeur The firefighter assigned to drive and operate the engine or the truck.

can man The firefighter on a ladder truck assigned to the fire extinguisher and inside team of the company.

control man The firefighter on an interior attack team assigned to make the hydrant connection, open the hydrant, make sure all doors are chocked open, and assist in advancing the line to the fire.

department radio The connection between dispatch and fire apparatus when they are on the road. Provided by handset to the officer in the cab. Geographic range is city-wide coverage. Not to be confused with handie-talkies, which provide person-to-person communications on the fireground.

defensive attack A strategy deployed to isolate, contain, and stabilize a fire to let it burn itself out. Defensive operations consist of deploying large master streams outside the fire building and placing fire streams between the fire and other exposures to prevent fire extension.

dispatch The common reference to the fire dispatch office where emergency calls are received from the 911 emergency notification system and from which emergency response orders are transmitted to fire stations and houses.

door man The firefighter on an interior attack team assigned to ensure the slack is out of the line from the street to where it enters the building and to control the door leading into the fire area to ensure unimpeded advance of the line toward the fire.

EMS Emergency Medical Service.

EMT Emergency Medical Technician.

engine A fire apparatus designed to primarily engage in fire suppression. It is equipped with hoses, nozzles, water tanks and pumping compressors, and all equipment necessary to provide water and extinguishing agents to put out fires.

engineman A firefighter who is assigned to an engine company.

exposure A building or structure exposed to a fire. On a building or structure each side is identified by a number starting with 1 at the side of the building facing the street on a clockwise basis (i.e., left side of the building is "exposure-2 side" and the building to the left is "exposure 2").

FDNY Fire Department of the City of New York.

fire The light and heat manifested by the rapid oxidation of combustible materials, many times manifested by flame, but not always.

fire tetrahedron The four-sided geometric representation of the four factors necessary for fire: fuel (any substance that can undergo combustion), heat (temperature, energy sufficient to release vapor from the fuel and cause ignition), oxygen, and a chemical chain reaction, also known as an ignition source (reaction energy sufficient to produce ignition). Removing any of the four factors will prevent or suppress the fire.

first due engine Refers to either the first apparatus arriving on the scene of a fire or the area in which a company is expected to be the first to arrive on a fire scene; sometimes referred to as the "attack engine," it is primarily tasked with initial command, fire suppression and control.

fire hydrant A pipe rising from an underground water main that has capped openings used by firefighters to gain access to pressurized water for use in fire suppression activities, also known as a "spud" or a "plug."

flashover During a fire, all contents of the fire area are gradually heated to their ignition temperature, then simultaneously ignite. It is caused by excessive buildup of heat, and the flames fully involve an entire area of surface. Anyone in the fire area when it "flashes" is highly unlikely to survive.

flashover simulator An enclosed container with doors and a stovepipe that is used to simulate fire conditions up to a flashover condition. The simulator is used to familiarize firefighters with conditions leading up to a flashover to alert them to either eliminate the flash-over condition or evacuate the fire area.

gated-wye An appliance with a valve to control water distribution that takes one hose line and divides it into two hose lines.

grab A rescue of a person or persons from a fire or other emergency.

halligan tool A multipurpose tool used for prying, twisting, punching, or striking. It consists of a claw (or fork), a blade (wedge or adze), and a tapered pick, which is especially useful in quickly breaching many types of locked doors.

handie-talkie A hand-held radio with a keyed mouthpiece that is carried by officers and firefighters. Geographic range is limited—typically hundreds of yards or dozens of floors in a high-rise—and communications may break down beyond these distances due to building materials.

Hurst tool A hydraulic tool consisting of mechanical blades and scissors used to extricate trapped occupants from automobiles, vehicles, and other confined spaces.

highrise pack also known as a **roll-up** A coiled fifty-foot section of hose with a smooth-bore nozzle attached, and a spanner wrench used for fighting fire on upper floors.

hydraulic ventilation The process used by an interior hose team by which air is drawn into a fog stream to help push smoke and heated gases out of a structure.

hydrant wrench A large wrench with an octagonal head carried on a fire engine used to open a fire hydrant.

irons The term for when a halligan tool and a flat-head axe are married for carrying.

irons man The firefighter on a ladder truck assigned to conduct forcible entry duties and carry a halligan tool and a flat-head axe (the "irons").

jammed up Slang for getting killed or gravely injured.

a job A working fire.

the Job Reference to the fire service by those who are employed in the profession.

JP-8 A jet fuel used widely in commercial and military aircraft.

K12 saw also known as a "**partner saw.**" A large hand-held circular saw equipped with a 14-inch blade. The saw is designed to cut through roof sections and structures of differing materials during ventilation or entry work.

the knob slang for the nozzle.

line also known as **hose line** A line of fire hose comprised of 50-foot sections of hose of different diameters such as 1¾-inch, 2½-inch, 5-inch etc., categorized as either "attack hose" or "supply hose". Smaller diameter hoses are utilized in attack lines; larger diameter hoses in supply lines.

mutual An agreement between firefighters to swap assigned work shifts ("tours").

nozzle man The firefighter on an interior attack team assigned to the nozzle end of a fire hose who is responsible for fire suppression. It is one of the most respected and hard-earned assignments in the fire service.

NYPD New York Police Department.

officer The firefighter with the rank of lieutenant or higher who is responsible for the operation and safety of one or more fire apparatus and their crews.

outside vent man (OVM) The firefighter on a ladder truck assigned to ventilate the fire from outside and perform any immediate rescues with the assistance of the truck chauffeur if possible.

personal alarm safety system (PASS) A personal safety device used by firefighters. The system triggers a loud audible alarm when a firefighter remains motionless for thirty seconds or more. The system also emits a flashing beacon when it is operational.

pike hook also known as a **wooden 6' hook** A firefighting tool of lengths between 4 and 12 feet consisting of a pike and hook on one end and a rounded nub on the other, used for prying roofs, pulling ceilings, and breaking and clearing windows.

probie A probationary firefighter; a firefighter who has been employed for less than a year; also known as a "johnnie"; a rookie.

pyrolysis The term for the process by which gases evolve from solid fuels when they are heated.

rescue rig A fire apparatus designed primarily to respond to any emergency in which persons are trapped or incapacitated and in need of rescue. The rescue apparatus is specially designed to enable its crew to meet any circumstance or emergency.

rig Informal name for any fire engine or truck.

the Rock The informal name for the FDNY Fire Academy located at Randall's Island in New York City.

rollover A phase of fire which occurs when unburned combustible gases which accumulate at the ceiling level are pushed into uninvolved areas where they mix with oxygen and, upon reaching their flammable range, ignite and expand rapidly, rolling over the ceiling. Unlike a flashover, only the gases are burning, not the contents of the room.

roof hook or **"OV hook"** A firefighting tool used for multiple purposes including pulling and prying, composed of a long shaft with two triangular-shaped ends jutting in opposite directions. One is angled at 45 degrees, the other at 90 degrees.

seat of the fire The area where the main body of the fire is located, as determined by the outward movement of heat and gases; where the fire is deep-seated.

second due engine Refers to the second fire engine arriving on the scene of a fire or the area in which the company is expected to be the second to arrive on scene; usually assigned the task of water supply to the attack engine.

self-contained breathing apparatus (SCBA) also known as a "**mask**." The device worn to provide breathable air in an atmosphere that is immediately dangerous to life and health. It consists of a backpack and harness, an air cylinder, a regulator and a facepiece.

Siamese The connection to building standpipes and sprinklers, sometimes equipped with a clapper valve, that takes two or more hose lines and forms them into one hose line.

smoothbore nozzle also referred to as **solid-bore nozzle** A smooth-surfaced nozzle that produces the greatest reach per gallons per minute (gpm) compared to other nozzle types. The smoothbore produces maximum reach and penetration to the seat of the fire.

spanner wrench A two-pronged wrench used to tighten and loosen hose couplings.

standpipe A vertical pipe extending from a water supply, especially one connecting a temporary tap to the main commonly found in apartment buildings and high-rise structures.

"suckin' the nails" Slang for an interior attack crew crawling along the floor advancing toward the seat of the fire, underneath heat and toxic gases.

TAC Tactical Support Unit truck that carries specialized tools and equipment not carried by ladder trucks, engines, or rescue apparatus.

truck A fire apparatus equipped with ladders, both portable and hydraulic, saws, hooks, pike poles, extinguishers, tools, and rescue equipment necessary to enable firefighters to vent fire buildings and rescue trapped civilians.

truckie A firefighter assigned to a truck company.

ventilation The process of removing smoke, heat, and toxic gases from a burning building and replacing them with cooler, cleaner, oxygen-rich air. A fire in an enclosed structure emits toxins and flammable gases creating heat and potential flashover conditions. Ventilation reduces the build-up of heat and toxic gases and improves conditions for interior firefighting operations through the introduction of fresh air.

vertical ventilation The process of opening a roof or existing roof openings to allow smoke and heated gases to escape. Vertical ventilation is accomplished by opening roof doors, skylights, hatches, scuttles, and chases, or by cutting a hole in a roof and pushing down ceilings beneath the roof.

IN MEMORIAM

On September 11, 2001, more than 200 FDNY units, approximately half of all units in the department, responded to Box 55-8087 at the World Trade Center. Of the more than one thousand FDNY personnel who answered the alarm, three hundred and forty-three would give up their lives that morning. Line of duty deaths included the chief of department, twenty-one chief officers, twenty-one captains, forty-seven lieutenants, and two-hundred-and-fifty-three firefighters. Losses were claimed from all levels of the department, including its seventy-one-year-old deputy fire commissioner, a departmental chaplain, a fire marshal, and six probationary candidate firefighters who had not yet graduated from the FDNY fire academy. On November 2, 2001, these six were awarded their diplomas posthumously.

FDNY CHIEF OF DEPARTMENT
Peter J. Ganci Jr., 54

FDNY FIRST DEPUTY COMMISSIONER
William M. Feehan, 71

FDNY CHAPLAIN
Rev. Mychal Judge, O.F.M., 68

FDNY FIRE MARSHAL
Ronald P. Bucca, 47

CITYWIDE TOUR COMMANDERS
Chief Gerard A. Barbara, 53
Chief Donald J. Burns, 61

BATTALION 1
Chief Matthew L. Ryan, 54

BATTALION 2
Chief William McGovern, 49
Chief Richard Prunty, 57
Faustino Apostol, Jr., 55

BATTALION 4
Lt. Thomas O'Hagan, 43

BATTALION 6
Chief John P. Williamson, 46

BATTALION 7
Chief Orio Palmer, 45
Lt. Stephen G. Harrell, 44
Lt. Philip S. Petti, 43

BATTALION 8
Chief Thomas P. DeAngelis, 51
Thomas McCann, 45

BATTALION 9
Chief Dennis L. Devlin, 51
Chief Edward F. Geraghty, 45
Lt. Charles W. Garbarini, 44
Carl Asaro, 39
Alan Feinberg, 48

BATTALION 11
Chief John M. Paolillo, 51

BATTALION 12
Chief Frederick C. Scheffold, Jr. 57

BATTALION 22
Lt. Charles J. Margiotta, 44

BATTALION 43
Lt. Geoffrey E. Guja, 49

BATTALION 47
Lt. Anthony Jovic, 39

BATTALION 48
Chief Joseph Grzelak, 52
Michael L. Bocchino, 45

BATTALION 49
Chief John Moran, 42

BATTALION 50
Chief Lawrence T. Stack, 58

BATTALION 57
Chief Dennis Cross, 60
Chief Jos. R. Marchbanks, Jr., 47

DIVISION 1
Capt. Joseph D. Farrelly, 47
Thomas Moody, 45

DIVISION 11
Capt. Timothy M. Stackpole, 42

DIVISION 15
Chief Thomas T. Haskell, Jr., 37
Capt. Martin J. Egan, Jr., 36
Capt. William O'Keefe, 46

ENGINE 1
Lt. Andrew Desperito, 43
Michael T. Weinberg, 34

ENGINE 4
Calixto Anaya, r., 35 (Prob.)
James C. Riches, 29
Thomas Schoales, 27
Paul A. Tegtmeier, 41

ENGINE 5
Manual Del Valle, Jr., 32

ENGINE 6
Paul Beyer, 37
Thomas Holohan, 36
William R. Johnston, 31

ENGINE 8
Robert Parro, 35

ENGINE 10
Lt. George A. Atlas, 44
Jeffrey J. Olsen, 31
Paul Pansini, 34

ENGINE 21
Capt. William F. Burke, Jr., 46

ENGINE 22
Thomas A. Casoria, 29
Michael J. Elferis, 27
Vincent D. Kane, 37
Martin E. McWilliams, 35

ENGINE 23
Robert McPadden, 30
James N. Pappageorge, 29
Hector L. Tirado, Jr., 30
Mark P. Whitford, 31

ENGINE 26
Capt. Thomas Farino, 37
Dana R. Hannon, 29
Robert W. Spear, Jr., 30

ENGINE 33
Lt. Kevin Pfeifer, 42
David Arce, 36
Michael Boyle, 37
Robert Evans, 36
Keithroy M. Maynard, 30

ENGINE 37
John Giordano, 47

ENGINE 40
Lt. John F. Ginley, 37
Kevin Bracken, 37
Michael D. D'Auria, 25 (Prob.)
Bruce Gary, 51
Michael F. Lynch, 30
Steven Mercado, 38

ENGINE 54
Paul J. Gill, 34
Jose Guadalupe, 37
Leonard Ragaglia, 36
Christopher Santora, 23

ENGINE 55
Lt. Peter J. Freund, 45
Robert Lane, 28
Christopher Mozzillo, 27
Stephen P. Russell, 40

ENGINE 58
Lt. Robert B. Nagle, 55

ENGINE 74
Ruben D. Correa, 44

ENGINE 201
Lt. Paul R. Martini, 37
Gregory J. Buck, 37
Christopher Pickford, 32
John A. Schardt, 34

ENGINE 205
Lt. Robert F. Wallace, 43

ENGINE 207
Karl H. Joseph, 25
Shawn E. Powell, 32
Kevin O'Reilly, 28

ENGINE 214
Lt. Carl J. Bedigan, 35
John J. Florio, 33
Michael E. Roberts, 31
Kenneth T. Watson, 39

ENGINE 216
Daniel Suhr, 37

ENGINE 217
Lt. Kenneth Phelan, 41
Steven Coakley, 36
Neil J. Leavy, 34

ENGINE 219
John Chipura, 39

ENGINE 226
David P. DeRubbio, 38
Brian McAleese, 36
Stanley S. Smagala, Jr., 36

ENGINE 230
Lt. Brian G. Ahearn, 43
Frank Bonomo, 42
Michael S. Carlo, 34
Jeffrey Stark, 30
Eugene Whelan, 31
Edward J. White, III, 30

ENGINE 235
Lt. Steven Bates, 42
Nicholas P. Chiofalo, 39
Francis Esposito, 32
Lee S. Fehling, 28
Lawrence G. Veling, 44

ENGINE 238
Lt. Glenn E. Wilkinson, 46

ENGINE 279
Ronnie L. Henderson, 52
Michael Ragusa, 29
Anthony Rodriguez, 36 (Prob.)

ENGINE 285
Raymond P. York, 45

HAZ MAT OPERATIONS
Chief John Fanning, 54

HAZ MAT -1
Lt. John A. Crisci, 48
Dennis M. Carey, 51
Martin N. DeMeo, 47
Thomas Gardner, 39
Jonathan R. Hohmann, 48
Dennis Scauso, 46
Kevin J. Smith, 47

LADDER 2
Capt. Frederick J. III, Jr., 49
Michael Clarke, 27
George DiPasquale, 33
Denis P. Germain, 33
Daniel E. Harlin, 41
Carl Molinaro, 32
Dennis M. Mulligan, 32

LADDER 3
Capt. Patrick J. Brown, 48
Lt. Kevin W. Donnelly, 43
Michael Carroll, 39
James R. Coyle, 26
Gerard Dewan, 35
Jeffrey J. Giordano, 45
Joseph Maloney, 45
John K. McAvoy, 47
Timothy P. McSweeney, 37
Joseph J. Ogren, 30
Steven J. Olson, 38

LADDER 4
Capt. David T. Wooley, 54
Lt. Daniel O'Callaghan, 42
Joseph J. Angelini, Jr., 38
Peter Brennan, 30
Michael E. Brennan, 27
Michael Haub, 34
Michael F. Lynch, 33
Samuel Oitice, 45
James J., Tipping, II, 33

LADDER 5
Lt. Vincent F. Giammona, 40
Lt. Michael Warchola, 51
Louis Arena, 32
Andrew Brunn, 28 (Prob.)
Thomas Hannafin, 36
Paul H. Keating, 38
John A. Santore, 49
Gregory T. Saucedo, 31

LADDER 7
Capt. Vernon A. Richard, 53
George Cain, 35
Robert J. Foti, 42
Charles Mendez, 38
Richard Muldowney, Jr., 40
Vincent Princiotta, 39

LADDER 8
Lt. Vincent G. Halloran, 43

LADDER 9
Gerard Baptiste, 35
John P. Tierney, 27
Jeffrey P. Walz, 37

LADDER 10
Sean P. Tallon, 26

LADDER 11
Lt. Michael Quilty, 42
Michael F. Cammarata, 22 (Prob.)
Edward J. Day, 45
John F. Heffernan, 37
Richard J. Kelly, Jr., 50
Robert King, Jr., 36
Matthew Rogan, 37

LADDER 12

Angel L. Juarbe, Jr., 35
Michael D. Mullen, 34

LADDER 13

Capt. Walter G. Hynes, 46
Thomas Hetzel, 33
Dennis McHugh, 34
Thomas E. Sabella, 44
Gregory Stajk, 46

LADDER 15

Lt. Joseph G. Leavey, 45
Richard L. Allen, 30 (Prob.)
Arthur T. Barry, 35
Thomas W. Kelly, 50
Scott Kopytko, 32
Scott Larsen, 35
Douglas E. Oelschlager, 36
Eric T. Olsen, 41

LADDER 16

Lt. Raymond E. Murphy, 46
Robert Curatolo, 31

LADDER 20

Capt. John R. Fischer, 46
John P. Burnside, 36
James M. Gray, 34
Sean S. Hanley, 35
David Laforge, 50
Robert T. Linnane, 33
Robert D. McMahon, 35

LADDER 21

Gerard Atwood, 38
Gerard Duffy, 53
Keith Glascoe, 38
William E. Krukowski, 36
Benjamin Suarez, 34

LADDER 24

Capt. Daniel J. Brethel, 43
Stephen E. Belson, 51

LADDER 25

Lt. Glenn C. Perry, 41
Matthew Barnes, 37
John M. Collins, 42
Kenneth Kumpel, 42
Robert Minara, 54
Joseph Ravelli, 43
Paul G. Ruback, 50

LADDER 27

Jon Marshall, 35

LADDER 35

Capt. Frank Callahan, 51
James A. Gilberson, 43
Vincent S. Morello, 34
Michael Otten, 42
Michael Roberts, 30

LADDER 38

Joseph Spor, Jr., 35

LADDER 42

Peter A. Biefeld, 44

LADDER 101

Lt. Joseph Gullickson, 37
Patrick Byrne, 39
Salvatore B. Calabro, 38
Brian Cannizzaro, 30
Thomas J. Kennedy, 36
Joseph Mafeo, 31
Terence A. McShane, 37

LADDER 105

Capt. Vincent Brunton, 43
Thomas R. Kelly, 39
Henry A. Miller, Jr., 51
Dennis O'Berg, 28
Frank A. Palombo, 46

LADDER 111

Lt. Christopher P. Sullivan, 39

LADDER 118
Lt. Robert M. Regan, 48
Joseph Agnello, 35
Vernon P. Cherry, 49
Scott M. Davidson, 33
Leon Smith, Jr., 48
Peter A. Vega, 36

LADDER 131
Christian M. O. Regenhard, 28

LADDER 132
Andrew Jordan, 36
Michael Kiefer, 25
Thomas Mingione, 34
John T. Vigiano, II , 36
Sergio Villanueva, 33

LADDER 136
Michael J. Cawley, 32

RESCUE 1
Capt. Terence S. Hatton, 41
Lt. Dennis Mojica, 50
Joseph Angelini, Sr., 63
Gary Geidel, 44
William Henry, 49
Kenneth J. Marino, 40
Michael Montesi, 39
Gerard T. Nevins, 46
Patrick J. O'Keefe, 44
Brian E. Sweeney, 29
David M. Weiss, 41

RESCUE 2
Lt. Peter C. Martin, 43
William D. Lake, 44
Daniel F. Libretti, 43
John Napolitano, 32
Kevin O'Rourke, 44
Lincoln Quappe, 38
Edward Rall, 44

RESCUE 3
Christopher J. Blackwell, 42
Thomas Foley, 32
Thomas Gambino, Jr., 48
Raymond Meisenheimer, 46
Donald J. Regan, 47
Gerard P. Schrang, 45

RESCUE 4
Capt. Brian Hickey, 47
Lt. Kevin Dowdell, 46
Terrence P. Farrell, 45
William J. Mahoney, 37
Peter A. Nelson, 42
Durrell V. Pearsall, 34

RESCUE 5
Capt. Louis J. Modafferi, 45
Lt. Harvey Harrell, 49
Lt. Joseph A. Mascali, 44
John P. Bergin, 39
Carl V. Bini, 44
Michael C. Fiore, 46
Andre G. Fletcher, 37
Douglas C. Miller, 34
Jeffrey M. Palazzo, 33
Nicholas P. Rossomando, 35
Allan Tarasiewicz, 45

SAFETY BATTALION
Robert J. Crawford, 62

SPECIAL OPERATIONS
Chief Raymond M. Downey, 63
Chief Charles Kasper, 54
Capt. Patrick J. Waters, 44
Lt. Timothy Higgins, 43
Lt. Michael T. Russo, Sr., 44

SQUAD 1
Capt. James Amato, 43
Lt. Edward A. D'Atri, 41
Lt. Michael Esposito, 41
Lt. Michael N. Fodor, 53
Brian Bilcher, 37
Gary Box, 37
Thomas M. Butler, 37
Peter Carroll, 42
Robert Cordice, 28
David J. Fontana, 37
Matthew D. Garvey, 37
Stephen G. Siller, 34

SQUAD 18
Lt. William E. McGinn, 43
Eric Allen, 44
Andrew Fredericks, 40
David Halderman, 40
Timothy Haskell, 34
Manuel Mojica, 37
Lawrence Virgilio, 38

SQUAD 41
Lt. Michael K, Healey, 42
Thomas P. Cullen, III, 31
Robert Hamilton, 43
Michael J. Lyons, 32
Gregory Sikorsky, 34
R. Bruce Van Hine, 48

SQUAD 252
Tarel Coleman, 32
Thomas Kuveikis, 48
Peter J. Langone, 41
Patrick Lyons, 34
Kevin Prior, 28

SQUAD 288
Lt. Ronald T. Kerwin, 42
Ronnie E. Geis, 43
Joseph Hunter, 31
Jonathan L. Ielpi, 29
Adam D. Rand, 30
Timothy M. Welty, 34

EMS BATTALION 49
Paramedic Carlos R. Lillo, 37

EMS BATTALION 57
Paramedic Ricardo J. Quinn, 40